SH[...]

Quint gather[...] and took her to his [...] the door, she stirred. [...] Quint's neck and she snuggle[...] slumber.

She had an instant effect on him. His heart started pounding in his chest and his blood raced through his veins. Quint lay her down on his soft feather mattress and, after disrobing, followed her there.

The highly aroused male felt Rebecca tense and try to pull away. As he ran his tongue down the side of her neck she mumbled indistinctly, "No, no. I don't want this."

He whispered back, his voice husky with desire. "Yes, you do. You want me as much as I want you."

Even as he loosened her chemise and nibbled her soft flesh, she pushed against him. "No, we must not . . . I can't let you do this."

He kissed his way back to her lips. "Yes, we can. You want me to do this, Rebecca. You want it, and you know you do. Say you do."

Rebecca muttered a sleepy phrase, lost herself to the pleasure of his kisses and swooned with the sensuality of his embrace. Yes, she wanted what he could do to her and she wanted it now . . .

ZEBRA'S GOT THE ROMANCE
TO SET YOUR HEART AFIRE!

RAGING DESIRE (2242, $3.75)
by Colleen Faulkner

A wealthy gentleman and officer in General Washington's army, Devon Marsh wasn't meant for the likes of Cassie O'Flynn, an immigrant bond servant. But from the moment their lips first met, Cassie knew she could love no other . . . even if it meant marching into the flames of war to make him hers!

TEXAS TWILIGHT (2241, $3.75)
by Vivian Vaughan

When handsome Trace Garrett stepped onto the porch of the Santa Clara ranch, he wove a rapturous spell around Clara Ehler's heart. Though Clara planned to sell the spread and move back East, Trace was determined to keep her on the wild Western frontier where she belonged — to share with him the glory and the splendor of the passion-filled TEXAS TWILIGHT.

RENEGADE HEART (2244, $3.75)
by Marjorie Price

Strong-willed Hannah Hatch resented her imprisonment by Captain Jake Farnsworth, even after the daring Yankee had rescued her from bloodthirsty marauders. And though Jake's rock-hard physique made Hannah tremble with desire, the spirited beauty was nevertheless resolved to exploit her femininity to the fullest and gain her independence from the virile bluecoat.

LOVING CHALLENGE (2243, $3.75)
by Carol King

When the notorious Captain Dominic Warbrooke burst into Laurette Harker's eighteenth birthday ball, the accomplished beauty challenged the arrogant scoundrel to a duel. But when the captain named her innocence as his stakes, Laurette was terrified she'd not only lose the fight, but her heart as well!

Available wherever paperbacks are sold, or order direct from the Publisher. Send cover price plus 50¢ per copy for mailing and handling to Zebra Books, Dept. 2745, 475 Park Avenue South, New York, N.Y. 10016. Residents of New York, New Jersey and Pennsylvania must include sales tax. DO NOT SEND CASH.

CAPTIVE INNOCENT
ALLISON KNIGHT

ZEBRA BOOKS
KENSINGTON PUBLISHING CORP.

ZEBRA BOOKS

are published by

Kensington Publishing Corp.
475 Park Avenue South
New York, NY 10016

Copyright © 1989 by Allison Knight

All rights reserved. No part of this book may be reproduced in any form or by any means without the prior written consent of the Publisher, excepting brief quotes used in reviews.

First printing: August, 1989

Printed in the United States of America

Dedication

*To my mate, Hank, with all my love,
for all the lessons of joy and sharing
you've given
through the years*

Chapter One

"Come on! If we don't get started soon, you'll miss your ship," Arthur Ranserford pushed his younger sister toward the carriage.

"I haven't said good-bye to Peter or his daughters, and I really don't care if I miss the ship or not." Rebecca glared at her brother and flipped her head toward the waiting carriage. Arthur's plans were something she would rather not think about. At least he was going to keep his word and take her to the ship, as he had promised.

Immediately after breakfast, even before she started telling her servants and the tenants good-bye, he had loaded her trunk and now he was pushing her toward the door of the carriage. She glanced past him at the estate. Would she ever see her home again? Something inside her twisted painfully and she stumbled into the carriage. She blinked her eyes rapidly; Arthur must not see her tears.

They traveled for miles before Arthur said a word. Then he turned to her with a grim, determined look on his face and stroking his new black velvet jacket, said, "Make this marriage work. Without a dowry and at your age, this will be your only chance."

Rebecca wanted to reach across and strike his smug face. She was only a year and full score and it wasn't her fault there was no dowry. He was the one who misused the funds. He should have seen her properly married two or three years ago, but he had been much too busy playing in London. Now, it was too late, too late for her, or any future for her. He was such a coward, her brother.

Rebecca's black eyes glistened with anger and she jerked her chin as she gritted her teeth. Arthur was even more of a coward than she thought. She looked around at the tiny room on the ship. He brought her to the ship, saw her to this room and then he disappeared. He was supposed to introduce her to the captain, and he should have said goodbye, but he had simply left her. She was furious and she admitted, frightened, too. Her whole life was in turmoil. Everything had changed.

Before today, she had never seen a ship and now she was on one. She tried to take a deep breath but a putrid stench drifted into the cabin from the harbor and it mingled with the cloying mustiness that surrounded her. She raised her lace trimmed handkerchief scented with her favorite fragrance to block the smells. It didn't help at all.

Above her head the thudding and thumping of boxes and trunks dropped on the wooden deck combined with the groans and creaks of the ship created a cacophony that irritated her beyond words. Sounds seemed to explode in her head. Six weeks? Perhaps, two months? Never! She would go mad. "How will I survive?" she moaned.

There was no way she could stay in this tiny closet for another minute. She grabbed for her shawl and headed toward the stairs. At least in the fresh air, the smell of the harbor might not be so overpowering. She would have a chance to see her beloved England for one last time. She rushed through the corridor, up the steep stairs and onto the main deck.

Confusion was everywhere. Sailors were rushing in every direction and several passengers were leaning against the deck rail waving to a small cluster of people standing on the dock. Still others were watching the crew load the last of the cargo. One of the sailors appeared to be checking ropes that were coiled all over the deck. Rebecca stepped over to the railing and watched in fascination. Above her, more sailors were hanging from long pieces of wood that seemed to form a ladder into the sky. They were gathering yards and yards of fabric against the wood. She muttered softly, "How ever will they get this ship away from the dock with such confusion?"

She pushed herself back against the railing away from the men rushing back and forth with barrels and boxes as the chaos continued. She spotted two well-dressed men at the rear of the ship talking quietly. The older of the two pointed the sailors to one area of the ship and then another, directing their movement. Rebecca watched him orchestrate the confusion and decided he was the captain.

The captain! Arthur was supposed to have introduced her to the captain. Arthur was supposed to have done so much. Instead, he had put her on the block and sold her like a Christmas goose. Months before, he stressed that the income from the estates was gone, where she didn't know. At Christmas, he said there was nothing for a dowry, something about heavy business losses. Marriage to a gentleman of property was out of the question, he told her. She had nothing to bring to the union.

She really had no feelings, one way or the other about marriage. She supposed that eventually she expected to get married, but in truth, she had given it little thought. But Arthur was obstinate about the whole matter. All of a sudden, long after he should have found her a husband, when the estates stopped providing the funds necessary to supply a dowry, he insisted that they talk about marriage.

Somehow, some way, Arthur found a man from the brand new country across the sea who needed a wife badly enough to pay for one. She wiped at the tears that started to form in her eyes again. When the ship moved away from the dock in London, it would carry her away, too, far from England and the life she knew to the city of Philadelphia in a country called the United States. And, she was going to have to marry a man she had never seen. In fact, the only thing she knew about him was his name. Master Stephen Hill of Philadelphia!

Rebecca shook her head in amazement. Why was Arthur so interested in getting her out of England? She raised her hands to her temples, her face a mask of agony for a second. If she was out of the way, he could lay claim to the rest of the estate, sell it and gamble it away, until it, too, was gone. It had taken her the better part of three months but she found out only ten days ago that the estate was producing more than enough in the way of funds. The trouble was Arthur! He was spending it, gambling it away faster than the farms were making it.

She groaned aloud. There was nothing she could do. Her father was dead, killed in a hunting accident six years ago, and her mother had died ten years before. Arthur was her legal guardian. There wasn't even an aunt or uncle to come to her aid. Arthur was her only living relative.

She ordered herself not to think about her situation and she concentrated on the two men at the rear of the ship. She would not cry, she despised women who sobbed at every little thing. Instead, in the half light of twilight, she studied the man she thought might be the captain. He was hatless, and his graying hair waved against his head. He was tall, at least as tall as Arthur and his muscular arms were bound up in a dark jacket. In the gathering gloom of dusk she couldn't make out the features of his face.

The second man was much younger, even taller, and had very broad shoulders. In the light colored breeches he wore, she could see the leg muscles ripple as he moved back and forth to avoid the busy sailors. His features were completely hidden in the shadows of his tricorn.

As she watched, the two men separated and the younger man stepped to the opposite rail to gaze west while the older man moved forward to stand with another sailor at the ship's wheel. As Rebecca waited, the ship's lines were thrown from the pylons and the gangplank removed. Sailors, who minutes before were scurrying about the deck now climbed hand over hand up the ropes to the tall poles and released the gray fabric that shuddered in the wind.

A sigh slipped past her lips, as she forced herself to concentrate on the activity around her. She didn't want to think about what might lay in store for her at the end of the voyage.

Rebecca stood at the ship's rail as the last light of day faded and the twinkling heralds of night married the sparse glow from the river bank. The soft lamp lights guided Rebecca back to her cabin.

She glanced around the room. Arthur was undoubtedly responsible for this pathetic little space. Her fear was forgotten and her anger grew. Soft light from the lamp outside her door bathed the room in a uncanny glow. She glared about the room. She would need a great deal more light to unpack than that dingy little lamp. The tiny room was so dark and gloomy that she knew she would find it impossible to store any of her things in the unfamiliar space.

She stepped back to the bunk and rummaged through her bag until she found the small silver box the household staff gave her as a farewell gift. Sally showed her how to use a tinderbox before she left but Rebecca doubted her own ability. She turned the box over and over in her hands. "Well, it won't light itself," she mumbled. She picked up the flint and pushed it against the metal. Nothing happened. Again, she tried, and again, but she couldn't get a spark. She bit her lower lip in frustration and a look of dismay crossed her face she pushed the flint across the metal over and over. She twisted the box in her hands as she considered her problem. Unless she could find someone to help her, she would never have any light nor would she get her things unpacked.

She heard a noise from the passageway and she rushed to the door. A lad no taller than herself was making his way down the passageway, wearing the uniform of the sailors she saw on deck. When he reached Rebecca, she cleared her throat and stepped into the passageway, "Could you help me, sir? My lamps need to be lit and I haven't been able to get a spark." She held up the tinderbox to illustrate her problem.

The lad looked at her with concern and then amazement in his face. Rebecca was afraid that she would have to pour out her whole life story before he helped her. A shudder traveled down her spine as she wondered if she had committed some unpardonable crime by requesting his aid?

Without a word, he stepped into her cabin, lit her lamps and then left to continue down the passageway. Following him out the door, she offered her thanks but he only nodded. As she watched, he moved on past the next two doors then glanced back in her direction. "I *did* do something wrong," she mumbled as she moved back into her room and looked at the area that was to be her home for the next several weeks. She felt sick as she glanced about the room.

There was a line of drawers that took up all the space under the narrow bunk that was supposed to be her bed. More small drawers filled the cabinet under the washstand that was no bigger than a dog's bowl. Two narrow cupboards occupied the little bit of space at the end of the bunk. Even at that, she doubted she would be able to get half of her clothing into the drawers. A dingy mirror, no more than six inches square, hung above the washstand. It was too small to be of any value. She glanced around the room once more. There wasn't even a chair or stool in the cubbyhole. In fact, with the exception of the bunk, there was no place to sit at all.

She looked at the bunk; she certainly couldn't sit there. There was a wooden railing that extended ten inches above the thin mattress. She stared at the railing. What on earth was that for?

Thank goodness she was short. If she were more than her five foot one inches, her bonnet brim would brush the ceiling. And, if she held her skirts and was very careful, she found that she could just turn around without bumping into her trunk and valise. Grinding her teeth, she muttered, "Arthur, you will have much to answer for."

"Well, Rebecca," she said aloud, "Are you going to stand here and feel sorry for yourself or are you going to do something constructive?" She grinned. If anyone heard her, they'd think that she was a victim of some mental disorder. "I'll unpack," she answered herself. As she reached for her valise, she consoled herself; it made more sense to busy herself than to stand and fume about things that could not be changed.

When she opened the bag, her eyes fell on her jewelry case nestled in the colorful splash of one of her cotton skirts. She was certain that she packed it in the trunk. A shudder of apprehension passed through her as she reached for the velvet box. Holding her breath, she opened the clasp and pulled the miniature door out of her way. Her heart fell. The case was empty. Arthur had stolen her jewels!

She sank to her trunk. That was the last straw. She

dropped the empty case and pounded her fists on the trunk in frustration. There was nothing in the case worth much, but those things were special. There was a small diamond brooch and earrings, a gift from her father on her fourteenth birthday; her tiny black enamel dog with ruby eyes, her mother's last gift to her when she was three; her mother's garnet studded locket; and four gold chains. Her fingers strayed to the single strand of pearls she wore. They were her grandmother's and now, that was all she had left. Her brother had taken everything she had: her land, her farms, her friends, her jewelry, and now, her freedom.

All the pain and frustration of the past six months pressed on her. Arthur's crimes paraded before her blinking eyes. There was Sally, her maid. Rebecca sank her teeth into her bottom lip as she remembered. Seven weeks ago, Arthur had dragged her into the parlor and informed her that he had found her a husband. She was going to Philadelphia to be married. Then he ordered Sally to mend and pack all of Rebecca's clothes, and then, her own. His orders were so clear. Rebecca was to help Sally with everything they had. Both girls worked together, cleaning, stitching, and packing their belongings, and while they worked they planned their journey.

But Arthur ruined even that. Three days before they were to sail, he barged into her suite, and announced, "I want to talk to both of you, now! Is Sally packed?" He waited for an affirmative nod, "Good. Two days from now, she'll be reporting to Princeton Hall for her new duties as upstairs maid."

Rebecca sat very still, "Why, she is traveling with me to Philadelphia."

"No! You don't need a maid. I'm not paying extra for her so you can enjoy a sea voyage."

Rebecca stared at Arthur in horror, "I . . . I . . . she . . . but . . ." She was so angry none of the words came out. Finally, she managed to scream over the tight lump at the back of her throat, "You can't do this!"

Sally rushed from the room as Rebecca staggered to her feet and stood in front of her brother. Her fists were clenched into tight balls at her sides, "No lady travels alone.

It isn't done. Even I know that. I must have my maid." The words rushed out, "What will the other passengers think, what will Mr. Hill think? If you don't care what people think, I most certainly do!"

"You will travel alone. I'll not pay good money for a maid when it's totally unnecessary. The ship is small, and I'll take you there myself. This particular ship even has a special room for dining, and a cook so you won't have to worry about meals. Surely, you can dress yourself, you're old enough! You don't need a maid," Arthur said matter-of-factly.

"But I need a maid. I do!" she whispered, brushing the welling tears from her eyes. "What will people think?" she repeated as she stood before him. "If I travel alone, they'll think the worst. They'll think I'm a joylady, or . . . or a . . . someone's mistress. It won't matter what I say or do, without a companion I'll be suspect. You can't do this to me." She dropped her voice, ashamed to beg, "Arthur, please don't do this."

"You're being ridiculous. You'll conduct yourself as befits your station. You will talk to the other women on board and eat your meals with the other passengers."

"And, what about the sailors or the other men on board, do I talk to them?"

"Rebecca, silence! You will be under the protection of the captain. He'll watch out for you. He'll see that no harm comes to you."

"And who will protect me from the captain?"

Arthur scowled at her, turned on his heels and walked out of the room. He refused to discuss the matter again, even though she tried to reopen the conversation twice more that day. To him the matter was closed. She wiped away the tears that threatened to fall. Her anger bubbled up inside her. He had disappeared before he even saw the captain. How could people as wonderful as her parents sire such a miserable human being as her brother?

She jerked the bow of her bonnet, yanked the hat from her head, then hurled it into the far corner of the bunk. She clenched her fists, wanting something to throw. "Arthur has no right, no right at all," she shouted to the empty space around her.

Rebecca stared down at the partially empty trunk, and then around the cabin. Just as she guessed, there wasn't nearly enough room for her things. She closed the lid and sat perched on the trunk, trying to decide what to do. Obviously she couldn't live out of a trunk, not for two months. Only the things she needed for the journey would go in the drawers, everything else could stay packed away until she arrived in Philadelphia.

Smiling grimly, she surveyed the trunk. It would serve nicely as a bench. She pushed it against the wall and stood back to view her efforts. That should work satisfactorily, she nodded her head in approval.

She sat down on the trunk and glanced around her. Everything that could be unpacked was stowed away, now what was she to do? Long before they quit the Thames, Rebecca undressed and crawled under the faded blue blanket of the bunk.

Above Rebecca, Quint McQuade stood at the rear of the ship and stared toward the sea, west to his home. The captain of the ship was personable but more important, Quint was satisfied that he knew his business. The man was capable! Quint leaned forward to rest his arms on the rail. As he felt the ship shudder and then move with the tide, his full lips thinned in anger. He shouldn't even be on this vessel. He should have been on his own ship laying two hundred yards away, still fully loaded. His dark handsome face now wore an angry scowl. With all of his business unfinished, his cargo unsold, and no new cargo secured he was forced to go back home to Philadelphia and all because of his mother. A pox on her and damn all women!

Chapter Two

For hours, Rebecca rolled to the right and then the left trying for some kind of softness in the thing called a bed. In spite of her fatigue, she had never been so uncomfortable in her life. Gritting her teeth, she grumbled, "It's like sleeping on a board." And the motion of the ship as it rode the waves was anything but pleasant. Why were men obsessed with the sea, she wondered. She certainly was not impressed.

Shortly before dawn, she gave up the idea of sleep altogether and crawled out of the bunk. "Agh!" she growled to the somber morning and glared at the bunk. The only way in or out of the thing was to crawl over that ridiculous railing. Forcing her anger aside, she grabbed for her tinderbox. What would she do if she couldn't get the lamps lit?

Pleased that for once something in her life worked properly, Rebecca dressed carefully by lamplight, intent on making a good impression on the other travelers. Then she tackled her long tresses. After she tried to style her hair and found it impossible, she gave up and braided the ebony strands. "Impossible," she muttered. Sally had always done her hair because Rebecca had no patience to work with the thick straight strands. She sighed; Sally wasn't here.

She tried to give herself a careful perusal in the mirror, but she couldn't see enough to determine if she was acceptable or not. She decided it was too early to matter and she left her room in search of the dining room Arthur told her about. As she tiptoed through the passage she wondered if he had lied about that.

* * *

Quint found little comfort in his bunk that night and before dawn he struggled into his clothes. He moved toward the small room set aside for passengers' meals. He growled at the thought of waking to a cup of tea. With any luck, the coffee would be ready.

The coffee was ready and with a mug of the stout stuff in his hand he straddled the bench. His problem, he decided was that he was feeling guilty, guilty because he didn't feel something more. Susannah's note was plain: he must come home immediately; his mother was dying. His mother may have given him life, but that was where it ended. Not once in his nine and twenty years had she ever given him the impression that he was a son to her. No, he was the payer of her bills, the provider, but never the son.

He was going home because Susannah asked him to come and for no other reason. A grin spread across his tired face. He'd sail around the world if Susannah asked it. Every man should have a sister like Susannah. If there was another woman as capable and loving as she, he would have married her long ago.

Some of the exhaustion left his face as he thought of Susannah and George Beal, her husband. George was a good man, a good father, and Quint had sensed it as soon as he met him. Over the years they had become good friends and Quint grinned as he thought of the postscript George had scrawled across the bottom of Susannah's note: "We'll finish the keg of rum when you arrive. By then, we'll have a need." George would have need of the keg long before the ship arrived, if he dealt with their three older sisters and Mary Elizabeth, herself.

At the thought of the matron of the McQuade clan, Quint winced. Could his mother actually be dying? Susannah would not have sent for him if she wasn't seriously ill. By the time he got home, he would probably find that she'd recovered, or . . . . He stirred the liquid in his mug trying to remember something pleasant about his mother.

In the center of the vessel, Rebecca found what seemed to be the dining room. It was almost as small as her own room and contained two narrow rough hewn tables complete with benches. But it wasn't empty. She eased onto one of the benches and watched the only other occupant of the room. He was hunched over the other table with his back to her and the entrance. She couldn't help but notice his enormous shoulders.

Before she had a chance to determine anything else about the man, the boy who helped her with the lamps the evening before stepped up to her table. "We 'ave tea and biscuits this morning, Ma'am." She blushed as she nodded her head to the lad, missing the quick glance of the man.

For the few minutes she waited for her tea, she kept her eyes lowered. She certainly wanted no conversation with anyone this morning, especially not a gentleman to whom she had never been introduced.

Suddenly, a voice at her side said, "Cap'n wants ya to join him."

She jerked her head up with a start. Captain? She glanced at the man. Surely, this wasn't the captain. She could have sworn the captain's hair was gray. This man's hair was a dark rich brown and for some reason she thought he was younger and taller than the man she named captain the night before. Perhaps she made a mistake. Arthur had not taken the time to introduce her. She relaxed. It would be perfectly proper to sit with the captain. He was probably trying to overcome Arthur's oversight. She glanced at the man quickly and then turned to the lad and said softly, "Tell the captain I'd be delighted if he chooses to join me."

The boy turned to the man, then looked back at Rebecca, shrugged his shoulders and headed back toward the food preparation area and the fireplace Rebecca saw in the background.

Quint turned on the bench to better survey the young woman who had, however graciously, just put him in his place. He stared at her. The quick glance he took moments before did nothing to prepare him for the vision who sat at the second table. She was small with a delicate bone structure. Her shining raven-black hair was braided and twisted around her head like a crown. Her complexion was not the pallid, eggshell white of the fashionable ladies of London but had a hint of color, a natural pink and cream that was flawless.

As she turned away from him, he caught a glimpse of her profile. Her short, dainty nose had an upward tilt to it and her eyes were edged with the longest black lashes he had ever seen. She had high rounded breasts and even in her gown, Quint could tell they were full and mature. As she raised her tea cup, his eyes followed to her heart shaped mouth. He glanced at her long slender fingers. She wore no jewelry of any kind. Was she married?

"I'm sorry if I offended you. It was not my intention," he suggested quietly.

Rebecca was startled by the richness of his voice, "I was not offended, sir."

Quint was aware that he was having difficulty breathing properly, but he had never seen a woman as beautiful as this creature. He stood up, picked up his mug, and moved to her table.

It was Rebecca's turn to stare. He was gigantic, well over six feet in height and perhaps a head taller than Arthur. His shoulders were even wider than she suspected. She wondered, for an instant, if he had to stoop to get through the doorways on the ship. His bright blue eyes sparkled and there were tiny laugh lines at the corners of his eyes. His full lips were curved in a friendly smile.

This man is dangerous, especially to women, she thought as he turned to pull out the bench. His face was square and she could see a strong jaw line. The hair on his head was the color of the warm beaver fur that all of England wanted from the colonies and just as thick. It hung in a queue at the back of his neck but, there was a tendency for it to curl and the soft waves gave him an impetuous look. He was by far the handsomest man she had ever seen. In that instant, she was aware of her femininity and of his masculinity as she had never been with another man and she felt weak.

As he sat down, he said, "You did say that you would be delighted if I joined you." His words hung in the air for a fraction of a second too long, as she stared at him. Her wide doe-brown eyes glared at him for a second more and then with a blink they turned almost black and he was instantly aware of her irritation. He grinned, enjoying her discomfort. She has quite a temper, he thought.

Rebecca fought to control her irritation. This man was supposed to be her protector? He was arrogant and much too self-assured to her way of thinking. She turned her attention to her cup of tea and the hard heavy circles that were called biscuits.

As she picked up the biscuit, Quint's blue eyes twinkled with amusement. "They're better if they're dunked. The cook is satisfactory, but baked goods are not his specialty," he offered.

Rebecca looked up quickly, "We haven't been introduced, yet, Captain."

Quint hurried to correct her mistake, "Oh, I'm not the captain of this vessel, but I do have my own ships." He smiled easily and Rebecca felt her heart flip. If he wasn't the captain, then she should never have encouraged him. What would he think of her?

She tried to smile back, she really did, but something was very wrong. Her heart was beating much too fast and she felt like she was trembling inside. Mentally, she shook herself. He was a man, a very good-looking man, but just a man, nevertheless. No man, however, had had the effect on her that this one was having. She tried to brush away her confusion by telling herself that it was simple apprehension. She should not have talked to him. He was not her protector.

She dunked the biscuit, took a dainty bite, then took a sip of tea. "An improvement, let me assure you," Quint said, still smiling.

Rebecca finished the biscuit and her tea and turned to the stranger, "The biscuit was tasty. Thank you, sir."

"Please. My name is Quinton McQuade. I'm from Philadelphia and we are not quite so formal in our new country and less so on a ship. Please, call me Quint. Now, what's your name?"

Rebecca twisted her hands together, and glanced away nervously, "My name is Rebecca Ranserford. I come from Hertford, north of London. I'm traveling to the colonies to be married." There, she thought, that ought to discourage him. Now, she would not have to talk to him, she told herself.

Quint watched as she twisted her hands in one direction and then the other. It was an arranged marriage, judging by the nervousness of the lady, he decided. Her obvious discomfort suggested that she did not know the man, had never met him. Such a pity, too. She was incredibly beautiful.

"You should use caution when you call the new nation, "the colonies," especially to some of its citizens, Mistress Ranserford. Some of them fought hard for their freedom and they might take offense," he grinned down at her. She had the most expressive eyes he had ever seen and his breath seemed to catch in his throat for a second or two as he gazed into them. What would happen when the crew got a good look at her? he wondered. He dismissed the thought, grateful that it was not his problem.

For a second, it seemed she might take offense at his reprimand, then she attempted an apology, "I'm sorry. I know little about the country to which we're traveling and even less about ships." She seemed genuinely sorry that she had so little knowledge.

"Well, it would be my pleasure to correct your lack of education on both counts. In fact, I would be honored to answer any questions you have." He watched her closely, smiling warmly, and asked gently, "What can I explain?"

Rebecca hesitated, thinking about the evening before. Would he think her too bold if she asked him if she had done something wrong asking for the cabin boy's help? She took a deep breath, "There is one thing," she paused once more, not sure she should continue.

Quint pasted on his friendliest smile and leaned forward, "Yes?"

"I . . . I . . . asked the young serving boy to light my lamps, last evening ... in my room." It didn't sound quite right to her, and she blushed. "He—he seemed, well, he acted so surprised. Did I do something wrong?"

"You did nothing wrong. I imagine he was only concerned that your maid had no tinderbox," he looked at her closely as a dark flush spread up her neck, coloring her cheeks. She was squirming uncomfortably on her bench.

"Wasn't your maid with you?" Quint asked innocently. He realized his mistake the instant the words left his mouth. The girl actually winced.

Rebecca wanted to run, but she sat there, staring down at her tightly clenched hands. She was certain that her face was bright red. Silently, she cursed Arthur for denying her Sally. She could tell by the tension in the air that this man was questioning her morals. Now, her reputation was in question, just as she told Arthur it would be. For the first time in her life, she told a blatant lie. She mumbled, "She became ill the day we were to sail. There was no time to replace her."

Quint sat very still, trying to hide his shock. The girl was obviously lying. She never had a maid or companion for this trip. A lady, even one from one of the very humble houses, would not consider a trip without a maid. Yet, her manners were genteel and she was well dressed. Unless she was a commoner . . . Quint scowled, that seemed very unlikely. Could she have been some man's mistress? It was not at all uncommon for a man to arrange a satisfactory marriage for his mistress when the affair came to an end.

A hard gleam settled in Quint's eye. He would never consider seducing a virtuous young woman, but another man's mistress, especially if the affair was ended, was fair game for all. He could certainly do with some female companionship on this particular voyage, and she was a beautiful woman. His expression changed as he tried to imagine what she would look like without her clothes. In a husky voice, he asked, "Do you have any other questions at the moment?"

Rebecca wanted to run and hide, but she stood her ground, her eyes black, "No, nothing, sir." She would not use his name. She would not be that informal. "Thank you for your time. I want to take a walk and then return to my room," she said in dismissal.

Quint refused to be dismissed. "On board a ship, your room is called a cabin," he corrected. Quint chuckled to himself, imagining the long lovely hours he would spend with this woman. "Now it's time for your first lesson about a ship. Come! Since you planned to walk around the deck, I'll escort you and tell you about topside."

He grasped her elbow to guide her toward the door. A thousand tiny pinpricks seemed to travel up her arm from the point where his fingers touched her. Her gaze flew to his face and she was amazed that he looked as startled as she felt. Frantically, she pulled away from him. They stared at each other for several seconds.

Quint was the first to regain his composure. Speaking as if nothing extraordinary had happened he began to explain the different levels of the ship. His deep rich voice shot through her like an arrow. Rebecca, she chided herself, get a grip on yourself, he's only a man. His voice rolled over her and she forced herself to listen. ". . . two more decks below. One is the living quarters for the crew and some cargo is stored there. The lowest deck holds the bulk of the cargo, the hold, and some of the ship's stores." Without touching her again, he directed her toward the stairs.

As she followed him up the steps, she vowed that the lesson was going to be very short. The sooner she got back to her room . . . no, cabin, the better off she would be. She reached the last step of the gangway, and Quint stood, holding out his hands to assist. She glared up at his grinning face. Even if she fell flat on her face, she thought, she would not touch him again.

Quint gestured about the deck, "Now, we're topside."

Straining to see above her, she peered up at the yards of gray fabric strung across the wooden beams and held in place with endless lengths of rope. As she watched, brisk breezes swirled over the deck and fluffed the gigantic sheets above her head into pillow form. "Exhilarating, isn't it?" Quint added quietly, watching the display himself.

A mist from the spray of waves wet her face and she tasted the salt. Around the deck, neat coils of rope, like enormous snakes ready to strike, drew her attention. She had to watch where she stepped or risk being snagged. Everywhere, the crew seemed intent on scrubbing or polishing everything in sight.

Quint seemed to feel an explanation was needed, "Cleanliness and neatness are inherent in a well-run ship." He chuckled, "And, this is a well-run ship!"

Just then she stumbled over one of the coils of rope. Quint grabbed her arm. "You better hang on to me, until you get your sea legs." For the next hour, he held her arm tightly as he guided her around the ship, pointing up, down, or to the side as he explained the function of each section of the ship. If she had not been so conscious of his arm holding her so tightly, or the erratic beating of her own heart, she would have enjoyed the lesson. She was uncomfortable, though, and the occasional furtive glances she got from the crew alarmed her even more. She had never been in such a masculine environment. She didn't like it.

She didn't like the fine mist from the waves that soaked her red wool dress, either. Suddenly, she shivered violently. The reaction was as much from the glances she was getting as from the ocean spray, but her trembling drew Quint's attention. "Here, now. Are you cold? You didn't bring a shawl, did you? Do you want to go below? You need some hot tea. We'll have you warmed up in no time at all."

Rebecca nodded and shook her head at the appropriate times and eagerly headed for the stairs. Anything to get away from the sailors' leers and from Quint McQuade. The emotional upheaval of the last weeks, the sleepless night just past, and the tension generated by the man next to her combined to make her very tired, exhausted, in fact. She thanked Quint and mumbled something about needing a nap. She rushed back to her own cabin, threw off her dress and petticoats and crawled into her bunk. Lulled by the slow rhythm of the rolling ship, she sank into a deep sleep.

For the next several days, Rebecca rested in her cabin, introduced herself to Ephram Hemphill, the captain of the ship, and met the other passengers. She was not surprised to find that she was the only single woman. She knew Arthur gave no thought to her comfort. There were two families on board traveling back to Philadelphia after visiting families in England. The other three families were going to America for the first time.

She spent a good deal of time with the other women. While they visited, though, she watched Quint. She kept her eyes on him as he moved around the deck, talked to the other travelers, and inspected the vessel with the Captain.

For some reason she didn't understand, she was fascinated with him. She made a conscious effort to keep her mind on the conversation that whirled around her and her eyes on the women, but Quint kept creeping into the corners of her vision. Several times, she caught him watching her as well. That pleased her tremendously and was even harder to explain.

When she was alone in her cabin, she lectured herself, "You're engaged, even if you've never seen the man. You shouldn't be looking at another man and he certainly shouldn't be watching you. In fact, you shouldn't even be thinking about Quinton McQuade." Her lectures didn't help at all, she still watched him. She couldn't seem to help herself.

One evening, after dinner, Rebecca was on the deck with her new friends taking the air. Quint approached and asked her to join him for a tour of the deck. Rebecca glanced at the other women and knew instantly that they thought the worst. She refused him quietly, but as she looked at her companions, Rebecca knew the damage had been done.

"I'll stay here, in my cabin," Rebecca said as she undressed that night. "Or at least I'll stay here morning and evenings." The weather was turning warmer and she knew she couldn't stay in the tiny enclosure during the hottest part of the day. But, as the days dragged by, her self-imposed retreat affected her disposition and once more, she grew furious. Her anger kept her confined as nothing else would have.

After dinner on the eighth day out, she couldn't bring herself to go back to her cabin. Instead, she climbed the stairs to the main deck and wandered to the bow, where she sat quietly on a coil of rope and tried not to think about anything. The harder she tried not to remember, however, the more the memories demanded attention.

She could see her father, his tall elegant figure striding through the house at Hertford. She could almost feel him holding her on his lap and telling her about the mother she didn't remember. She pictured him as he had been, tall and straight, as he rode with her across her lands. And, they were her lands, in spite of Arthur. Her father had given them to her on her fourteenth birthday as her estate. She was to keep them even after she married and they were to go to her children. The carriage accident had taken his life, though, before he saw his lawyer, and she was left with Arthur and a will that hadn't been changed in years.

Arthur knew of their father's desires, but he ignored them and insisted that the terms of the will be met, which meant that he handled all funds, the estate, and the farms. According to the will, when Rebecca married, the estate and the farms went to Arthur and if she did not marry then at twenty-five, all of the property was to be divided between them. She scowled at the setting sun, Arthur was going to make sure that she married long before then.

For the moment, the sun brought her back to the present and she sat fascinated as the sea swallowed the brilliant orange ball. It struck her that she was very much like the sun and Arthur the sea. She wondered if she would someday rise again, as the sun must the next morning. She grew angrier still.

The moon was an indistinct crescent in the sky when she left her place on the ropes and moved to the rail. The night was warm and the soft trade winds from the south blew gently across her face and swished through her cotton gown. Waiting for the night to quiet her anger, she let her mind wander back to her farm and she was so absorbed in her own private world that she failed to hear the muffled footsteps approach her place of refuge until a deep cough alerted her to the presence of a man.

She spun around and glared at the tall broad form of Quint McQuade. A groan slipped from her lips when she realized that he must have come searching for her. As she looked at him, for some strange reason her knees felt peculiar and she had the distinct impression that they might not hold her weight.

"Good evening, Mistress Ranserford. Are you all right?" he bent his head toward her. She said nothing, nodded her head and turned back to the sea.

Quint moved next to her at the rail, "Peaceful, isn't it?" he said quietly and then continued without waiting for her answer, "I think I like the evening hours aboard ship the best. There's something about the vastness of a dark sky, studded with stars and the ever-moving water that makes personal problems so remote." He turned to the shadowed face and breathed in the soft fragrance of dusky spring roses that she wore.

Rebecca wondered if he, too, had personal problems, but before she could phrase a question, Quint slid one hand about her waist and with the other he tilted her face up to his. He looked deep into her eyes, glistening in the soft glow of the celestial canopy. Slowly, he lowered his head to touch his lips to hers.

Rebecca was too stunned to move. Something passed between them when he looked in her eyes, and she could not draw away. She knew he was going to kiss her, but she didn't care. There was such a thrill of savage anticipation that any movement away from him was completely impossible. It mattered not that she had never been kissed before, nor that she was a woman pledged to another. At that moment nothing mattered.

His first kiss was a soft brush of her lips, but before she could regain her composure, he kissed her again. His second kiss was nothing like the first gentle brush, but a demanding kiss, a kiss that made a devastating claim on her delicate mouth. Her whole body tingled. She melted into him and without willing it to be so, she felt her arms move up to twine about his neck. The kiss went on and on and she never wanted it to end. Suddenly, the face of Arthur danced before her eyes. She stiffened and dropped her arms, then pulled away from him and turned back to the railing.

Quint sensed the tension before she dropped her arms, and when she stepped away from him, he let her go. Damn. He'd already decided that she had to be wooed gently, even if others had known her first. She was such a delicate creature and he'd intended to go slowly, convinced that she was not over the desertion of her lover. He wondered if he had ruined his chances.

Lifting his head, he smiled at her, delighted that she stayed at the rail instead of running for her cabin. In a husky voice, he apologized, "I'm sorry. It's such a pleasant night. I'm afraid I let your beauty and those softly glowing stars rob me of my senses. Will you forgive me?"

Rebecca stared at him, her eyes blank. She had never been faced with such a situation, and she didn't know how to respond. She was trembling and she was angry, angry with herself for the way she responded. She accused, "Sir, you shame me. I'm an engaged woman! You had no right."

To cover his own feelings, he snapped, "Oh, come now! It was only a little kiss, and you enjoyed it as much as I did."

Rebecca stood frozen to the deck for a second and then her anger flared. How dare he insinuate that she was the kind of a woman who enjoyed a stranger's kisses. Why, it was clear that he thought she was a . . . was a . . . She struck out at him with her anger, anger at Arthur, anger at her situation, and anger at what Quint did. The slap sounded like an explosion in the quiet night. Rebecca stomped to the stairway and disappeared below deck.

Bewildered, Quint rubbed his cheek as he watched her go. He had only kissed her, but she reacted like a virgin. Her response delighted and surprised him, but it left little doubt that she was exactly what he thought. No, the lady was not untried, not the way she rubbed herself up against him and twined her arms around his neck. He scowled, but no woman of his acquaintance had ever cracked him across the face after she enjoyed one of his kisses. Was it possible that this girl was not what she seemed? There was the missing maid. He was willing, though, to take an oath that she lied when she told him the maid became ill. No, he was right the first time. She was someone's ex-mistress and this marriage had been arranged to get her away from her lover for whatever reason. Still, it wouldn't hurt to ask Captain Hemphill what he knew of the girl.

Quint pulled out his pipe, carefully filled the bowl from his bag of tobacco, and striking his flint against the dried leaves, pulled deeply against the stem. She was certainly a strange one. He watched her watching him while she talked to the other women. And, just tonight, when most of the other women he knew would have run for their chambers, she held her ground. Damn it! There was a spark there that had never been there before with other women he met. No, there was an attraction to this girl he didn't understand. Perhaps he should have gone with his first instinct and ignored Susannah's letter. He would still be in England with his own ship. He never would have met Mistress Ranserford. She was a puzzle and he didn't like puzzles.

Chapter Three

Rebecca reached her tiny cabin and, shaking violently, threw off her clothes and crawled into bed. Horrified at what had just taken place, she refused to acknowledge to herself that she had kissed the man back, that she had wanted the kiss. No, the scoundrel kissed her, and she was an engaged woman. Somehow, that made it even worse. Did all colonial men make a habit of grabbing any women available and forcing their attention on them? Was this why they were considered savages? They were certainly a different breed of men than the gentlemen of England.

Never once did she consider that she had no knowledge of men at all. The few men she knew either worked for her father or lived in the small village she called home. Arthur had refused to consider a season for her, and she never met any of his friends. He stayed in London at his townhouse and she stayed on the farm, directing its everyday affairs. Rebecca Ranserford had never been courted, and she had never been kissed.

She squirmed in her bunk trying to get comfortable. As she stared up at the wooden ceiling above her, her thoughts raced over the events of the night. Obviously, if he kissed her once, he would try again. She must not allow that to happen. Somehow, she had to stay out of his way and the only way she could do that was to stay in her cabin and venture out only when she was positive that the other families were on the deck as well. She had her books and her sewing to occupy her time, she could stay in her cabin. Content that the problem was solved, Rebecca rolled over and tried to go to sleep.

The next morning, Rebecca waited until she heard the laughing voices of some of the children before she headed for the dining room. It was too crowded to be comfortable. Quint was nowhere in sight. She went back to her cabin and dragged her books out of the trunk. For the next three hours, she worked on the handwritten treatise that her tutor had given her as a farewell gift. She remembered how excited she had been at the time, for it was a gift of incomparable value for her. It was a study of the native herbs in Pennsylvania.

Herbs and their healing power had always been fascinating to her. Long before her father died, she had been hungry for knowledge of medicine and medical treatment, but her father discouraged her. Ladies were not interested in such things. After his death, she pursued a limited study with her tutor. He would get the book and she would read and take notes.

Those notes proved their worth when she started accompanying the local doctor around the farms. When any of the tenants were injured or sick and the doctor was called, she went, too, and he even taught her how to set broken bones and stitch up wounded flesh. He taught her how to detect infection and she helped with all of the serious injuries on the farms.

Then, one afternoon, their relationship came to an abrupt end. Rebecca remembered the argument as if it had happened only a day ago. One of her father's grooms had been severely kicked by a foaling mare. He was bleeding badly and the surgeon insisted that the man be bled. Rebecca screamed at him that the man had already lost too much blood. When the doctor pushed her out of the way, his bowl in hand, she lost her temper completely. She pushed him out of the barn, yelling that he was a barbarian, a quack. She gave him five minutes to get off of her property. He never came back.

She took his place. On two separate occasions, she had even helped the midwife with a difficult birth. There were times when she didn't know what to do, and her books and notes gave her no clues. Never would she forget the angelic face of the first child who died in her arms. His parents had waited too long to summon her and there was nothing she could do then. She brushed a tear from her eye and wondered what her people were doing now for their aches and pains. She wondered if Arthur told the man she was going to marry about her healing skills?

As she worked, she made a note to tell Captain Hemphill that she had such knowledge and would be glad to be of assistance if he needed her, that is, if she could ever find him alone, without Quint McQuade at his side.

As she worked she fought a continual battle to keep the rogue from her thoughts. When she least expected it, his face would appear above the book she was studying, or the sensation of his lips on hers would make her lose her place. Even when she lay in her uncomfortable bed, his blue eyes would dance out of the dark corners of the cabin. She couldn't remember when she last had a good night's sleep.

Because of her lack of sleep and her lack of companionship, her spirit lagged. Each day, getting dressed was a chore and she missed several meals because she couldn't hear the children's voices that had become her signal. On a particularly gloomy day, she returned to her cabin intent on working at an embroidery she brought to pass the time. As dark as the cabin was, she needed both lamps to sew but she couldn't get the spark she needed from her flint to light one lamp let alone two. "Arthur," she mumbled, "Right now I'm very close to hating you." She slumped down on her trunk and gave into a feminine habit she always despised in others. Tears of frustration and helplessness streamed down her face and she started to sob.

Quint was on his way to his cabin when he heard the muffled sobs of a woman. He traced the heart wrenching sounds to Rebecca's cabin. Standing there, trying to decide what to do, he thought of the information Captain Hemphill had shared. She had been entrusted to the captain by a man claiming to be her brother. She was to be delivered to Stephen Hill of Philadelphia as his bride. Quint frowned. That supposed brother was probably the man she loved, and it was clear to him that she was attempting to recover from her loss. Her heartbreak stirred some protective instinct in him and as he listened to her sob, a physical need to comfort her almost overwhelmed him.

Without a thought to the consequences, he tapped on the door and waited for a response. None came and the sobs continued. He tapped louder. There was still no answer and the sobs continued. Cautiously, he pushed the door open and stood in the opening for several seconds.

Rebecca sat huddled in the corner on her trunk, her slender hands covering her face while her small frame shook with the pain and the desperation she felt. Quint moved quietly from the door to the trunk. He knelt down and drew her into his arms whispering soft words of comfort. He was amazed at his own feelings. Never before had a woman's tears affected him and he had seen enough of his mother's and sisters' tears to know. Something about this black-haired beauty moved him to a tenderness he had never experienced before. He had to comfort her, hold her in his arms and soothe her.

Without realizing what she was doing or who was providing the comfort she needed, she leaned into his chest and sobbed her heart out. She was frightened and felt so alone. The need to be held as she had once been held in her father's arms, was overwhelming. At the moment, she needed comforting and she was too absorbed in her misery to question the strong masculine arms that gently lifted her and cradled her in his lap.

When her sobs slowed, Quint removed his handkerchief and tilted her chin up so that he could wipe away the remaining tears. She blinked her eyes and stared at him for a second before she stiffened. Trying to pull away, her voice caught, "You!"

Quint held her firmly while she struggled against him trying to free herself. In a husky voice he said, "Please, no more crying. I'm sorry. I feel some responsibility for those tears, at least some of them. Let me show you that American men aren't the savages I'm sure you think we are. Although, some of us act like it at times," he added, his voice full of irony.

Bewildered, Rebecca gazed at him and thoughts careened through her head. Had she misjudged him, or perhaps made more over the matter than was warranted? Was he as harmless as he seemed at the moment, or a monster? Finally, she whispered, "Your apology is accepted, sir," and turned her head away.

Quint sighed in relief. She had stopped crying and she accepted his apology. Suddenly, he realized that she was in his arms and he was holding her tightly. The desire to tighten his hold and kiss that exquisite little mouth left him breathless. With more will power than he thought he had, he set her on her feet and stood himself. He moved to the door and struggling for a normal tone of voice he asked, "Will you walk with me after the evening meal?" Noticing her hesitation he added, "The captain will join us."

She looked at him suspiciously but she nodded her head in agreement. She would walk with him after dinner.

The weather for the next three days was nearly perfect, and Rebecca was glad to get away from her tiny cell. She spent most of her time on deck, enjoying the sun and the fresh air. She was delighted with Quint's attitude to her. He treated her with complete respect and almost solemn courtesy. He introduced her to both of the men from Pennsylvania and suggested that they tell her much about her new home. Often, he began the discussions that took so much of the day. He encouraged her to ask questions.

She asked a thousand. Both men delighted in telling her about the part of the country that was to be her home. She listened carefully to the comments made about the French territory and the Spanish claims in the southern part of the new nation. As she listened to the descriptions of the country, she wondered aloud at its size. One of the men tried to draw Rebecca a map of some of the area known to him. She shook her head in disbelief, "It can't be that big. I just can't believe that such an area of land exists. You'll have to give me some kind of proof."

The men and the women, too, agreed that although the map was not completely accurate, it basically represented the land mass of the country and the territories under dispute. Rebecca was speechless; the country was enormous. No wonder these Americans were so arrogant. As if he could read her mind, Quint grinned at her and said, "We're a proud people."

It wasn't just the size of the country that fascinated her so. She found that the tales about the savages that first occupied the land aroused her interest and terrified her even more. They're exaggerating, she decided as they described the tortures some tribes used. As she listened, they extolled the skills used by the Indians who served during the war, and she became confused. Weren't all of the Indians alike? Were they applauding the tortures, and the savages' way of life? Were the Indians friends or foes?

She raked her memory to find the comments that her tutor made when he told her about the three American Indians he'd seen in London. It was his opinion that the savages lacked only the white man's education. Except for that, he told her solemnly, there was little difference. Rebecca held on to that bit of wisdom as she listened to tales of recent trouble along the frontier.

When she wasn't discussing the frontier with the couples from Philadelphia, she talked with the other women new to the country. They discussed the latest fashions and the dresses they would copy when they were settled. They shared letters from family or friends about the homes that were waiting for them. Rebecca tried to hide her amazement. Arthur had told her that the country was backward and her need for new clothing was ridiculous. How could he have been so wrong?

One afternoon, almost two weeks into their journey, a child became sick. Several hours later, one of the women fell ill. Even though the weather had been near perfect for days, the captain blamed their complaints on Mal de Mer. That evening, though, another child and one of the men took ill. By the next afternoon, three more passengers and a sailor were confined to their bunks, retching uncontrollably.

Rebecca offered her knowledge to the captain immediately, but he ignored her just as he had when she initially told him about her skills. He went below, inspected the food and the water, pronounced both good and ordered the burning of ashes. Broth was made for the sick passengers but they couldn't hold that down. By evening, two more children were violently ill, and the first sick child was close to death.

Rebecca pleaded, "Please, let me try to help them. I do have some skills, and I have herbs with me that might help. At least let me try. It's better than doing nothing."

He scowled at her and nodded, "Go ahead. But, I doubt it'll do any good." He turned away so that she could not see his worry. He knew of entire shiploads of people, passengers and crew alike, who died of strange maladies while at sea.

Rebecca gathered her herbs and descended into the kitchen to brew tea. She smiled grimly as she worked. At least she could do as much as the captain and the cook had done. Through the long night and into early morning Rebecca spooned the bitter brew between the weakly protesting lips of the Prescott child. Together, Jane Prescott, his mother, and Rebecca sponged the child down. Slowly, he grew less restless and finally slept.

Rebecca ordered a gallon of tea to be prepared and distributed to all the ailing passengers. Then, she went on a food hunt. She discovered that all the passengers who became ill had eaten the same fish. With the cook howling his protests, Rebecca threw the remaining fish overboard and went to check on her patients. Everyone of them was improving. She tried to explain to the captain and then the relatives of those afflicted how she figured out the fish was responsible, but they weren't interested. She was a miracle worker. Even the sailors treated her like some kind of goddess.

Each day blended into the next as the ship sailed West. Rebecca spent more and more time in the company of Quint. He made sure they dined together, that she had a daily turn around the deck, and when the weather was unpleasant, he told her more about ships and her new country.

In spite of Quint's attention, Rebecca could not shake a certain amount of melancholy. There was something, too, about the way he looked at her when he didn't think she was watching, almost as if he could devour her as she stood, that made her very uncomfortable. One afternoon, she found a spot on deck beside some of the coiled ropes that had so intrigued her that first day on the ship. She wanted some small amount of time alone. Perhaps, she admitted to the cloudless sky, I'm a bit homesick. Whatever the reason, she was depressed and she wanted no conversation with anyone. The reason that she was on the ship in the first place held a death grip on her consciousness. Into what kind of a marriage had Arthur sold her?

She stood at the rail and watched the brilliant blood-red ball sink into the silver waves. Once more, she was lost in her concern about what waited for her in the new country to which she was traveling. Long after the globe of fire had faded beneath the sea, Rebecca stood in the darkness frozen with fear for her future. What if the man to whom Arthur was sending her was a cruel man, or a grotesque creature, someone no other woman would consider? Her fears poured panic through her body like oil spreading across water. Dear God, what would she do if she could not marry the man? Indeed, did she have any other choice?

Quint cleared his throat so that he wouldn't surprise her as he had before. There was a wistful quality about her that drew him closer and closer. For days, he had been fighting the urge to grab her and force her body against his, but something about the way she looked at him had held him at bay. But, in the darkness, he couldn't see her face. Tonight, he would claim her. She would be his for this night at least.

He stepped up beside her and gently placed his arm around her narrow waist, "So sad tonight. Missing home?"

Rebecca let his deep mellow voice roll over her. Somehow, he had guessed. She nodded her head in answer and for a second she allowed his arms to circle her in comfort. "I should go below," she whispered softly.

"No," he whispered back, "Stay with me for a time."

Rebecca knew she should pull free from his hold, but she felt weak, detached. She couldn't move away from him, not just yet. She looked out into the darkness, "For a time."

At first, as the minutes slipped by, Rebecca was comfortable in their quiet companionship. But, for some reason, she gradually became aware of Quint's labored breathing and the erratic beating of her own heart. Suddenly, nothing would do except that he put his arms around her and draw her close. As if he could read her mind, his arm tightened around her waist and he pulled her into his arms. She tried a feeble protest, but even to her own ears it sounded most unconvincing.

If he heard her murmured rejection, he gave no reaction. Instead he lowered his head, and brushed her lips with his own. The gasp that left her lips did not go unnoticed, however. He mumbled, his voice husky in the night, "You wanted that, as much as I wanted to kiss you."

She tried to shake her head, but he held her face still with his hand and once more his head dropped so that again his lips touched her. But this time, Rebecca felt her knees give out and vaguely she wondered how she could still be standing. Then, she thought of nothing as warm pulsing pleasure twisted through her small frame. A warm glow seemed to envelop her as Quint's kiss went on and on. He pressed the tip of his tongue against her lips and she opened for him. The glow burst into flames and Rebecca knew that she could not pull away from him, even to save her life.

Quint pulled away from her so that he could take a breath. Rebecca laid her head against his chest and her soft rose fragrance blended with the smell of the sea creating an enticing perfume that threatened to intoxicate him. He touched his lips to her thick black hair and told himself that once he had sated his desire for her, he would not find her so intriguing.

Rebecca rested her head against his chest and tried to force the fog of desire from her own mind. What was happening to her? Why couldn't she resist this man and the pleasure that being in his arms brought her? As her mind cleared and she could once again breathe in a normal fashion, she became aware of his hand trailing up and down her spine. His hand drifted down toward her buttocks and she tensed. He shouldn't be touching her there. He shouldn't be holding her, either, or kissing her! What was she allowing him to do?

She jerked away from him. "I . . . I must go below. I . . . I should go to bed. I . . . I shouldn't be here with you. You must not kiss me." She knew she was making little sense but she had to get away from him.

As she started to move toward the stairs, Quint grabbed her arm, "Stay with me. I want . . ." he let his voice trail off.

"I can't stay with you," she answered stiffly. "I am betrothed to another." As she turned to start down the stairs she heard Quint mutter, "Damn you."

For several days Rebecca avoided Quint again, but once more they fell into the previously established patterns, as they sailed west. On the thirty-first day of the journey, the cry "Land, ho!" split the air. Captain Hemphill pulled Rebecca aside, "My dear, this island, far from the continent, is my home. I insist that you join me at my plantation."

"You live here?"

The captain smiled down at her, "When you see my island paradise, you'll see why I choose to make this my home."

Rebecca thought of his words while she smiled lazily in her first fresh water bath in a month. It was a paradise. The sea provided a delightful breeze all through the day. The captain's beautiful red-headed daughter accompanied her to the open markets in the small village. Rebecca had never seen anything like it. The dark-skinned natives hawked their wares under brilliantly colored canopies and the air was fragrant with the strange smells of native food. She saw nothing of Quint McQuade, for he accepted the offer of the first mate who also had a home and a wife on the island. She told herself that she was extremely glad that she didn't have to concern herself with him as she enjoyed the captain's hospitality.

She did enjoy his home and the feather bed she lazed in each morning. Even the dark-skinned servants who saw to her every need were gratefully accepted as she luxuriated for the first time in years. For the four days that they were there, Rebecca felt somehow reborn. Perhaps her future was not as bleak as she suspected.

Early on the thirty-fifth day from England, they prepared to leave the island and with each step Rebecca took back to the ship, she felt her spirits sag. Her future was already decreed. She was going to meet some kind of monster and there was nothing she could do to avoid the marriage Arthur had arranged. As the ship sailed away from port, the dark ominous clouds hanging heavy over the small island mirrored Rebecca's mood.

Chapter Four

Rebecca stared at the dark clouds that followed them and thought about the captain's comments as she boarded the ship. He'd told her quietly that they were only about ten days from the port of Philadelphia and she wondered if the clouds would delay their arrival. Even in the farmlands north of London tales of storms at sea and lost ships circulated. When she questioned him, however, the captain explained with confidence, "The clouds will break. It's too early in the season for a real storm."

Rebecca watched the clouds collect and grow darker and darker. Silently, she doubted the captain's words. As the sky grew black, the wind filled the sails, pushing the small ship through the ever-increasing waves. When the captain suggested that the passengers seek their cabins, Rebecca just stared at the man, her eyes wide with fear. One of the women tried to assure the frightened girl, "The fall storms are much worse. There are many more ships lost in the fall storms."

Quint volunteered to take Rebecca to her cabin, "It might be a little rough for a while, but the vessel is seaworthy and the captain is competent. We should ride out the waves with little trouble."

Rebecca kept thinking of Quint's words as she clung to the railing in her bunk. She had soon given up the thought of sitting on her trunk in the dark cabin, for the ship pitched and rolled so violently she feared for her safety. She thanked the Almighty for the railing that had perplexed her the first day on the ship. Without it she was sure she would have been thrown to the floor countless times. She thought about the woman's words, "Nothing could be worse than this," she muttered, her voice shaking.

She was terrified. She was going to die. As the ship lurched and creaked, she muttered, "Arthur, you've condemned me to a watery grave."

For what seemed like an eternity, the ship struggled through the churning sea. At one point, there was a deafening crash, and Rebecca steeled herself for the end. But, it never came and somehow, even with the ship bouncing and pitching, she fell asleep.

A distant banging brought Rebecca awake with a start. The floor seemed to be at a proper angle and the ship was no longer making the crunching sounds that she was sure spelled the end. She shook her head to clear the fog and the banging grew louder. Someone was pounding on her door!

She groped her way to the door. When she threw it open Quint greeted her, his face anxious. "One of the beams split and the cabin boy, Jimmy, was trapped," Quint explained, his voice full of concern. "His leg is badly injured. Is there anything you can do?"

"I'll need to see him," she answered softly. As an afterthought she asked, "Are we through the storm?"

Quint held the door for her, before he turned to answer, "Most of it. It was worse than any of us thought, and the seas are still heavy, but the storm is to our north now. Unfortunately, we were blown off course. It will add several days to our voyage, I'm afraid."

"Come," he said and led her to the flight of stairs that led to the third level of the ship. She looked at him in surprise as he started to descend. "We carried him to one of the officers' cabins," he explained while she was making her way down the steps. At the bottom of the stairs, he took her arm and guided her through the opening. Jimmy was lying on a bunk that was smaller than her own, in an area half as large as hers. She glanced at the boy lying in his bunk, his face a grayish white in the light of the lamp. His face was covered with small beads of perspiration and he groaned in agony.

Rebecca turned her attention to the bloody leg that she had been called to tend. "It's broken and the wound must be cleaned," she explained slowly. She leaned over and whispered something in Jimmy's ear as she soothed his forehead. He quieted down and tried to smile at her.

She patted his shoulder and returned his smile, then moved to the door. She signaled Quint to follow and once they were both outside Jimmy's hearing she turned to the tall man at her side, "We'll need some strong spirits to set his leg." She frowned, "I'll need someone to help. In fact, I'll need at least two people, someone to hold him down and someone to help me with his leg."

As Quint led her to the stairs, he assured her, "I'll help and I'm sure one of the officers will come."

Hurrying to her cabin, she grabbed her herbs and started back to the steps. Quint met her at the stairway, a bottle of rum in his hands, "The first officer will be down shortly. He's volunteered to help."

Together they made their way back to the small room where Jimmy lay. "Mr. McQuade," she said as she glanced around the room, "I'm going to need a lot more light than this. Could you get me more lamps?" She glanced at the large open space where the officers took their meal, eyeing the large lamp that hung above a table in the center of the officers' mess. "Actually, can we move him to that area? There isn't enough room to work in here."

First Officer Landis arrived and as Quint explained what was needed Rebecca spread blankets out on the table. When everything was ready, Rebecca waited beside the table while the two men gently carried the moaning boy to the table. The bright lamps flooded the room with light and Rebecca winced as she looked at the bloody wound and the twisted leg. After she said a silent prayer, she took a deep breath and went to work.

She worked quickly and cleared the dirt from the wound, then packed the place with crushed herbs. Then she turned her attention to the break. While she explained to Quint what he must do to help her, Mr. Landis filled a cup with rum and succeeded in getting Jimmy to swallow several small draughts. Rebecca moved up to the boy's head, "Jimmy?" she smoothed his feverish brow to gain his attention, "I'm going to pull on your leg and it will hurt terribly but only for a minute. If I don't do it, you'll never walk again and you might lose your leg. Remember, just for a minute and if you want to yell, go ahead. All right?"

Jimmy tried to smile, "All right," came the weak response. Quint watched, amazed. She radiated calmness and when she spoke the boy tried to smile. He turned his attention to her words, as she gave orders to the two men.

After the instructions, Rebecca grabbed Jimmy's leg and he screamed and fainted. The crunch of bones going back into place broke the silence in the room and Rebecca heaved a sigh of relief. Quickly, she placed two boards on either side of the leg and while Quint held them in place she secured them. Next, she fixed a poultice and placed it over the gaping wound, wrapping it tightly. "It would be best to move him back to his bunk while he's unconscious," she suggested to the two men as she started cleaning up. When everything was cleaned up to her satisfaction, Rebecca dragged a chair from the eating area and sank down beside the bunk. Quint offered to sit with the boy so that she could go back to bed, but she stubbornly refused to budge. "Someone can take over for me in several hours," she whispered, "But not just yet."

Reluctantly, Quint left her sitting beside the boy. As he turned to go up the stairs, he looked back toward the cabin. There was something very special about the woman. Shaking his head, he moved up the steps. Even if she had been someone's mistress, she was one of the most caring people he'd ever met. He couldn't help but wonder if her intended knew how very special she was.

For the next week, Rebecca spent most of her day with the injured cabin boy feeding him, trying to take his mind off of his pain, and reading to him. When she found that he could not read himself, she began to give him reading lessons.

Quint watched her with a touch of jealousy. In days, the trip would come to an end, and Rebecca Ranserford would leave the ship to become Mrs. Stephen Hill. His face wrinkled in displeasure as he admitted that she was the kind of woman who would honor her pledge. He would have liked to spend more time with her, he decided as he glanced up to see the object of his thoughts take the lunch tray from the cook, balance the book she was carrying, and start toward the door.

"Mistress Ranserford, here, let me carry that for you."

"Oh! Why, thank you, Mr. McQuade."

Quint took the tray and started for the stairs. She never called him Quint. Once Rebecca was at Jimmy's side, Quint climbed the stairs to the main deck. They were south of their destination by three, maybe four days, but they should sight land soon, he thought, as he remembered his conversation with the captain the night before. Perhaps he should have mentioned that to Rebecca. After all, she seemed so anxious about his country.

Rebecca was too busy helping Jimmy with his reading lesson to think about her destination. After lunch, they read for an hour and when Jimmy tried to stifle a yawn, Rebecca closed the book, picked up the tray and bade her patient a good rest.

She closed the door and with the tray in hand, she started for the stairs. Lounging against the stairwell frame was one of the sailors. She had noticed him before and Quint had introduced him to her on one of their many trips around the deck. His name was Bud Worthman, and he, too, was originally from a farming town north of London. He was not very tall, perhaps only five or six inches taller than she, but as with most of the men on the ship, powerful muscles rippled across his back and arms when he moved. She remembered him because his chest and his arms were covered with dark thick hair. He wore a beard but the hair on his head was thin and he was growing bald. He never seemed interested in any of the passengers, in fact, he had never shown any interest in Jimmy before, either.

"Strange," she mumbled as she gathered her skirts to climb the steps. Why suddenly had Bud decided to keep an eye on the boy? She glanced around, something wasn't as it should be. Then she realized that there was no noise. This section of the ship was usually very noisy but today there wasn't a sound.

A prickly feeling ran up her spine and she glanced at Bud in alarm. Something was definitely wrong. As she lifted her foot for the first step, she caught a movement out of the corner of her eye. He grabbed at her from behind and the tray clattered to the deck. Slamming his hand across her mouth, he stilled the scream that was about to erupt. For an instant, she froze. Why was he doing this? Then she felt him start to pull her toward the bowels of the ship. She squirmed and twisted, but he was so much stronger than her.

As he forced her down into the lowest level of the ship, he muttered against her ear, "If ya don't scream, then I'll take my hand away. I only wants a little of the lovin' ya be wastin' on young Jimmy there. And I'll love ya good, little girl. Just don't yell none!"

They reached the bottom of the stairs and he yanked her up against him and ran his hand across her buttocks. She struggled, fighting him and the waves of nausea that crowded in upon her. She started to gag and he laughed. He dragged her away from the stairs around a cluster of boxes piled high against the rope railing. "So, ya goin' to fight me are ya? Well, we'll see about that," he slurred, then shoved her around the corner, knocking her against the wall. Her scream died on her lips as her head thudded against the wall. As she sank to the floor, she heard the sound of boxes falling.

For a second she was stunned. In the next instant, he quickly fell on her, grabbing her head. He forced her head back and planted a wet sickening kiss on her lips. She felt his tongue jabbing at her lips. Trying to twist her head away she felt, rather than heard, his growl. Suddenly his tongue was in her mouth and she bit down hard. She could taste the salt of his blood and she gagged. He cursed in pain and struck her across the face. The slap was vicious but it cleared her head. She screamed with every ounce of strength she had.

He clutched at her trying to get his hand over her mouth, but she fought for her life. She struck out at him, scratching and clawing. He would not take her, she would not let him take her. Somewhere in the back of her mind, she knew that if someone didn't come soon, she would be lost. Her voice broke in a sob. Where was everyone?

Once more he reached for her. She rolled away, but his fingers were tangled in the lace of her bodice. The rending sound silenced her for a split second, but only for an instant. She was sobbing, "Help me, someone. Please, help me!"

Quint stood on the deck as passengers and crew alike responded to the call, "Land-ho!" He glanced around. Rebecca was not in the crush of passengers. Of course, if she was still with Jimmy, she hadn't heard the shout. He'd have to go below and get her, or she'd miss the first sighting of her new home.

He was starting down the second flight of stairs when he thought he heard the muffled screams of a woman. The hair on the back of his neck stood up and he leaped down the stairs to the third level. He saw Jimmy trying to crawl toward the stairway, dragging his splinted leg behind him. The anguished sobs were not his imagination. They were coming from the hold. He roared at Jimmy, "Stay!" Then, he took the last flight of steps two at a time.

As Rebecca struggled, she managed to topple several more boxes. She bit and scratched, but Bud's hands continued to clutch and grab her. He kept trying to squeeze the breasts he had bared when he ripped her gown. Suddenly, he was gone, flying into a stack of barrels lined against the wall.

Someone had saved her! She glanced from Bud who was propped against a barrel, shaking his head, to the tall man standing over him. She sank to the deck as her saviour reached down and pounded his fist into the face of the fallen man. As Rebecca watched, Bud slid down the side of the barrel and slumped into unconsciousness.

She stared up at the man before her and was surprised that his face was ashen and his mouth looked very grim. Pulling at the torn dress, she tried to cover herself. Slowly the realization of what had happened hit her. Her eyes glazed over and her face turned from red to a sickly white.

Quint glanced around to see if she was all right and his heart caught in his throat. Her dress was almost torn in half and the color of her face changed from a deep blush to pallid pale. He jerked off his jacket and moved to her side. Carefully, trying not to alarm her, he draped it about her shoulders, pulling it together to cover her nakedness. As his hands touched her shoulders, she started to tremble and Quint stared into her glazed eyes.

Quint cleared his throat and asked in a husky voice, "Are you all right?" Even before the words were out of his mouth, she turned her head and against her pallor, he could see the ugly red marks of the hand that slapped her. As gently as he could, he cupped her chin and forced her to turn toward him. "Oh, my God!" he breathed as he looked into vacant eyes. His voice shaking in concern, he whispered, "Are you all right? Rebecca, are you all right?"

She opened her mouth as if to answer, but not a sound crossed her lips. She stared at nothing. Quint scooped her into his arms and started for the stairs. He wondered if he had been too late.

"What happened?" Mr. Landis stuck his head through the hatch. "I heard thumping noises and found Jimmy lying on the floor. Did she fall? Is she all right?" He looked at Quint in confusion. He backed out of the way as Quint came up the stairs.

"Get the captain. And have him bring one of the women to Rebecca's cabin, and be quick about it." Rebecca was lying in his arms, her eyes open but there was no reaction to the first officer or to Quint's directive.

As he carried her gently to her cabin, he swore softly. Her perfect oval face was gray and her unblinking black eyes looked blank. The girl was in shock. His mouth was a grim white line and his eyes were dark blue with anger. This was not his ship and he wondered how this captain would mete out justice. On one of his ships the man would surely receive the cat.

He laid Rebecca on her bunk as gently as he could, covered her with a blanket and only then did he remove his jacket. Quietly he stood in the open door, glancing in her direction frequently while he kept watch on the stairs. In minutes, he heard the swish of a woman's skirt and saw the bright cotton fabric descending the stairs. The captain's

48

concerned voice blustered behind the woman, "Did she fall? Is she hurt?"

Quint walked to the stairs and stopped the woman, forcing Captain Hemphill to wait on the steps. "She's in her cabin. I don't think she's . . . hurt. She was attacked in the cargo hold by one of the sailors. I think she's in shock." Quint glared at the captain. Why he was angry with the captain he didn't quite know, but he was.

The woman rushed past Quint and he realized it was Jane Prescott. Mr. Landis was, it seemed, an astute fellow. "The cargo hold? What was she doing in the hold? Where's the sailor? Who is it?" The captain's puzzled voice drew Quint's attention.

"This way," Quint growled. Captain Hemphill followed Quint down the second flight of stairs. The young man was angry, he mused, much angrier than he should be unless . . . Had he missed something between Quint and Rebecca?

Mr. Landis met them at the stairs. "Jimmy heard him drag her down the stairs. He says she did a lot of screaming before you came." The first officer's face was red and his eyes were snapping. It seemed that he was as angry as Quint.

When the three men were in the hold, Quint explained what he saw and what he did, as he pointed to the unconscious form still heaped up next to the barrels. Before Quint finished, the captain was glaring, his lips thin and his expression deadly. He produced a large key and slipped past the younger men to a door marked "Ship's Stores."

The long whip with the small lead balls secured to the ends of the leather straps was in his hand before he slammed the door. "Gentlemen, after you," he said in a voice of deadly calm.

Even before Quint's head surfaced above the hatch on the main deck, word had spread that something had happened to the pretty lady passenger. The captain barked orders to sailors and passengers alike and concern for the woman was replaced by a feeling of imminent danger, if not for the whole ship, then at least for someone on the ship. Several sly glances fell on Quint. There was no chance for speculation as the captain ordered the women and children below.

After they were gone, four sailors disappeared and in minutes they returned with Rebecca's attacker, thoroughly drenched, yelling and screaming curses at everyone. As Bud was secured to the center mast of the ship, Captain Hemphill explained to the men on deck what was going to happen and why. The main deck grew hushed as the captain handed the second officer the whip and gave the order, "Nineteen strokes, sir!"

The hand raised, the whip unfurled and the leather descended upon the bared back. Bud screamed a list of profanities. The thongs descended again and then again. The screams died and Bud Worthman lost consciousness once more that day. As the lead balls tore the flesh from his back, several passengers, unable to watch any longer, bolted to the railing. The only sound was the second officer counting the strokes and the hiss of the whip as it passed through the air.

The nineteenth stroke was called and in the hush that followed, the captain ordered, "Cut the man down." Then he added as brusquely, "Into the brig with 'im." Even Quint groaned. In the dark hole in the stern of the ship, the man's back would fester from the musky dampness. He would probably be dead, or dying, by the time they docked in Philadelphia.

The punished man was carted away and the crew returned to their duties. In the unnatural quiet, Ephram Hemphill's words sounded loud and hard, "Ugly business. Would you care for a drink, captain?" and he waited for Quint's reply.

The answer came quickly and it, too, sounded harsh, "Yes, thank you." Both men left the deck and moved down to the captain's cabin in the stern of the ship.

Once inside the sparse room, Captain Hemphill opened a large cabinet and removed a bottle. He poured a dark amber liquid into the two tankards on his desk, then handed one to Quint. For several minutes Hemphill rotated the mug in his hands, watching the liquid swirl around the container. He looked at Quint and clearing his throat he muttered once more, "Ugly thing." He was shocked by the bitter gaze on the younger man's face. McQuade was more affected by the afternoon's events than one would suppose, unless, as he suspected, his two passengers were taken with each other.

He was seized with concern, but he reasoned quickly that they were both adults. He believed, as Quint did, that the girl in question had been the property of another man at one time. No, as long as he fulfilled his part of the bargain, and she arrived unharmed, he really didn't care what Quint and the girl did.

Quint watched the closed face of the *Venture*'s captain as he sipped his rum. He would be willing to wager a sum that the older man had more to say, and he glanced down at his own mug and then at Ephram Hemphill. Yes, he had a lot more to say. He was an imposing man, almost as tall as Quint, but he was a full score older. From his years at sea, his face was weathered and his skin was dark from the sun. His thick silver hair waved around his head. Under bushy brows, his wide-set steel gray eyes could look right through a man and he had the strength to back up any order he gave. His shoulders were wide, his waist trim, and he was heavily muscled. Hemphill could probably show a much younger man a thing or two in a fight, Quint decided.

His reputation as a just man was well-earned, and when Quint checked with those who knew, the man's sailing record was spotless. There were also few discipline problems on board the *Venture*. Captain Hemphill was a strict master, but his crew respected him.

"Do you think our little English lady was harmed?" The captain's question broke the silence. He pulled out a chair for himself and indicated to Quint that he should sit down as well.

"No, I think she is very frightened and also very embarrassed. Nothing more," Quint replied in a firm voice.

Captain Hemphill glanced at him and Quint was surprised to see the relief in the man's eyes.

"This whole affair has not been to my liking," he continued. He began to chuckle at Quint's puzzled expression and said, "I have a great deal of money invested in that little lady." Quint's interest was aroused. The captain took out his pipe, filled the bowl and lit the tobacco. He glanced over at Quint and drew deeply on the stem. "Mr. Stephen Hill, a leading citizen of Philadelphia—I know the man myself—approached me last fall and asked if I would bring his bride back with me this spring. He even authorized me to pay the bride price her brother was demanding. Imagine, a bride price in our society. It amounts to little more than selling the woman. Barbaric!" he paused for another drag on his pipe. "If she does not arrive unharmed and healthy, I forfeit her passage and the fifty pounds sterling I advanced to the man, Arthur."

Quint let out a thin whistle. She was a purchased bride, and a very expensive one at that. And, although it was not an uncommon practice, when the woman was so young and so beautiful . . . Quint shook his head. Usually the woman brought the dowry into the marriage. There was something very peculiar about the whole situation.

Chapter Five

Rebecca recovered quickly from her attack, thanks to the help and support of Jane Prescott. Two days later, the *Venture* sailed into port. The women had said their good-byes after dinner the night before. Rebecca and Jane promised to keep in touch. And, although he tried several times to see her, Rebecca refused to talk to Quint, to tell him anything. The day after the attack, she composed a brief thank-you message and when the first officer came to check on her he promised to deliver it. That would have to do, she told herself.

Early in the morning, word spread that they were finally entering the port and would soon tie up in Philadelphia. Rebecca went topside to watch the ship dock. It was the first time she left her cabin since the attack, and she self consciously stayed off to one side of the deck by herself, away from the leering glances of some of the sailors and one of the passengers.

As soon as the ship docked, she strolled back to her cabin. When she finished packing she sat forlornly on her trunk listening to the clamor above her head as the passengers prepared to disembark. She couldn't bring herself to go back to the deck. Everyone on board had family or friends waiting for them. The man that was coming to get her she knew nothing about, had never seen. A violent shudder shook her slender body. The rest of her life she would belong to him.

She waited quietly, her mind in turmoil. How terribly frightened she was, too frightened to be angry. She felt so alone. Finally, she went to lunch but it was much too early for anyone else to eat and she sat by herself in the empty cabin pushing her food around on her plate. Whether it was the early hour or her nerves, her appetite was non-existent. She went back to her cabin to wait some more.

When she could stand the suspense no longer she left the cabin and climbed to the top deck. "Surely," she mumbled, "Mr. Hill has sent some kind of a message by now." Captain Hemphill told her the night before that they were two days late. The awful tension had to be relieved, somehow. She had to talk to someone.

Cautiously, she approached Mr. Landis. "Where might I find the captain?"

The first officer smiled warmly. "He's in his cabin. There's much paper work to be completed before he can have his lunch and see to the unloading of the cargo, but I'm sure he'll talk to you."

She hurried back down the steps and when she arrived at the captain's door, she hesitated. She knocked timidly and waited several seconds before she raised her hand to knock again. Just before her hand touched the door an impatient voice gruffly ordered, "Come in!"

Rebecca pushed the door open and stood waiting to be invited into the captain's quarters. She glanced at the sparsely decorated room and the large desk in the center littered with slips of paper and a thick logbook. Captain Hemphill's elbow was touching a decanter and his gray head was bent over his log.

Without looking up the captain mumbled, "Yes?" and continued with his work. When he received no answer, he glanced up and saw Rebecca standing in the open doorway. "Oh, Mistress Ranserford. Mr. Hill hasn't arrived yet."

Rebecca felt a trifle nervous but her need to find out more about her situation pushed her anxiety to the shadows of her mind. When the captain pointed to a chair, then turned back to finish his entry, Rebecca moved forward and slid into the seat, folding her hands in her lap. She had to know, and he could tell her. She was willing to wait until he had the time.

He laid the quill pen aside and glanced at the girl before

him. She was distressed, of course, because the man had not arrived, but he sensed something else. Her visit had to do with more than Mr. Hill's tardy appearance. "Well, my dear, can I answer some questions or offer assurance?"

Rebecca relaxed slightly, took a deep breath, and asked softly, "Will Mr. Hill be told about . . . the . . . the . . ." her voice trailed off.

So that was her problem. She was concerned about what Stephen Hill's reaction would be to her near-rape. He tried to put some reassurance into his voice. "I see no need to mention it to him. I wouldn't want to distress the man when nothing happened, do you?"

Rebecca shook her head and let a sigh slip pass her lips. She smiled ever so slightly and asked, "Do you know the gentleman, sir?"

"Well enough!"

"Is he an older gentleman?" Rebecca concentrated on her folded hands clutched in her lap.

Ephram Hemphill was startled. Had the brother who made arrangements told her nothing about the man she was to wed? "I don't know his exact age, but I suspect he is about my age, two score and ten."

Rebecca's shoulders slumped. He was fifty years to her twenty-one, a man old enough to be her father. Another sigh slipped out. She could have expected something like that from Arthur.

The captain watched her carefully. What could he say that would ease her obvious distress? "He's a man of influence in Philadelphia, and he's known for his generosity. He also has a fine sense of humor. A woman could do much worse for herself," he offered softly. "You'll see when you meet him."

Rebecca wanted to ask a dozen more questions, but the captain was not the man to ask. In fact, he might take offense if she asked why such an outstanding citizen bought a wife from England. No, she couldn't ask him that kind of a question.

He stood, as if to indicate that the discussion was finished. As he moved to the door, Rebecca was sure that he was dismissing her. His words confirmed it, "Now you must excuse me. I have to get this cargo to the warehouse. I will let you know just as soon as Mr. Hill arrives. He probably doesn't know that the ship has docked."

Rebecca followed him to the door. "Thank you for your time," she murmured.

When Captain Hemphill closed the door quietly behind her, he stood for several minutes, his heavy brows drawn across his forehead. Where was the man? He figured that he would be standing on the dock before the ship tied up. Stephen Hill had seemed so anxious before the *Venture* sailed. Was it possible that he changed his mind? That thought was worrisome. When financial arrangements were first proposed, Ephram worried. Something about the advisability of using his own money to bring the girl to Hill troubled him. "Stephen Hill is an honorable man. I'm borrowing trouble." He slumped down in his chair and stared at the clutter on his desk. But where was the fellow?

All through the afternoon, Rebecca asked herself, where's the man who had been willing to pay Arthur for her hand in marriage? According to Captain Hemphill, he was a honorable man, and the captain said she could not do better for herself. It hurt more than she was willing to admit that the man Arthur had chosen for her was old enough to be her father, but he obviously was a good man. Where was he, then? Why hadn't he come forward to claim her hand? She couldn't bear it if he had had a change of heart.

After lunch was served to the sailors, she asked if she could leave the ship and walk on firm ground for a while, but the captain seemed reluctant to assign her an escort. When she protested that she wanted to walk by herself, he admonished her. "Your memory is short, my dear. I do not intend to let you out of my sight and you WILL NOT leave this ship without an escort."

She dragged herself back to the tiny cell that was her cabin and tried to nap. It was useless, and in less than an hour she was up walking the deck. Suddenly, in the bright afternoon sunshine of the upper deck, Quint McQuade's face with his twinkling blue eyes appeared in her mind's eye. Why was his image coming to haunt her? What had the man done to her? She should be thinking about Stephen

Hill, the man she was pledged to marry, and not another. "I don't know Stephen Hill," she told the gulls who kept her company on their perches about the deck. Somehow, she felt disloyal.

As the afternoon dragged on, Rebecca tried to read but the words blurred after a page or two. If she just had someone to talk to! The captain, the first officer, and most of the sailors were still on board, but Rebecca didn't feel that she could bother them.

When Rebecca saw the black carriage rolling toward the dock, her heart lifted and fell in one motion. Had Stephen Hill finally arrived? The creature that climbed down from the conveyance however was a small wiry woman. As she started up the gangplank, Rebecca looked down to see a thin hard face with wisping gray hair. The tiny woman insisted in a nasal twang that she be allowed to see the captain immediately. Rebecca stared in fascination. She sensed disaster. Something was very wrong. She slipped away to her own chamber, but she left her door ajar just in case something was said about the woman within her hearing.

The woman met Captain Hemphill only feet from Rebecca's door and Rebecca strained against the wall so that she could hear what the woman had to say. "I'm Mistress Rachel Hill, and Stephen Hill was my brother. We must talk." Rebecca heard the sharp taps of the woman's heels as they moved down the corridor. Rebecca wondered at the past tense the woman used but gave it little thought as she remembered the woman's face. No wonder Stephen Hill sent to England for a wife. If Mistress Rachel Hill lived with her brother, no other woman would dare.

Rebecca left her listening post and slumped down on the trunk, a feeling of doom descending. She heard the tapping of the old woman's heels and the sounds told her that the stringy little lady had taken herself from the ship. Soon, Rebecca told herself, she would know. Breathlessly, she waited.

The minutes dragged by into what seemed like eternity and Rebecca waited for her summons. Finally, the first officer tapped at her door and identified himself, "Rebecca,

Captain Hemphill would like to talk to you."

Half in hope and half in fear, she started for his cabin. For just a second, panic seized her. Her legs, now like jelly, no longer seemed able to support her. She clenched her hands into tight fists and took several deep breaths. Back in control, she continued to the rear of the ship with a small degree of grace.

The captain came to the door quickly and ushered her into his room. He escorted her to a chair, then turned to a decanter on his desk and poured her a glass of wine. She read nothing in his blank face, but his actions spoke eloquently. She had guessed correctly; something was terribly wrong.

He said quietly, "Mistress Ranserford, I have some bad news for you. Mr. Hill will not be coming for you. He was killed several weeks ago in a carriage accident." He paused and watched her closely.

She gave him a forlorn look, set her untouched glass of wine on the table next to her chair, rose, and walked to the door. "I did not know the man, but I am sorry," she said, then left the cabin quietly.

Back in her own cabin, she sat on her trunk in a daze wondering what she should do. She was in a foreign land, had no money or friends, and did not want to return to England. If she went back home, Arthur would only find someone else who would marry her and pay him in the bargain. No, she decided, England was not the answer. She made her way up to the deck and sat watching the afternoon sun make its way across the sky, conscious of the groups of sailors walking past the ship.

She ignored the sailors and gazed at the city of Philadelphia for the first time. People mingled on the street, carriages moved back and forth, and she could see the groups of buildings that marked the beginning of a new nation. She thought back over the discussions held on that very deck and the resiliency of the people who lived here, the plans the newcomers had, and Quint McQuade's statement, "We're a proud people."

Well, she had pride, too. She sat up straight, squared her shoulders and took a deep breath. If those individuals who sailed with her could begin again, certainly she could do the same. She was strong, young, and intelligent. She would survive. Arthur couldn't take her education away from her, like he had everything else. Suddenly, an idea drew her straighter still. Her education! That was the answer. She took a deep breath and exhaled slowly. She could teach. Surely she could earn more than enough to support herself and she would never have to return to England and Arthur.

Rebecca stood up and glanced around. She gritted her teeth and clenched her fists. After all, England had once been ruled by a woman. Women could manage, if they were given a chance. She would have to insist that she be given her chance. She tossed her head in the air and fluffed her skirts as if to announce to the world that from that moment on she was in control of her own destiny. It was time to tell the captain that she wanted to leave the ship. She started for his cabin.

After Rebecca left his cabin, Ephram Hemphill scowled at nothing and filled his mug from a bottle on his desk. He wondered if the brother would willingly return the pieces of silver when he returned the girl. He slammed the tankard down on the desk. What rotten luck that Stephen Hill got himself killed. That sister of his took such pleasure in informing him that any contract made with Stephen was null and void upon his death. Ephram's frown deepened as he sat down at his desk once more to work on the ledgers stacked up to his right.

Rebecca's knock interrupted the captain at his work. As he sat back in his chair he made a mental calculation. It was almost time for the evening meal. After his visitor left he would call for his dinner. He sighed, then grumbled, "Come in."

Rebecca stuck her head around the door, "Captain, I have to talk to you."

"Oh, Mistress Ranserford, please come in. Yes, we do need to talk."

Rebecca made her way into the room and eased herself back into the chair she had vacated less than an hour before. "Sir," she clasped her hands together to give herself courage, "Tomorrow, I'll be leaving the ship. I want to thank . . ."

"You'll what?" he asked, puzzled. Where was she planning on going? He cleared his throat, "Mistress, we won't be sailing for England for several weeks. I know that the ship is not the best place for a young woman and I'm sorry that you must stay on board . . ."

"You misunderstand, captain," Rebecca said softly. "I'm not going back to England with you. I'm staying here."

"With whom?"

"With no one. I am going to find a position and tutor. I'll make my own way." She raised her head and felt her confidence build as each second passed.

"Mistress Ranserford," Hemphill stated in surprise, "I'm taking you back to your brother. My agreement with him was that I was to deliver you to Stephen Hill. Stephen Hill, poor devil, is no longer with us. I can't deliver you, so I'll take you home."

"No!" Rebecca cried. "He'll only sell me again."

Ephram was fast losing his temper, "He'll not sell you, not till he pays me."

Rebecca stared at the man. "What do you mean? What agreement did he make with you and why should he pay you?"

Ephram Hemphill's fingers tightened around the tankard he held in his hand, and with his face dark red in embarrassment, he turned away from her. She knew little about the arrangements that affected her future. He moved around his desk and stood looking out the window toward the sea. He should have had better control over his words. It was just that as a man of the sea, he was not accustomed to dealing with women. He even found himself floundering when he tried to reason with his own daughter.

He turned back to the young woman and began slowly, "I best tell you the whole of it. Last spring, Mr. Hill came to me and told me of his correspondence with your brother concerning you. Mr. Hill was willing to pay the bride price your brother was asking. He approached me and . . . I . . . I'm handling this all wrong. I can see it in your face."

Almost all of the color faded from Rebecca's cheeks at the mention of the previous spring. Arthur made these arrange-

60

ments over a year ago. A whole year! And he had never said a word to her. She had never been so mortified in her life. Rebecca's gray face turned to a bright pink and her dark eyes became wide black orbs. "How much?" her voice was shaking. "How much do I owe and to whom must I pay? Certainly, not that little lady who was here today."

The captain turned back to the window. "I advanced your brother the funds. You owe me nothing. I'll return you to England and settle with your brother. You? You owe me nothing."

Rebecca laughed, bitter and harsh, the noise a sharp grating sound, even to her own ears. "My brother has spent the money. He won't pay you back. He'll have to sell me again to get the funds."

"NO!" roared the captain. "I should never have mentioned it. I will discuss this matter with your brother."

"No, captain," Rebecca stated firmly, "You'll have to discuss it with me. I will have to pay you back, because I am not returning to England so that Arthur can do this to me again." Rebecca was getting angry and her voice was growing loud and hoarse. "*I will not go back to England.*"

Ephram spoke quietly. "You have no choice."

"I do, I do," Rebecca swiped at the angry tears forming in her black eyes. "I will indenture myself and pay you before I return to my brother," she was shouting. "I will not return to Arthur."

"Please, Rebecca! Calm yourself. We'll think of something."

She glared up at him. "I will be leaving your vessel in the morning. I will find someone who will pay whatever my brother owes and then let us see you try to take me back."

The color of the captain's face was fading even under his tan. "Mistress Ranserford, what has happened to you? You seemed like such a nice obedient girl at the start of this trip. Surely your brother will arrange a nice marriage for you."

Rebecca drew herself up to her full height. "Sir, I am, by most standards, an old maid. I am one and twenty and before you could return me to England, I would be two and twenty. You see why I want to make my own way, don't you?"

The captain only shook his head, he didn't understand, and he certainly couldn't let her leave his ship. For one thing, the docks were not the place for a fragile young woman who had been gently reared. If he let her walk off his ship, in days she would be dead or in a place where death would be a welcome visitor. No, with her looks, making her own way would put her in some lecherous old man's bed, and he couldn't allow that to happen. She left him no choice, he would have to lock her in her cabin until he could decide what to do.

Ephram suggested they go to dinner and after a quiet meal he walked her to her cabin. Satisfied that he was going to let her go in the morning, Rebecca proceeded him down the hall, content with her plans for the moment. She hadn't given serious thought to the idea of indenturing herself until she mentioned it to him in anger, but it did have some merit. She was anxious for some quiet time alone, to explore all of the possibilities that such a step might provide. The first and the most obvious consequence was that Captain Hemphill would not be able to take her back to her brother. No, she needed some time alone to think this concept through completely.

They reached the cabin door when Rebecca realized that Ephram Hemphill never answered her original question. "Captain?" she asked quietly, "How much does my brother owe you?"

Without thinking, he answered, "Fifty pounds and the cost of your passage."

"Fifty pounds?" Rebecca was stunned. Where would she ever get that kind of money?

Once more that day, Hemphill turned red in embarrassment. His mind had been churning over what to do with the wench and again he had not guarded his tongue. Damn. He never should have mentioned money to her in the first place. Now what was he going to do?

Rebecca stumbled into her room and sank down on her trunk, stunned. She was so shocked that she was not even aware that the captain had closed her door and turned the key in the lock. Slowly, she shook herself out of her mental fog and loosened her clothing, then crawled into her bunk.

Fifty pounds! What would she have to do to earn such an enormous sum? Finally, frustration, anger, despair all combined and Rebecca Ranserford gave in to the trait she so disliked in others. She cried herself to sleep.

While Rebecca cried herself to sleep, Ephram Hemphill kept his own lonely vigil as he walked the deck of his ship. Everything the woman said was probably true. Her brother would probably sell her again, especially if the captain demanded payment himself. The girl was not his problem, he told himself as he walked. His agreement had been with Hill and now Hill was dead. He had no obligation to the girl. He should not even worry about her. No, he should only worry about getting his money back from her brother.

But he liked the girl. She was a fragile thing, beautiful in a special way, and she didn't deserve the kind of treatment she was getting. Still, it wasn't his problem. The more he walked, the more he worried and the more concerned he became. He couldn't keep her locked up until he sailed for England. That was weeks away. What would he do with her? Finally, as the night grew old, he realized that he could not make this decision alone. The one other man who was in a position to advise, who had ships available, and who seemed remotely interested in the young woman's welfare was Quinton McQuade. He would send for Quint in the morning. Together, they could decide what to do about Rebecca Ranserford.

Chapter Six

Long before the ropes were slipped over the pylons, Quint was packed and waiting to leave the ship. For an hour he debated whether he should try to see Rebecca once more. "For what purpose?" he asked himself. Her future husband was about to arrive and there could be no further association.

With the order, "Let go the lines," Quint grinned and turned his attention elsewhere. He was home! He made his way through the excited passengers waiting for the gangplank to be lowered, to Captain Hemphill. After the customary pleasantries, he made his way down the plank, watching the milling throng for a glimpse of Susannah or George. Quint fully expected to be greeted by his sister with the news that dear Mother had recovered and he had wasted his time and money. He spotted his brother-in-law standing at the edge of the crush of people moving toward the ship.

With his feet on firm ground, he turned and looked back at the ship. He caught himself looking for Rebecca. A touch of a smile crossed his lips as he realized what he was doing. Even if she had been another man's mistress, she was quite a lady. He wished her well.

Quint ambled toward the spot where he had seen George, still looking over the crowd for his sister. George met him halfway and grabbed his outstretched hand, clasping it warmly in both of his. He swung his arm around Quint's shoulders and affectionately patted him on the back. "She's waiting in the carriage," George said in answer to Quint's puzzled expression. "Come on, it is over there," George pointed to a group of carriages waiting across the street.

Quint started in that direction when one of the carriage doors flew open and Susannah rushed out. She threw her arms around her brother and hugged him tightly. Quint disengaged her arms and kissed her on the cheek. He grinned down at the woman who was his senior by three years. "Hi, sis!" Quint said warmly. He looked her over carefully. Susannah Beal was a handsome woman. She was taller than most men, had curly hair, almost as dark as his, and she had the same dark blue eyes, which were more widely set than his, though. Her brows were thin and arched. She had the straight classic nose that marked the McQuade side of the family and her full lips were curved in a happy smile.

"Oh, Quint, I'm so glad you're home."

Quint glanced down at the dress she wore. He couldn't remember Susannah wearing black, except, of course, when Father died. She looked tired, too. Quint looked at her in confusion. "I'm sorry," her smile faded, "Mother died four weeks ago."

He stood there staring at his sister, waiting for some grief, some sorrow to flood through him, but there was nothing. His own mother was dead and he felt . . . He frowned, he felt relief? Guilty that there were no other emotions surging through him, he stared off in space for several minutes. Then he turned his attention back to Susannah. "Was it bad?"

Susannah only nodded. She would explain later, he knew. Quint said quietly, "Let me send word to the office that I'm back, then I'll go out to the farm with you for a few days." As George threw the valise into the boot, Quint helped his sister into the carriage, then he and George climbed in.

Once the carriage started down the cobblestone street, George leaned toward Quint, "Susannah is staying with one of her friends in the city. I wasn't certain that you'd arrive today, so I arranged for a bed at one of the local inns. Perhaps you should stay with me. The apartment has been closed up for months and you may not want to open it up today. You made it in time for the reading of the will. I

65

tried to delay it, but it seems your sisters could wait no longer to hear the good news. Oh, and you better know that Mary Elizabeth changed her will no less than nineteen times in the last three years."

Quint stared at George, his mouth open in astonishment. Finally, he growled, "Nineteen times? My God, what are the lawyers' fees for all of that?" Grimly he remembered that George had never called the woman "Mother," instead preferring her Christian name. Quint glanced at Susannah, "How are the girls taking all of this?"

Susannah shrugged her shoulders, "Oh! You know . . ." George squeezed her hand gently and smiled down at her. "Well, it has been interesting," he said.

"Now, George," Susannah said.

"Sweetheart, he had better hear it now," George put his arm up around her shoulder and squeezed her arm as he drew her closer to him. The carriage came to a stop before the shipyard office and Quint ducked out of the carriage.

Quint watched the display of affection between his brother-in-law and his sister, and he felt a tug of jealousy. It must be wonderful to have such love for one another. "Give me a minute," he mumbled and headed toward the office.

When Quint climbed back into the carriage, George grinned at him and took a deep breath, "Let me fill you in. It seems that Elizabeth Ann has decided that since she is the oldest, she should get the largest share. If she doesn't, she's already said she'll contest the will." Quint groaned. "Oh, it gets better," George continued, "Margaret admits that if age were the determining factor, then Elizabeth Ann should receive the larger share, since she is older than Margaret by two years. However, Mary Elizabeth died in Margaret's home. For that, Margaret says, she should get it all. There is also some dribble about Margaret being promised everything years ago. And Mary Jane feels that since your mother stayed with her more often than with the other two, she is entitled to the greatest share. You, my friend, have a battle on your hands."

Quint groaned loudly and squinted at George. "Thanks!" he said. The trio sat quietly, each absorbed in their own thoughts as the carriage rumbled through the streets of

Society Hill. Quint glanced over at Susannah and a small smile played at the corners of his mouth. He remembered an afternoon, long ago, when he and his mother sat together in a similar carriage across from Susannah and George. The couple had been sitting then just as they were now, holding hands. Mary Elizabeth, scandalized, had whispered, "Quint, say something to George. He is entirely too forward." Quint remembered his response, "My God, Mother. They are married." He and George laughed over that for weeks. And his sisters were as bad as their mother. At least the next several days would not be dull.

He could use a day that was decidedly dull, he decided the next morning as he crawled from the bed. He growled at George about tightening the bed ropes and left his still sleepy brother-in-law sitting on the edge of the bed. Damn George Beal! The two of them had talked and drank long after midnight. He wondered how much rum they had consumed. It wasn't the rum, Quint thought painfully. It was the ale they had had with it.

Blearily, he remembered that in the predawn hours, he woke from a nightmare, the shadows of which still teased his memory. In the fog of sleep, a tiny black-haired creature, much like Mistress Ranserford, kept holding out her arms to him and just as he was about to reach her, one of his sisters or his mother would grab her and yank her away. Constantly in the dream, Margaret's grating laugh sounded above the crowd. He tried desperately to shake the dream. What could it mean? Was it premonition? How could it be? Rebecca was soundly sleeping in her new home and would rise to a day full of wedding plans.

Trying to dismiss Rebecca Ranserford from his mind, he made his way out to the well. After a dozen minutes and as many dunkings, Quint, feeling just a bit more human, splashed more cold water in his face. He could well imagine what this day would bring. Back in the room he changed his clothes, brushed his wet dark locks into some kind of order and followed George across the hall for a hearty breakfast. He grinned when he remembered George describing the fight he had over determining the appointed hour for the reading of the will. All three of the ladies in question declared that eleven o'clock was not a decent hour to conduct business. Quint shook his head. No, this would not be a dull day. They were going to be difficult. He could sense it.

Dressed in somber gray breeches and black coats, Quint and George rode back to the edge of Society Hill to the home of Susannah's friend. Susannah was dressed and waiting, still wearing a black dress. Even in mourning clothes she looked especially good to Quint and he said so. "Quint, if any one hears," she murmured but her eyes shone with pleasure.

"A brother should be able to compliment his own sister," he reminded her, adding, "You sound like Mary Elizabeth when you say things like that."

A quick frown crossed Susannah's face as she let George help her into the carriage. When Quint swung himself up and took his seat opposite them, scowling, George tried hard not to laugh in his face. "Now, Quint, it may not be so bad."

"It could be worse. In fact, I'll bet cash money that it will be terrible," Quint growled.

Susannah grinned at Quint and then her husband. "Oh, Quint! It's so good to have you home. I really don't think I could have gone through this without you." Leaning forward she patted his knee. Quint growled something under his breath and George turned to the window, intently watching the passing scenery. He struggled valiantly to confine the chuckles that fought to erupt. Quint was not handling this well at all.

But Quint was right. It was much worse than either man expected. They arrived at the lawyer's office a full forty-five minutes before the appointed time, for the expressed purpose of meeting the lawyer before the older women arrived. But, it was not to be. All three older sisters were waiting with their husbands at their sides. Quint scowled at two of the men; he hadn't seen those worthies for five years.

Even before he removed his hat and great coat, Margaret came charging forward, her husband following in her steps. "I want to make this clear before we start. If we don't like what we hear, we'll contest the will." Quint shrugged. If that wasn't bad enough, each husband took turns pulling Quint aside, demanding that his respective wife was much more worthy than the other two and should have the bulk of the estate. Quint stared at them. What did they think, that Mary Elizabeth had a fortune? My God, he thought, with the exception of the farms, I paid for most of what she had.

The lawyer was the final straw. He was a full hour and fifteen minutes late. By the time they adjourned to the office for the reading of the will, Elizabeth Ann and Margaret were no longer speaking to the rest of them.

Quint was livid as he took his seat in the back of the room beside George and Susannah. His sisters were behaving like a bunch of scavengers fighting over remains. If there was any way he could have gotten up and left the assembled group and retained any dignity, he would have done so. He felt trapped as he glared at the gray-haired barrister.

When the lawyer was satisfied that he had their attention, he took out the folded parchment, and started to read, "The last will and testament of Mary Elizabeth McQuade, given this day . . ."

Quint stared in horror as the words droned on and on. His mother left all of the property to him. Susannah was given all of the woman's personal effects, stating that she was to keep what she wanted and give the remainder to any charity of Susannah's choosing. His older sisters were given one dollar each. Their indignant gasps didn't even penetrate Quint's shock.

He dragged himself back to the present as the lawyer read, "This will differs from the others only in the amount of money left to my three older daughters." The lawyer lifted a stack of parchment from the desk and read dates and amounts. The amounts never varied a great deal, first a penny, then a dollar, then two pennies, and so on. Quint sat in his chair stunned. He could not move.

He didn't need to move. His three older sisters descended upon him before he drew a deep breath, and they were breathing fire. Margaret was the last to accost him. When she had her say, she started for the door, glaring. Just before she reached her destination, she spun around and took a step backward. With pure rage in her voice, she flung her words at him, "You'll be sorry, little brother, very sorry."

Margaret's words never registered as Quint stared after her, his expression confused. The lawyer leaned down and said something to him, but Quint couldn't seem to focus on the man. Susannah reached over and touched his arm. Quint looked at her with dazed eyes as he realized that she was trying to tell him something. He forced himself to concentrate.

"Quint, we're leaving now. Quint? Quint, do you hear me? We're leaving." Quint rose automatically and followed her from the room. He shook his head, aware that George was not at his side. He turned back toward the office and noticed that his brother-in-law was in conference with the lawyer.

They reached the walkway in front of the carriage when George came bustling out of the door. "We'll meet with the lawyer again in two days to finalize the deed transfers and the distribution of Mary Elizabeth's things," George said as he took Susannah's arm and escorted her to the carriage. When they were all seated in the carriage, he continued. "The lawyer will be coming to us. I've made the arrangements. Now, we're going home." He rapped on the ceiling of the roof and settled back next to his wife. He took her hand and smiled down at her, "Are there many things of Mary Elizabeth's you want?"

Susannah frowned, "I don't know. I never thought about it. I didn't think she would leave me a thing."

"That's obvious," he grinned at her. "Quint, what about the property?"

"George, I'm as surprised as Susannah. I have to think." He lifted his hand to rub his palm against his forehead. "I have to think," he repeated, as if to himself.

The ride to the farm took all afternoon and most of the evening. Once, just before sunset, they stopped for dinner, then continued on. Quint had little to say, simply staring out the window at the passing landscape. Several times, when Susannah attempted to draw him out, George told her quietly, "Let the man alone."

It was almost too dark to travel on when Quint spotted

the farm and looked over at George in surprise. George chuckled softly, "Welcome back."

"Sorry," Quint muttered, "I've been trying to sort it all out. I was sure that she hated us both. I never dreamed she would do this. I don't even want those properties! I have more than I can handle with the ships and the shipyard. Why, I'm gone half the year as it is. What do I know of farming? And I don't need another apartment in the city. My rooms by the yard are more than adequate." He ran his long fingers through his thick dark hair in frustration.

George watched his friend in sympathy. "Perhaps she was trying to tell you that it's time for you to settle down."

Quint shrugged and for one fleeting moment he saw the face of the beauty who shared his voyage from England. He almost choked as he mumbled quietly, "I've found no one yet with whom I want to share my life."

As the coach pulled up in front of the large stone house, Susannah leaned over to retrieve her hat, gloves, and purse. She paused to pat her brother's knee, "Your room is ready. You'll stay at least a week, won't you?"

Quint nodded his head and moved toward the house. Out of the shadows of the front door a man appeared. "Cap'n?" he questioned softly. "Cap'n McQuade? Sir, it's Pauley. I got's this here note for you. A Captain Hemphill of the *Venture* wants you to come back to Philadelphia, sir, right away, sir!"

"Captain Hemphill?" Quint didn't try to keep the annoyance out of his voice. "Well, I'm not going any place until tomorrow. Whatever it is, it will have to wait until I've had some sleep."

Quint was up with the sun and studied the confusing note that Pauley had surrendered the night before. The impression Captain Hemphill gave was that a matter of life and death was threatening someone on the *Venture*, but the captain failed to name the person in trouble. Was someone that Quint knew making life dangerous for the captain and he didn't want to name the person in a message? No, that was too ludicrous to even consider. Still, the missive was about someone in serious trouble.

"I'll have to return to Philadelphia. I'm sorry, George, but

I'll make arrangements to see the lawyer in town after I've cleared up whatever problem the good captain has," Quint apologized as he packed his valise.

While he waited for the horse that he kept stabled with his brother-in-law's, he tried to explain to Susannah, "I'll come for a visit in a week or two. The man needs help and he brought me back from London on the spur of the moment, Sis. If he's in real trouble, then I must see what I can do," Quint hugged his sister and kissed her on the forehead. "I'll send word, just as soon as I know I'm free."

Quint arrived in Philadelphia early in the afternoon, and he sent word to the *Venture* that he was in his office at the shipyard. He could come to the *Venture,* or if it was more convenient, Captain Hemphill could come to the shipyard. Quint ordered a pot of hot coffee and sent two of his younger workers to his rooms to open up the place and air out the chamber.

When his messenger returned from the ship, Captain Hemphill was with the man. Quint ordered two tankards of ale and the men sat opposite each other in Quint's large comfortable office. "I'm deeply sorry that I had to send for you," Ephram began, "but the more thought I gave to the problem, the more certain I was that you can help."

Quint frowned, "What problem is so difficult that you can't solve it yourself?"

"Right now, I have Mistress Ranserford locked in her cabin on board the *Venture.*" Captain Hemphill ran his hands through his hair, his eyes betraying his loss of composure.

"Has she refused to marry the man, or did he refuse her?"

Captain Hemphill looked puzzled for a moment. "Oh, didn't I mention that Stephen Hill is dead? He died several weeks ago in a carriage accident. I intended to take Mistress Ranserford back to her brother, but she has this hairbrained idea that she is leaving the *Venture*. Only an hour ago she was screaming at me that she was going to indenture herself to pay her brother's debt, but she is not going back to England. Captain, I'm sorry I've involved you in this mess, but I thought you might have a suggestion or a solution.

The girl has been locked up for almost two days and I'm beginning to feel like a jailor. I can't keep her locked up for three more weeks and I can't leave for England until I've unloaded and sold all of my cargo and contracted for another. You have a fleet of ships. Could you take her back?"

Quint stared at the man. He had to be joking. He sent for Quint because Rebecca Ranserford was threatening to indenture herself? Surely there was more. He cleared his throat. "I'm not returning to England for another six to eight weeks. I've a Caribbean trip planned first. Perhaps, Captain, you should start this tale at the beginning."

Ephram bristled at Quint's remark. It seemed that the young man was not interested in Rebecca Ranserford at all. He gritted his teeth and explained in crisp tones what had happened in the last two days. "Right now," he continued, "I'm concerned for the girl and her health. She is angry, she refuses to eat, and whenever I unlock her cabin door, she dashes for topside. Only this morning she got half way down the gangplank before my first officer caught her. I tell you, man, it doesn't look good for the *Venture,* for passengers and sailors alike to see or hear either me or my men chasing a stubborn English wench."

Quint shook his head. It was obvious that the older man was at his wit's end. No wonder he sent for him. Quint doubted that the man knew other citizens of Philadelphia well enough to burden them with this kind of a problem. He chuckled at the grim face of the older man. Capt. Ephram Hemphill was beside himself.

"Captain," Quint said softly, "Why don't we have dinner on board the *Venture* this evening and I'll talk to Mistress Ranserford. Surely, two intelligent men can convince the young woman in question that England is the place for her." As Quint uttered the words, something told him he didn't really want Rebecca Ranserford in England, not even if that truly was the place for her.

Chapter Seven

While Quint waited in the dining room of the *Venture*, Captain Hemphill stood at Rebecca's cabin door. He knocked gingerly, remembering the yells and unladylike words she had thrown at him only four hours before. "Mistress Ranserford? Quinton McQuade has joined us for dinner. I'm going to unlock the door now, and I want you to accompany me to dinner."

He unlocked the door and slowly pushed it open. Rebecca sat on her trunk, her arms folded in her lap, her expression grim, "I do not want to join you for dinner. I most certainly do not want to see Mr. McQuade tonight, or ever. When are you going to allow me to leave, or has Mr. McQuade been summoned to take me back to England immediately?"

Ephram winced as she phrased her question. The girl was too astute for her own good. He cleared his throat. "I asked him to have dinner with us. My hope is that he can make you understand why you must return to England."

Rebecca stood and shook out her dress. Tonight she was hungry enough, she thought, to endure the men and their righteous comments. She glared up at Captain Hemphill and marched from her cabin. She was staying here. Neither man could say a thing that would change her mind.

The meal was a solemn affair. Rebecca answered one of two questions and then refused to say another word. Quint talked about the dangers of a woman alone in a strange land, and Captain Hemphill commented about women's place in the scheme of things. What Rebecca needed, he said softly, was a husband and eventually a child or two and only her brother could arrange that. Rebecca tried to close her ears and concentrate on the food on her plate, but before the meal was finished her hunger took flight as their words weighed her down. She tried twice to excuse herself, but Quint wouldn't let her.

"You must agree to go home with Captain Hemphill." Quint glanced at the captain and suddenly a thought gave his argument direction. "Rebecca, the captain has spent much of his own money bringing you here. The only way he can recoup his investment is to take you back to your brother."

Quint watched as Captain Hemphill dropped his head in his hands and groaned. He wondered if the man had already tried that tack and failed. One glance at Rebecca's face told him he had just commented the blunder of the night.

She stood up from her place at the table and glared at him. "Sir, you are as heartless as the captain. Don't you realize that my dear brother," Rebecca's voice was growing louder with each word, "will only sell me again." She was screaming now, "I will not go back to England!"

Quint asked as quietly as he could, "And how do you expect to stay? You have no family, you have no friends, you have no way to support yourself. I would offer to keep you until you could find work but . . ." he grinned as she stood shaking her head, "No, I thought not."

Rebecca took a deep breath. It was time for both men to know that she made up her mind and her course, no matter how offensive to them, was decided. "I plan to indenture myself for several years. I am educated. I am intelligent. I speak several languages. I can cipher, read, write, and I most assuredly can teach. I will find a family that needs a tutor and offer my services."

"No!" Quint's voice was almost drowned in the bang of his fist hitting the table. "Women do not tutor. You would be abused in no time. I'm sure I speak for both the captain and myself when I say no, you will not offer your services. If you are so determined to stay here, then, damn it, I'll pay the fee. I'll buy you, if that is what you want. At least the good captain will know that you are not being mistreated."

Quint glanced at Ephram and the captain did not look as convinced as Quint hoped. Well, what did he expect, Quint wondered, as he realized to what he had committed himself. The wench was bound and determined to stay here, she would not go home. In his care, she would at least enjoy some wealth and it wouldn't be much different from the life she led at home. And she probably guessed correctly about her brother. The man would only sell her again. She had a right to decide her own fate. In time, he would find a decent husband for her. For some reason, he winced at the thought.

Quint turned to the older man. "Draw up the papers. I'll get the funds from my business and I'll be here tomorrow. I'll set her up in my apartment while I'm at sea and when I come back, I'll take her to the farm I've just inherited. I'll find something for her to do."

Rebecca brushed at the tears in her eyes. This was not turning out as she hoped. "I want to tutor," she whispered.

Quint turned back to her. "I don't think you have much choice. If the dear captain wanted to press the matter, you have cost him a considerable sum. I will pay the price, and at least we will know that you will come to no harm."

Rebecca raised her chin and her eyes snapped black. "I want to make my own decisions and choose my own fate."

Ephram grunted in dismay, "Women do not choose their own fates."

Quint shook his head, wondering if in a moment of temper, he had saddled himself with a small tiger. "I'll return tomorrow afternoon. Be packed and ready. Now, Captain I'd like to retire to your office and draw up the papers." Quint stepped away from the table and left the room, leaving Rebecca standing beside the table.

Early the next morning, Quint made a hurried visit to the lawyer. When the two men were comfortably seated in the lawyer's office, Quint gave his thanks that the man was willing to see him. "Your mother and father were friends of mine. I don't mind explaining the terms of the will to you.

In fact, there are several things I should tell you."

"All I want to know about right now is the farm," Quint stated.

"Not one farm, two," the lawyer corrected. "Mistress McQuade made that clear. And, if you refuse the two farms or the townhouse, they are all to be given to charity. Take one, take them all. But, it's not an impossibility. In fact the family farm, the one I believe you grew up on, is a productive farm. The tenant still lives there with his family. I believe you know the man," the lawyer started paging through the notes on his desk.

"Yes, I know John and Bette, go on."

"If both farms are refused, John and Bette will have to go. At present, John sees to the house and lives off the produce he grows and the game he hunts. I've taken a look at it myself. It could be made very productive if you spent a little time there. Now, the smaller farm will never earn as much, but it could be made profitable if you choose."

"I really only want the family farm, but I knew she'd make me take it all when I heard the will," Quint grumbled.

"She had your best interests at heart. She knew you would take the farms if John and Bette were involved. I think she wanted you to settle down now."

Quint frowned, "Why did she do this? She gave nothing to the three older girls and I was sure they would get it all. They were, too."

The lawyer sat back in his chair and placed the fingers of both hands together, then stared at the tent they made. "Quint, let me tell you something about your mother. I think Mary Elizabeth McQuade felt very guilty. In fact, within weeks after your father was buried, she came to me and told me how you blamed her for his death. She also told me about the fights you had concerning the apartment she wanted in the city and the clothes she made you pay for. She told me many things, things that I'm going to share, now that she's gone.

"Your mother never could show her emotions. In her own way, she loved your father, but I don't think she ever figured out how to tell him. Let that be a lesson to you. You find a woman to love, you tell her. If she can't say the words back,

I think I'd steer clear. I know that your father would have given anything if your mother had just once told him how she felt. Instead, he gave her things, things that she didn't need and never wore. She accepted every one and thanked him continually. On more than one occasion, even before he died, she showed me some of the things he'd given her, and she thanked him in my presence a dozen times. I think it was the only thing she knew how to do. Your father seemed to understand this."

"Did she tell you about the fight we had over the mourning clothes the day Father died? The dressmaker arrived before we had him laid out. I left home that day," Quint frowned, "And, I swore I'd never go back to that house again."

"She told me. The correct dresses were her way of showing respect for your father. Clothing meant a great deal to her. She was a strange woman, but she tried to make it up to you and Susannah. She wanted you to have the farms and the apartment in Philadelphia. It's beautifully furnished, by the way."

"It should be," Quint said. "It cost enough."

"Go see the farms. Take a look at the apartment." The lawyer handed Quint a bunch of keys. "Remember, you must keep all three to get the farm." The lawyer stood and walked to the door. "Come see me in a week."

Quint followed the man out the door, "I need the farm, or rather, I . . ." Quint paused. He didn't want to tell the man that he was about to claim a beautiful mistress, somehow he was sure the man would give him a lecture about a time in a man's life when marriage was more desirable. That obviously was what his mother had in mind. For some reason, the thought of his mother still trying to dictate to him rubbed him the wrong way and he scowled at the lawyer. Rather than explain, Quint muttered, "One week." He left quickly, and threw himself onto his horse. "Damn." In less than three days time, he was stuck with two farms, two apartments in Philadelphia, and one beautiful, but stubborn English wench. What happened to his quiet captain's life. "Damn!" he said loudly.

By two o'clock he had the fifty pounds that he insisted he

pay Captain Hemphill. His three rooms, two blocks from the shipyard, had been cleaned and aired. He sent one of the men to hitch up one of the smaller wagons.

At three o'clock, Quint stood in the office of the chief officer of the *Venture*, Mr. Landis in attendance, as well as one of his own men to witness the paper that placed Mistress Ranserford in his care for five years. He frowned as he thought of the implication of the bond. Well, no matter. He would see her properly married before the time was gone. He was sure to tire of her long before five years was up.

After the coins exchanged hands and the papers were signed and witnessed, Rebecca's trunks were carried to the wagon and she said a quiet good-bye to Mr. Landis and Captain Hemphill. As she started down the gangplank after Quint, Ephram strode forward, "Rebecca, if you change your mind, I'm sure Mr. McQuade would insist that I take you back to England."

Quint turned around and shot the man a questioning look. Neither man gave Rebecca a glance. She straightened her back and glared ahead. If Mr. McQuade turned out to be an abuser of women, she would never ask to be taken home. She could not convince either one of them that she did not want to go back to England and Arthur.

Quint took Rebecca to the apartment close to the docks. He left her with her trunks to unpack and instructions that he would bring the evening meal with him when he returned. She sank down on the small settee in the parlor. The rooms were sparse and small. The best word she could find was drab. The whole apartment was drab and she was stuck here for she knew not how long. Some of her new found courage left and she sobbed into her hands. What had she gotten herself into?

But a mile away, in a decidedly poorer section of Philadelphia, Bud Worthman was sobering up from the drunk his shipmates provided when he was let go from the *Venture*. Captain Hemphill had made it clear that Bud Worthman would not find a bunk on any of the ships in Philadelphia at the time. Every captain in the harbor would know of his attack on the English wench by now.

He would have to lay low, take some menial job until the *Venture* and the other ships left port. His back needed time to heal and while he was in town, he thought with a smirk, he could find out all about Quint McQuade.

The man's name turned his stomach. Somehow, he would get Quint McQuade and even up the score. The ship builder would suffer for every twinge Bud felt through his back. In time, he would know where Quint was most vulnerable and where he could feel the most pain. It would take time, but the one thing he had now, thanks to Quint McQuade, was time.

Bud Worthman moved up from the pallet slowly, dressed carefully, and splashed water over his face. He smoothed back the little bit of hair he had on the top of his head and made his way down to the dining room. He had a few pennies left for an ale and then he had to start thinking about work. He ordered and sat listening to two old crones talking about the inns in the neighborhood. "But, Sally, me love, Jenkins told me hisself, that he ain't aworkin' for the man. No man has lasted more than a month at Nicholas' place. Atween Hilda and Nicholas, there ain't no peace."

Bud turned to the old woman. "What inn you talkin' 'bout, Mother."

"Why, I speakin' of the "Crossed Winds." It be about a half a mile north. But if ya think ya can find work, ya best make up to Hilda. She's the one who rules the roost."

"Hilda?"

"Yeh! Nicholas Gibson ain't worth much. Hilda pushes him around."

"His wife?"

Both women started to cackle, and the woman named Sally responded between giggles. "Better not say that to Hilda. She thinks that man is 'bout as good as a pissant."

Bud left the two old women and gathered his meager possessions into his duffle. Before the sun started to sink into the west, he wanted to find the "Crossed Winds." He needed a job and he needed a place to stay before he could see to Quinton McQuade.

Rebecca found herself alone in the apartment long after the sun had gone down. She had already put all of her clothes away in the small closet and prepared a pallet for herself in the corner of the parlor. She had no illusions that Mr. McQuade would give up his bed for her, in fact she wasn't even going to ask. Her bed was ready for her and far from his bedchamber. She sat in the tiny parlor and waited for the man who now owned her for the next five years.

Quint finally arrived after nine by his clock above the fireplace. He did bring a pot of chicken and dumplings and a pail of cold milk. Tucked under a box in the closet he called his kitchen he dragged out a loaf of bread. "I figured that you couldn't cook." She nodded her head, not willing to answer his sarcastic remark. "What can you do, by the way?"

"I sew," she whispered, realizing that wasn't going to impress the man. "I am skilled in healing, but you already know that. I'm educated," she tensed, "I'm a lady. I never thought to learn how to cook or clean. I had a houseful of servants to care for those tasks. I directed the servants." Somehow, she knew that he wasn't impressed.

"Well, Rebecca Ranserford, I'm not sure what all you'll do here. I suppose you could help with some of my correspondence, perhaps with some of the billings. I'll have to think about it," Quint ran his hands through his thick dark locks.

Rebecca raised her chin an inch or two and glared at him with black eyes. "I planned to tutor."

"And just who do you think you'll tutor. I've been to school."

Rebecca clenched her fists, struggling with the desire to slap him across the face. She remembered the time she had struck him and she knew instantly that things were not the same. She couldn't strike him now. Instead, she left her food and nearly ran into the parlor. Before Quint could follow she was curled up in the corner on her pallet. Quint shrugged. After a night or two on the floor, he was sure she would accept his invitation to sleep in his bed. He chuckled at the small lump on the floor. Oh yes, she would welcome his bed.

The sun was setting when Bud Worthman found the "Crossed Winds" on a side street. He sat at a small table and watched the comings and goings of the staff for the better part of two hours before he decided that the big raw-boned woman with gray hair was Hilda. The short dark-haired little man who fumbled with one thing, then another had to be the Nicholas Gibson the old women had mentioned.

There were two young girls waiting on customers and as Bud glanced around he realized that the inn had an abundance of customers. He had the quarter for a plate of food, but he hadn't recovered enough from his three days of rum to spend his meager funds on food. But he could tell from the smells, and the satisfied looks on the faces of the sailors and the business men in the house that the cook in this place was superior.

He watched Hilda as the woman moved around and talked to a few of the guests. What about the woman could he use to get on her good side? He obviously had to impress her. It was easily apparent that Nicholas Gibson had little say in the running of the inn. As Bud listened, he heard her utter a bitter slur against the Spanish sailors as she offered sympathy to a man who claimed he had been mistreated. That, he decided, was the way to reach the woman. If he could convince her that he had been abused by a Spanish captain . . . Think of Spanish names, he told himself, as he groaned loudly, beginning his charade.

Jarrez was on his tongue as he allowed himself to slide from his chair. He didn't take the time to judge the surrounding area and he hit his back on the edge of the next table. A sudden real blackness closed in and Bud Worthman lost consciousness.

He came to in a large cozy room. As he forced his eyes to focus he realized that he was in the kitchen and from the stack of plates on the table, it had to be the kitchen of the inn. Had he said anything as he lost consciousness? He had intended to tell the big woman that the Spanish had stripped the skin from his back. Had he lost his chance?

He groaned at the thought and suddenly a husky voice murmured, "Hurt ya must, but careful I be."

Bud frowned, and tried to roll over, forgetting his back for a fraction of a second. "Damn," he mumbled and noticing the skirt beside the bed, he instantly mumbled a hopefully contrite, "Sorry."

He worked himself up into a sitting position and glanced up at the big woman he guessed was Hilda. "I ain't meanin' to be trouble, Mam," he said softly.

"Out there," she pointed to the dining room, "About somebody name Jarrez you swore. Your back, did he do that?"

Bud breathed a sigh of relief, and nodded. The woman waited as if she expected more of an explanation. Nothing much came to mind so Bud told her how he noticed one of the Spanish sailors following a young girl down the steps of the ship he was on. When the man tried to hurt the girl, Bud explained, he had tried to stop the man. But, the sailor was Spanish and he was not. The captain, who was also Spanish decided that the Spanish sailor could not have hurt the girl, that the English man had. Bud got carried away with the story and thought of Quint McQuade and the brutal punches he felled Bud with in the hold.

"Someday I'll get 'em," Bud snarled. Hilda's grip on his arm drew him back to the kitchen and the present.

"Not good is revenge. Here is better for you to stay. Work you must and forget this revenge. Come, help we need and your back I can care for."

Bud smiled his best smile. It had worked. Hilda wanted him to work at the inn and she would take care of his back. He lowered his eyes, afraid that she might see the gleam of satisfaction that he knew he couldn't hide. Women were all the same, gullible to a fault. Tell them a good story and they'd believe most anything.

Chapter Eight

Quint rose with the sun the next morning and was stunned when Rebecca greeted him with a cup of hot tea. The girl looked the worse for wear, Quint thought to himself, and he wondered how much sleep she got on the thin pallet on the floor. "This won't do," he said as he looked around the tiny rooms of his apartment. He shook his head in disgust. Already his life style was changing. These rooms were much too small for them. He would have to move Rebecca into his mother's apartment. At least there they would have enough room.

He tried to remember how Susannah had described the apartment after Mary Elizabeth insisted she visit. Quint smiled grimly. He had refused the woman's invitations countless times and, at the moment, he was almost sorry he had not seen the rooms himself.

If he remembered correctly, there were two bedrooms, a room that could be used by a maid, a kitchen, a dining room and a large parlor. It was on the second floor and at the opposite end of the docks. There was even a stable and a large barn for a carriage and wagon. It would be less convenient for him, but it would be much better for Rebecca. He would go there after lunch, and if the lads were available to open these rooms, they could move to the large quarters that afternoon.

He made arrangements with Rebecca, grabbed his jacket and left to find one of his sailors. "They're not going to be too pleased to play nursemaid to the girl. I had better think about a housekeeper, or at the very least a cook," Quint grumbled as he ambled toward the office.

It was late afternoon before Quint made his way back to Rebecca and his small rooms. She was sitting on the settee waiting for him. "We're moving tonight," Quint informed her as he came through the door. "I have a much larger apartment several miles from here. We'll both be more comfortable."

Rebecca said nothing, went to her trunks and packed the few things of hers that rested on a nearby table. She placed her shawl over her shoulders and sat back down. "I'm ready."

"Then you don't object to moving?" he asked sarcastically. For some crazy reason, he wanted more of a reaction from her, even if it was anger. She only shook her head. Quint threw the door open and yelled for one of the men he brought with him. Within the hour, they were on their way to the new place.

The candles burned low before Rebecca and Quint were settled for the night. He glanced around the bedroom that held some of his possessions. In the next day or two, he would get most of his things from the other rooms, the things he didn't want to take to the farm. An uncomfortable thought had been nagging at him all day. He couldn't take Rebecca with him to the farm, it wouldn't look right. She was his servant, in time, his mistress, and it would not do to introduce her to the people at the farm or in the village. She would have to stay in Philadelphia.

Rebecca's large bedroom was flooded with morning light when she stretched and crawled out of bed the next day. Oh, it had felt so good to sleep in a decent bed with fresh linens. It seemed like years since she had enjoyed such luxury, instead of two months. In the bright light of the summer day she looked around the pleasant peach room. It was a woman's room, decorated with more frills than Rebecca liked, but it was a pretty room. She wondered how Quint had found the rooms so quickly and so well-decorated.

She slipped into her dress and strolled through the apartment. She glanced at the kitchen and wondered about meals. Surely, the man who was lord and master within these walls knew that she could not cook. She had told him as much. Would he provide her with a cook, or was she expected to learn the art of meal preparation? If he insisted that she cook, she was certain that with her new independence she'd find a way to learn. She straightened her shoulders and grinned at nothing. She could do anything.

She found fresh fruit and a note on the dining room table. Her meals would be brought to her, the note said, and one of Quint's men would see to bringing the rest of the things he wanted from the old apartment. She was to make herself comfortable, unpack, and do whatever ladies did. He had property to check on and would be out of town for the next two days.

Rebecca smiled to herself. Being a bondservant wasn't bad. She had little or nothing to do and her master wasn't even at home. She hummed as she unpacked her trunks.

The whole day passed quickly, and Rebecca learned the name of the young boy that was to bring her her meals and see to her care. Harry Jamison was a tall thin lad of fourteen, and he blushed a shocking coral when his voice floated up and down, out of control. Rebecca smiled her encouragement, and talked about several of the young boys who worked on her farms. In minutes Harry relaxed, and Rebecca thanked him for seeing to her care.

"Oh, it ain't nothing, Miss. Mr. McQuade, he's a good man to work for, and he helps my Ma." He glanced at her in embarrassment, as his voice refused to stay where he wanted it.

Rebecca patted his arm, "Harry, I can't thank you enough. Perhaps, when Mr. McQuade returns, I could meet your mother."

Harry smiled, his thin face wrinkling in delight, "I'd like that, oh, yes, I'd like that."

The second day passed much more slowly than the first, and Rebecca found herself wandering around the rooms, staring out the windows, and praying that Quint would return early enough for them to talk a little bit. Was she desperate enough, she questioned, to talk to Quint McQuade? Yes, she needed someone, anyone, with whom to talk. Harry was only a boy; he did a great deal more blushing than talking.

She debated whether she should go to bed or wait up for Quint, but her bed beckoned and she finally gave in to sleep. Despite her boredom, she rested well and was up the next morning bright and early. There was no sign that Quint had returned.

She gathered her courage and knocked on the closed door of his bedroom. Silently, she waited for his growl, but it never came. When her nerves were stretched as tight as young saplings, she eased his bedroom door open a crack. His bed was undisturbed. The bright day lost some of its appeal, and she wondered what she would do all day. An unhappy thought struck her. Mr. Hill had been killed in a carriage accident, only weeks before. Could something have happened to Quint?

Panic clawed at her throat, no one knew she was there. No, she reasoned, Harry knew and Quint left word at the ship yard. His workers knew about her. If something happened to their boss, they would come to tell her, surely. Yet even as she logically explained the situation to herself, over and over, a part of her fought fear all through the day. She did not attempt to go to bed. She sat stiffly on one of the chairs in the parlor, hours after the sun went down, a single candle burning low in the late night hours.

Quint returned to Philadelphia, tired but content. The lawyer had been right about the farm. The smaller one could easily be made productive. He had no time to travel to the larger of the two and talk to John and Bette, but he had glanced at the records the lawyer gave him. He was pleased. The farms would make a nice addition to his investments. And, if he ever tired of the sea, he could turn either place into an adequate home for himself.

He turned the wagon over to Harry Jamison, who had been staying in the stable until his return, at Quint's insistence. It was almost midnight, but Quint told the lad to take the horse and go home. Quint wondered if Rebecca had found enough to keep her busy while he was gone, and if she had thought of him as much as he had thought of her. She had never quite left his thoughts, much to his dismay. He couldn't stop thinking about her.

He didn't expect to find the object of his thoughts slumped down in one of the parlor chairs. Why hadn't she gone to bed? He glanced at her bedroom. The room was dark. He looked over at his own room.

The covers of the bed were turned down and a small fire burned in the back of the hearth giving the large room a soft friendly glow. He picked up the sleeping girl and started toward her room. The soft fragrance of spring roses teased at his memories of a night not too long ago, on the deck of the *Venture*. How he had wanted to love the girl in his arms. That was probably why she occupied such a constant part of his thoughts. If he slept with her, he would be able to put her out of his mind.

He grinned to himself. Why not tonight? He started for his own room. Carefully, he placed Rebecca on the soft feather mattress and as soon as she touched the surface of the bed, she curled up on her side. Smiling to himself, he discarded his shirt and shoes and then turned his attention to Rebecca.

He released the hooks of her gown and untied her petticoats. Gingerly, he rolled her to her back and pulled the gown, then the petticoats from her. Slowly, he slid her slippers from her feet and pulled her black stockings from her legs. He yanked off his breeches and slipped into the bed beside her. In the soft light he looked down at her, clad only in a frequently mended and very thin chemise. Her delicate female form was almost completely visible and her full breasts swelled above the ancient fabric. He was dazed by her beauty. She had to be the most perfect woman he had ever seen. His heart swelled with pride knowing that she was legally, totally, and completely his. He fought his baser need and reminded himself that he had decided to go slowly with her, or he would lose her.

He pulled her gently into his arms, feeling her warm flesh pressed to his own aroused body. His conscience, long ignored, teased at him. He could not continue, at least not until she had agreed. Sleepy, yes! Dazed, all the better, but sound asleep? No, that wasn't fair to her. He raised himself up on his elbow and looked in the shadows of her face. Gazing down at her, he whispered softly, "Rebecca,

Rebecca! I want you so much. If you don't want me, then tell me now, before I do anything."

She didn't make a sound, but she did smile softly without opening her eyes. She snuggled up against him, even closer than she had on the trip from the wagon to the house. His heart skipped a beat and he gently ran his hands over her shoulders and down her arms. He smiled, she wanted him, that was evident, even if she could not bring herself to say the words. Her body had answered for her, as he knew it would. He dropped his head and gently caressed her parting lips, enjoying her instant response. She stirred against him and pushed her arms up around his neck. Quint never bothered to look at her closed eyes.

He kissed her forehead, then her lips, moving next to her ears and back to her mouth. Her lips parted and he allowed his tongue to caress the soft lips, then, growing bolder, he tentatively probed with his tongue. She murmured against the pleasant invasion and pushed herself up against the warm body next to her.

Accepting her invitation, Quint grew bolder still and slid his hand down her body across her firm breasts, covered by the thin fabric. He molded the fullness in his hand as his tongue wandered through the moist playground he had already entered. Drawing away from her for a fraction of a second, he loosened the chemise and dragged it from her shoulders. He wanted not even the thin material to separate him from her warm flesh. In his arms, Rebecca sighed, but Quint was too consumed with his own love play to recognize the sound as a sigh of sleep. He dragged his lips from her mouth, past her chin, over her neck to dwell between the warm flesh of her breasts.

He nibbled up one hill, over the peak, and down the other side, before he traversed across the other mound. Working his way back to the nipple which was rigid now, he pulled on it, twirled it in his mouth, and then sucked slowly, until he had the whole hard nub in his mouth.

Rebecca stirred again and pushed herself up against him. She had not even been aware of his first gentle kiss, and if she could have awakened enough to think, she would have realized that she was not engrossed in a dream of unreal pleasure. Slowly, she felt the growing flush of passion's first stirrings, but she could not reason. Gradually, a spreading warmth filled her and she responded. Her mouth, her neck, even her breasts were each in turn, being loved and she pushed herself up to allow the warm pleasure to spread through every part of her.

With her innocent response, Quint was beside himself, fighting a monumental battle for control. As she pushed against him in her attempt to gain more pleasure, he gave up. He nudged her thighs with his knee, and when they opened willingly for him, he carefully placed himself between her shapely legs. He pressed forward. When he met the small obstruction he tried to check his forward momentum, but it was too late.

In her dream, her legs were being spread apart and the very center of her became a molten mass of desire, desire for the unknown, like nothing she had ever experienced. Then, abruptly, the dream was gone. She felt as if she was being served upon a sword and the sharp cutting pain between her legs forced her awake. As she struggled from sleep, she realized that this was no nightmare. She screamed and jerked her eyes open. Peering into her eyes were the startled eyes of Quint.

He stared down into dark eyes, now filled with pain and saw the tears start to form then roll from her eyes into her tussled hair, even before she turned her head away from him. He rolled over to his side and pulled her into his arms. As he held her shaking form tightly against his naked body, a thousand questions rushed through his mind. If she was a virgin, she couldn't have been some man's mistress. The man she was to have married rejected her, but she was a virgin. She sold herself as a bondservant, but she couldn't have known what that would mean. For a second, he was angry. She should have told him that she had never known a man. Instantly the anger was gone and he was filled with remorse. Should he beg her forgiveness? He gazed down at her, and she pulled away for just a second to look at him. The pain and despair he saw in her eyes spoke volumes. Unconsciously, he sought to at least wipe the pain from her eyes. Tenderly, he kissed her hair, then her wet eyes, trying to erase the agony he had seen there. His lips brushed hers again and again, softly like a brush of spring snow. He offered comfort to them in the only way he knew. Slowly, she began to return the feathery kisses and once again, she wrapped her arms around his neck.

Rebecca had been dazed as she pulled away from him. She recognized the torture in his face, and for a second she wondered if he hurt as badly as she did. The thought was gone, as he brushed soft kisses against her lips over and over. The pain was forgotten and in its place was the same surge of warmth that she had felt before. Without thinking, her arms slid up around his neck and she began to return his kisses. She had no idea what was happening to her, but she knew that she did not want him to stop with his tender attentions. But, as suddenly as before, his kisses were no longer tender but spoke of a hunger she didn't want to understand. She tensed and tried to pull away from him.

He held her gently, and whispered in her ear, "I won't hurt you again, never again." Somehow, those words touched her fear, and she surrendered once more. She closed her eyes and let his kisses relax her. He was holding her face with one of his hands and his tongue gently pushed against her lips, begging for entrance. She opened to him and the pleasant warmth of her dream came flooding back. She felt his hands roaming over her curves and she delighted in the caresses he lavished on her breasts. The nipples hardened under his touch and instinctively she pushed against his hands.

For once in her life, Rebecca let her senses rule her body. She felt, she smelled, and she tasted but she would not think! Her breathing was ragged and she could feel her heart pounding loudly in her chest. As if he could hear it, too, Quint lowered his head to the hard peaks above the noise. When he touched each one with his tongue, the pleasure curled through her, from the point of his mouth, through her breasts, down her stomach, through her belly to a point between her legs. Everything seemed to move toward that point.

She felt his hands stroke over her hips, across her legs, and then up the insides of her thighs. She wanted to cry out, to beg, but for what? Slowly, his fingers were drifting over her firm flat belly to the dark curls between her legs. She tensed again, afraid for a second, but Quint kissed her deeply, holding his hand still against her warmth. As she relaxed, he let his fingers gently wander where the pain had been but was no more.

Rebecca was nearly mindless. There was no explanation for any of this, and she wanted none, not now, not when her whole body was crying for a release. Quint rolled her to her side and lifted her leg so that it rested above his hip. He continued the gentle exploration of his fingers as his mouth sought out her very depths and his tongue played again in the sweet cavern under her lips. Very slowly, so as not to break the mood, he removed his fingers and gently pressed forward. He began to move. Each thrust brought her pleasure, and she moved toward some unknown goal.

Suddenly, she was on her back, Quint above her, and she felt a need to move against him. Almost frantic now, she arched up, trying to put out the burning fire that threatened to consume her. The end of all of this was surely her own death, but still she moved against him, seeking more. There was an instant of hesitation and then it came, wave after tumultuous wave of pleasure as her world teetered between past and future. She was swept up into a shower of stars that blazed through the vastness of her mind and her whole soul careened up and out of her. She was somehow aware that he had surged forward one last time and then he, too, had collapsed.

Slowly, she opened her eyes, almost afraid that she had left the world. His dark head resting next to hers brought reality back a second at a time. Weak at the moment, prickly thoughts trickled into her head and she could not stop them. What had she allowed him to do? She closed her eyes against the flood of wetness that gathered there.

While his breathing slowed and then returned to normal, he held her tightly against him in the aftermath of love's storm. He stared out the window into the dark of the night. Never before had he experienced such a feeling, never such an intensity or completeness. It could not have been because she was a virgin. At that thought, the situation forced itself into his brain and he glanced at the small woman in his arms. He was filled with grief, guilt, and shame at what he had done. This exquisite little creature in his arms had been bought and sold, perhaps abused, but through it all she had remained an innocent. He was the one who had willfully and intentionally seduced her. Turning toward her, intent on apologizing, he attempted to smile. He looked down into her eyes and realized she was crying. Tenderly, he brushed the tears from her eyes and pulled her even more tightly against him.

"Rebecca," his voice was hoarse, "There is no way I can say I'm sorry. I'm not even sure I am sorry," he admitted honestly. "Perhaps we should marry," he murmured almost to himself.

She tensed, "Marry? Why should we marry? You own me for the next five years, don't you?" The bitterness of her words loosened Quint's hold. Her tears were falling faster now. "Just leave me alone, please. Just leave me alone."

Quint rolled away from her and sat on the edge of the bed, confused and concerned. She rolled away from him and stood up, glancing around the room for her clothes. Quint watched as she jerked her gown over her head and into place. As she moved toward the door, he jumped up from the bed and rushed to her. Grabbing her arm, he pleaded, "Rebecca, don't leave yet. I want to speak with you."

"We can talk in the morning," she said firmly and jerked her arm from his restricting hold. Quickly, she was out of the door. Quint started to follow her but realized as he stepped to open the door she had just closed that his naked state might make matters worse. He moved back into the room and sank down into one of the chairs in the room.

For a long time he stared out into the night. Rebecca said firmly that he owned her, and he did. She was his, so why did he feel so guilty? Other men, some good friends, owned bondslaves and they used the women to serve their needs. He was within his rights. Why then did he feel like a spoiler, a defiler of women, a cad of the worst kind? Because Rebecca had forced the bond, not knowing or even imagining what it could mean. He had not meant to seduce her.

Of course, he told himself, trying to salve his conscience, she had responded to him. He even took time to see to her own pleasure as well as his. He climbed back into bed, and sank down under the covers praying for sleep. It didn't come quickly. Rebecca's tortured face kept reappearing before him. He could feel the wetness of her tears against his cheeks, on his lips, against his chest. Repeatedly, he told himself that she was a bondservant, but that knowledge did not make him feel any better. Somewhere in the back of his head a tiny laughing voice repeated over and over, "She's special. You knew she was special, very special. Now, she'll hate you."

Chapter Nine

Rebecca was too tired not to sleep. She crawled into bed and forced all thoughts from her head. In the morning, then, she would deal with her problem. Whatever could be done, could wait for another sunrise, she told herself as she sank into the soft feather mattress. Tomorrow!

She woke with the sun and the cruel happening of the night before flashed before her mind. She was no longer a maiden. She rolled over and groaned. For the next five years she belonged to the man who had taken her virtue. There wasn't a thing she could do about it. She had no one to blame but herself. It was she who insisted that she leave the *Venture* and indenture herself. Quint only took her up on her offer.

In her disgust with herself, she pounded on the pillow. This was not the independence she thought she would claim. Now she belonged to the arrogant Yankee in a way that would never be changed, not in five days, five months or five years. Soon she would have to leave her bed and face him across the dining room table. She felt her cheeks grow warm. No, she couldn't do it.

She shrunk down into the quilts, trying to sink into the mattress. Of course, if she didn't get out of bed, would he think that she was ill? He might come to check on her, and when he found her in bed, he would . . . She was out of bed in seconds. Dressing took very little time. He would not find her in bed.

She came from her room to find the door leading to his bedroom closed. No sound issued from within. A deep furrow wrinkled her brow. Was he up and out already, or was he still asleep? Perhaps she would find the answer in the kitchen, she thought, as she headed toward that unfamiliar area.

Quint heard the door across from his room open and close and he lay rigid in his bed waiting for sounds of sobbing. He heard nothing except the rapid fall of her footsteps as she started down the hall toward the kitchen. Strange, the last room he thought she would visit would be the kitchen.

He rolled toward the edge of the bed and groaned. Now by the light of day he vacillated between guilt and anger. She should have told him; she should have stopped him. How was he to know that she had never known a man? He was angry at himself because he should have asked instead of assuming as he had done. He felt guilty above all else. She had been a maiden! He couldn't send her back to her brother, not anymore. At the moment, he forgot that she had vowed never to return to Arthur. He neglected to remember, also, that he originally had no interest in letting her return to England.

He rolled out of bed and sat at the edge, holding his head in his hands. If he slept at all, it had only been for a few minutes, and even before he got home, he was exhausted from the trip to and from the small farm. Now this! He had no answer for the problem. What should he say to the girl, and what kinds of plans could he make, now that he had ruined her? Damn, he thought, as he struggled into his pants. He grabbed for his shirt and his eyes fell on the dark stains in the middle of the bed. He rushed from the room, his boots in hand, prepared to make almost any kind of concession, if it would ease his guilt. Quickly, he made his way toward the parlor. Rebecca was not there. Surely, she was not still in the kitchen, but in case . . .

Rebecca sat at the table for the longest time, wondering what she would say to Quint McQuade. Should she say anything? What little she knew about indenture was not encouraging at the moment. He bought her for five years, and the agreement she read said nothing about duties. Simply that she was owned by one Quinton McQuade for five years. At the end of her time, she was to receive enough funds to begin her life in this country. Perhaps what happened the night before was what happened to bondslaves.

No! She could not believe that. Rebecca stood and glanced around the room. Maybe she wouldn't have to face him for the moment, not if he had already left the apartment. There was a tea kettle at the edge of the hearth, but there were no hot coals that would indicate that someone had fixed tea. The table held a fresh bucket of water, but had Harry brought that up for his employer? "I certainly cannot go knocking on his door," she muttered as she glanced around the room one more time.

A soft voice questioned, "Why not? I'd knock on your door if I was concerned about something, as you seem to be."

Rebecca blushed and wanted to crawl between the boards of the floor. Not only did she have to face him now, but he had found her talking to herself about him. She wondered if she could dissolve into nothingness if she wished hard enough.

Quint chuckled. She was most embarrassed at being caught talking to herself. He wondered if she did that all the time or only when she was upset. She was clearly upset. He had glimpsed her frown before he replied to her comment. Instantly, he felt his guilt growing heavier and heavier. What could he say to her? He tried to speak above the lump in his throat. At the moment, he had better say nothing, he decided. He walked to the rear entrance and opened the door. "Harry," he yelled down the back flight of stairs, "Fetch breakfast, will ya?"

He turned back to begin the apology that he knew he had to make. Rebecca was no longer in the room. Well, he shrugged his shoulders, if she could not stand to be in the same room with him, then the apology could wait.

Quint made quick work of dressing and he was almost ready to make his way to the shipyard when Harry returned with their breakfast. Quint gave instructions to Harry and left the apartment eating a hot bun. He was certainly not going to wait until Rebecca felt like talking to him before he went to the shipyard. He had three days of work waiting for him at the office.

It was almost ten o'clock at night when Quint returned to the apartment. There had been several problems that he elected to solve that day rather than face the girl to whom he needed to apologize. Fortunately for Quint, she had already retired when he got to his rooms. For the next four days, Quint left before Rebecca was up and returned long after she had retired. He had to talk to her on the fourth night, though, because in the morning he was going to leave for a week. He had to see the big farm. Susannah had issued one of her rare ultimatums, and the lawyer was insisting on a decision. He left the shipyard about four.

Rebecca was nearly frantic with boredom. Quint left early and returned very late each day and the only person she saw was Harry Jamison and he was a child. She took a nap intending to stay up until Quint came home, no matter what the hour. He had to allow her to leave the walls of the apartment before she lost her mind.

When Quint arrived late in the afternoon, he found Rebecca in the large sunny parlor. He stood at the doorway and watched her pour tea for herself before he cleared his throat. She nearly dropped the tea cup, and it rattled when she sat it down on the tea cart in front of her. It was obvious that she did not expect him. He frowned wondering how she had spent her time.

Rebecca saw his frown and her anger surfaced. He had no right to frown at her, no matter what he thought she had done. She glanced at the tea set before her. Perhaps there was something special about the service, but he had said nothing to her about the things in the apartment, so how could she know what to use and not use?

Quint watched as Rebecca's expressive brown eyes darkened and once again snapped black. He was positive that she was remembering that he had abused her and became angry himself. Damn it, she had no right to be angry when she didn't bother to explain anything to him.

They glared at each other. The tension in the room was almost volatile when Rebecca backed down a bit, "Would you like a cup of tea? I made this moments ago."

Quint answered stiffly, "Yes, a cup of tea would be

pleasant." He took a chair opposite Rebecca.

"Lemon or cream?" Rebecca asked.

"Plain," Quint said and added, "No sugar."

Rebecca made a face and handed him the steamy brew. "You don't care much for tea, do you?"

"No, I've developed a taste for coffee. I prefer that beverage."

"Rebecca," Quint began. Once again, she almost lost the cup. "Tomorrow, I have to leave Philadelphia for my large farm. My sister insists that I stop to see her and my lawyer is demanding my attention. I will be gone for five or six days, perhaps a week."

Rebecca stared at him in dismay. He had left her alone for five days, and now he showed up to tell her that he was leaving her alone for another five days, perhaps longer? Was he trying to drive her insane? She was bored out of her mind already, and the thought of another week closeted in this apartment forced words from her mouth before she had a chance to think. "And what am I supposed to do while you are gone?"

Quint looked stunned. Was she saying that she missed him? He looked at the black eyes snapping in anger and decided that she was not missing him at all. "What do you mean?" he asked hesitantly.

"I have nothing to do here. I am not accustomed to such inactivity, and I have no one, not even a maid to talk to," she answered her voice breaking.

Quint stared at her. What on earth did he know about what women did? His mother and sisters liked to buy things, perhaps that would keep her happy. Maybe she would feel more a part of his world if she decorated the apartment. "Tomorrow, I'll have Harry take you shopping. I'll make a list of the places where I have an account and I'll leave some coins in case you see something you want and I don't have an account with the proprietor."

"What will I buy? I don't need anything," she answered with some confusion.

"Well, this is your home now," Quint indicated the apartment with his right arm, "Decorate it!"

Rebecca looked around at all of the beautiful things in

the apartment. Surely, he was jesting. Everything in the apartment was new and tasteful. Her farms at home were not as elegantly furnished and she could not imagine the need to buy anything. She looked back at him, more confused than ever.

"I want to leave early in the morning," Quint said. "I'll talk to Harry tonight, and he can take you around tomorrow. Now, I'd like to have dinner and get a decent night's sleep." Rebecca flushed as he mentioned sleep.

Quint left the next morning shortly after Rebecca had risen and dressed. No sooner had he ridden off than Harry was at the door, "I've got a list of stores here. Mr. McQuade ses ya want to do some shoppin' and we can go right after I get yer breakfast."

Rebecca blushed again at the mention of Quint McQuade. "Harry, I don't want to go shopping. I would like to walk around, perhaps visit a farmers' market and get some more fresh fruit, perhaps some flowers. In England, we can buy flowers at the markets." Harry nodded his head, it was the same in Philadelphia.

Rebecca ate much faster than usual, anticipating her opportunity to leave the apartment, and in less than a half an hour, she tugged on her bonnet and grabbed her shawl. "Let's get started," she said as she thrust her arm through the handle of a basket.

Harry stood very still. Rebecca Ranserford was beautiful, tiny but gorgeous, and her smile lit her expressive brown eyes. He wondered if he was strong enough to protect her.

Rebecca meandered through the stalls at the market, fingering one thing, then another. She couldn't remember when she enjoyed something as much as she enjoyed walking through the display of farmer goods, flowers, herbs and the sundry other things that the locals were selling in Philadelphia. She purchased a loaf of crusty bread, several small tart apples, and a large bunch of summer roses. She turned to Harry and nodded. She was ready to go back to the apartment.

From out of nowhere, two boys, thinner than Harry and not quite as tall, dashed around her. One boy bumped her from the right and the other boy pushed her from the left.

As she lost her balance, she shrieked and dropped her basket. The boy on her left grabbed for the purse that hung from her left arm. Rebecca wasn't certain what happened next but the large woman next to her swung her own basket at the boy and he stumbled, then fell, dropping Rebecca's reticule. The big woman scooped up the linen bag and thrust it at Rebecca, as Harry reached out to help the girl back to her feet.

Rebecca smiled at the woman, "Thank you." She whispered, almost ashamed that she had to admit it, "Those are the only coins I'll have for the week."

The woman smiled back, "Try that stunt before, I've seen those two. Hurt are you?"

Rebecca stood staring at the woman, startled. She was saying everything backwards and with a heavy German accent. "Are you from Germany?" Rebecca asked.

"No," came the accented reply. "Hilda Winkelblake I be. And, from Amsterdam I come, about fifteen years before."

Rebecca looked surprised, "You're not an American. I haven't met an American yet, except for Harry and the man who employs him."

Hilda looked offended, "An American I be. I serve my time and a citizen I am." She smiled and her whole face lit up, her dark eyes twinkling in her round face. "An American you've met."

Rebecca grinned at the woman. "Mistress Winkelblake, could you come to my apartment for a cup of tea? I would like to thank you properly."

Hilda looked at the small woman smiling up at her. The girl needed a friend. It was written all over her face. She seemed genuinely pleased to be able to offer a cup of tea. Hilda glanced up at the sun. Lunch was simmering away and Bud was there to stir it when it needed it. She could have a cup of tea. "Yes, a cup of tea I'll have. Thank ye!" She fell in step with Rebecca, and Harry led the way back to the apartment as Hilda and Rebecca shared information about how they traveled to the United States.

Back at the apartment, Rebecca heated water and prepared the tea leaves. Hilda worked with the flowers Rebecca had purchased, and soon the two women were stirring tea.

101

Rebecca eagerly explained to Hilda all that had happened to her since she boarded the *Venture* in England. She avoided telling the woman about the sailor on the ship who tried to rape her, and she said nothing about her night with Quint. The hour they spent over tea passed much too quickly for Rebecca. "I've done all the talking. I didn't let you tell me anything about you," she wailed in horror, when Hilda said she must leave.

Hilda smiled down at the girl, "Come tomorrow I will, if you'll have me. And tarts I bring for our tea. Early afternoon be best."

"Oh, would you came back? I want to hear all about you and what you think of this country and where you work, and everything," Rebecca blushed. Her mouth was running away with her in her excitement. Hilda probably thought she was a dunce.

Hilda chuckled, "Be back I will. Two o'clock tomorrow?"

Rebecca was much too excited to answer, and she nodded her head. After Rebecca showed Hilda out, she danced through the rooms, her excitement growing. She had made a friend. She was going to have someone with whom she could talk. Perhaps, with a friend she could manage to live through these next five years.

Chapter Ten

The next morning, Rebecca could hardly contain her anticipation. She was entertaining. With her guest in mind, she dusted and cleaned, admitting as she worked that it was really not needed.

At two o'clock, Rebecca answered a sharp knock on the door and admitted her grinning friend. "Come I did, and bringing some things, I am. Tarts for to make the tea a treat, and little cakes for your evening meal I bake. You cannot cook, I remember."

Over tea, Rebecca learned all about Hilda Winkelblake and the "Crossed Winds Inn." "I don't think I would like this owner, Nicholas Gibson. He sounds like he is very lazy and would want others to do his work."

Hilda smiled slightly. "Another job I'd take, if I could find one. Just inside the law, the man moves. One day, and not too far away, he gets caught. Then, the Crossed Winds will be all gone."

Rebecca nodded sympathetically. Perhaps she could help find Hilda another position. The woman was illiterate, however, and she did not wish to move, either. "A job where I have to move, I not take. Travel, I will not," Hilda muttered. Rebecca looked surprised. "Sick it makes me!" Hilda offered in explanation.

Hilda stayed for over an hour and then hurried back to the inn where she had to prepare the evening meal. Before she left, she assured Rebecca that she would return the very next day, so that they could enjoy a cup of tea together. "Coffee, I like, more than tea," Hilda said softly. "Coffee, I make also."

"Oh, Hilda, Mr. McQuade likes coffee ever so much more than tea. Could you teach me how to make it?"

Hilda grinned in pleasure, "I teach!"

Hilda came each afternoon, and Rebecca didn't mind in the least that Harry, after the problems, refused to take her back to the farmers' market. Instead, Rebecca sent the boy out for coffee, a coffee grinder and a coffee pot, after Hilda explained what she needed for a good pot of the brew. Rebecca didn't like the taste at all, even when Hilda told her to add cream and sugar. "It's so bitter," she said, grimacing.

Hilda laughed, "Coffee that makes it!"

On her fifth visit, Hilda brought a fresh raisin pie, several apple tarts and a dozen oatmeal cakes. "Come I can't for the next two days. The inn is full and food I must prepare. Bring enough for several days I did."

Rebecca thanked the woman and brushed the tears from her eyes. However would she manage the next several days without Hilda to confide in? She said as much to the round faced woman who, in a matter of days, had become her closest friend. Hilda patted the girl's hand. "Walk me home, Harry can, and then you he brings for tea, day after tomorrow. Time we'll have there. To take time to leave the inn, I cannot. Talk we can, then."

Rebecca beamed, "I'd like that."

Hilda left with Harry in tow. When they arrived at the inn, Hilda insisted that Harry come into the big sunny kitchen for a glass of cool milk and a platter of oatmeal cakes. "Energy for the walk back," Hilda grinned. Harry sank down at the long narrow table and munched on the cakes and drank his milk. He was almost ready to leave when one of the other employees of the inn came strolling into the kitchen.

"Picked up another stray, Hilda?" the short dark man asked as he looked Harry up and down. Harry noticed the dark beard and what long dark hair he had tied in back of his head. His shirt was open a bit and Harry was amazed that a man with so much hair on his body would be balding. The man was not very tall, but Harry was struck with the muscles that fairly bulged through the man's shirt.

Harry thought to himself that he wouldn't want to tangle with that man in a dark alley. He grabbed his glass, drained the last of the milk, and thanked Hilda. "We'll be here day after tomorrow."

Bud watched the boy practically run from the inn, "The boy comin' to work?" he asked, not pleased that Hilda was offering something to a young lad who would be more than eager to work him around the table.

Hilda laughed, "No, coming for tea are friends of mine. To be concerned about, you need not be."

Harry hurried back to the apartment, told Rebecca he knew how to get to the Crossed Winds and added that it seemed a clean enough place. "But, we ain't staying very long."

Rebecca watched the boy as he collected the dishes and left to obtain her evening meal. It was obvious to her that Harry wasn't happy about something at the inn, and for an instant she wondered if Quint McQuade would approve of her going out for tea. "He did say that I could go shopping. Surely a stop for tea is not unreasonable, and I do know Hilda," she said as she arranged the baked goods under a linen cover.

She crawled into bed that night arguing with herself over a visit that would not take place for at least a day and a half. She had been asleep for several hours when an unusual sound brought her instantly alert. Shaking with fright she listened carefully. Someone was in the apartment with her! Trying to move without making a sound she scooted out of bed and tiptoed to the door, but her heart was beating so loudly that she was sure she was announcing her presence to whomever was on the other side of the door.

Still trying to move without a noise, she grabbed at one of the candlestick holders that rested on the table next to the door. It would make an adequate weapon, she thought. Gingerly she removed the candle and laid it down on the table. However, the candle did not stay put, but rolled to the edge and fell to the floor with enough of a clatter that Rebecca shrieked and dropped the brass holder.

A man's voice shouted, "Rebecca, what's wrong?"

Rebecca winced. She had completely forgotten that Quint

was coming home today or tomorrow. She wrapped her robe around her small frame and pulled the door open a fraction of an inch. "I'm all right," she said, her voice still shaking. "I didn't know you had returned."

Quint frowned. She had scarcely left his thoughts and she was saying that she wasn't expecting him? That thought made him furious. He slammed his door as he entered his bedroom. Had he made a serious mistake allowing her to leave the apartment? Had she met someone else that appealed to her more? Well, he thought as he threw his jacket in the general direction of his chair, she was bound to him for five years and she better not even so much as look at another man.

Rebecca fumbled around in the dark until she had the brass base and the candle in hand. After setting them on the table, she made her way back to bed. She could not imagine how she could have ever let Quint McQuade slip from her mind. Yet, since she had wondered if he would object to her visiting Hilda, she had given him no thought. Well, she sighed, she didn't have to worry about what he thought of her traveling to the inn now, she could ask if she could visit. In minutes, she was sound asleep.

While Quint slept late, Rebecca was up with the dawn determined to make amends for not anticipating his arrival. She fixed a pot of coffee as Hilda had directed and laid out some of the fresh baked goods from the day before. Then she slipped back to the kitchen to await the rising of the master of the house.

Quint rolled over in his bed wondering why the smell of fresh coffee had awakened him. He shrugged out from under the light blanket and reached for his clothes. Surely Rebecca wouldn't have hired a cook, not without his permission. Perhaps she felt it was the thing to do. Well, he muttered to himself as he dressed, he was the master here, and he would do the hiring.

When he strolled into the dining room and saw the array of fresh pastries, he knew she had hired someone and his temper flared. She had no right, she was only a bondservant herself. He would set her straight as to her role in his household. He slumped into a chair. What was her role in his household?

Suddenly Rebecca stood beside his chair, "I have coffee."

Quint glared up at her angrily. "I didn't tell you to hire a cook."

Rebecca glared back. "I didn't hire anyone."

"Who made the coffee?" he snapped.

"I did."

She almost threw the pot on the table and stomped out of the room. So much for making the man a pot of coffee. She was only trying to apologize for forgetting his arrival, but he didn't appreciate her efforts at all. She slammed the door to her chamber as loudly as she could. There was simply no way she and Quinton McQuade were going to be able to coexist for five years. It was impossible!

She sat and thought about the tortures she would like to see inflicted upon him, until she heard "Rebecca?" followed by a sharp rap on her door. "Rebecca?" the voice came again. "I'm sorry. I thought you couldn't make anything but tea. I appreciate the coffee, really I do, and I didn't mean to get angry with you."

Rebecca sat up straight. Why was he apologizing? Suddenly, he was saying that he didn't mean to get angry with her. Why didn't she believe him? Harry! Harry must have told him about Hilda. That would explain why he was willing to excuse her. Well, it wouldn't make any difference to her. She had tried to make up for forgetting his return, but with his reaction she wasn't sure that she wanted to remember him at all. She tried to ignore the voice that kept calling her. "Rebecca? Come on! Say something! I know you're in there. Rebecca?"

She jerked the door open and stared up into Quint's concerned face, her eyes narrowing and turning black. He should not have questioned her, she told herself as she tried to ease past him.

Like a snake, his arm uncoiled and trapped her in his clutches, but the heat that permeated her skin from his mere touch confused her and she stared up at him with uncertainty written on her face. He dropped his hand and stepped away from her. He looked every bit as confused as she felt. Was he as affected by that touch as she was? She shook her head, bewildered. What was happening to her?

Quint stepped back and let her pass. This tiny creature was tearing his world to bits and he had no explanation for it. For the past six days he was unable to stop thinking about her. When finally in her company, he insulted her. Now he touched her and her skin seemed to burn through his own flesh. Was Rebecca Ranserford an English witch, sent to tease him beyond reason?

Quint made arrangements to spend several hours at the shipyard and he left instructions for Rebecca. That evening, she would be accompanying him to a local inn for dinner. She needed to get away from the apartment and although he didn't mention it, he thought he might be less tempted to drag her back to his bed with people around them. He promised himself a dozen times while he was seeing to the farms that he would not compromise her again.

The day dragged by as Rebecca tried to busy herself with her preparations for that evening. She examined one of her better gowns and although it was terribly out of style and almost shabby in appearance, she spotted and pressed it. It would have to do, she told herself. She bathed early and dressed carefully. She braided her hair, wrapping the thick plaits around her head like a crown. Shortly after Quint arrived back at the apartment, she pronounced herself ready.

The carriage was waiting for them and Quint smiled as he handed her into the carriage. "Several of my men have told me about an inn here in Philadelphia. I thought we would dine there. It's not far."

When they arrived, it was already too dark for Rebecca to notice the name of the place which she decided wasn't important anyway. The meal they shared was to Rebecca's way of thinking one of the finest meals she had ever had. There was roast duck and several kinds of bread. Roasted potatoes and carrots glazed with dark sugar graced the table and Rebecca sighed with pleasure as the serving girl brought out cups of bread pudding covered with a thick brandy sauce.

In a far corner, unnoticed by either Quint or Rebecca, Bud Worthman drank an ale and cursed the man and the girl. He would find a way for both of them to suffer, he thought as he flexed his back muscles and clenched his fists against the pain that lingered in the flesh across his shoulders. As he watched, he thought of the two characters who tried to get a free meal from Hilda earlier in the evening. He wondered if they were still outside the inn and if they would be willing to take on Quint McQuade. The only way to find out was to check. He slipped from his table and in the dark shadows of the large room he found the side door and eased out the door, his mind already busy with what he would do to both of the young people.

Quint grinned at Rebecca, "I think we had better walk some after this meal. The exercise will do us both good." He took her arm and led her through the door, positive that she had enjoyed the meal as much as he. As they stepped out to the cobblestone pavement, her delicate rose fragrance drifted up to him, and her warm soft body pressed close to him, stirring a protective urge that he could not explain. Rebecca Ranserford did something to him, but he was too content tonight to try to understand what there was about the girl that affected him as no other woman had.

They moved away from the door and as he placed Rebecca's delicate hand on his arm, Quint was alerted by a movement in back of them and to their side. He grabbed Rebecca and pushed her into the street, "Stay there," he bellowed as he yelled out. Rebecca turned in panic and saw the carriage they had ridden to the inn move up quickly.

Rebecca glanced from the carriage coming down the cobblestones to Quint who was swinging at two men. One of the men darted past Quint and lunged for Rebecca. She felt the fabric of her gown tear and in slow motion, she sensed the ground rising to meet her. She hit the pavement with force and felt a hard weight press her down. The odor that eminated from the man above her made her shut her eyes and swallow hard. The smell of smoke, stale rum, and an unwashed human body stunned her for a second, then she felt her head collide with the ground. Darkness surrounded her.

As Quint's stocky driver joined the fray, Bud rolled away from Rebecca and disappeared into the inn swearing as he went. Those two fools were so drunk they did nothing but make McQuade angry. He certainly was going to have to plan much better if he was going to get the captain. Spur of the moment actions would never do. And the girl! It seemed that McQuade was only playing the very cool gentleman on the *Venture,* just so that he could have the girl to himself. She was more beautiful than Bud remembered and very soon he was going to have her.

Even over the noise of the meals being served and the pewter mugs and plates clanging together, Hilda heard the commotion in the alley next to the inn. She wiped her hands on her white apron and stepped to the open door. She watched as a tall young man and a stocky older man routed two very drunk sailors. As her eyes drifted over the scene she spotted the petticoats of a woman lying on the stones in back of the fight. She ducked out of the door and around the swinging men until she reached the side of the woman. Stunned, she stared down at Rebecca's dirty face. Hilda stooped down and gently cradled Rebecca against her knee.

She yelled for help and quickly two girls from the inn joined her. They picked up Rebecca and moved toward the inn as Quint disposed of the more obstinate of the two men who attacked him. The first man laid at the feet of Quint's driver. Quint glanced around. "There was a third man. See what you can find out. Where are you taking the girl?" His last remark was directed at Hilda who was ordering the help to place Rebecca on a bench in the kitchen.

Rebecca groaned and opened her eyes. Hilda and Quint were over her and she turned her head, trying to decide from the unfamiliar surroundings where she was and what had happened.

Hilda answered her questions before Rebecca had a chance to ask, "Into the inn I bring you. To the ground, somebody knocked you, but all right you'll be now."

"Is this your inn, Hilda?" she asked softly.

Hilda nodded and Rebecca glanced up at Quint who now wore the puzzled expression. "I met this woman when I went shopping. She has been having tea with me and we have become good friends," Rebecca explained.

Quint nodded in the direction of the woman, his expression still puzzled. "I'll tell you about her later," Rebecca said as she struggled into a sitting position. "Could we go to the apartment?" she whispered as she pulled her torn gown together in embarrassment.

Quint nodded and helped her to her feet, "I have to thank this Hilda. Let me get you in the carriage." He led her through the door and helped her into the cab, then disappeared back into the inn. In a short time he was back, and he sat next to her, instead of across from her as he had on the ride to the inn. He placed his arm gingerly around her shoulder and murmured softly, "Why don't you try to relax? It will be a good half an hour before we're at the apartment."

Rebecca didn't try to respond. Instead, she snuggled into his shoulder and tried to still the shudder that ran through her. His husky voice whispered in her ear, "Are you alright?"

She couldn't speak over the knot in her throat, but instead nodded her head against his chest. What was there about men that made them force themselves on women? The memories of another time, in another dark place flooded her mind and she shivered again. Quint reached down and pulled her onto his lap. He put his arms around her and held her tightly against him.

As he held her he thought about his plans for the evening. He had taken her out to dinner so that he would not be alone with her, so that he could avoid the temptation she presented. Now this! He would not be able to let her out of his sight, not because he couldn't find some of his men capable of caring for her, but because he would worry himself to death. After all, something like this could happen again and the next time she might be seriously hurt. He tightened his hold. Rebecca snuggled closer to him and Quint gritted his teeth. If he lost this battle, it would not be his fault, he told himself grimly, as he fought to control the effect she was having on him.

On the ride home, Rebecca rested in his arms, occasionally shaking violently. While Quint held her, he wondered if she would shake apart and then he berated himself for even considering a walk home. He should have been more aware of the possible danger. Rebecca could have been seriously hurt in the fall to the pavement, or the men could have succeeded in separating them, and then what would have happened to the girl? Quint tightened his hold on her once more.

As he stared out the carriage window, he admitted to himself that what had just happened was more than a little suspicious. He had enemies, everyone in business had some enemies, but he didn't think there was anyone who would profit enough from his demise to attempt murder. Yet, someone obviously tried to harm him. Could it have been a simple robbery attempt? The Lord knew there were enough of them in the city these days.

He shoved the disquieting fears away and let Rebecca's soft rose fragrance fill his troubled head. She was good for him, even if he didn't want to admit it. And he wasn't really ready to admit to himself how wonderful it was to come back from a troublesome trip and find her waiting, despite the fact that she had forgotten he was returning yesterday.

The carriage pulled up in front of the apartment, and Quint shook Rebecca gently. "Rebecca, are you asleep? We're at the apartment. Come on, brown eyes, time to leave the carriage."

Rebecca sat up with a start. She had dozed off and at first she couldn't imagine what she was doing in Quint's arms in a carriage. Then, the events of the evening came flooding back and she lurched off his legs and leaped for the door. Quint threw out his arm to prevent her from falling from the carriage. "Whoa! Let me get out first, and then I'll help you down."

He didn't miss the look of panic that spread across her face for a fraction of a minute. He moved quickly, and had her back in his arms before a minute had passed. He spoke quietly to the driver, "Put the carriage away, then go on to your home. I won't need you anymore tonight. See you in the morning."

In minutes Quint had Rebecca in the apartment and he was placing her on her feet at the door to her room. As he argued with himself, though, she tightened the hold she had around his neck. The evening, even Rebecca herself, were conspiring against Quint and his good intentions. He lifted her back into his arms and turned from her door to his own. Damn his good intention, he thought as he kicked his bedroom door open. He knew he would feel like an animal in the morning, but tonight . . . tonight he would enjoy the beauty in his arms.

Chapter Eleven

Quint eased Rebecca down on his bed and sat down next to her. She pulled away from him and he saw her anxious eyes. He pulled her into his arms and tenderly touched her lips with his, then he traced the line of her jaw to her shell-like ears. His words, merely a breath in her ear, begged for what he wanted, "Let me love you, Rebecca. Let me help you forget. Let me take you to another world."

Rebecca sighed and leaned into him. She should push him away, but not yet. In a minute she would stand and leave his side. But first, she wanted his kisses and the tenderly whispered words that made her feel secure and safe. She turned her head to meet his and her nose touched his. She sighed once more and let his gentle kisses cover her face. Again, his lips touched hers and as his tongue invaded hers, a thrill shot through her. She couldn't deny him. She couldn't pull away and leave his side. Not tonight, not for her very life. She melted against him.

Quint felt her sag into his arms and he sensed her surrender. For a fraction of a moment, guilt flooded through him, but he pushed it aside. For days he had thought of little else but Rebecca Ranserford and now she was in his arms, offering what he wanted. He would not turn away. He ran his hands over her shoulders, down her arms, then gently grasped her waist and lifted her into his arms while his tongue busily explored the moist cavern behind her lips. Tentatively, he ran his tongue over her teeth, around the underside of her lips and dueled with her tongue. He felt rather than heard her sigh and he lifted his head so that he could take a much needed breath.

"Let's get rid of these," he muttered as his hands grabbed for the buttons of her bodice. She raised her hands and rested them on Quint's wrists, but she did not attempt to pull them away and Quint released several buttons before he lowered his head. He didn't bother pushing her chemise out of the way, but nibbled at one of her erect nipples through the fabric. Rebecca closed her eyes and fell back against one of his arms, no longer able to sit upright. She gave herself up to the intense pleasure he was creating and simply tried to breathe, because what he was doing to her was making breathing difficult.

She pulled air into her lungs and felt his lips touch hers again. His hand was where his head had been and he was rolling the moist bud between his fingers. She sighed into his mouth. He pulled away and mumbled, "Rebecca, it is time to undress."

She opened her eyes wide, reality trying to push past the sensual atmosphere Quint had created. He sensed it and pulled her back into his arms, kissing her hard, his tongue mimicking the invasion he sought. Once again, she closed her eyes and melted against him. In a matter of seconds, he had loosen her bodice and was untying the tapes of her petticoats. She felt the cool air brush against her naked skin but it took her a moment to realize that Quint had removed all of her clothing and was lowering her to the bed.

His hands traveled over her skin, touching her breasts, tickling the skin across her stomach, and tracing her legs to her knees. He followed his tracings in reverse, and Rebecca became aware of the coarse texture of his naked body against hers, as he leaned over her to kiss her deeply. She kept her eyes closed, allowing herself only to feel. Deep in her center, a throbbing was quickening. Part of her wondered how he had created such a sensation, when he had done little more than kiss her, but before she could wonder more, he was poised above her.

She could feel the heat radiate from his body and she reached up to draw him down to her. As his lips met hers, Rebecca felt a hard object pressed against her leg. She tensed remembering the pain she experienced when she had lain beneath him before.

He felt her tighten up and he whispered against her lips, "I won't hurt you."

Suddenly, Rebecca felt him penetrate her, possessing her as no other man had done, and the exquisite sensations he was creating surprised her, so much so that she gasped. Quint understood what she felt, and he gathered her up in his arms as he rolled to his side. He positioned her leg over his thigh and stroked her shoulder, her back, her buttocks as he rocked gently against her. It wasn't enough, though. He rolled her back under him and began the ancient dance of love. Now it was his turn to gasp, as he fought against the desire to loose himself immediately.

He concentrated upon bringing her more and more pleasure and her panting breath assured him that she was close to climaxing. She tensed and Quint groaned as he felt the waves of pleasure course through her. There was no way he could hold back on his own release and gasped as ecstasy clasped his body tightly against hers. For long minutes, Quint held her against his chest, waiting for reality to touch the corners of his mind. Never in his wildest dreams had he imagined a woman pleasuring him so. He stared down at the creature beneath him. Had she felt the same thing?

Rebecca's eyelids fluttered opened and she gazed up into Quint's stunned expression. For a second she wondered if she had done something wrong. He had just given her a small piece of heaven and she wondered if he knew, but she couldn't ask him, not tonight. Perhaps tomorrow she would ask. Her eyelids drifted closed and she smiled, feeling sleep's gentle arms pull her into unconsciousness.

Quint watched as she shut her eyes. He wondered at the small smile that played at her lips, but as her breathing evened out, he knew she was asleep. He drew her close and let his own body relax. Never before had he felt as complete as he did at that moment. Rebecca was truly a special woman, and as sleep teased him, he wondered if he could ever get along without her. For almost an hour, Quint held the delicate woman in his arms and thought about their future.

When Rebecca awoke in the morning, she was startled to

find that she was still in Quint's bedroom. What would Harry think of her, she wondered, if he knew that she had spent the night here. She blushed scarlet as she struggled out of the bed. Quickly, she donned her clothing and slipped from the room and across the hall into her own room. She should never have let Quint carry her into the apartment. He had no better control of himself than she did, she admitted shamefully to herself as she poured cold water into the bowl on the washstand. Somehow, she really didn't know how, she was going to have to keep her distance from Quint McQuade.

On the kitchen table, next to an empty coffee cup and a crumpled napkin, Rebecca found a brief note. Quint explained that he had a great deal to do. One of his ships had a cargo to take to the Caribbean and he would be gone all day. She was not to expect him until late that night. Tomorrow they would discuss the hiring of a cook.

Rebecca smiled slightly and wondered if Quint would object to the plan she had. Hilda wanted another job, and with Hilda in the apartment, Rebecca knew she would be able to stay away from the tall man who destroyed her self control. Of course, she wasn't going to tell him that, but if he hired Hilda, Rebecca would have a friend close at hand. Still smiling, she made her way out to the kitchen to fix herself tea.

The day passed slowly for Rebecca as she tried to plan her best course of action. The truth was always the best she decided, and she mentally arranged her arguments so that Quint would agree that Hilda was the perfect choice for a cook and companion for her.

Rebecca would have been surprised and pleased if she knew that Quint was wondering if Hilda would accept a position in his household. Rebecca seemed fond of the woman but after Harry had explained in some detail what happened in the market and how well Rebecca and the big, raw-boned woman got along, Quint knew he would offer her the position of cook. "I'll let Rebecca go with me when I make the offer," he thought as he dug through the bills of lading he needed for the next trip.

His frown grew deeper as he thought about the voyage.

He really didn't want to go, but there was no other way of seeing the matter disposed of properly. There were also the farms that had to be taken care of in the next several weeks. "Damn," he muttered, as he realized he was going to have very little time with Rebecca. He could always take her with him, but, his frown now a scowl, there was no room for a woman on the ship and he didn't want his neighbors at the farm talking about a woman who was not his wife. Then, too, there was always the possibility that George and Susannah would come for an impromptu visit. It certainly would not do to have his mistress in his house with his sister in residence.

It was almost midnight when Quint returned to the apartment from his office at the shipyard. Most of the matters left to be handled before he sailed were last minute items he could address for another three days. His crew was being rounded up and he could think of nothing that could postpone his departure. He had spent a tiring day but Rebecca had been at the fringe of his mind for the seventeen hours he had worked. The small clock on the mantle rang the witching hour before he was ready to retire. "It wouldn't do to wake her up," he told himself as he tiptoed into his own room.

The sun was making a rapid assent in the sky when Quint crawled out of his bed the next morning. The fragrant smell of coffee told him that Rebecca was up and moving around. "Today," he mumbled as he dressed, "we see about a cook."

Rebecca was indeed up and dressed in one of her plainest dresses. Until she could convince Quint that Hilda was the cook he needed, she was going to dress in her simplest gowns. All day yesterday she had talked to herself, frequently out loud, and her own ears had burned with her words. She had to stay away from the man. There was an unbelievable attraction between them and although she couldn't deny it, she certainly didn't intend to encourage it.

"Good morning," she greeted Quint softly.

"Good morning," he responded, his voice husky with sleep.

Rebecca poured his coffee and placed a plate of sweet

buns before him, then she sat back and waited for him to finish the buns. After she poured a second cup of coffee for him, she decided it was time to have her say. "The woman who took care of me at the inn is a friend of mine," she tried to explain.

Quint smiled, "I know. Harry told me all about that misadventure my first day back. He told me about this Hilda. I'm just sorry I didn't realize who she was at the inn."

Rebecca smiled back. "She is a very good cook. She doesn't like the man she works for now. I think she might come to work for you with the proper incentives."

Quint stared at the girl. Surely, she hadn't tried to hire the woman. Had the two of them schemed to get Hilda the position? That would be just the kind of thing his older sisters would have done.

Almost as if she read his thoughts, Rebecca replied, "I told her that I would help her place an advertisement in one of the local newspapers. I said nothing about being a cook for you."

"I'll do some checking and perhaps I'll talk to her." Quint glared at the empty cup before him. After he bathed and dressed in more formal attire, he left the apartment with the purpose of hiring a cook. He talked to several business friends only to discover that people with those kinds of skills were in high demand. He spent the afternoon checking on the "Crossed Winds" inn and both Nicholas Gibson and Hilda Winkelblake.

Nicholas was a small time rogue. He had been before the magistrate a number of times, but the cases had been dismissed because there was little evidence against the man. Hilda apparently was only his cook. She came years ago as a bondservant herself and Nicholas had paid off her bond and hired her as his cook when he opened the "Crossed Winds." The only thing he knew for certain about Hilda Winkelblake was that the woman was a marvel in the kitchen. The whole dock area of Philadelphia knew about the meals at the Crossed Winds.

By the time he got back to the apartment Quint had made up his mind. He would offer the position as his cook to Hilda. If the older woman was a friend of Rebecca's that might induce her to accept the offer more quickly. Then he could get started for the Caribbean.

Quint said little to Rebecca that night but told her that he had an early afternoon appointment the next day and he wanted her to accompany him. "Be ready to leave about half past one," Quint instructed before he set off for the shipyards the next morning.

Rebecca was surprised that Quint said nothing more about a cook. "Perhaps," she told herself glumly as she tried to arrange her hair, "he's decided I'm too much trouble."

She knew that he could sell her bond to anyone who wanted to buy it and for several minutes she sat chilled with horror. Whatever had made her come up with such a scheme? She shook her head, trying to dislodge the feelings of gloom that surrounded her. "You know why you did what you did. Now, take command. He hasn't sold you yet," she muttered out loud to the black-eyed girl staring back at her from the mirror.

At one o'clock Quint returned and had the carriage brought around. He still offered her no explanation and she was afraid to ask. They left the apartment with only a terse greeting between them. Rebecca sat stiffly in the carriage, watching the parading scenery as the carriage moved briskly down the street.

The cab was slowing when Quint looked over at her and with a grim face he announced, "Now, let's see if we can hire a cook." He stood and before the carriage had come to a complete stop, he swung down to the street and waited to help Rebecca from the conveyance. When she saw the sign above her head she wanted to squeal with delight. She tried to contain the smile that played at her lips. He was going to ask Hilda to take the job.

From the side door of the inn, Bud saw the carriage and when the tall occupant swung down from the door, Bud swore a vulgar oath. He had only started to put the plans he made into order. He was days away from getting the revenge he wanted. Watching carefully, he saw Quint aid the dark-haired beauty down to the street. There was no preventing it. For the moment, Bud decided he had to disappear. At least with McQuade at the inn, he could check out the rumor he heard about the man sailing for the islands. He grinned as he remembered the look of fond appreciation and something else that graced Quint's face when he helped Rebecca from the carriage. Bud wondered if his revenge against the girl might prove a greater pain to the man. It was clear that the girl meant something to McQuade. He smiled. Hilda would tell him what Rebecca meant to Captain McQuade. He took off in the direction of the docks.

When Bud made his way back to the inn late that afternoon, he was more than disgusted. Quint McQuade had more champions than any man had a right to. He had tried to ask some discreet questions about the woman he had seen at Quint's side and the sailors of Quint's ship took exception with his remarks. He barely escaped with his life. He found out that the man was indeed going to the islands and would be gone for several weeks. If he was going to get McQuade it would have to be in the next day or two, because the ship would sail on Friday.

He planted himself at the big table in the kitchen and batted his eyes at Hilda. "That there stew were the best I ever ate."

Hilda smiled her thanks. "Sorry I am to say this to ye, but enjoy while ye may."

Bud groaned. "Nicholas ain't gonna fire me is he?" he asked, trying to remember if he had failed to do something Nicholas had instructed him to do. He couldn't think of a thing.

Hilda sighed and Bud glanced over at the woman. She seemed happy and sad all at once. "No, fire you he ain't. It's me."

Bud grinned up at her. "He sure can't fire you. Don't you go be scaring me like that."

"Another job I take. Day after tomorrow, I start."

Bud stared at the woman. Surely he had misunderstood. "Another job?" he croaked.

Hilda nodded her head. "Happy I am with the job, but of all the people here, I think, and sad I am."

Bud continued to stare. "What job?"

"Well, meet her you didn't, but a young English lady and a captain, a cook they need and they want me."

Bud's suspicions started to grow. "What captain?"

Hilda looked at him, a frown creasing her broad brow, "A job for you, he does not have. A job you have here, if you do the work."

Bud attempted a chuckle to distract from his questions. "I don't want you being taken advantage of, Hilda. I ain't gonna let no one treat ya bad."

Hilda was distracted. "Quint McQuade is an honorable man. Worried you don't need to be."

Bud worked at keeping his face a blank. Quint McQuade was gathering more and more sins that he would have to be punished for, Bud decided as he left the table. Wishing the big woman luck took all of his effort. Now, he would have to get the man before Hilda changed jobs. He couldn't have her going off to work for someone else.

Bud thought about his feelings the next morning as Nicholas Gibson put them to words. Hilda had just told him she would be moving on the next day. "Ya ain't quittin' me. I don't care iffin' he does pay ya more. Ya ain't gonna be leavin'."

Hilda glared at the short dark-haired man, "Leaving I am, and I go today!"

She whirled around and headed out of his office. With her hand on the knob she turned around and growled, "Stop me you can't, and don't you try!" She slammed the door in her anger.

Quint was not in the best of humor when Hilda arrived at the apartment later that morning. Rebecca had refused to let him touch her and in spite of the fact that he had hired her friend, she had slept in her bed and he slept in his. That was not what he had planned. And, if the truth were known he had done little sleeping. The voyage ahead of him was not something he wanted to do, but he couldn't figure a way out of it and that made him angrier still.

"Quit I can't, Mr. Gibson says, so I come today," she offered when Quint asked what she was doing there. "Wait I must 'till next Tuesday, to get all my things. To the market he goes every Tuesday. A wagon I'll borrow, and get my things."

Quint nodded with a groan. His life had been so simple

before he went to England. Now, he had ships, and land, and servants, and farms, and a beautiful mistress that didn't know she was a mistress. Well, with Hilda in the house, he could leave a day early. He grumbled as he left the apartment, "If the crew is sober enough, I may leave today."

Quint didn't leave that afternoon, even though the crew had been assembled and everyone from the oldest to the youngest was very sober. But by high tide of the next afternoon, Quint's ship left the dock of Philadelphia with his mind at peace. He had taken the time to explain to Hilda some of his fears, and the woman was very perceptive. She had nodded her head, "More than pretty she is. The wolves she will draw. Alone, she cannot be. Out of my sight she won't get."

Quint explained to both Hilda and Rebecca about the trip, "I'll be gone for about two weeks. I have a cargo to deliver and I'll have to find one there to bring back. I've left instructions with Harry to help with the shopping and Pete Moran is a good man. He's second to the foreman at the yard. He'll take Hilda to the inn on Tuesday and fix anything that should require attention."

He left funds for the market and shook hands with Hilda. He tried to kiss Rebecca, but she managed to twist her head so he only grazed her cheek. With Hilda standing next to Rebecca, he had to be satisfied.

As the ship sailed out, the heading plotted, the sails set and the wheel in the capable hands of the second mate, Quint leaned against the rail and thought about the girl who slept in his apartment. When he told her that he had to take one of the ships to the islands, she had seemed so relieved. Even though she tried to hide them, however, her eyes misted with tears. She wanted him to go, but she obviously didn't want him to go.

He slammed his hand on the railing thinking of the whispered scene he had had with her the night before. She had once again refused to come to his bed. "Not with Hilda in the apartment," she had hissed.

"What has Hilda got to do with this?"

"I don't want her to think badly of me. We aren't married, you know! What you want me to do should only be done by married couples."

Quint remembered his feelings of frustration, "You don't believe that anymore than I do."

Rebecca stood her ground. Quint slept alone that night and he hoped that she slept as well as he did, which was poorly. He stared back in the direction of Philadelphia, and at the brilliant sunset. He had a feeling that he was going to regret having Hilda in the apartment, unless she could change Rebecca's mind. If it weren't for the talk that would result, the farm would be the perfect solution.

He turned away from the railing and made his way to his cabin. With his lack of sleep for the last two nights, he was certain that this night he would sleep like a log.

Miles west, Rebecca was getting ready for bed as well. Quint had judged her feeling very accurately. She was very relieved to have him gone for several days, but another part of her didn't want him gone at all. She had a terrible time refusing him the night before, even with Hilda in the house. "What is to become of me?" she asked out loud as she donned her night dress. In spite of her tiredness, sleep came slowly as Rebecca tried to answer her own question.

A mile from the apartment, Bud Worthman was nearly wild with disgust. "The bastard!" he shouted at the empty room. He had given two weeks pay to the little gray-haired man with the blade. The old man promised to slice Quint up good, cutting on his face once he got him down. Bud had checked on the old man, too. He was as good as he said he was. But now McQuade was gone. "Damn!" Bud slurred at nothing. He had to start over with his plans. He would get the girl. McQuade would be gone for several weeks, and with a sea voyage there was no guarantee he would come back. Bud could get to the girl. Somehow, he had to get to the girl!

Chapter Twelve

Hilda had been at the apartment for ten days when the message she had been waiting for finally arrived. She handed the poorly penned note to Rebecca, blushing as she explained, "Read, I can't."

Rebecca took the card and read aloud, "Boss goes market Friday," It was signed, "your friend".

Hilda sighed and nodded her head, then she mentioned quietly, "About my things I must see. Go, now I can and get my things."

Rebecca smiled at her friend standing in the door frame of the kitchen, remembering her anger the week before. Hilda had left with Pete Moran early in the morning, set on bringing all of her personal items back to the apartment. Much to Rebecca's surprise, she was gone less than an hour and there was no mistaking the woman's anger when the first floor door slammed, shaking all of the windows in the apartment.

Rebecca remembered how she had rushed out to the parlor to see Hilda standing in the middle of the room, her round face, a bright red. Her large arms were folded over her chest in an attitude of defiance and her dark eyes were slits. For a moment, Rebecca wondered at whom the Dutch woman's anger was directed. "Hilda," Rebecca spoke softly, "Whatever is wrong?"

Hilda glared at her and Rebecca watched her jaw work as if she were trying to translate words with her mouth. *"Schwienhound,"* she slurred in accented German. Rebecca gasped, remembering the expression from her Prussian farmers.

"Hilda!" Rebecca admonished.

"Well, he is!" Hilda announced with venom.

It took Rebecca the better part of the next hour to drag the facts from the cook. Hilda had gone to the Crossed Winds, certain that Nicholas Gibson had gone to the market as he always did, prepared to pack her things and tow them back to the apartment. But, it seems the woman's former boss was waiting. "A friend, a message will send when the man is gone," she choked out when Rebecca insisted they both go back to the inn and get Hilda's things that day. Hilda refused to go and she refused to tell Rebecca anything more.

Rebecca sent Harry to bring Pete Moran back to the apartment and Rebecca was stunned when the short little man shifted from one foot and then the other, "I ain't never seen anything like it, Mam. They got to yelling at each other about what was hers and what was his and she hauled off and hit him on the chin. Knocked 'im flat she did. Then, he shouted about bringing in the law and I grabbed Hilda and pushed her out the door. She didn't want to go, and I don't want you tellin' Capt. McQuade, Mam, but I was afraid she was a gonna hit me, too. She can't go back there if he's there. One of the other employees talked to her after I got her outta there. He promised to send word when the boss goes to market."

Rebecca handed the grubby paper back to Hilda, "Let's make sure Pete Moran is available for tomorrow before you make plans. How long will you be gone?"

"Nicholas goes early to market. Early I go to inn. Spend the day I will not! But pack I must and sort things. Four hours, maybe five it will take. For me, Mr. Moran can return. At the time, I'll tell him."

Rebecca smiled wondering if Pete would understand Hilda well enough to determine when she wanted to return to the apartment. If Pete stayed at the inn with her, he would be on hand to pull Hilda out of the place if Nicholas Gibson returned early from the market. Rebecca decided that she would prefer to have the man with Hilda and would tell him herself when he picked up the woman the next morning. Rebecca thought about Harry and mentally made a note to tell him to go along, too. The sooner Hilda got her things packed and out of the place the more relieved Rebecca would feel.

Rebecca saw the three off about an hour after dawn the next morning. Hilda had argued but in the end Rebecca won and Harry, Pete, and Hilda climbed into the wagon. "You'll be back for lunch, I'm sure," Rebecca called after them. "I'll have coffee ready." She retreated back into the apartment, and sat down for an unhurried cup of tea. She had mending to concern herself with until Hilda returned.

Rebecca pulled out her sewing box and had just settled herself down in the parlor with a stack of things that needed mending. One thing she could do better than any of the Americans she'd met, she thought with a grin, was mending clothing. Of course, she'd had enough practice, she grimaced, picking up a bodice that needed repair.

Rebecca didn't get her needle threaded before a loud banging at the lower door forced her to lay the fabric aside and see to her visitor. "Surely Hilda hasn't had trouble?" she muttered as she crossed to the stairs.

She opened the door to a short little man, one she knew she had never seen. "Beggin' yer pardon, Mistress," he said bowing his head, "Captain McQuade sent word that you and Mistress Winkel - a - the cook, are to go to the farm."

Rebecca smiled at his attempt with Hilda's name but when she realized what the message meant, she blurted out, "But, Mistress Winkelblake is not here."

The sailor looked surprised, "Where is she?"

Without a thought, Rebecca responded, "Pete Moran took her to the inn this morning."

"And Pete didn't say anything. He knew about this here message. He knew we had to start real soon, or we won't make the farm. He must be taking this Hilda to the farm hisself. I'll take you and he can bring the cook." The little man smiled up at Rebecca, and she wondered if the missing teeth were what made the smile look like a leer.

"I think I better wait for Hilda," Rebecca said softly.

"Well, I ain't comin' back tomorrow. And if Pete takes Hilda to the farm . . . By the way, where's the boy?"

"Harry?" Rebecca asked cautiously, not sure about the

man at all.

"Did Pete take him?" When Rebecca nodded, the little man pushed open the door, "Well, that proves it! Git yer things together, Missy. Captain said enough for a couple of weeks, then he'll see to the dressmaker."

Rebecca was torn between wanting to stay right where she was and doing what she thought she had been ordered to do. Obviously, she told herself as she followed the man up the stairs, Quint had forgotten to tell her about the move. "Should I bring my herbs?" she asked as she climbed up the last several steps.

"Yer to pack whatever you'll need for about two weeks. The Captain'll send fer what ever more ye need," he answered with some finality. "But, I told ya, I want to get a move on. It'll take pert' near all day to reach the place and I don't like travelin' at night."

Rebecca nodded, convinced that the man had come from Quint McQuade, "It won't take long. I don't have that much." And, Rebecca sighed with satisfaction, it didn't take long. She was packed and ready in less than two hours. The little man was nearly beside himself with the time she did take, however, and shouted a dozen times during the last hour, "Hurry up!"

Rebecca ended his shouting by glaring at him then commenting, "If you'll quit shouting, I'll get finished much sooner."

Minutes later she was ready to lock up, when once again the little man shouted at her. "The other shipmates will lock up. They got to clean up, and pack up what ya didn't take and bring the captain's stuff. Now, come on, let's get outta here." Rebecca felt a shiver of apprehension dart up her back. The sailor looked like he was about to come unstrung.

Rebecca positioned herself on the wagon seat with her trunk on the wagon bed and watched the sailor clamor up to take the reins. Was Quint really sending her to the farms, she wondered. And why hadn't he explained it to her?

* * *

It was nearly two by the time Harry jumped down from the wagon and ran ahead of Pete who was steering the vehicle to the barn. For over two hours, he listened to Pete and Hilda arguing over the things that she was packing. Hilda brought with her what she claimed were her things: a coffee grinder, a set of knives, several skillets, two big iron pots, and a dozen old utensils that mystified Pete. "Mine, they are. Bought them, I did, with what little money that man gave me," she shrugged her shoulders toward the main room with the office. "With me they go."

Harry smiled as he remembered Pete muttering about arguing with her until the sun went down. He could almost understand why Nicholas had threatened Hilda with the Constable. Pete told him he didn't want Nicholas Gibson arriving and another argument beginning. Even if the woman insisted on taking half the kitchen with her, Pete groaned, he wasn't going to object.

When they arrived at the door of the apartment, hands full of boxes and cartons, a deep masculine voice boomed down the stairwell, "Well, it's about time. Where in the hell have you been?"

Hilda started up the stairs, "Where we were, Rebecca knew. Why she not tell you?"

Quint stared at the woman who handed him an enormous bag, "She's with you, isn't she?"

Hilda shook her head and stood at the top of the stairs frozen in position. "Harry and Pete, they take me to Crossed Winds to get my things. Rebecca, here she stays."

Quint growled back, his bright blue eyes clouded with confusion, "Well, she's not here now! Where is she?"

Inside of fifteen minutes a dozen sailors from the shipyards had been summoned and Quint McQuade was organizing a search. Hilda had gone to check in Rebecca's room for some clue. She came back quickly. "Something is smelling here. Her trunk is gone. Most of her clothes she takes, but her herbs she leaves."

Quint stared at Hilda trying to put that information into what he could only guess had happened to the young English lady. "Who did she know? Who could have taken her away? None of this makes any sense."

Pete Moran was standing next to Hilda scratching his thick graying curls. "This ain't connected, I don't think, but there's been a sailor around the dock asking questions and making comments. Hell, one night a couple of weeks ago, he started insinuating something about you and Mistress Rebecca and I thought some of your men were gonna take his head off."

Quint looked confused, "What'd he look like?"

Hilda was listening, too, and Harry had turned his attention to Pete as well.

"Well, strange thing about the man, he had lots of black hair, chest, arms, face, but not on the top of his head," Pete touched his pate in demonstration. "He was nearly bald."

"Bud," Hilda squealed.

"Worthman," Quint moaned.

Pete nodded his head, "He called himself Worthman."

Quint turned to Hilda, "Whom did you say?"

"Bud Worthman, he called himself. Months ago, to the inn he came. A job Nicholas gave him and his back I fixed up. A cruel Spanish captain, a whip to his back he took."

Quint stared at her, Horror and anger flicking across his face, "Captain Hemphill stripped his back for attempting to rape Rebecca. I caught him in the hold of the *Venture* slapping her around. You took care of Rebecca's worst enemy."

"Now, Capt'n," Pete said quietly as he looked at Hilda's crumpled face, "She didn't know."

Quint attempted to apologize, but Hilda's tears and sobs prevented his words from being heard. "Tell her what I said and let me see what I can find out," Quint ran down the stairs to the street. Hilda dried her tears and followed him out.

Quint went to the house next door to ask for information, but before he could knock he saw Hilda pounding on the door of a house three doors from the apartment. "Hilda," he called, "What are you doing?" He made his way to her.

"In every neighborhood, one there is," she hissed at him. Stay, see you will." As the door opened, Hilda smiled at the woman who stood with her hand on the knob. She spoke

130

softly, "Mistress Langdon, my employer this is. Wondering we were if you saw his young ward today. Mr. McQuade for her he has been waiting, and she hasn't come."

The woman straightened her shoulders with self-importance and said, "What makes you think I saw her?"

Hilda looked disappointed. "Mr. McQuade, I told about how observant you were. Please, something you must have seen."

The woman looked a bit guilty and offered a weak smile. "Well, I did notice that the sailor was loading a wagon with her things. They left about three hours ago."

Hilda smiled triumphantly at Quint. "The sailor, please, about him you tell Mr. McQuade."

Within a matter of minutes, Quint knew exactly what the man looked like, how much Rebecca took and even in what direction they went from the apartment. He thanked the woman and complimented Hilda on her knowledge of the neighborhood when they were out of the woman's hearing. "How did you know that she would have watched?" Quint asked intrigued.

"Before, through the glass, watching I've seen her. She everybody's business must know."

"But," Quint frowned, "Rebecca left with someone other than Bud. Maybe Bud has nothing to do with this at all. Maybe," his voice grew husky, "she left to get away from me."

Hilda looked up at him grimly, "Bud Worthman, involved he is. Paul that sailor is called. Bud for meals he brings him all week before I left." Hilda swiped at a tear, "If Rebecca I've harmed, myself I'll hate."

"Hilda, I didn't mean what I said. None of this is your fault. You know that don't you?" he asked her softly as he patted his cook's broad shoulder.

She tried to smile up at him, but her face fell. "Where she is, we don't know?"

"No," Quint replied, "But we know who took her and what direction they started moving. We'll find her, " he whispered.

Hilda looked up at him with a glint in her eyes, "Another might know. For a meal, another sailor Bud brings

131

with him. Arnold Schmidt he called himself."

Harry had followed them down the stairs and heard the name Hilda mentioned. "Arnold Schmidt! Arnold Schmidt lives with his sister. Just down the street from my ma. I talked to him night before last."

"Let's go," Quint grabbed Harry. "Hilda," he shouted back at the cook, "Pack some food. We may be gone for awhile."

Harry's home was only blocks from the apartment and Quint's horse came to a stop before the small cottage where Arnold Schmidt lived. Luck was with them when Arnold himself came to see who was banging on his sister's door. His face lost all of its color when he recognized Quinton McQuade. "I ain't had a thing to do with it," he groaned, as if he knew what Quint was doing there.

"I want to know what you know," Quint pulled out a pocket watch, "And in about one minute."

Arnold was shaking. "I ain't had no part in it. I don't cotton to kidnapping, not a lady, I don't. I told him I ain't doin' it. But, Paul, he ses he'll do it. He done it, didn't he?"

Quint nodded his head, "I want to know where he was taking her. That's all I need to know."

Arnold grimaced. "I ain't supposed to tell. If he finds out . . ." his voice trailed off as if the thought was too horrible to contemplate.

Quint grabbed the short little man by the shirt front, "I'm a lot bigger and can be a lot meaner than either Bud Worthman or your friend Paul. I'll see you pulled apart, literally, my friend, if you don't tell me where they've taken her."

Arnold's face turned gray and his lower lip trembled in obvious terror. "Paul has a cousin what's got a tavern outside of Bristol. Bud was meeting him there tomorrow night. Paul wasn't too sure he could get started with the girl soon enough to make the tavern tonight. I didn't do nothing. I tole ya, I don't cotton to stealin' women." His eyes blinked rapidly as he watched Quint clench and unclench his fist. "I didn't do nothing," he whispered as Quint moved closer.

"I need a name, either the cousin, or the inn," Quint

snarled, reaching for the front of Arnold's shirt once again.

"The White Gull," Arnold shouted at him, "The inn is called the White Gull."

Quint pushed the man away in disgust. "If she's not there, or if she's been harmed in any way," Quint said through gritted teeth, "Your life is over. Do you understand?"

Arnold was shaking visibly now, "Paul weren't to touch her. Bud ses that plain. She's there and she can't be hurt none. Bud ain't paying if she has a scratch."

"You better hope so," Quint yelled over his shoulder as he stomped away from the man. In seconds he was back on the big bay, racing back to the apartment.

Rebecca tried to relax on the wagon seat, but as they moved out of Philadelphia, she couldn't shake the feeling that something was wrong. Surely, Quint would have mentioned a trip to the farm before he left. Why had he changed his mind and more important, when? He wasn't due to arrive back in the city until the end of next week. Had he arrived and sent word through one of his men? She was very confused.

"What is your name?" she asked softly as they reached the edge of the city.

"Paul, Mam," he answered, never taking his eyes from the road.

"Paul, when did Mr. McQuade get back? Why didn't he come to tell me himself?"

Paul blushed and stared ahead, "I wish ya hadn't asked, but I guess ya have a right to know. I made up all that stuff about the farm, 'cause I didn't want to hurt ya. But, I guess ya have to know." Paul took a deep breath, as if what he had to say was going to hurt him, too, "He sold ya. I'm taking ya to yer new owner. He owns a tavern in Bristol."

"He sold me? That's not possible. He didn't want me to indenture myself to begin with. I don't believe you," she shouted at the man beside her.

"I got the papers," Paul patted his pocket soundlessly. Rebecca sat very still, hoping against hope that what the man said was not true. Somehow, it made sense. Quint hadn't wanted her to begin with. She was probably putting a strain on the way he lived. She had forced him to hire help.

Afternoon turned into early evening as Rebecca sat on the seat of the wagon, bouncing and weaving with the motion of the vehicle as it traveled over the rutted trail that passed for a road. The long gray afternoon turned into a chilly starless night, but still the wagon banged along in mind-numbing monotony. Rebecca refused to give in to the panic and fear that she felt. Instead, she kept reminding herself that she had been used again.

Her rage spawned tears, but they were tears of anger as she recalled each man who betrayed her, beginning with her father. His betrayal came in the form of his sporting nature. He should never have gone hunting. He betrayed her by getting shot, and by not rewriting his will, leaving her in the hands of Arthur. Her list continued. Each man she had ever met, to her way of thinking, had treated her poorly. She simmered with anger.

When the wagon finally stopped in back of a large white building lit with several oil lamps, she glared at the man beside her, "Are we there?"

He nodded and led her to the door. His cousin was told to have an attic room ready for the runaway wife of a friend. The boss better get here soon, Paul thought, as he led Rebecca through the door. "They've got a room ready for ya," he muttered as he sat her down at the big table in the kitchen. "I'll get the key."

Rebecca sat at the table and tried to eat the bowl of stew the serving girl placed before her, while Paul carried her trunk up to the room she had been given. He said nothing more to her and except for the strange looks the serving girl gave her, no one seemed to be the slightest bit interested in Rebecca Ranserford.

After the meal, Rebecca followed Paul up the steps. The tiny attic room was cold and dark, but Rebecca was too devastated to care at this point. She didn't even bother to tell the sailor a good night and she forgot to ask for the key to the room. In fact, the fact that he had locked her in didn't register for a minute or two. "Well," she muttered as she stumbled onto the mattress filled with corn husks, "They're probably afraid I'll run away." She clenched her teeth and closed her eyes. She couldn't do anything unless she was rested. Tomorrow after a decent sleep, she told herself, she would decide what to do.

At dawn, a rustling noise disturbed her sleep and Rebecca stretched on the lumpy mattress. Still half asleep, she glanced at the closed door. On the floor near the door was a tray containing a pitcher and a small pot. Next to the pot was a covered plate. She shook her head, trying to clear the sleep from her brain. Slowly the events of the previous day seeped into her head and she jumped up from the bed and ran to the door. Hesitantly, she reached out to turn the knob.

The ball turned but the door would not budge. She muttered, "It's stuck. Don't panic. Pull hard!" The last she said as she gritted her teeth and yanked on the door, hard. Nothing happened. Why had they locked her in?

Something was not right, here. Well, she thought, at least I won't starve. She couldn't help but wonder when someone would come to check on her. "I better be ready to go," she mumbled as she slumped down on the bed to consume the contents of the tray.

After she ate, she made up the bed, washed, and dressed quickly, stopping often to listen for noises that would tell her someone was coming. Still, noon came and she heard nothing. What she needed, she thought, was some idea of where she was. She glanced up at the high ceiling. There was a small window in one of the eves. If she could reach that she could at least get some idea of the countryside. She tried to arrange something in the room that would let her peer out of the tiny window, but nothing got her close. There was nothing she could do but wait and wonder at her fate.

Quint and three of his sailors loaded the small skiff that Quint had chosen for the trip up the Delaware River. All of his men knew about the White Gull. It was a cheap inn a block from the docks but they served a decent stew, Pauley said. The sailors all agreed that they watered the grog, and in their eyes that made it an inn of thievery. "They better not have hurt her," two of the men stated as they discussed the place that Rebecca was to have been taken.

They sailed off just as the sun was setting and Quint thought back over his plans for the evening. It certainly hadn't included trying to rescue Rebecca. He wanted nothing more than to try another of Hilda's marvelous meals and to sit quietly and tell Rebecca about his trip to the islands. He hadn't even tried to get a cargo to return to the mainland. He had missed her too much and when they unloaded the goods they brought, Quint arranged payment and loaded his ship. He was on his way back to Philadelphia before the return tide, with his men shaking their heads and grinning at him in disbelief.

"Damn," he muttered as he gave the orders to trim the small sail, he had wanted Rebecca in his arms this night, not in some tavern north of the city. His brow furrowed. He'd better get to her before Bud Worthman showed up. As he watched the chill wind fill the small sheet of sail, he thought about Bud Worthman. This time the man was not going to get away with what he'd done to her. Quint would see him locked safely away, possibly for a dozen years. No, he was going to find Rebecca, and catch Bud Worthman red-handed. Quint would see the sailor that helped Bud in the arms of the law as well. Quint leaned back in the skiff and made his plans.

Chapter Thirteen

Quint glared at the dull gray disk of the late fall sun and swore softly. Everything about this trip was fast becoming more than he could bare. He turned his anger on the crippled wooden structure that was to have carried them quietly up the river. What a disaster the whole plan had turned out to be. They had been on the water less than an hour when the wind died down completely. Dark clouds obliterated the sliver of a moon and then the wind picked up, this time announcing a storm.

For the next three hours, they put into shore to wait for the storm which moved through quickly. Unfortunately, the storm north of them had been much worse and without some stars or the light of the moon. Quint did not see the trunk of the tree that slammed into the skiff. They barely made it to shore with all of them bailing. The men were wet and cold and without transportation.

He swore again, and moved closer to the small fire he had built after he sent Pauley out to round up a wagon and a team of horses. He glanced at the rising sun. Already they had been stuck for six hours. They had at least ten more miles to travel before they got to Bristol. If Bud Worthman arrived at the White Gull before he did . . . He could not finish the thought.

Quint shivered in apprehension. What if he didn't get to her in time? Wrestling with his nightmarish vision, he lunged from his seat before the fire and strode up the slight rise that marked the river's edge. He stared at the road in the distance. Where in the hell was Pauley? The man should have been back hours ago. Quint leaned toward the road and listened intently. Was he hearing the soft tinkle of the trappings of a horse and wagon. Please, he prayed silently.

A half an hour later, Quint sat behind a sway-back nag, questioning Pauley's knowledge of horseflesh. The old mare would make it for a few miles, but she would never be able to travel to Bristol. Quint swore viciously.

It was almost dusk when Quint and his men found the White Gull. It had taken a long discussion with a farmer of some wealth before Quint convinced him that he could honor the paper he gave the man for a massive stallion to take them into Bristol and back to Philadelphia.

When they arrived at the inn, Quint stationed the men around the fringe of the tavern to watch and wait, at least for a short time, until he could decide how best to proceed. If Worthman had arrived, he would spot Quint and he might hurt Rebecca before Quint had a chance to help her. He had no idea if Rebecca knew why she had been brought to the inn and he doubted that he'd have the time to find out. He heard the soft clop of a nearby horse and rider as someone approached.

He signaled his men to hold their positions and he hid himself, stretching from his place behind a bramble bush. Biting down hard, he stilled the curse that wanted to gallop over his lips as the visitor reined his horse to a stop before the inn. Bud Worthman had arrived.

Rebecca spent the morning moving around the tiny room, restless and anxious. She fought back tears when she thought about Quint McQuade. The question of why had he sold her kept creeping into her mind and although she answered it a dozen different ways, none of her answers cut through her despondency. "Why?" she mumbled as she sat down on the bed for the hundredth time that day.

Slowly she watched the shadows shorten and she judged

that the sun had to be at its zenith, still, no one came for her. She watched as the shadows lengthened and her anxiety grew. Late in the afternoon, she heard steps on the stairs and she jumped up, eager to find out what was happening. The door creaked open a fraction of an inch and a small female voice pleaded, "Don't try nothing. I got your supper."

Rebecca watched as a small tray with a bowl, a hunk of bread and a mug slid past the door. As quietly as it opened, the door closed and Rebecca stood still, not able to believe that her only contact with a person had come to an end. The retreating steps brought her to reality, "No," she yelled, "No! Don't go. Wait!" The sound that answered her call was the sound of running steps, moving away from her prison. She glared at the tray and realizing her helplessness, she fought a depression every bit as deep as the one that occurred when her brother told her she was leaving England.

She sank back to the bed and tried to regain the independence that she had felt only a day before. Suddenly, she was poor little Rebecca Ranserford, the purchased bride of a man she never met. The tears ran freely down her cheeks and she paid them no heed. Once more, her world was in ruins. Could she survive yet another time?

She didn't bother to look at the bowl or the mug. She was consumed with despair, and food was the furthest thing from her mind. No, she didn't want food, she wanted out of this room, away from Pennsylvania, away from the sea and back on her farms in England. Her head fell to her chest and her thick black locks hung free to her waist. They covered the face that was streaked with another waterfall of anguish as Rebecca sank deeper into despair.

An hour later she had no more tears to cry and she was talking out loud to herself. A token amount of her independence had been restored, when a voice startled her, "Missy, you come with me. Your husband is here, and I don't want no trouble."

Rebecca's head snapped up in astonishment. Husband? Good Lord! Someone had made a monumental mistake. They had her confused with someone else. "I have no husband," Rebecca said to the voice on the other side of the door.

The door swung open and Rebecca stared at a dowdy woman scarcely an inch taller, with gray wisps of hair straying from her mobcap, and rough red hands twisting in her gray stained apron. Rebecca said more firmly, "I have no husband."

The woman turned and started down the steps, "Your husband," she said, in a loud voice, "has come for ye. I don't want no trouble. I'll lock ye back in that room and he can come fer ye hisself."

Rebecca followed, "Please, someone has mistaken me for someone else. I am not married. My name is Rebecca Ra . . ."

"I knew who you is. Yer name's Ranserfer, er—something like that. Now, no trouble, Mistress." She stepped into the hall and reached for a paneled door. "He's waiting, in here." She pushed Rebecca through the doorway.

Rebecca glanced into the room and the figure she saw standing in the room next to the fireplace chilled her bones. For an instant, she froze, recognition clear in her eyes. Never would she forget the man who tried to force himself on her in the hold of the *Venture*. Somehow, she pulled a breath past the knot in her throat. "No," she whispered; "No!" she said with more volume; "No!" she screamed as she lunged for the door.

In that second, Bud grabbed at her, catching her wrist as she whirled to escape. She fought the fog that threatened to consume her, then she regained her will to fight, but it was too late. Bud had pulled her off balance. She yanked away from him but in so doing, she fell in the other direction. The side of her head hit the edge of a table. A merciful black fog closed in before she hit the floor.

Quint heard Rebecca's scream and signaled his men that their wait was over. He flung open the back door to see Bud leaning over Rebecca where she lay on the floor next to the table, a vivid red mark on her temple, darkening as Quint watched.

"What did you do to her, you bastard?" Quint roared as he threw Bud in the direction of his men. Kneeling at

Rebecca's side he placed his fingers on her neck. Her heart was beating, at least she was alive.

The mistress of the inn stuck her head around the door. "Sir, what have you done? What happened to his wife?" she nodded her head in Bud's direction.

"She is not his wife!" Quint said with emphasis. In quick succession Quint procured a bed for Rebecca, had a man go find the constable and a physician and had Bud Worthman lashed to the center post of the inn's back porch.

The wife of the owner of the inn was more than apologetic. "I didn't know, sir. He said she was a runaway wife. He gave her name and paid the bill."

Quint glared at her. "The coin was great?"

The woman only nodded.

"When there is a great deal of money involved, woman, I suggest that you consider whether or not the transaction is an honest one," Quint lectured.

The constable arrived and with Quint's sworn statement, Bud Worthman was taken into custody. Quint assured the lawman he would sign a formal complaint in the morning. The physician arrived and Quint refused to leave the man alone with Rebecca.

"She should be bled, and then the waiting begins. With head injuries . . ." the man began to pull his knives and the bowl from his bag.

Quint stated quietly, "I don't believe in bleeding a patient and the young woman you were called to treat does not believe in bleeding either."

The physician raised one eyebrow. "Sir, if you did not want my help—"

Quint interrupted, "I don't want her bled."

The physician turned and stuffed the equipment back in his bag. "When you decide to let me be the doctor, send for me!" He marched out of the room in a huff.

Quint stood at the end of the bed, gazing down into the pale face of Rebecca. She probably should not be moved, but he knew of no one to help with her care. He should send for Hilda, but that would take too long. The roads were impossible, but the river had calmed since the storm. If he could get a large enough vessel, Rebecca could be transported to Philadelphia. The roads were much better in the city and a comfortable carriage could see her to the apartment with ease. He strode out of the room, leaving Pauley and the innkeeper's wife at Rebecca's bedside.

Quint found a friend in Bristol and with his help, Quint had a large skiff secured in less than an hour. At dawn the next morning, Quint had signed the complaint against Bud Worthman, paid the innkeeper for Rebecca's care, gathered Rebecca in his arms and made his way carefully to the skiff. The mark on the side of her face was a colorful blue, black and purple. Just a glance at the bruise made Quint want to rip the soul from Bud Worthman's body. The mistress of the inn, and even Quint's sailors, were very concerned with moving Rebecca, but he was not to be deterred.

She had not regained consciousness, but she had grown restless twice during the night and she groaned several times on the way to the skiff. He felt that it would only be a matter of time before she woke, but he still was not certain that her head injury was the only pain Worthman had caused. No, he wanted her in Hilda's hands as soon as possible.

The trip down the river, moving with the current was accomplished in less than six hours. The ride was as smooth as glass, for the river had calmed down considerably. Quint guided the skiff to the northern docks away from the main traffic, so that the waves of the larger vessels would not disturb Rebecca. Once they were tied up, he sent Pauley scurrying off for a carriage.

Before the afternoon was over, Rebecca was bathed, in a clean gown, and resting in her own bed. She awakened with a king-sized headache. Hilda assured Quint that Rebecca had received no other injuries, and the cook fixed her a powder for her head and a cup of herb tea to help her sleep. Rebecca hurt too much to ask why she was back in her bed, or how she got there. After she struggled through some of the broth Hilda insisted she eat, she sank back to sleep, grateful to someone, she didn't know whom.

Quint paced the parlor floor, thoroughly disgusted with

the events of the last several days. Obviously, a woman of Rebecca's beauty and stature, could not protect herself from the riff-raff that populated the streets of Philadelphia. Despite what the neighbors or Susannah thought, Quint was going to have to take Rebecca to the farm. At least in the country she would be safe. Of course, Hilda would go with her, so there would be a chaperone at the farm. Quint was not honest enough with himself to admit that he wanted to spend the next several months at the farm and he did not want Rebecca sixteen miles away.

Before the cook went to her bed, Quint told her of his plans. "We'll leave late in the morning, after Rebecca has had a chance to sleep. If we go slowly, she shouldn't suffer too much." He went on to explain to Hilda his reasons for the move, stressing the dangers he thought Rebecca faced.

Hilda nodded her head. "Safe she is not. Much too pretty. Travel, I don't like. We go tomorrow and there we stay?"

Quint nodded. Tomorrow evening they would be at the farm. He left it to Hilda to explain to Rebecca that they were going to his farm. Hilda had always been very sensitive to her role as cook and companion to Rebecca but in this she felt Quint would want to explain his thoughts to the girl as he had to her. Quint would tell Rebecca that they were going to the farm for her safety. As a result, neither one explained anything to Rebecca. Her head hurt too much, however, to be concerned with anything. She was aware that they were leaving the apartment but where they were going she didn't feel up to asking.

Quint loaded the few things Rebecca had left in the carriage with the few things of Hilda's that they could carry. Hilda asked about Rebecca's trunk and Quint said, "I left the damn thing at the White Gull. I forgot about it in the rush to get her back here. I doubt that the thing is still there. We'll have to see about a wardrobe when we get to the farm."

Finally, Rebecca was carried down the stairs and carefully placed in the carriage. Hilda climbed in beside her and Quint took his seat behind the horses, assuring both the women that he would drive as carefully as he could.

Hilda and Rebecca both frowned. Rebecca was sure that her head could take very little bouncing and Hilda was certain that her stomach would complain before they were out of Philadelphia, but Quint McQuade had made up his mind. He was going to the farm!

The bright moonlight made their journey fairly easy and long before the moon set, Quint's large farm house with its surrounding buildings stood out against the hills. The pale shimmer of moonlight gave an almost ethereal glow to the area. The only sign of life, as they neared the house, was the ribbon of silvern smoke silhouetted against the dark sky, trailing from the large chimney at one end of the dwelling.

Quint pulled the carriage around to the back of the house and before he climbed down, he said loudly enough for Hilda to hear, "Wait here until I get the lanterns lit." Hilda sat with the sleeping girl held tightly against her bosom. Soon a warm yellow glow was welcoming them from several windows in the house and Quint was back beside the carriage. He opened the door and lifted the sleeping girl into his arms. Cradling his light burden, he told Hilda to follow him and hurried to the house.

He moved through a large hallway and led the way to the first door at the top of the stairs. He waited for Hilda to open the door and then gently laid Rebecca on a large bed. He stepped back, "You'd better sleep in here with her tonight, in case she wakes up. I'll get her things." He turned and left the room.

Hilda glanced around the room. In the soft glow of the lantern, the room appeared to be very large. The canopied bed was draped in dark cotton and several chairs were placed in front of the cold hearth. To one side stood a large wardrobe and a table with pitcher and bowl. Even in the dim light, Hilda could see a thick layer of dust on everything. Quinton McQuade needed more than a cook, she thought. He definitely needed a housekeeper and very quickly.

By the time she finished her quick perusal, she heard Quint trudging up the stairs. He brought the valise into the room and removed his coat, then set about arranging a small amount of dried kindling from the box on the hearth. Striking a flint, he soon had a fire blazing in the fireplace. Picking up his coat, he moved to the door, "You can have the room next to this one tomorrow."

Hilda glared at the man moving toward the door, "A cook I am. By the kitchen I sleep." She paused at the look on his face. "Tomorrow," she added softly.

Quint ignored Hilda's comment and made his way to the study. A small fire flickered in the fireplace. Sam, the oldest son of one of his farm hands, was curled up asleep in a chair. He smiled as he woke the lad responsible for the fire and sent him home. Pouring himself a whiskey, he sat down before the fire to consider the condition of the young woman asleep upstairs in Susannah's old room.

The study had been his father's and especially in the late evening, the room seemed to radiate Samuel McQuade's quiet personality. Quint loved the room because in it he felt close to the man who died so quietly five years before. Quint couldn't help but wonder what his father would say about his present situation. Here he was, an unmarried man and in one of his upstairs bedrooms was an educated young woman, paid for in his coin and indentured to him for five years. His father, Quint admitted, never condoned the business of indenture or for that matter slavery of any kind. He shook his head in confusion. He wasn't sure how he felt about this particular young woman, either. Oh, he was infatuated with her, infatuated to the point that he couldn't even concentrate on business. He groaned, he could almost hear her lilting voice and see her soft brown eyes darken in anger. Closing his own eyes, he remembered the feel of her and the smell of her as he held her in his arms.

He sat up in his chair. This was insanity! he thought. He had bedded women before. It almost boggled his mind to be so affected by one woman. The attraction would cool, surely. He would be able to forget her, or would he? Maybe, he grinned, he wouldn't have to forget her. Then he reprimanded himself, he couldn't keep her forever. Well, he wouldn't be leaving for almost four months. Perhaps, he would discover that she was no different from the other women he knew. In the meantime, there was a great deal to be done to make the farm a paying enterprise. He blew out the candle and made his way upstairs to his room and his bed.

Chapter Fourteen

It was late morning when Quint finally crawled out of bed. The room was chilly but the clear fall sky, visible through his window, gave promise of a sunny day. He dressed quickly, hurried downstairs and into the dining room at the back of the house. He started for the kitchen and nearly ran into Rebecca carrying a collection of brooms and brushes. They stared at each other for several long seconds before Rebecca lowered her eyes. In a flat voice, she muttered, "I thank you, sir, for my second timely rescue." She didn't look up at him as she pronounced each word carefully.

Quint stood for one more second, speechless, then as she tried to push past him, he grabbed her by the waist and pulled her back toward him. When she was close enough, he lifted her head so that he could look into her eyes. They were almost black and they were flashing bits of fire. "You are angry!" he exclaimed in astonishment. Looking down into her wild eyes, he almost shouted, "Why are you so angry?"

"I do not like being bought and sold like a piece of baggage, sir!" came the hard cold reply. With that she pushed away from him and started back toward the kitchen. When she got to the door, she paused and glared back at him. "You only got half of what you paid for. All of my clothes are in the trunk in that attic." Turning, she ran back through the door to the kitchen.

Quint stood very still, stunned. Then anger flooded through him, and for a second, he was so angry he couldn't focus his eyes. Surely, she couldn't have wanted the attentions of that slimy bastard. Her words about being sold resounded in his head. What did she mean? He bought her indenture months ago and her brother sold her, he hadn't. "Should I have left you there?" he yelled at the empty space she had occupied a moment before. He had pulled her from the clutches of a man who wanted her for a less than honorable reason and she was angry with him! "Women!" he scoffed, his voice too loud, as he tried to bring his anger and frustration under control.

He took his seat at the dining room table, pondering Rebecca and the possible cause of her anger. Hilda came bustling through the door. She practically threw the plate from the tray she held in front of him. "I wait, but you no come, so I the kitchen find and fix breakfast."

Quint frowned as he looked up at her. She seemed to be angry, too. Looking back at the plate, he saw a large steak, fried potatoes, and apple slices. "No butter, no eggs, no sugar, no flour! Cook I cannot, with no food," she said in a huffy voice. She slammed down the coffee pot, cup and saucer, and left for the kitchen. Quint stared at the food before him and glanced up at the rapidly disappearing figure of the woman, shaking his head. Maybe the whole thing was a disastrous mistake.

After he had broken his fast, he sat back in his chair, a satisfied smile playing at the corner of his mouth. If nothing else came of this arrangement, he had hired an excellent cook. The food, what there was of it, was superb. Leisurely, he sipped his coffee. It, too, was perfect. Few people could do a satisfactory job with the brew, and he for one liked the beverage.

His coffee finished, he pushed himself away from the table and ambled through the house. His father had built the house for his mother many years ago. It was all stone and was large compared with the houses of the neighbors. The first floor was comprised of a sitting room, dining room, formal parlor, and study. A large entry hall with the stairway to the four upstairs bedrooms cut the house in half. The kitchen was a separate building set away from the house due to the heat generated by the big fireplace and the ovens. The building consisted of two rooms, the actual cooking space, and a second room, just as large, which at one time was used to feed the hands that farmed the land. In the center of the second room was a large opening in the floor covered by a heavy door that led to the well that supplied the water for the household and functioned as a fruit cellar as well. It also provided safety from the Indians that attacked during the late 1760's when the house was first built.

Several rows of large maple trees surrounded the kitchen and lined the property in the back of the house. There were no leaves on the trees now, but in the summer the entire back of the big house was shaded from the warm rays of the hot Pennsylvania sun.

Quint opened the door to the kitchen and found Hilda going through jars and containers. Leaning his large frame back against the door jamb, he said, "Breakfast was marvelous, and the coffee was . . . I never asked where you learned to make coffee?"

Hilda's cheeks turned pink with pleasure as she listened to his compliment. She smiled up at him and then made a little formal curtsey. "Thank you, sir. And, coffee, I like. For me, I make it."

Quint glanced around, then frowned, "I want to talk to Mistress Ranserford. I don't know where she is, but would you tell her, when you see her, that I'll be in my study," he spread his large hands out before him in a gesture of request. As he turned to leave, he glanced back at Hilda. "Make a list and I'll take you shopping this afternoon. We'll get all of the things you think you need: herbs, sugar, flour, whatever. Then, tomorrow, I'll expect a feast." Before she could mention that she couldn't make a list because she didn't know how to write, he was out the door.

Rebecca returned from the well just as Quint left the room. "What did he want?" she asked trying to keep the disgust out of her voice. When she had risen that morning, Hilda explained what had happened to her. As she worked around the house, she decided that all men were less than honorable and none of them were to be trusted ever again. Not one of the men she had dealings with were anything but despicable, not even the good Captain McQuade. First, he bought her, then he sold her, and now she was with him again miles from anything civilized. She could only guess at what other trauma he would cause in her life.

Hilda was still blushing from the compliments she received and the prospect of shopping for her kitchen produced an enormous smile. She glanced at Rebecca with some concern. "In the study, he wants to talk to you," she said quietly. But, when Rebecca ignored her words and started to fill the bucket with hot water from the kettle on the fire, Hilda protested. She took the kettle and pushed Rebecca toward the door. "Now!"

Hilda watched as Rebecca wiped her hands on her apron and walked stiffly from the room. The cook shook her head. Whatever had gotten into the girl? McQuade did not seem a bad sort at all and he did appear taken with her. He had gone after her the minute he found her gone and he seemed genuinely concerned over her injuries. No, Quint McQuade was not nearly as bad as most.

Rebecca held herself together tightly and walked to the study. She and Hilda had already toured the lower floor when they got up that morning, long before the master of the house came down for his breakfast. There was something warm and inviting about this house, but Rebecca refused to dwell on it. She thought of the rooms she saw as she moved toward the requested interview. Each of the four rooms had a large fireplace and although there was an accumulation of dust on everything, the comfortable furniture appeared well made and hardly used. Each room had several windows and all but the sitting room at the back of the house had blinds for coverings. They were open now so that the sun flooded each room with warmth and made the layer of dust that much more visible.

For some reason, Rebecca was delighted that he had not picked the sitting room for her interrogation. She had liked the looks of the little room, even with the closed shutters, and some noticeably worn furniture. It will be my room, she thought, as she resigned herself to her long term of indebtedness.

She moved slowly through the dining room, into the hall and to the study which was on the opposite side of the house. The solid oak door was closed and she hesitated for serveral minutes, before she timidly raised her hand to knock. For a second she was transported back in time, when she stood in front of a closed door, and Bud Worthman waited before the fire on the other side of the door.

She had not confided to Hilda that Quint had sold her and then changed his mind. Nor could she describe the horror she felt when she saw Bud Worthman standing in the kitchen of the inn. All of her new independence deserted her then. She felt like a limp rag whenever the thought came to mind, and the thought would not be dismissed now. Before she could gather what little courage she had left, the door swung open, and Quint started out the door, almost running her down.

"I was coming for you," he explained as he grabbed her hand and pulled into the room. She tried to resist, but it did no good. When they reached the center of the study, he gazed down at her for a moment and then releasing her hand, he asked her to be seated. He walked to the window and looked out over the front of the farm to the hills in the distance. A thousand questions ran through his mind as he tried to arrange his words so she would not be offended.

He was struck with a myriad of feelings ranging from anger to the need to protect her from any more abuse. He didn't understand any of his own feelings. When he finally turned to face her, there was a frown on his face and he could not hide the puzzled look in his eyes. "I want to know why you are so angry at me. What do you think I've done? What didn't I do that you think I should have done?"

Rebecca winced. He did not mince words when he wanted information. She lowered her gaze to her hands which were tightly clasped in her lap. She didn't want to be in this room answering his questions. The tight knot in her throat made speaking an effort. Her heart pounded, but she took a deep breath and whispered above the lump in her throat, "You had no right to sell me to Bud Worthman."

Quint saw red. Just the suggestion that he could do such a thing drove his blood past the boiling point. He shouted at her, "I didn't sell you to anyone. You belong to me."

In a soft voice without emotion, she replied, "Your man said you had sold me. He was taking me to my new owner."

Quint watched as she closed her eyes and tears slid down her face. He felt as if he had just been kicked in the stomach by a mule. Staring at her, with her tears streaming down her cheeks, not making a sound, something inside him twisted. He struggled against an urge to take her into his arms and promise her anything, to protect her from everything. He wondered if Bud had been at the inn the evening before. Had the man forced himself on her before Quint got there? Furious with himself and not sure why, he addressed her a bit more brusquely than he intended, as he handed her his handkerchief. "I would appreciate it if you would stop crying!"

She sat stunned, not daring to look at him, but feeling as if she were a child, a child that had just been punished for something she hadn't done. Drying her eyes, she tried to make her mind blank. Anger at her situation, at the men who used her, at Quint for being a man, bubbled up to the surface and she snapped, "Then don't ask me any more questions!"

Quint stood his ground. "If I can't ask you what has happened to you, then how will I know how to help you?"

Rebecca lifted her chin and her eyes were no longer a dull brown but an angry black. She glowered at the man standing at ease before the window. "I do not want, nor do I need your help."

Quint turned his back to her and glared out the window. "Look, this is going badly. Something must have happened when you were taken from the apartment, and for some reason, " his voice faded to a whisper, full of confusion, "I want to make up for the hurt that you have suffered."

Rebecca's sharp intake of breath signaled her loss of control. He should not have been concerned for her. It was her undoing. Sobbing, she jumped up from the chair and tried to run from the room.

Quint heard the gasp, and before her first sob, he spun around from the window. He was beside her in three steps and just as she reached the door, he gathered her up in his arms. As he carried her back into the room, to a large leather chair, he cradled her in his arms. Rebecca sobbed against his chest. Holding her on his lap, he smoothed her hair and kissed her forehead and the top of her head, as he tried to think of something, anything, that would stop her crying.

At long last the sobs slowed and Quint lifted her chin so that he could look into her tear-filled eyes. They were once more a soft shimmering brown. These were the eyes that had plagued him across the Atlantic and allowed him no peace. Without conscious thought, Quint lowered his head and pressed his lips against hers in a soft gentle kiss. She responded completely and her arms slid around his neck. Gently, he pulled her back for just a minute and gazed into her astonished face. At least, he told himself, she had not rejected him, but he couldn't continue to hold her on his lap and keep his self-respect. She was having a decided effect on him and this was not the time to make love to her.

With her still in his arms, he rose from the chair and carried her across the room to a couch. Carefully, he sat next to her. He took her hand. "Rebecca," he started softly, "This is my farm. My mother left it to me when she died recently. I want you to stay here. Hilda has agreed to stay here as cook and your companion. I'll get one of the tenant's daughters to help with the cleaning. I want you to stay here as my . . . my . . . " Suddenly, he realized that he couldn't ask her to be his mistress.

Rebecca stared up at his confusion. "I want to teach. It was with teaching in mind that I suggested to Capt' Hemphill that I indenture myself in the first place." Her eyes filled with tears again.

Quint panicked. She wouldn't want to stay at the farm unless she could teach. Then an idea started to form in his agile mind, and he smiled at her. "And, teach you shall! I'll arrange for the children of the tenants to come to the house several times a week and you can teach them to read and write. You will have your own school." A pleased expression tugged at the corner of his mouth. "Will you stay and teach the children for me?"

"Do I have a choice?" she asked in a flat voice.

"No, not really," he answered. A part of him was pleased that indeed, she had no choice, but another part was disgusted that she showed so little enthusiasm. Pulling her to her feet, he added, "Now, we need to travel into town and let Hilda get what she needs for the kitchen. Both of you need the services of the local dressmaker."

At the mention of the dressmaker, Rebecca stiffened. The tears started once again. "All of my clothes are at that inn. You left my trunk there. I want my . . . . . . clothes."

Quint watched with alarm as she wilted back into the couch. "I'll buy you new clothes. You don't need the things at the inn. I'll get you more."

"I can't pa . . . pa . . . pay for them," she sobbed.

"We'll work something out," Quint muttered between clenched teeth. A flood of tears over some clothes, he thought with disgust. He really had hoped that she was different from the rest, but here she was traumatized over the loss of her wardrobe. Well, he offered to buy her a new wardrobe, didn't he, so why was she still sobbing her heart out? She never seemed to react as he expected her to. Here he was, standing in the middle of the room, feeling woefully inadequate because he failed to bring her trunk with them. None of this mess was his doing, he mused. Yet, for some inexplicable reason, he felt guilty as hell.

Awkwardly, he patted her hand. "Go freshen up and we'll leave in about thirty minutes. I'll go tell Hilda to get ready. As soon as I get the horse hitched to the wagon, we'll leave." He helped her to her feet and followed her out of the room. As she gracefully mounted the stairs, he shook his head. Well, he was in up to his neck. The next question had to be, into what?

Quint started for the stables. It had been several years since he visited the local dressmaker. At one time, he spent a goodly number of hours with the woman, arguing with her over the cost of his mother's clothes. He almost regretted that he was forced to take Rebecca and Hilda to her shop, since the woman was also well-known for her gossipy tongue. Perhaps, going to the dressmaker's shop was not the best of plans. No, there had to be a better way.

In less than thirty minutes the horses were hitched to the wagon, and he pulled up to the back door of the house. Hilda came out pushing a reluctant Rebecca in front of her. Once they were seated, Rebecca nudged the woman and Hilda said softly, "To the dressmaker's, she no go."

Rebecca settled herself in the wagon beside Quint and watched him closely from under her thick dark lashes. She had not yet shown her gratitude for his timely arrival at the inn, but for some reason, she could not bring herself to say a simple thank you. Very much ashamed of the tears she shed in the study only a short while before, she wanted to avoid direct conversation with him. She was confused at his tenderness and frightened half out of her wits at the way she responded to him. There was no question. No matter what the cost, she must avoid him.

The ride into town was pleasant in the warm fall sunshine. Rebecca tried to relax and enjoy the hills and the neat farms set back from the road. Quint and Hilda carried on a lengthy conversation about the countryside and the neighbors closest to him. Quint told them both about the farm and the family that worked his property. He described the town where they would do their shopping, a tavern, an inn, a mercantile, two tailors, a printer, and a general store. The town had one dressmaker, but Quint passed over that information since he had decided on a different tack. He told them they would go the general store where Hilda could find about everything she wanted.

When they arrived, Quint talked to the owner for a few minutes, introduced Hilda and Rebecca, then told the two women he would be back in a little while. Rebecca watched him leave and walk toward the printer's shop, then disappear from sight. Hilda was already discussing her order with the clerk as she named the staples and herbs she needed.

Quint came back to the store before Hilda finished and he wandered about poking into barrels and boxes as he ambled through the small building. When Hilda finished, Quint spent several more minutes with the clerk adding more items to the growing list of supplies. Arrangements were made for delivery and the three shoppers left the store.

All Rebecca could think of was the impending visit to the dressmaker. She wondered how angry Quint would be if she refused to see the woman. If she stubbornly held her ground, she suspected that he might pick her up and dump her unceremoniously on the floor of the shop. She steeled herself for what she knew would be a battle. As they drove down the street Quint made no comment to either of the women and Rebecca sat stiff and straight, looking ahead at nothing. As the wagon bounced and jumped over the holes in the road, Rebecca realized that they were already out of town and traveling on the road they had traveled only an hour before. They were not going to see the dressmaker! She released an audible sigh of relief. Quint glanced down at her and chuckled. "Don't worry," he whispered, "The dressmaker is coming to you. She'll be at the farm in several days."

Chapter Fifteen

The next two weeks passed in a flurry of activity as two young women, daughters of local farmers, arrived and set about cleaning, polishing, sweeping, and scrubbing the house from top to bottom. Quint asked Rebecca to supervise the cleaning and Hilda was content to cook away in her kitchen. Rebecca made a conscious effort to avoid Quint at all cost and for the afternoon meals, Rebecca always found some unfinished chore that demanded her immediate attention, so she was spared eating her meals with him. Then, when the task was finished, she ate in the kitchen, alone, or with Hilda. Rebecca congratulated herself on her skill at avoiding him, never realizing that Quint was very busy himself.

One of the first things Quint did was make arrangements for the classes that Rebecca wanted to teach. School, he decreed, would begin for the children two weeks after the new year. Then, he set about making preparation for spring planting. Fields had to be cleared, rocks removed, and the soil tilled before the ground froze. While he was busy with the farm, things at the shipyard also demanded constant attention. His goal, he kept repeating to himself as he stilled a yawn and groped his way to bed long after midnight, was to make this farm as profitable as the shipyards had become. He probably would have to take up residence for the spring planting and the fall harvest of each year, but he was certain that he could run the shipyards from the farm until planting and harvest were complete. At the moment, every spare second had to be used to concentrate on securing seeds, equipment, oxen, and hiring men to help the tenants. He silently admitted that he was even too busy to coax Rebecca back into his bed.

In the busy days that followed the trip into town for supplies, Rebecca put the dressmaker's visit out of her mind. Before they had returned from shopping, she decided that she was not going to spend another year or perhaps two in slavery to pay for clothes she hadn't requested. As the days flew by with wagons and carriages coming and going, loaded with things for the farm or with people anxious to see Quint about the shipyards, she forgot about the dressmaker. Late one morning, she was surprised when Hilda came trudging up the stairs to get her. "The dressmaker, she comes," Hilda told her quietly.

Rebecca stopped cleaning and stood straight. "Tell Mr. McQuade that I don't need his charity." Her eyes started to darken as she resumed her task.

"I don't consider it charity," a familiar low voice responded. Rebecca trembled as Quint strode into the room. It had been days since she saw him and she had forgotten how just the sight of him left her shaking. He stepped before her, "I will not have my *property* dressed in beggar's rags."

His property? Rebecca bristled with the reminder and was about to tell him exactly what she thought but she wasn't sure how he would react. She hesitated, then pointed to herself. "These are the clothes of common, hard-working folk, and they are fine for me." She smoothed the skirt of her worn black dress and moved away from him.

Quint took a step, glowering at her, "They are *not* fine with me." He grabbed her wrist and started pulling her toward the door. Hilda, forgotten in the verbal exchange, started pushing Rebecca from behind.

Rebecca twisted around and glared at her companion. "You — you're a traitor!" As they passed the large fourposter bed, Rebecca grabbed one of the posts with her free hand and tried to wrap her arm around the column.

Quint was too quick for her, though, and he hoisted her into his arms. At first she was too stunned to attempt to free herself, but by the time Quint reached the stairs she had started to struggle.

Quint warned quietly, "If you keep wiggling, I'll probably end up dropping you. You may even break your pretty neck." Rebecca stopped moving and glanced up at his flushed face. She shivered as she realized that he was every bit as angry with her as she was with him, but he was much bigger.

When they reached the small sitting room of which Rebecca was so fond, Quint deposited her in front of a small thin woman. Rebecca glanced everywhere but at the woman, taking satisfaction in the clean little room that gleamed in the winter sun that filtered through the leafless trees outside the windows. As Quint released her, she realized that her heart was pounding, but she didn't have time to wonder why, for Quint was introducing her and Hilda to the amused dressmaker. Rebecca tried to pull away but Quint said quietly, "They will both need to be measured for complete wardrobes." After he looked at Rebecca's belligerent face, he added. "I'll be back in a few minutes to make the selections."

Rebecca was past furious. It was bad enough to be carried into the room in the man's arms, with her heart pounding, probably from fright, but to listen to him tell the woman that he would personally pick out her wardrobe was a slap in the face. The dressmaker probably thought that she was a complete simpleton. Embarrassed and almost afraid of what Quint might do, Rebecca stood quietly for the measurements. I'll hate this room from now on, she thought to herself.

Just as the seamstress finished with her tape, Quint returned, and Rebecca looked at him suspiciously. She wondered if he had been waiting outside the door. She looked at him as calmly as she could and asked in her sweetest voice, "Are you ready, sir, to make your selections?"

Quint gazed down at her sweet smile and her flashing

black eyes and responded softly, "Yes! Yes, I am!"

Rebecca turned on her heel and as she fled the sitting room, she shouted over her shoulder, "Good, make your selections, and you can wear them too! I don't have time for this foolishness, I have work to do."

All three people still standing in the room, watched Rebecca disappear. The thought shot through Quint's mind that he should go and drag her back, but a small smile spread across his face and broke into a broad grin. He'd pursue another course. Turning to the dressmaker, he glanced at Hilda, rubbed his hands together, and stated energetically, "Ladies, shall we get to it?"

Hilda looked at Quint, then at the open door, and shrugged her shoulders. Sometimes that girl lacked any sense at all, she thought to herself, knowing that Rebecca needed the clothes desperately. Hilda turned her thoughts away from Rebecca and back to the dressmaker who was already unpacking her valise, pulling out plates, sketches, and swatches to spread out on the table. Hilda spoke softly, "I've a need for one more dress."

Quint leaned forward to examine the display. "Oh, I think not. At least three, perhaps four, new day gowns, one special garment for church, something for shopping, and at least one ball gown. You're Rebecca's chaperone," he said, his engaging grin winning Hilda over. So, for the next hour, he discussed style, line, and color with the dressmaker, while Hilda kept interrupting that it must be dependable. She smiled in delight, pleased that he was so knowledgeable about fabric and style, for her own experience was so limited. She had no qualms about taking his advice. In fact, she glowed with anticipation. Never in her whole life had she time to think about clothes. To be in the enviable position to have a dressmaker construct five or six new garments for her . . . Oh! Such joy!

Without warning, Quint watched as a frown creased her brow and her face disintegrated into panic. Quint suggested quietly that they go out to the kitchen for refreshments. He unwound his long frame from the chair and started for the kitchen, certain that he knew why the distress signals were emanating from her.

Just inside the kitchen door, she turned on him, "Sir, I have no coin. Pay for those clothes, I cannot." Her chin quivered slightly.

"Hilda, I know that," Quint leaned toward her, "But, remember, I hired you as a cook with wages and room and board. Alas, I have also given you a job that I'm beginning to think will take a great deal more of your energies than cooking meals. You are also Rebecca's companion and that may be the harder of the two positions. I never offered any compensation for that task. We'll let the clothes be compensation for the second responsibility and you need the clothes, for appearance's sake. We must consider what people will think. Now, how do you suppose it would look, if you, as Rebecca's chaperone, were poorly dressed? No, if you're to be effective and keep gossip at a minimum, you must be dressed like a chaperone."

Hilda beamed. It certainly made sense to her. The man was a gentleman, and he had a rich purse. The citizens of the village just might talk. No, Quint was right about how important it was for both of them to be well dressed.

Quint turned to walk back to the sitting room. "Bring a pot of tea for the dressmaker and coffee for me." He grinned broadly at her as he paused at the door. "I'm going to select Rebecca's wardrobe and Hilda, when the new things arrive, I want you to promise me that you will personally gather all of her old clothes and burn them."

Hilda stared at him, bewildered. Then, as she caught on to his plan, an enormous smile filled her face. She nodded her round head in agreement and purred, "Burn them I will and now tea I make, and for you, coffee. And, a few cakes I serve." She headed for the hearth smiling happily.

When Hilda served the beverages and her delicate little sugar cakes, Quint was deep in discussion with the dressmaker. He offered no explanation as he selected day dresses of cotton and wool, dinner attire and ball gowns of both silk and velvet. As he made his decisions, the woman mentally calculated the amount of cloth and stitches he was ordering, and she couldn't help but remember his apparent stinginess with his own mother and his sisters. She sat stunned. The difference was staggering. This Rebecca must be very important to him, she thought. And, she was such a beauty. Her dark eyes and that black hair set her apart from most women. And, her figure would be the envy of every woman for miles. The seamstress ached with curiosity. What was this girl to McQuade and who might she ask?

After all of the undergarments and nightgowns were selected, two cloaks, and the necessary slippers and bonnets coordinated, Quint stood and leaned against the table that held the coffee and tea service. "Madame," Quint said quietly, "I know that you'll be the epitome of discretion. If any word of what has transpired here today becomes common knowledge, I personally will hold you responsible and I will see that you do no more business in this area."

She stared up at him, her face reflecting fear. Quint quickly turned the conversation to scheduling fittings and discussing payment, then he showed her to her waiting carriage with another warning, "Now, not a word!"

He seemed to be waiting for her response. She looked at him in agony, "Not a word, sir." To have such a tidbit of gossip and not be able to utter a word was asking too much, but her business was thriving and McQuade was wealthy enough to destroy her if he chose. She gritted her teeth and picked up the reins, chiding herself. Business first. Perhaps someday she would be free to mention that Quint McQuade once had a mistress.

Later that evening after dinner, Rebecca sat at the huge kitchen table mending a tear in her threadbare cloak, smarting over her friend's betrayal. "And when will you get your fine new wardrobe?" she asked. Hilda only smiled and continued with her preparation of food for the next day. Rebecca stuffed her cloak into the sewing basket she confiscated from the sitting room and angrily marched off to bed.

"She be one to cut off her nose to spite her face," Hilda giggled to herself. "And I'll probably earn every penny that Mr. McQuade spent for those clothes," she laughed out loud.

The day after the dressmaker's visit, Quint announced that he must return to Philadelphia and the shipyard. He had business to attend to and would be gone until February. For the next month Rebecca cleaned and prepared the small room behind the kitchen for the classes that were scheduled to begin the first week of the new year. She gathered slate, chalk, and printed books until she was satisfied. When she pronounced the classroom ready, the three boys and two girls that Quint told her would attend, arrived. It took her minutes to discover that her work was cut out for her as only one of the boys had any skills at all and those were with numbers.

For three weeks Rebecca worked with the children and by the end of the third week, they could all read and write their names. Quint returned and on his first day back he visited the classroom, but he quickly realized that was a terrible mistake. Rebecca was so upset that he pledged he would stay far away from the schoolroom and leave the children in her care.

The second morning Quint was home, snow started falling and the wind blew from the north. There was nothing to be done but cancel school. The snow drifts were so high that Quint said no school for a fortnight. By the end of the two weeks, the weather had warmed, the snow was melting, and Quint left for the village to check on supplies and his advertisement for workers for the spring. Hilda and Rebecca had spent the time working in the kitchen, sorting through supplies, and making jellies and jams from the fruit that was starting to turn.

Hilda had just finished cleaning the chicken that would soon be the afternoon meal, when one of the little boys from Rebecca's class dashed to the house. Rebecca grabbed the child and dragged him to the kitchen. The lad was crying in anguish, "Got to get Mr. McQuade, got to find him."

Rebecca tried to calm the boy and when he stopped trying to wriggle out of her arms, she said with authority,

"Tell me."

The boy looked up at Rebecca and something told him that he would be freed only after he explained. He took a deep breath, "My pa and Clem and Pete was over in them woods, cutting down trees. Pa hit his leg with the axe. He's bad hurt. Got to get Mr. McQuade!" He struggled to get free.

Rebecca tried to restrain the boy for another minute, and her words stopped him completely, "Mr. McQuade is not here. He went into town this morning and he's not expected back until late tonight." Rebecca dropped her hands but the small boy just stood and stared at her. She ducked into the kitchen, wrapped her cloak about her shoulders, and grabbed her bag of herbs and medicines. In an instant, she was back and the boy was standing just as she left him, "I can help. Take me to your father."

When the boy continued to stand frozen before the kitchen door, tears rolling down his face, she pushed him gently, calling to Hilda that she was needed. Rebecca's gentle shove seemed to break through the lad's reserve and he started off, scurrying toward a distant stand of trees. She followed him across the frozen field. They were half way across the field when the boy broke into a run. Rebecca had no choice, she ran to keep up with him.

The sharp pain in her side slowed Rebecca as they came to the edge of the woods. The boy bolted ahead, but Rebecca saw the horse and wagon directly ahead. She found the boy's father lying on the cold ground with the snow around him stained red with his blood. Two of his young sons stood beside him, their fear written across their faces. Quickly, Rebecca knelt in the pool of blood and studied the deep gash in the man's leg. "I have some healing skills," she told the frightened man as she looked into his pallid face. "It's a bad cut, but I have seen worse. This should not be that much of a problem."

Thankful that the day was not too cold, she grabbed her bag, and dug around until she found a thick pad of cotton. Placing it over the jagged flesh, she bound it tightly into place. She turned to the boy who looked like he might be the older of the three and said softly, "We must get your father home. He needs warmth and I must dress his wound."

With quiet authority she ordered the boys to carry their father to the wagon which had yet to be loaded with timber. They laid him down gently and Rebecca climbed into the wagon and wrapped a blanket around the man, while the two younger boys lifted themselves up onto the seat. The older boy led the nag toward a small house in the distance.

Before they got to the house, a small gray-haired woman met them. Her anguished cry split the afternoon air, "Oh, my God! John, what happened?" They got John out of the wagon and into the house, and without a word, Rebecca started cleaning the wound. While she worked, she heard the older boy explaining what happened to his mother. After Rebecca took several stitches with rum soaked thread and fixed an herb poultice which she bound on the wound, she turned to the woman of the house. She smiled at her, willing her to calm down before her husband and her sons.

"Your husband should be fine," she said quietly. "He'll likely be weak from all the blood he's lost, but unless he develops a fever in the leg, he should heal just fine." As she cleaned her hands and packed her herbs into her valise, she instructed the little woman about the food that John would need for the next several days. She asked the oldest boy to see her back to the house, when a loud tapping at the door startled everyone.

Quint was ushered into the kitchen and he walked over to John's bedside. "Bette, have you met Mistress Ranserford formally? She is the teacher I told you about," he smiled down at the anxious little woman. "Of course, you couldn't know, but she is also quite skilled in the art of healing." Quint went on to tell them about the broken leg. He grinned at a red-faced Rebecca. "If Mistress Ranserford says he'll be fine, then he'll be fine."

Quint waited until Rebecca made arrangements to return the next day and change John's bandage, then he took her arm, gently propelling her toward the door. "I'll see her home," he said quietly. He helped her into the waiting wagon and climbed up himself watching her expression of surprise. The day was gone and night had fallen on the farm.

"I didn't realize it was so late," Rebecca muttered, almost to herself.

Quint turned to her, but in the darkness she couldn't see his face. "Thank you," he said out of the darkness, "John has been here as long as I can remember. Will he recover with no problem?"

"It's a bad cut, but if he stays off it for several days, and doesn't take a fever, he should be fine." She spread the skirt of her dress across her knees, acutely aware of the dried blood and dirt that covered the fabric. Struggling against a yawn, she pulled her cloak up around her shoulders and realized that she was very tired. She was hardly able to keep her eyes open but she forced herself to sit in an upright position as the wagon jostled along. It was nearly hopeless. Every time they hit a bump, she rocked into Quint. After her fourth or fifth yawn, Quint put his arm around her shoulders, pushed her head against his chest and whispered, "Rest! It's too dark for the horse to do anything but walk and it'll take some time to get back to the house." Her eyes closed and slowly she let sleep take her into its peaceful void.

Quint smiled down at the nodding head resting against his shoulder. He was assailed by her fresh womanly smell as she nestled against him. Her nearness invaded his sense, and he felt the stirrings in his loins. For three months he had stayed away from her. He fought against the idea that he should carry her up to his bedroom tonight and make wild passionate love to her. He rationalized, telling himself that she had responded to him before and if he didn't rush her . . .

He shook with desire. Oh, he wanted her, wanted her with a desperation he had never experienced with another woman. And, she was his, legally his, paid for and bonded to him. If he wooed her slowly, he was sure she would respond. Leering at nothing in the darkness, he acknowledged that he had talked himself into a soft warm bedmate for the night. He wanted to urge the horse to a faster pace but he had to travel slowly, for the sake of the horse as well as his own. Something told him that if she were jolted awake his plans would be ruined. He grinned to himself in the darkness. She was like an angry kitten when she was awake, claws bared, hissing at him until she got her way. It would be infinitely easier to manage her if she slept until he had her in his bed.

Chapter Sixteen

Before Quint had finished convincing himself that she was his for the taking, Rebecca slid down to lie across the seat, curled up against him. He took the extra blanket Hilda had thrust on him when he left the house and covered her up, tucking it around her. She needed her sleep, he told himself, smiling at his generosity.

It took forty-five minutes before Quint impatiently guided the horse into the stable yard. Sam, now in permanent residence in the stable, came forward, rubbing the sleep from his eyes. Quint jumped down from the wagon and in hushed tones told the boy to see to the horse and be quiet about it. He gathered the sleeping girl into his arms, moved quickly across the yard and let himself into the house. As he shifted Rebecca in his arms to open the door, she stirred. Her arms slid up around his neck and she snuggled closer in her slumber.

She had an instant effect on him. His heart started pounding in his chest and his blood raced through his veins. Even his breathing was uneven and labored. Rebecca weighed scarcely more than a bag of grain, so he knew the burden in his arms was not what was causing the reaction. He glanced around for Hilda, but it appeared that the cook had already retired for the evening. Grinning, he carried Rebecca up to his chamber. Hilda wouldn't have understood, he admitted as he moved quietly into the room where a fire burned in the back of the hearth, giving the large room a friendly glow. He laid Rebecca down on the soft feather mattress and as soon as she touched the surface of the bed, she curled up like the small kitten he had compared her to in the wagon.

He smiled to himself as he quickly disrobed. With only his breeches still in place he padded to the bed and as carefully as he could he began to remove her clothing. When he realized that she was staring at him with her eyes wide open, he pulled her to him and kissed her as swiftly as he could. He put everything he could into that kiss, for he did not want the delicate creature in his arms leaving his bed that night.

He felt her tense and try to pull away. As he ran his tongue down the side of her neck she mumbled indistinctly, "No, no. I don't want this."

He whispered back, his voice husky with desire, "Yes, you do. You want me as much as I want you."

As he loosened her chemise and nibbled the soft mound of her breast, she pushed against him. "No. We must not . . . I can't let you do this."

He kissed his way back to her lips. "Yes, we can. You want me to do this, Rebecca. You want it, you know you do. Say you do."

She muttered an indistinct phrase and her arms slid up around his neck. There was no denying that what he did to her made any rational thought impossible. Once more she was lost to the pleasure of his kisses. She gave herself up to the delicious feelings that were coursing through her body at his command. She wasn't aware that his fingers were pulling the remaining clothes from her frame until she felt his warm sensual hands drift across her bare skin. His name passed her lips in a husky whisper as her body arched toward his in passion. Yes, she wanted what he could do to her and she wanted it now.

She snuggled closer to him, amazed that she fitted against him so perfectly. She felt the rapid beat of his heart and she wondered if her own was beating as quickly. She had no time to wonder because the intense pleasure he was creating as he ran his hands across her flesh, from the tips of her breasts to the caps of her knees, was leaving her dazed and panting. All she could do was glory in the rapture he was creating.

When he stopped his kisses, she sighed in disappointment and then caught her breath when his head lowered to one of her breasts. Her squeal of delight as he pulled her nipple into his mouth surprised her more than it did him and he chuckled with knowledge. The woman in his arms was pleased with what he was doing. Rebecca liked his type of loving. Confident that what he was doing was arousing her more, he ran the top of his tongue around and around before he flicked it across the tight tip. He smiled as she shuddered in his arms. Oh, yes, she loved the way he loved her.

He turned his attentions to the other mound and caressed it slowly. Just as slowly, he let his fingers trail across her ribs, over her waist, down her flat belly and into the black curls that covered his ultimate destination. He then moved his hand back the way it had come. She was going to have to beg him to take her. Then there could be no denial on her part. He wanted to be able to remind her that she wanted him as much as he wanted her.

As he fingered the warm skin between her breasts and her thighs, he heard her moan. Before long, she would plead with him for that special joining that brought a contentment he had never experienced before with another woman. He dragged his fingers across the inside of her thighs and she moaned more loudly. "Say it, Rebecca. Tell me what you want," he prompted in a deep and guttural murmur. "Tell me."

Shaking her head from side to side, she sought to deny him, but he lowered his head back to her breast and she was lost. "Oh, take me. Take me now," she mumbled as her heart heaved in her chest. She was dizzy with want, and could no longer ignore the twinges between her legs that screamed for release. She had to have him. Opening her legs, she arched against him. "Now," she commanded.

Quint smiled and placed himself between her legs. He groaned as he sank into the warm haven she provided, and for a fraction of a second he wondered if he could maintain his control. Perhaps, he thought as he concentrated on her, he should not have waited for her quite so long. He stayed poised above her for minutes until she opened her confused eyes and stared up at him. His face was a sheath of tight muscles as he fought with his own desires. He had to pleasure her as well.

Not sure why he wasn't offering her the relief she wanted so desperately, she whined at him and pulled his head down to kiss her lips. He sighed in surrender and began to thrust forward and draw back, giving in to the instincts that drove her. She moved with him, certain the ceiling of the room was parting from the walls and together they would ascend into the heavens. Slowly, an incredible pressure built and Rebecca wondered if she would live through the explosion that was sure to follow.

And explode she did, not even aware that in her pleasure she cried out. Quint caught the end of her cry with his lips and gave himself up to a pleasure as intense as hers must have been. Dazed, she snuggled against him even before he had gathered the strength to roll to his side. He pulled her into his arms, sensing that she was fast asleep. In seconds he joined her in a contented realm of unconsciousness.

Suddenly, a sharp stab jarred Quint out of his sleep. He rolled over and glanced up at Rebecca who was sitting in the bed, her eyes wide and a look of horror on her face. He gazed at the dark windows and at the embers glowing in the fireplace. They could only have slept several hours. It was still a long time until dawn.

Rebecca inched her way to the edge of the feather mattress. "How could you! I told you I did not want this."

There was not enough light in the room for Quint to prove it, but he knew her eyes were black, she looked angry enough. "You wanted me just as much as I wanted you," he managed as he raised himself up on his elbows and glared back at her. He was not going to take the blame this time. After all, she had begged him.

"I know what happened. I remember what you said. You were leading me," she yanked the quilt up around her breasts and crossed her arms to hold it into place. "If you had been any kind of a gentleman you would have taken me to my own room, not yours."

"Shhh. You'll wake up Hilda. Look, I know you want to deny it, but there is a special kind of. . ."

"Don't you tell me there is anything special in this . . . this . . . lust you practice on me."

"Rebecca, Rebecca. Did Bud Worthman's kisses make you tingle. I know what happens to you when I . . ."

"Nothing happens to me," she snapped as she stepped from the bed.

Quint tried patiently to make his point. "I have a little experience in these things, Rebecca and I know what is happening. I can tell from the way you react."

She grabbed for her dress, holding on to the quilt, "You force yourself on me. I know nothing of the flesh," she turned back to look at him, her face wet with her tears, "I was a vir-virgin before you took me. You may make my body respond, but I will continue to deny you! I want you to leave me alone! My husband should have taught me the things you are teaching me." Her shoulders started shaking with her sobs.

Quint tried to disavow her words but he remembered his thoughts in the wagon and he cringed. She was right. He had talked himself into seducing her once again. Reaching up to run his hands through his hair, he argued with himself. She had responded to him, even if she wanted to refute the passion that he had created. The passion he—he stopped breathing. He was completely responsible for what had taken place in this room only several hours before. "Rebecca," Quint started to move out of the bed, "We have to talk. I mean, a very serious discussion must take place." And I have to figure out how to apologize, he thought to himself.

"Not tonight," she whispered, her words dripping with the tears he could not see. She managed to pull on her dress and one of her petticoats before she started for the door.

Quint jumped out of bed and started toward her. "Stay

away from me," she begged, "Just stay away." She backed toward the door, reached in back of her, and felt for the door knob. As Quint struggled frantically with his breeches, he heard the door swish shut. Rebecca was already out of his room.

He turned and stared at the door. If he followed her out of the room, he would probably have to explain everything to Hilda. He wasn't in the mood to defend his actions to both women, not in the middle of the night. Perhaps he would be in the morning, after he had a decent night's sleep. He shrugged his shoulders. He hadn't had a decent night's rest since that dark-haired English wench had wandered into his life.

He yanked off his breeches and stumbled back to his bed. He was not going to chase her through the house at two or three o'clock in the morning. She could wait until dawn, at least. And then, by damn, they would talk!

Morning came, and Quint struggled from his warm bed aware that the small amount of sleep he had gotten was far from its usual quality. He dressed quickly and started for the dining room, muttering to himself, "I might as well face both of them right away and get it over with." In the dining room he sat resolutely at the table waiting for Hilda to appear and give him the dressing down he was beginning to think he deserved. Instead, she came bustling in, coffee pot in hand, and peered at him suspiciously. "Bad you look, but Rebecca, she look worse. What happened? Did the man die?"

Quint stared up at her trying to figure out what on earth she was talking about. He couldn't remember a man dying. His mind spun around the events of the previous day and he suddenly remembered John. He drew a deep breath. Obviously, the cook had no idea that she spent a small part of the night in his bed.

"The man's name is John. I guess it was a bad cut, but Rebecca thinks he'll be all right. She told him to stay off the leg for several days. By the way, where is she? I have to talk to her."

Hilda frowned. "She in the sitting room be. She say

she's too tired to go to bed, so she sleep on the couch. I tell her to stay abed, she looks that bad."

Quint tried to shake his feelings of guilt and picked up his cup and saucer, mumbling, "I better check on her. Don't want her getting sick when she tries to help others." He walked away from Hilda without looking at her directly. Damn, he felt like a naughty boy of eight.

When he reached the sitting room, he found Rebecca on the couch with a quilt tucked around her. Her eyes were closed, the streaks of tears from the night before still marking her cheeks and even in her sleep she looked pained. Quint sat quietly in a chair watching her. When she finally woke, she would have to talk to him. Perhaps, after they talked, he wouldn't feel like such as cad.

He sipped his coffee enjoying the opportunity to observe her without her knowledge. She was uncommonly beautiful. Although he thought she was thinner now than when she was on the ship, her face was still full and her complexion was unmarred by her trials. The small, luscious, heart-shaped mouth was relaxed and he ached with the need to cover those lips with his own. Remembering that he gave into his desires the night before with disastrous results, he sat quietly, longing to touch her, but holding himself in check with stoic control.

Rebecca drifted in and out of a restless sleep. She stirred, for even in her sleep she felt that someone was watching her. She opened her tired red eyes and glanced around the room. When she noticed the long legs of a man sitting in a chair, she gritted her teeth. He was watching her intently. With her voice barely above a whisper, she asked, "Did you come here to torture me more?" Her eyes filled with tears.

He felt as if she had stabbed him with an invisible knife. "Tortured? If I recall, you enjoyed what we did," he replied in a voice that grew softer with each word. His comments brought back the exciting memories of the night just past and his desire stirred. The need to hold her close was overpowering and sheer willpower held him in his chair. "You said that we would talk today, so I'm here to do just that. We will talk, and nothing more," he tried to keep the regret out of his voice.

Rebecca swung her slender legs to the floor and Quint was allowed a quick glimpse of her trim ankles as she arranged her dirty skirt about her. She raised her soft, warm brown eyes and stared into his shining blue ones. As she looked at him, her eyes began to darken, "What do you wish to discuss, or do you have more orders for me?"

Her remark made him pause. "Have I given you orders? I don't believe I've ordered you to do much of anything." He took a deep breath and in a weary voice he continued, "I'm not here to spar with you, Rebecca. I want to talk about the future, your future." He wasn't ready yet to admit to her, let alone himself, that her future might include him.

Her eyes snapped black and she blurted out, "I have no future!" She looked away and her voice broke, "Not now."

"Rebecca," he said, more upset with himself than with her at the moment, "I told you I was sorry. What more can I say?" He paused, struggling with the feelings of anger that surged through him. Damn it, it was partly her fault. She responded to him every time he got near her. Why, last night, she urged him on! He ran his hand through his hair. No, she hadn't seduced him; he seduced her, after he made his careful plans in the wagon.

His voice was softer as he returned to the subject at hand. "For the next several weeks, we'll be here together," he said, watching her eyes narrow. "I'll try to stay away from you, but . . ." his voice trailed off. How difficult that would be. "You have the children to teach and I would like you to continue with the classes. John will need your care for several days and I expect that we'll have visitors soon. Yesterday I sent my sister and her husband word that I wanted them to come. Knowing Susannah," Quint's face brightened considerably, "she'll be here by the end of the month."

Rebecca gasped, "Your sister! You asked your sister and her husband to come here? Why?" Rebecca stood up quickly.

"Why, to meet you, of course," Quint said softly.

Rebecca looked at him in dismay and without a word, ran from the room.

Quint followed her from the sitting room and watched as she raced up the stairs to her room. He called, "Sam will take you to John's whenever you're ready to go." He chuckled when he heard her door slam. Suddenly, he was ravenous and he smiled, anticipating the meal that Hilda usually served for breakfast.

As Quint ate, he wondered at himself. He was hungry and usually when he was upset or annoyed he couldn't eat, yet here he was, stuffing himself with nothing settled between Rebecca and himself. As he pondered his dilemma he thought of Susannah. If she knew how he had seduced Rebecca, she would be furious. Why, she would probably demand that he marry the girl, then and there. He laid his utensils down on his plate and wondered why his thoughts kept returning to marriage.

He sat quietly and pondered the way he lived his life. Most of the year he was at sea and even if he decided to make the farm a permanent home, he wasn't planning any drastic changes in his life style. He certainly wasn't considering marriage, at least not for several more years. So, why did he keep thinking of matrimony when he thought about Rebecca? He frowned at nothing. What had the little witch done to him? He didn't want to marry anyone! When Hilda brought his coffee and cleared the table, his dark scowl made her question, "Breakfast not good?"

Chapter Seventeen

True to his word, Quint stayed away from Rebecca for much of the following week. Late the first day after his troublesome interview with her, he called her back into his study. She hadn't left to tend to John yet, and Quint informed her in a stern voice, "I'll expect to have your company at the evening meal."

Her lips formed a tight line, "Is that an order, sir?"

"Yes, it is!" Quint shouted back at her.

She walked out of the room, head held high, picked up her bag of herbs, and climbed into the waiting wagon. Quint watched from the window as Sam guided the wagon to the winding path heading to John's cottage. Dinner time arrived but Rebecca had not returned. When Hilda asked about the meal, Quint said quietly, "Dinner will wait."

Rebecca stayed with John until the afternoon sun drifted toward the mountains. When Sam finally insisted that they return to the main house, Rebecca smiled to herself. She was sure mealtime had come and gone. When Sam pulled the wagon up in the yard, however, Hilda stomped out of the kitchen, dragged Rebecca out of the wagon and pushed her toward the dining room. Rebecca protested but Hilda would hear none of it. The angry cook pushed Rebecca into her chair and when she rose to leave, Hilda forced her back down. Growling, she said, "You eat. He says he eats with you, you eat now! My meal you not ruin!"

The meal was strained and quiet. Quint said little and

Rebecca admitted that in this she would have to give in. He would order Hilda to hold the meal until she was ready to eat. Making Quint angry was one thing, but facing a furious Hilda was something else. Rebecca made a mental note to arrive on time for dinner.

Her days were full. She spent most of the mornings working with her students and her afternoons were spent preparing lessons for the next day. Word of her successful treatment of John's leg spread to the other families and, surprisingly, she now had ten children in the classroom.

As busy as she was, she was still plagued by memories. On the few occasions when she got a chance to sit quietly in her classroom and watch the children work, or when she traveled silently in the wagon next to Sam on some errand or another, her thoughts drifted to the night she occupied Quint's bed. She could almost feel his hands running up and down her small frame or cupping her full breasts. Once she realized the direction of her thoughts, she would blush scarlet and look to see if anyone noticed.

If days were bad, the nights were worse. Frequently, she would wake in a cold sweat and without warning, her vivid dream would surface to her consciousness. She would find herself struggling from sleep, then she'd have to glance around the room in fear, certain that he had invaded her room. The sensations of his lovemaking had left her shaking and burning with desire. Somehow, he had touched the dark corners of her soul.

In her defense, she dredged up her anger. He'd used her, just like the other men in her life. She wailed at the shadows in the room, "Why can't I forget? Oh, why do I have to remember?"

Rebecca forgot about Susannah completely, and she wasn't even aware that Quint carried three dresses and part of her undergarments back from town on one of his many trips. As she had promised, Hilda gathered the clothing Rebecca wasn't wearing and took it down to the kitchen to burn it. Once it was disposed of she tackled the task of ridding Rebecca of the worn dark dress she always wore.

Hilda prepared the large copper tub with hot water and a bit of the oil of roses Quint bought and then went in search of Rebecca. "Why the kitchen? I always bathe in my room," Rebecca asked in surprise.

Hilda smiled slightly, "Company I want. Bathe in the kitchen, I say." Rebecca finally agreed and as she soaked in the tub, Hilda quietly gathered the old black dress and the thin chemise and threw them in the fire.

Rebecca glanced around at Hilda and spotted her dress, being devoured by the flames. "What are you doing?" she yelped.

Hilda grinned over at her. "Burn he says, so burn I will! Besides, a teacher now you will look."

Rebecca tried to be angry, but, as usual, Hilda was probably right. The dress was worn and faded and certainly nothing that would inspire confidence in her by her growing number of students.

At the end of the second full month of classes, Rebecca dismissed her students for six weeks. All of the children were needed in the fields to begin preparations for spring planting. When a lone carriage arrived late in the afternoon of the last day of class, Quint dragged her to the front of the house. She waited at the front door as he ran up the path to greet a tall woman and her taller husband.

As Rebecca watched, Quint clasped the woman in his strong arms and swung her around. He set her gently on the ground and grasped the outstretched hand of the man. Stunned, Rebecca suddenly remembered that Quint had asked his sister and her husband to come for a visit. All three people were smiling from ear to ear and hugging and kissing each other. As Rebecca watched, she felt a twinge of jealousy. Her brother hadn't even kissed her good-bye.

She watched as Susannah's husband leaned toward Quint and whispered something to him and Quint raised his eyebrows at his sister. Rebecca could see the questioning expression on his face and she wondered about the strange exchange, but she had no time to reflect on it because Quint was leading the couple toward her. She steeled herself for the censure she knew would come.

Trying to appear calm, she watched Susannah approach. The tall woman was a complete surprise. Quint had mentioned her once or twice on the ship when they discussed the role of women in the new nation. He talked about her arrival at the farm, but from his remarks, Rebecca pictured Susannah as a very plain, stern woman. The woman coming down the walk was anything but plain. She was almost as tall as her husband who was only an inch or two shorter than Quint. Rebecca stared at all three of them. I'm going to get a sore neck from looking up, she thought to herself.

Susannah and Quint were obviously related, Rebecca decided as she considered the soft luxurious dark brown hair that covered Susannah's head. As the woman came nearer, Rebecca noticed the same sparkling blue eyes and the classic nose. Susannah was slender but she had lacked no feminine asset that Rebecca could determine. "Why, she is almost regal," Rebecca thought as Quint led Susannah forward. "She's everything I'm not," Rebecca muttered to herself wanting nothing more than to turn and hide. The thought surfaced, what had he told Susannah about her?

Frozen in place, she acknowledged Quint's introduction. Susannah was looking at her solemnly and then she glanced back at her brother. She turned back toward Rebecca and smiled. Rebecca couldn't help but notice that brother and sister had the same impish grin, but Susannah's eyes were much more involved in her smile than Quint's were.

Susannah laughed a deep musical laugh, and watching Rebecca she said, "Quint was right. You are a beauty."

Rebecca stared at her for a second, then, a little self-consciously, she lowered her eyes and murmured, "Thank you."

Susannah leaned forward as if to share a confidence with her. "And, of course, my addlebrained brother never said a word to you about your beauty, did he?" Rebecca looked up, grinned, and shook her head. She knew she was going to like this tall elegant woman standing before her, and she knew instinctively that Quint would get away with nothing while his sister was visiting.

They went into the house and while the trunks were being unloaded, Quint showed Susannah and George around the rooms. Susannah murmured softly as they moved from room to room that she had forgotten how lovely it was. Quint dragged them out to the kitchen, introduced Hilda, and showed them the classroom behind the main room. Susannah grinned as Quint described Rebecca's ability with the children. As they toured the house, Quint pointed out all of the changes that were completed or planned, and almost everything he mentioned involved Rebecca in one manner or another. Susannah caught her husband's eye and his grin answered her unasked question.

When the couple retired to freshen for dinner, Susannah turned on George as he closed the door. "What do you think?" she questioned softly.

George turned to her with a grin on his face. "About what, love?"

"About Rebecca, of course!"

George put his arms around her slim waist and whispered, still grinning, "I think she's the one."

Susannah was pleased that she and George agreed, once again, but her brow wrinkled as she asked, "Do you think he knows?"

He kissed her nose, then laughed out loud. "No! In fact, I'll bet he's fighting it like a game cock."

Susannah admonished softly, "Now, George!"

George swung his wife around, "Come on sweetheart! Let's go down to dinner and watch the entertainment. This is probably going to be a most interesting week." He chuckled as he led Susannah out of the door and down the steps to the dining room.

Dinner was supposed to be an elegant affair, but before they had gotten through the soup it became apparent to Rebecca that this meal was going to be too much fun to be formal. Susannah teased her brother almost continually and Quint returned the same. Rebecca quickly relaxed and let brother and sister entertain she and George. George in turn, loudly praised Hilda's cooking and threatened to steal her from Quint. At first Hilda was terrified but when Quint refused a million pounds for her she realized that it was all in jest and she joined in the fun.

After dinner, Susannah made no move to leave the men to their brandy and cigars so Rebecca stayed as well enjoying an easy camaraderie. George and Susannah asked many questions about where Rebecca lived, how long she had been in the new country, and what happened to her fiancé, but Rebecca gave evasive answers or changed the subject.

The hour was late when Rebecca finished her twentieth or thirtieth cup of tea and she asked to be excused, adding that she had responsibilities to see to in the morning. Quint watched her leave the dining room and suggested quietly that George and Susannah might like to retire as well. Susannah looked at Quint then to the empty doorway and whispered clearly, "Not on your life. I want to know more."

Quint sighed. He knew Susannah well enough to know that she would not go to bed until she had more facts. "Well, then, let's retire to the study and I'll tell you what I know," he said.

They seated themselves around the blazing fire in the study and Quint told them about his voyage to the United States after Susannah's letter had urged him home. He told them of Rebecca's caring for the sick passengers and the cabin boy. He explained his conversations with the captain and the sailor's attack on the girl. Avoiding his own feelings and his original opinion of Rebecca, he reached over and retrieved her contract from its little pigeon hole in the desk. He tried to explain. "The man she was engaged to marry was killed in a carriage accident before she arrived in this country. The girl insisted that she would bond herself and repay the captain. We both tried to convince her that wasn't necessary, but Rebecca has a stubborn streak that defies description. The only way I could prevent serious problems for the girl was to accept her paper and pay her bills."

Susannah and George sat quietly for several minutes before George asked in a solemn voice, "Just what are your intentions concerning this girl?"

George and Quint had been friends for ten years, and for the first time in the acquaintance, Quint took offense at George's words. "How the hell do I know what my intentions are? And it's none of your damn business anyway," he snapped.

George said, "Under the circumstances, with your buying her and all, someone has to look out for her."

Susannah seemed to agree with George, "Quint, it is no good for such a beautiful young woman to stay here with you alone. You should be thinking of her."

Quint scowled, if his sister only knew. Instead, he replied, "She's not alone with me," making *alone* sound like a dread disease, "Hilda's here and she's Rebecca's companion and chaperone."

Susannah smiled slightly, "And any fool can see that you've charmed Hilda out of her mind." Her words eased some of the tension. But, Quint stared into the fire for several more minutes, before he turned to George and asked quietly, "Well, brother, what do you think I should do about this lovely creature I own? Sell her papers, or send her unescorted back to a brother who would doubtless sell her again?"

George thought about the question for a moment. "You might let her come stay with us for a spell. Of course, our children don't need a tutor yet." The trio sat quietly.

Susannah ventured softly, "Quint, you might ask Rebecca what she'd like to do."

"But she might want to leave!" Quint blurted out. Susannah broke into laughter. He shook his head, "It's too late to discuss this any further. Why don't we all retire for the night?" He didn't like the turn of the conversation in the least.

Susannah and George both agreed that the hour was late and bed was probably a very good idea. They said their good nights and left Quint toying with a half-finished snifter of brandy. Susannah wondered aloud if Quint shouldn't come to bed as well, as she and George made their way up the stairs.

George took her arm and started her toward their room. "We've given him a lot to chew on, love. Let it be for tonight." He fondled his wife's shapely form as they made their way to their bed chamber. Susannah was giggling as she struggled to control his wandering hands before they were secreted behind their own door.

Quint heard his sister's soft giggles and could guess at their play. He sat glumly watching the dying coals. He really didn't want Rebecca to leave. Even if she was there under protest, she was there. What on earth had happened to him? A piece of feminine fluff could make him snap at his brother-in-law and even resent his dear sister's soft words of advice.

Finally, knowing that he'd find no answers in the dark room, Quint gave up and sought his own bed. That night, just like so many nights in the past, Rebecca's smiling face returned to haunt his dreams. As he punched his pillow in desperation he wondered if he would ever be able to sleep well again.

The week went by swiftly, but Rebecca felt a certain amount of tension between George and Quint, even though they spent long hours together planning the management of the farm, ordering supplies and discussing the marketing of the expected produce. Rebecca couldn't speculate on what caused the tension, because she was occupied with countless tasks of her own.

On the last full day of the Beals' visit, Rebecca called a halt to her work and joined Susannah early in the morning. Their conversation at first was very general, about teaching and about Rebecca's knowledge and interest in herbs and Rebecca found herself talking about the books she brought with her from England. Susannah told Rebecca about Mary Elizabeth and Samuel McQuade and the building of the farm and then the shipyards. She reminisced about her childhood and what Quint was like as a little boy and then as a young man. They laughed together and compared notes on foods and household chores.

Susannah told Rebecca all about her children and grew wistful as she mentioned that she missed them terribly, even being away from them for only one week. By the evening meal they both felt as if they had known each other for years. Susannah even told Rebecca about the new baby on the way and asked her if she would come to visit before the baby arrived late in October.

Early the next morning, George and Susannah left with a large basket full of some of the food George had made such a fuss over. Rebecca and Susannah held each other and tears flowed down their cheeks. Susannah insisted that Quint plan a visit in the fall before the baby came to bring Rebecca. Grudgingly, Quint agreed.

After the carriage pulled away, Quint went out to the fields to tell John and the other tenant about the plans he and George had discussed. He was gone for many hours.

Rebecca spent a miserable day alone. She had no classes to occupy her time and she was depressed beyond anything she'd ever felt before. In the afternoon she walked around one corner of the farm, watching Quint in the distance as he walked and talked with his men. She walked further into the woods that bordered the farm, lost in her thoughts.

Somehow, Susannah's insistence that she come for a visit before the baby arrived made Rebecca keenly aware of her own small family and she was homesick for the servants and her few friends in England. She thought about Susannah, her husband, her children and the life she led. She realized that she would never have a home and a family of her own.

Even Hilda seemed preoccupied as she prepared the evening meal. She wasn't interested in taking time to talk. Rebecca fought her tears and wondered why she had no one with whom she could share her pain. She struggled through the woods, confused, hurt, and terribly alone.

After the noisy delightful meals of the past week, dinner that afternoon was a somber affair. Rebecca and Quint said little to each other, but Rebecca noticed that Quint lavished praise on Hilda. He complimented her meals for the Beals, her thoughtfulness at providing food for them to take home, and the elegance of this evening's meal. Before dessert was served, Rebecca asked to be excused and hurried to her room.

Rebecca escaped in the hope that she could sleep, but instead her mind was busy with thoughts of the meal she had just endured. It was very considerate of Quint to heap such lavish praise on Hilda, but he had only asked once how the last day of school had gone. She tossed and turned and discovered quickly that she could not sleep. Her bed chamber offered no comfort because Quint's face appeared in the fireplace. When she closed her eyes, he moved through her mind. She saw him walking in the fields, eating his meals, drinking his coffee, and bending over Hilda's cooking.

Gradually, she became conscious of such an emptiness that she wondered how she possessed any strength at all. Her eyes filled with tears and she tried to remind herself that her first year of slavery was almost over. She had to bear only four more years, then she would be free. Free to do what? If Quint decided to settle on the farm permanently, as he said he would eventually do, there was no place for her. Surely, he would marry. . . . At that thought the sobs began, and she could not stop. She curled up in the center of the bed and pulled a pillow over her head to muffle the sobs she could not control. In her frustration she pounded her feet against the frame of the bed.

Chapter Eighteen

After dinner Quint went into the study to work on the ledgers from the last voyage and the one that would leave Philadelphia at the end of May. He enjoyed the chance to reflect on the past week and the manner in which Susannah and Rebecca got along. It pleased him inordinately that his sister and his reluctant guest got along so well. He remembered Susannah's comments the night before and he grinned. His sister confided to him that Rebecca was a very special person and that she wanted her to visit the Beal farm and soon. Darkness settled over the study and Quint blew out the candles.

He made his way up the stairs, his mind busy with the things to be done about the farm before the seed could go into the ground. A contentment settled around him that he had never known. As he passed Rebecca's room, he paused. She seemed so distant at dinner, perhaps he should tell her how much Susannah enjoyed the visit. He listened, trying to determine if Rebecca was still awake. The noise he heard instantly peaked his curiosity. It sounded like someone was pounding with a velvet hammer.

Quint tapped gently on the door but there was no answer, yet the thumping noise continued. Quietly, he opened the door. His heart plunged to his feet as he heard her muffled sobs. He approached the bed, wondering how long she had been crying like that. Rebecca didn't hear him enter the room and she was too involved in her own abject misery to know that she was no longer alone.

Quint bent over her and gently pulled the pillow away from her head. Several seconds passed before she realized that the reason for her tears was bending over her. She went wild. She threw herself away from him and off the bed, shrieking like someone deranged. And that was exactly what Quint thought as he dropped the pillow and dashed for her. He got close enough to her so that her tightly clenched fists swung out at him savagely. Struggling against her blows, he succeeded in grabbing her shoulder and turned her around. Immediately, she started pounding at his chest and head. Grabbing both of her arms, he yanked them down at her sides. He pulled her taut body toward him and held her tightly until he felt some of the tension leave her. He glanced down at her face and couldn't drag his eyes away. Never had he seen anyone so white. A desolate look radiated from her eyes and he suspected that she would crumple at any second.

Quint stood in indecision. He had no idea what he should do. He sensed that she was near hysteria and, for the life of him, he was at a lost to explain what prompted her behavior. Without thinking, he scooped her up into his arms and strode down the hall to his own room and the crystal decanter of brandy that rested on the table next to his bed. Brandy was the only thing he could think of. It had to bring her to her senses so that he could get to the bottom of her anguish.

He sat her in one of the chairs in his room and grabbed the bottle from the table. He pulled the stopper from the container and poured a small amount into a glass. Carefully, he lifted it to her pale lips and forced a portion of the liquid into her mouth. He prayed as he waited for some of the warmth of the beverage to penetrate.

Rebecca coughed and sputtered and her eyes lost some of their wild expression. She willingly took another sip. Tears were still flowing down her cheeks, but pathetic sobs no longer racked her body. Quint breathed a sigh of relief, she hadn't lost her sanity.

Rebecca felt the liquid fire slide down her throat and she lifted her head, gazing into his concerned face as he knelt before her. She felt the water falling from her eyes, but she didn't seem to be able to gather enough willpower to stop the flood. In fact, she had no strength left to sob out her fears, or her despair.

Quint watched her carefully for several more minutes as he coaxed her to take a few more sips of the liquor. Her color returned slowly and her tears lessened. When he thought she looked at him with recognition he decided he could question her. Quietly, he pleaded, "Tell me, what happened? What made you so unhappy? I can help, but you'll have to tell me what's wrong. Why were you crying?"

Rebecca's eyes filled up with tears again and she looked at him with such pain that his heart twisted in his chest. She tried to explain, "Susannah . . . left . . . no one . . . classes . . . Hilda." She started sobbing again and tried between her sobs, "Can't have . . . family . . . no babes . . . no place." She took a deep breath and with a clear heartfelt plea, she cried, "I wish I were dead! Oh, let me die. Just let me die!"

Quint grabbed her from the chair and held her tightly as she sobbed. He sank into the same chair, cuddling her against him. Weakness flooded him. Never before had he heard such a wretched cry. Few of her mumbles made any sense but her last words were engraved on his heart forever. Was he responsible for that plea? She had to tell him what happened to her and who had hurt her so. She had to!

She wasn't going to be able to tell him anything. He would have to question her and hope that he could glean enough from her responses to give him the answers he needed. He took a deep breath and whispered, "Rebecca, are you crying because you miss England." She shook her head. He was elated. Obviously, he could reach her through his questions. His sister visited, perhaps she was missing her own brother. Continuing, he asked her tenderly, "Do you want to see your brother?"

Her sobbing answer was clear enough, "He'll only . . . sell . . . me."

Quint tried again, "Do you want me to release you from your contract?" There was a hesitation, then a slight nod, yes. "What will you do if I release you?"

The sobs came again, nearly as frantic as before. "Is that the problem? Are you sorry you bonded yourself and you want your freedom? Are you concerned about what will happen to you?"

Again, there was a slight hesitation, then she gave a quick nod, but it was followed by a vigorous shake, no. Quint set her away from him just enough so that he could look into her eyes, and in a voice shaking with emotion he replied, "We can make some arrangements. But I don't know what kind of arrangements you want." He couldn't say anything more. His heart was in his mouth and he felt sick. She wanted to be free of him. She wanted to leave! He held her and a surge of tenderness and the need to protect her from pain flooded through him leaving him weak from it. He pulled her back against his chest.

Suddenly, he was aware of her soft warm body, covered only with her thin gown of cotton lawn. He forced himself to keep a tight rein on his emotions. For a fraction of a second the desire to make her one with him consumed him.

He held her tightly, and breathing deeply to control his lust, he smelled the soft fresh fragrance of her hair. Unconsciously, he murmured into her ebony locks, "I want you so badly." She lifted her head and as she gazed into his eyes, his control snapped. He could feel all of her soft curves burning through her gown and he gently lowered his lips to hers.

That night, Rebecca reached the limit of what she could bear. She knew she had no home, not even a place to call her own and she had no future. Above all else, she needed love. When she pondered her problems, they only grew larger in her mind's eye. Now, thought was banished. Her inner soul knew that she could not reason or try to understand the desperation that whirled around her. Instinctively, she knew that Quint could give her a measure of peace, if only for a few hours. She would be his, and she would feel warm and cared for and loved. Tomorrow did not exist, yesterday was not a concern, only this moment, this day, this second mattered. Her arms slid up around his neck and she surrendered. He wanted her and he needed her, just as she needed him. It was enough!

Quint's lips met hers in a tender kiss that went on and on and she felt safe. She felt his lips part and she welcomed the gentle invasion of his tongue as it touched hers, sending shock waves up and down her spine. She clung to him, afraid that if he moved away from her, even an inch or two, she would be lost forever.

Quint slid his hand under her gown and found her soft warm breast. He molded his hand around it, and with his fingers he stroked the tiny nipple until it gradually grew erect and firm. A sigh slipped past Rebecca's lips, and Quint, almost at the point of sighing himself, sought to quell his own passionate moanings in the sweetness of her open mouth.

No longer comfortable in the chair, he scooped her into his arms and moved swiftly to the bed. Gently, he placed her on the feather tick and started to remove his clothing, but a tiny sobbing voice stopped him. "Don't leave me," she whispered.

He dropped to the mattress beside her and took one of her hands in both of his. He struggled with his conscience. The thought that, in her present state of mind she was beyond reason and no longer knew what she was doing, plagued him. If that were the case, he knew that he couldn't make love to her, no matter how much he desired her. She had to want him as much as he wanted her. "Rebecca," his rich, hoarse voice said in a throaty whisper, "I want you so much. But I won't touch you unless you want me, too. I'll leave now if that's what you truly want. Do you understand?" He looked down at her in the shimmering candlelight as the warm shadows danced across her face.

She nodded her head. She understood. "Do you want me? I have to know," he whispered, the lump in his throat making his voice break. She raised her arms and opened them to him. He wanted to shout with joy. Instead, he lowered himself to the bed and wrapped his arms around her, holding her as though he was afraid that she would dissolve into the shadows before his eyes. He kissed her hair, her eyes, her face, trying to kiss away all of the tears that still clung to her dark lashes. Drawing away so he could look into her eyes, he sighed, "Let me get rid of these," and began pulling at his shirt.

She shook her head and whimpered as he drew away. Throwing her arms around his neck she pulled him back down to her and with one hand she started to struggle with the buttons of his partially opened shirt. Their eyes locked as she pulled at the shirt. He freed one arm and then wrapped it around her as he shook the other sleeve free. When the shirt was no longer a problem, he reached down and drew her into his arms to kiss her again. Her gown separated them and it too, was removed and tossed aside. With one hand, he released the buttons from his breeches and worked his boots from his feet. When the breeches were gone, he took his place beside her on the bed.

Rebecca lay in his arms, her whole body quivering with waves of excitement. The harder he kissed her, the more she trembled. She waited, almost afraid to breathe, as pleasure spread over her breasts, through her arms, around her stomach and down to the center of her being. She clutched at his muscles, stroking the warm flesh of his back, willing him to return the same touch.

He did, touching her shoulders, her rib cage, her abdomen and then, he slid his hands down further toward his ultimate goal. Rebecca listened to his heart thundering out in counterpoint to hers, and she gasped for breath, spreading her legs to allow him access to her very center.

He teased and touched until she was mindless. She heard the words, "Please, now," and she wondered if she said them or if she only thought them. Rational thought had disappeared long before.

She was conscious of Quint's movement and then he was poised above her. Once again, she whimpered and arched toward him. He answered her wordless plea with a consuming kiss. At that instant, he entered her and she groaned in ecstasy. As he moved, she moved with him, absorbed into a world of bliss and each thrust brought her sweeter and more intense delight. Suddenly, she was catapulted into another world and she cried out in release. Quint held her and then, no longer able to hold his own need at bay, he covered her mouth with a frantic, devouring kiss and followed her into the stars.

He collapsed against her, waiting for his world to adjust to what was ordinary. Holding her tightly against him, so they would still be joined, he rolled over on his side, taking her with him. He continued to press light, teasing kisses to the raven locks of hair that surrounded them. Touching her eyes, her mouth, even her ears with his hungry lips, he wondered at the satisfaction he felt. He mumbled against her ear, "Rebecca—Rebecca. You are mine. Only mine. Mine, now, forever." The trace of a smile flitted across her lips and the soft arms of sleep pulled her down into a perfect pillow of contentment.

The new day was still young when Quint became fully conscious. Rebecca lay curled against him and she was breathing deeply, still sound asleep. Carefully, so that he wouldn't disturb her, he raised himself up on an elbow and watched her closely. What she needed, he thought, was more rest before they could begin the task of sorting through the emotions of the night before. That was what they would begin that very morning, he resolved. With as much care as possible, he rolled from the bed and dressed quickly, never taking his eyes from her sleeping form. He sighed in relief when he silently slipped from the room. She was still sound asleep.

He made his way down the stairs, through the house, and out to the kitchen. The second he entered the kitchen, he knew that Hilda was furious. Her lips were drawn into a tight line and her brow was creased. She glared up at him and slammed the bread pan in her hands down on the table. He walked to the hearth and lifted the coffee pot to pour himself a cup of the bracing brew. He didn't have to guess at the reason for her anger, he knew! "Well," he said softly, "Go ahead and tell me why you are so angry."

"You . . . you . . . you . . ." Quint grimaced as she sought the words to condemn him satisfactorily. "Coins I take from you, and a wardrobe you buy, so that protect the girl I will. From you, how can I protect her?" Her voice was full of scorn, "A good girl she be, and of men, she knows nothing. You know that. After her you race to save her from a beast!" Still she raged on, "You! For yourself you save her! You . . . you betray her!"

"How did you know?" Quint asked sheepishly.

"I go check up on her. She too quiet yesterday. In her bed she's not, nor in the other beds. Not in the sitting room, or in the study or classroom, she be. She was with you! You ruin her," her voice was a hoarse whisper. "Worse than . . . than Worthman, you be." She turned her back on him.

"Hilda," Quint tried to explain, his voice soft, poignant, "I have to leave in a few weeks. When I come back, I'll release Rebecca from her contract. But we'll make some decisions long before then. In fact, today I hope to get her promise that she'll stay with me. I came down here to get tea for her and coffee for me and to tell you that she and I have some serious talking to do." His eyes pleaded with her for understanding.

Hilda did not seem to want to understand, "She no be your mistress!" she snapped at him.

"I wasn't thinking about her being my mistress," he said quietly. "I want something more permanent than that."

Hilda's mouth formed a silent "oh" and then she

grinned at him. "Nothing I say, my mouth I keep shut," she said, busying herself with a tray, her face almost cracking from the grin that stretched from cheek to cheek.

Quint started to smile himself. A great weight was suddenly lifted from his shoulders. He chuckled to himself, as he thought about the way he had tried to deceive himself over the past several weeks. He hadn't been honest enough with himself to admit that he wasn't going to be satisfied with a temporary situation. He wanted her for his own, for always, as his mate, his love, his wife. Thinking back to the previous days, when his sister had visited, he wanted to laugh out loud. Susannah had taken an instant liking to Rebecca and now he knew why. His sister had known. George probably knew as well. It was a good thing the Beal farm and his were only separated by a day's travel. There would be a great deal of visiting between the two families. Just thinking the word *family* gave him a warm comfortable feeling.

He took the tray Hilda held out to him and pointed at a plate of steamy scones on the table. "Perhaps you should fix a plate of those. We have a lot to figure out and this may take some time. Hold breakfast for me?" he asked as he started through the door. With the tray in his hands, he made his way back to his room. He sighed in satisfaction when he saw that Rebecca was still curled up in his bed, dreaming away. He placed the tray on the table, and hurried around the room, completing the task he set for himself. When everything was ready, he sank into the chair next to the bed and watched the delicate creature sleeping soundly.

Shaking his head, he digested the fact that he was in love, helplessly in love for the first time in his life. A sudden thought chilled him to the core. He was taking for granted that Rebecca felt the same, that she would want him, as he wanted her. Holding her papers, he could force her into a relationship with him for the next four years, but if she wasn't interested in marriage, there was nothing he could do. There was an attraction there, he was certain of that, but he had awakened her passions. Maybe that was all it was. Maybe she was a passionate woman by nature and he was reading more into her response than there was.

He would make her love him. He wasn't without some redeeming features. His sister said that he was charming, she had even mentioned that to Rebecca. He tried to remember her words. There were countless other women that seemed more than interested in sharing his life, but had they been interested in him, or in his fortune? he wondered. He sat sipping his coffee, contemplating his best course of action, convinced that Rebecca would not be thrilled with his marriage proposal.

The only course was to take his time, he thought as she stirred in his bed. He would suggest that she think about a future together. Perhaps, after she had been at the farm through the summer, she would be willing to accept him as a husband if the farm came with him. Of course, there was always the chance that she would discover that she cared for him deeply. He smiled happily at the prospect.

It was that smile Rebecca saw when she opened her eyes a few minutes later, after she had awakened completely. When she had first stirred, she refused to open her eyes but instead she stretched, then let her body relax and sink slowly back into the thick feather tick. She delighted in the thought that for the first time in months she had slept very well and all night long. She stretched again and just then, a flood of remembrances came back. Her eyes popped open and she sat up like a shot. She was still in Quint's room, in his bed and she was naked. She yanked the quilt up to cover herself and then looked around. It took only a second to find him and he was grinning at her. Embarrassed by the thought that she was being studied by the man responsible for her night of sleep, she wiggled down into the bed and tried to hide.

"Good morning. I have tea and warm scones, if you're ready for something to eat," he announced as he pointed to the table and the tray.

Rebecca scowled at him and then rolled over to the edge of the bed holding the quilt tightly around her shoulders. As she thought of him, sitting here, looking at her as if nothing had happened, she groaned. She was mortified and she pleaded in a small voice, "Would you mind handing me my clothes, please?"

She glanced at him over her shoulder but he sat in the chair smiling at her in a strange way. He said quietly, "After we've talked."

Rebecca whirled around, glaring at him, angry now, "I have nothing to say to you. May I have my clothes, please?" She looked at his grinning face and then she glanced around the room. Nothing of hers was visible. "Where are my things? Did you hide my clothes?" His eyes said yes and she wanted to scream. She stared at him and yelped, "You did! You hid my clothes!" She started for the door, holding the quilt around her like a shield of armor. Glancing back at him, his lips curled into a rakish grin, she wondered why he looked so smug. "I'll just go to my own room, then," she announced and reached for the doorknob. She pulled at the door but it would not open.

"It's locked. We talk first," Quint said to her back, his tone grim.

"I'll scream!"

"I'm afraid it won't do any good, I've already talked to Hilda."

"She knows. . . ." Rebecca uttered an anguished cry and tried to bury her flaming face in her hands and keep the quilt in place around her slender frame all at the same time.

Quint left his chair and approached her. "Come, get back in bed and have your tea, while we talk."

"Don't touch me." She panicked and backed toward the hearth.

"Then, get in bed and have your tea," he growled in frustration.

Rebecca looked at him very skeptically. Bed was not where she thought she ought to be. She eased herself into a chair next to the hearth, but across from Quint and held the quilt tightly around her body.

Quint poured tea, placed a scone on a small plate, then brought them to her. As he stood waiting for her to accept his offering, he watched her dark eyes. She glanced up at him in confusion. There was no table beside this chair and if she took the tea she would only have one hand on the quilt. There was no way she could handle the quilt, the tea, and the plate.

"I'll get back in bed," she said in surrender, her voice wavering slightly.

When she reached the bed, Quint turned his back. She arranged the quilt and the pillows and then said in a timid voice, "I'll have the tea now."

Quint handed her the cup and plate and sank into the chair, stretching his long legs out in front of him, "Let's start with last night." As the color faded from her face, he added, "Before I brought you here for the brandy."

Rebecca at staring down at the cup in her hands, but she said nothing. Quint sat up and leaned toward the bed. "There must be something very wrong for a beautiful woman to want to die." Then he said, as if to himself, "And, I'm going to find out why if it takes all day."

Rebecca stuck out her chin. The only thing he was worried about was losing his bondslave, she thought, especially one who served in so many ways. Well, he could sit there all day, for all she cared, she wasn't going to tell him a thing!

Chapter Nineteen

Quint sipped his coffee and watched Rebecca over the edge of his cup. He thought he could tell where her mind had wandered just by the stubborn set of her jaw. He growled, "Last night has nothing to do with your present status as a bondslave. Of that I'm sure."

Rebecca glanced from her perch on the bed, from Quint to the door and back again. There was no question, she'd get out of the room only when she explained. Sighing deeply, she thought about the way he rescued her from Bud Worthman, his concern over what she did at the farm, and the dresses he brought so that Susannah's visit would not be an embarrassment. Grudgingly she admitted that she probably did owe him some kind of explanation for her behavior the night before. She closed her eyes, she wouldn't tell him everything, just enough to get her out of his bed and back to her own room. "Where do you want me to start?" she whispered.

He tried not to look as relieved as he felt. Now, he was going to get some answers, "Start at the beginning, in England with your brother."

Rebecca lowered her eyes, took a deep breath and began with Arthur. She told Quint about the gambling, her maid, her jewels, and her proposed marriage. Once she started, she found that she couldn't stop. She ended up confiding to him the betrayal she felt over the unchanged will, Stephen Hill's accident, even his own amorous pursuit of her. She didn't mean to mention any of it, but the words tumbled over each other as she explained how she made her decision to bond herself and Captain Hemphill's reaction. "You should have stayed out of it," she whispered and blinked against the moisture forming in her eyes. By the time she got to the kidnapping, she was crying and Quint couldn't stay in his chair. He was beside her on the bed, holding her in his arms. In a husky voice, he changed the subject, "Would you like to visit Susannah this fall?"

She looked up at him in surprise as she dried her tears. "I would like that very much," she said softly, her voice still shaky.

He maneuvered himself back into his chair, regretfully, and refilled both cups. Handing her the tea, he sipped his coffee and wondered how he should approach the subject of the farm. Go slowly, he cautioned himself. "Rebecca, while I'm gone I want you to think about something. Could you be happy here, could you . . . would you . . . stay here, live . . . here . . . with me?" he stuttered, watching her carefully. The expression on her face turned to worried concern, and his heart sank.

Rebecca wasn't ready to consider her future, which still seemed hopeless to her, and she looked for a way to redirect the conversation, "Where are you going? When?"

Quint was a little angry. She simply avoided his question. "I told you," he said, a bit of his anger showing, "I have to leave here at the end of May. I must take a ship to the Islands, pick up a cargo and return to Philadelphia. I'll return by the middle of September. Rebecca, I'll mark your papers paid in full when I return, but I want you to think about what I said." Quint's feelings were hurt and he was frustrated. She wasn't reacting as he hoped, that was for sure. He thought that she cared for him a bit, but she wouldn't even answer his questions. In the short time he had left, before he left for the Islands, he had to court her, he decided. He would get her to talk and then, he would convince her that marriage to him wasn't going to be unpleasant.

Rebecca sat very still in his bed and held her tea cup

tightly in her hands. If he would only ask her to marry him, her world would not seem so desperate. But, he obviously had never considered marriage and she couldn't live with him as a kept woman. There was nothing honorable about being a mistress. That was worse than being a bondservant. At least a bondslave had a definite time period to serve and then the slavery was over, but a mistress served until the man grew tired of the arrangement. No, she could never be anyone's mistress. What he said about her papers confirmed her suspicions, "What if I don't want my contract marked paid?" she asked a bit too sharply.

He looked at her with a puzzled expression on his face. "We don't have to decide anything until I return." He definitely didn't want to argue with her, not until he could figure out why she didn't want her freedom. He'd already indicated that he wanted her to stay with him. He sighed in disgust and took her tea cup and placed it on the tray. Walking to the bedroom door, he took a small key from his vest pocket and unlocked the door. He moved to the wardrobe and opened one drawer. Pulling her gown from the corner, he brought it back to the bed. He was plainly confused and she looked unhappy. Most of the enthusiasm was gone. "You get dressed. The dressmaker is due today for your final fitting and I need to see the workers I've hired. It's time for them to start in the fields." He tried to keep the disappointment out of his voice. "There is one thing I would like you to do for me, if you have the time. Almost every shirt I own needs repair and half of the jackets in the armoire could use a touch of the needle. I suspect you sew very well. Could you mend the things that need fixing?" Perhaps if she thought that he needed her, she would be more interested in his proposal.

Rebecca held her gown in front of her and nodded in surprise. Of course she could sew but why wasn't he going to have the dressmaker mend the garments that needed repair? It was a strange request in light of the comment that she be his mistress. She didn't think mistresses sewed for their gentleman. "Yes, I'll fix whatever needs work," she answered quietly.

He moved to the wardrobe. "I think," he said softly, as he pulled out the lower two drawers, "that everything in here needs something, a button, a bit of lace, a seam repaired." He pointed to a pile of shirts. Rebecca blinked, she could see herself sewing for months.

Quint left her then. Rebecca threw on her gown and ran to her room to dress. The morning passed quickly as Rebecca worked with Hilda to prepare a meal for the fifteen men that were working in the fields. Before she got a chance to examine the contents of the drawers he pointed out to her, the dressmaker arrived. Rebecca had no idea that Quint had purchased so many gowns and dresses for her and she was embarrassed at the extravagance. There were dresses in cotton, linen and silk, dresses for winter in wool and heavy cotton, day dresses, evening gowns, undergarments, petticoats and scarves. There were even two riding outfits and a cloak of velvet and one of serge. The fitting lasted all through the afternoon and by the time the dressmaker had finished, Rebecca was numb. Never had she dreamed of such a wardrobe. He had ordered silk hose, shoes, bonnets and several purses which the dressmaker left with her. It would be impossible to ever repay him for the clothes. She wasn't going to accept the wardrobe. Her anger came to her aid. He was not going to keep her enslaved with a bunch of cloth.

After the dressmaker left, Rebecca stormed through the house, looking for Quint. She found him in the study. "I will not accept all those clothes. I will let you buy me a dress or two, but that wardrobe is a waste. And it must have cost a fortune. I have no intention of working for another five or ten years to pay for clothes I don't need, can't use, and didn't order."

Quint said firmly, "The wardrobe is yours!"

She argued through the evening meal but he kept repeating, "Rebecca, everything is yours. You don't have to pay for it. It's a gift. I'm giving the wardrobe to you." Then he tried to change the subject.

Over dessert, he presented her with a small velvet box. Inside was a string of matched pearls and Rebecca blinked back her tears. Stunned, she sat perfectly still. All of a sudden, it made sense. First, the gift of the clothes and now jewelry. Already, he was treating her like his mistress. He wasn't going to give her a chance to refuse his offer. She was his kept woman and he was going to see that she knew it. Keeping her thoughts to herself, she pledged that she would not wear a single thing he bought. She had already accepted the three dresses he brought before Susannah came but that was all she would take, no matter what he said.

That evening she stored the pearls and the things the dressmaker left in a large chest in her room. She felt sick. If his intentions were honorable she would have enjoyed the new clothes so much. It had been so long since she had had anything new. Arthur allowed her little after her father died. She tried to make herself angry, telling herself how high-handed he was, but for once it didn't work. It simply hurt, hurt more than she thought anything could hurt. There was no time to try to figure out why she felt the way she did. She packed the things away and wiped the tears from her eyes. He wasn't going to find her crying again, either.

The next morning Rebecca was awakened by the shouts of serveral strange male voices. The day before, she had missed the arrival of the new workers while the dressmaker forced her to stand and twist and turn for the fitting. She dressed quickly and rushed down to the kitchen. Hilda would need all the help she could get feeding the army that arrived. For the next two weeks the farm took on the appearance of an English fair. Long boards were set up in the yard next to the kitchen. A covering was stretched over the boards like a tent in case of wet weather. Hilda, Rebecca, Bette, and two of Bette's daughters cooked from sun up to sun down. The workers were given all the food they could eat and very small wages. The work was backbreaking so the meals needed to be substantial. Rebecca rarely saw Quint as he directed the planting. She was as busy in the kitchen as he was in the fields.

One morning, without warning, the farm returned to normal. All but two of the extra men had moved on. Rebecca left the kitchen and retreated to the sitting room to begin the repairs Quint requested days before. She took six shirts from the drawer and stared at the remaining pile. It would take her weeks before she got all of the things in the first drawer repaired.

That evening at dinner there was another small box at Rebecca's plate. When Quint insisted that she open it, she tried to put him off, but when he sounded hurt she pulled the ribbon free and gazed at a small silver brooch set with saphires. There was nothing she could say to him to convince him that she didn't want the jewelry. After she thanked him, she tucked the brooch away with the pearls. She didn't want to be reminded of what she had become to him.

She kept the hurt to herself and went back to repairing his shirts. But, each day at dinner there was a small gift at her plate: a box of candies, a lace shawl, some fruit. All of the personal gifts she packed away with the original gift of pearls, the food she shared with Hilda.

With the household back to normal, Rebecca completely forgot about Quint's impending departure. She was busy sewing in the morning and in the afternoon she planned new lessons for the classes that would soon begin again. She thought about Quint and the lavish gifts he presented to her and the elegant wardrobe hanging in the closet in her room. He was charming, spending the late afternoons with her, talking to her as she sewed, joining her in the sitting room after dinner for his coffee and brandy. Rebecca could close her eyes and almost pretend that she and Quint were married.

Rebecca prided herself with the fact that she was honest, especially with herself. She was falling in love with the man who held her papers and nothing he said or did changed her feelings. She wanted nothing more than to have him take her in his arms, kiss her senseless and carry her off to his bed. Whenever she found herself alone, she would begin a stern lecture to herself. She should not love him, and she should not accept his gifts, there were strings attached to each one. Despite of the lectures, she was miserable.

When Quint walked into the room her heart fluttered, when he drew close, her traitorous heart skipped a beat, and if he touched her, her blood would race through her body with enough speed to make her dizzy. She wanted nothing more than to throw her arms around his neck and confess her true feelings, but she knew that would not do. Instead, she kept her eyes downcast and told herself over and over that she could not be his mistress. Each day, however, the words she preached became more obnoxious and her resolve slipped a bit more.

She knew she needed to talk to someone, but who? She couldn't talk to Hilda, the older woman simply would not understand. Rebecca wondered at times if Hilda wasn't a bit in love with Quint McQuade herself. She longed to talk to Susannah, but she knew that wouldn't do either. What could she say, "Your brother wants me to be his mistress. I think I'm falling in love with him, but . . ." No, Susannah was not the person to tell!

Rebecca was so involved in her problems that she lost all track of time and when Quint looked at her with regret in his eyes, one afternoon during dinner and whispered, "I have to leave tomorrow," Rebecca gazed at him in surprise and almost cried. It couldn't be the end of May already. "You're not leaving tomorrow?" she asked, the shock plain in her voice.

At first, Quint stared back, annoyed and then angry. "I told you that I had to take my ship to the Caribbean for supplies. I know I told you that I would leave at the end of May. Well, tomorrow is the last day of May."

He was furious because she forgot, but he was even more angry at himself. He didn't want to leave, and although she had given nothing substantial to hang on to, he felt he had been making progress with her. The most painful part of the situation was that he wanted her with a desperation he couldn't believe. He had no idea how he was going to survive the next three and a half months without her. In the weeks since their talk, he kept his hands to himself except for an occasional peck on the cheek. Now, he was leaving her and he didn't feel that he could pull her into his arms and kiss her the way he wanted. He frowned in frustration, she would probably slap his face.

The rest of the meal was solemn. Neither said much of anything and when Hilda brought dessert to the table they both declined. Quint finished his coffee and gazed at Rebecca who looked as forlorn at her end of the table as he felt. She did look upset, he decided, so she must be a little sorry to see me go. With burgeoning hope he asked, "Would you walk with me?" She nodded her head and rose from the table.

They walked out of the house and toward the setting sun. Neither of them said anything for a long while, but finally, Quint broke the silence, "I'll miss you. I'd take you with me, but there's no place on my ship for a woman."

Rebecca felt her body turn to stone and she stopped to stare at him. There! she told herself. He couldn't have made it plainer, if he announced it in the town square. He wanted her for his mistress and he was willing to tell the whole world. She almost choked as she hissed, "I wouldn't sail with you!" They walked on for serveral feet, both suffering deeply from the words just spoken. In a husky voice Quint began to explain about the arrangements he made for Hilda and her while he was away. John would check up on them, and anything they needed he would get when he went to town. Sam would care for the animals.

"Classes will begin soon," Quint continued, almost to

himself, "and if you want to travel to town for something else to do, Hilda can go with you." He waited for her to ask a question or comment, but she thanked him very quietly and turned back toward the house.

Quint followed her as they made their way through the vibrant trees, now full with their summer dress. Just as they reached the door, Quint mumbled something about packing and leaving at dawn. Darkness was closing in on them rapidly and Rebecca was grateful that the dusk hid her despair. Already, she was missing him, and he hadn't even left yet! She walked through the door. "I suppose I should retire, as well," she said. She started up the steps leaving Quint in the hall.

She got to her room with as much dignity as she could muster but as soon as she closed her door she dissolved into tears. If he stayed, she knew she would accept the role he outlined for her and when he tired of her, as he surely would, he only had to sell her or send her away. But, at the moment, just the thought of him leaving tomorrow was tearing her heart from her chest.

She swiped at her tears and started to undress for bed. As she hung up her dress, her eyes fell on the rainbow of colors created by the unworn gowns hanging in her wardrobe. Her tears started anew. She pulled her nightgown over her head and tried to ignore the flood that streamed down her face. A soft hesitant knock on her door drew a sob from her lips. Hilda undoubtedly was worried about her. She hadn't even said good-night. She hurried to the door.

Quint stood before her, his hand raised to knock again, his eyes filled with the anguish she felt. He lifted his hand and wiped away a tear. "You've been crying," he murmured. She turned away from him, but he followed her into the room and reached for her. His voice was husky with emotion, "I can't leave like this." He grasped her shoulder and turned her toward him. She collapsed in his arms.

They came together like a violent spring storm. In

seconds, her gown was gone and his clothes lay in a pile next to her bed. With a tenderness born of fear, fear for a love untold, she surrendered and he took but only to give. He kissed her gently, coaxing her from herself, begging her to meet him in the playground of stars where they had revelled before. She followed where he led. Giving no thought to the journey that would take him from her side, she touched and kissed as he touched and kissed.

She could taste her desire and this time, she knew her words as they fell from her lips, "Please, please!" He entered her then and she gloried in the joining, the sweet bliss that shook her from the crown of her head to the tips of her toes, and against his deep searching kiss she crested, exploding again and yet again.

She rested quietly in his arms, waiting for her breathing to steady, for her heart to slow its frantic cadence as he placed soft mindless kisses over her throat, her shoulders, the curve of her chin, her closed eyes. "May I stay the night?" he whispered in a hushed voice against her ear. With a sinking sensation she nodded agreement, knowing that she could deny him nothing. She loved him, and she knew instantly that if he asked, she would do anything, be anything he wanted as long as he held her. As she floated between the nether world of sleep and reality, she knew that if he asked her once more to be his ladylove, she would agree. The hours of self-conscious examination would count for naught. Ultimately, she would refuse him nothing. But, he didn't ask and she curled into his arms and slept.

Before the sun heralded the beginning of a new day, Rebecca stirred. The rustle of the bed covers in the stillness of the early hour brought her to full awareness and in that second she knew she was in bed alone. She opened her eyes and spied the tall manly figure gathering the articles of clothing that lay strewn about the room. Stretching, she sat up, intending to leave the warm bed and dress. She hated good-byes, but she would have to tell him farewell.

The tall figure approached and sat down on the edge of the bed. "Rebecca," Quint whispered tenderly, "There's no need. I'll be leaving very soon," he eased her back into the mattress, and leaning forward he brushed her lips gently with his own. Pulling her up and into his arms, he held her tightly for several minutes. Without a thought to what she was doing, she draped her arms around his neck and held on to him just as tightly. He kissed her deeply, as if he wanted to imprint her kiss at the back of his memory. His work-roughened hands ran up her back before he carefully pulled from her. "I'd rather you stay here," his husky voice betrayed his emotions and Rebecca sank back down into the cushion of feathers.

Before he went down the stairs, he came back into her room. She was still in bed, but now she was sitting up staring at the dark shadows of the room. He bent over her and whispered, "I'll be back in several months, in September. We'll go to Susannah's just as soon as I return."

She stayed in bed, her lips still warm from his kisses, and she listened to the noises from the first floor. She heard the carriage come around to the front of the house, the door open and close, and the clop of the horse as the carriage rumbled down the drive. Much later, as the sun peaked over the hills and slowly crept through her window to light the doorway through which Quint passed, she left her bed, a sad smile curving her lips. She dressed carefully, trying to concentrate on the task at hand. She didn't want to think, not yet, not for a long while.

Chapter Twenty

The days dragged by slowly and Rebecca tried to stay busy and not count the hours or the sunsets. She was in a turmoil. She admitted freely, at least to herself, that she was very much in love with Quint and a part of her wanted to deny him nothing. When she was free to think, she scolded herself for allowing him to take the liberties he had, but she couldn't have told him no. If he wanted her to be his mistress, a part of her was more than willing. That would not do, she berated herself. If she gave in to him, her love for him would eventually be destroyed, one way or another.

She relived their last night together and in her confusion, she decided that although he was physically attracted to her, her love was one-sided. Engrossed in her problems, she drew away from Hilda. The few times the cook tried to draw her out, Rebecca walked away from her without a word. With a sweet sadness, she moved through each day, giving her attention to the care of the large house she occupied, trying to still the frantic doubts that raced through her mind.

A week after Quint left, she thought about the trip to the Beals that Quint promised they would make when he returned. When she thought of Susannah growing large with a child, she paled. She had never considered the possibility of a child herself. With her knowledge, she realized that she could indeed be with child. For two weeks she suffered through each day, growing more sure that when Quint returned and found that she also carried a child, his, he would send her from the farm, far away, to have the child in shame. She became so tense and withdrawn that Hilda watched her, her own fear increasing. There was something very wrong with the girl and the only solution Hilda could come up with was to send Sam to the Beal farm for help. Suddenly, one morning, Rebecca's disposition improved dramatically.

Quint had been gone for four weeks when a group of men came up the road. George rode with them. When Rebecca opened the door to welcome them, George dismounted and the other riders continued north. He looked so solemn that Rebecca couldn't swallow. He was bringing news of a tragedy, she decided as she tried to force words of welcome over the strangling lump in her throat.

George tied up his horse, and when he glanced at the frantic look of anguish on Rebecca's face, he knew immediately what the girl was thinking. He smiled to himself, Susannah was right. Rebecca Ranserford was as much in love with Quint as he was with her. And, at the moment, she was certain that he carried bad news. Hurrying to eliminate her fear, he grinned at her.

As he strode up the walk, he remembered the night Quint stopped at the farm to ask if George would check up on the women who now resided at the family home. He wanted to laugh as he pictured Quint confessing that the vixen with the black hair had truly snared him and he was giving serious thought to settling down and beginning his own family. Of course, Quint was quick in telling Susannah that Rebecca was only fond of him, that she didn't return his feelings, yet, but he had hope.

Susannah had been overjoyed with Quint's conversation, it had been all she could talk about for days. She told him over and over that a sixth sense made her sure that Rebecca was as taken with Quint as he was with her. They didn't know it yet.

George was at the bottom step to the front door when Rebecca could hold her concerns no longer. She blurted out, "Is Quint, er . . . Mr. McQuade, alright? Has something happened?"

George's smile broadened, "No problems as far as we know. He's in familiar waters and fairly close. If there was trouble, we'd know in just a few days." When George was standing in the hall, Hilda came hurrying into the house. Her round face was lined with concern. George said, to relieve the anxiety on both women's faces, "I came to check up on you. I promised that worrisome brother-in-law of mine that I would drop everything and ride up here to make certain that you both were still in residence."

"Then, you'll stay the night?" Rebecca asked, her confidence showing in the relaxed smile she gave him.

"Leave without one of Hilda's fabulous meals? Woman, I may be addled enough to let my friend talk me into leaving my palace, but I am not without some intelligence." He grinned at both of them. "Of course, I'll stay the night and I expect a full course dinner and a man-sized breakfast."

As Rebecca led him into the parlor, she realized that she had not said a word about his wife. Her voice was low and embarrassed. "How is Susannah?"

George swore he could read her mind and he was forced to bite the inside of his cheeks to keep from laughing out loud. "Susannah is fine!" She was going to be elated when George told her about Rebecca and the girl's reaction to his visit. "Quint did mention that you two agreed to a visit as soon as he returns. Susannah is looking forward to that."

George was tempted to tell Rebecca just why Susannah was so looking forward to the visit, but he decided that Quint would not be pleased with his brother-in-law's attempt at match-making. No, Quint would have to do his own courting. "Well, young lady, if I'm to carry out the checking up I've agreed to, I suppose I'd better talk to John and Sam."

Rebecca smiled at him, "I'll send for them and you can talk in the study while I prepare your room." She led him into the study, comforted beyond measure. Quint was all right. She never thought to wonder how George arrived in the morning, when it took all day to travel from his farm to Quint's.

George spent several hours with John and then toured the stable and the fields, and met with the other workers before dinner. Hilda's dinner late that afternoon was a masterpiece, even though she complained bitterly that he didn't give her much time to prepare something special. After the meal, he insisted that Hilda join them at the table, something she usually refused to do. He looked so serious that Hilda forgot about the argument on her lips and brought her own coffee cup to the table. When she was seated, George explained one of the reasons he came when he did: "There's a group of young Indians, probably renegades, that have been raiding nearby again. They appear to be after horses and livestock. It's a small raiding party, and a few shots have been exchanged, but they don't do the usual damage." His voice was confident.

Rebecca's face lost all of its color. "Usual damage?" she whispered, her voice unsteady.

"Larger groups, sixteen or more, usually burn the farm and kill or capture those who are unfortunate enough to be around. But we haven't had those kinds of raids in several years now." He patted Rebecca's hand, "We have a well in our kitchen area just as you do. If a large raiding party should ever come, get to that well as fast as you can and bar the door. No matter what you hear or smell, you stay there for at least twelve hours." His voice carried a stern quality that Rebecca had never heard before and she knew that he was deadly serious.

His face relaxed as he continued, "Now this particular group is a very small raiding party and from reports, they are very young. Don't worry. John's boy, Clem, will move in to the classroom behind the kitchen. I've cancelled classes for a week, just in case, and Sam is moving in with Clem until the danger is past. If they come this far east, and I doubt they will, I don't want Sam in the barn. If they come, let them take the horses and don't do anything foolish. No guns! I've already told the boys, no shooting." George glanced over at Rebecca's ashen face, "I really don't think they'll come. But, I had to prepare you just in case."

She looked so terrified that for a moment George feared she might faint. "Rebecca, they raid for horses and cattle, two or three times a year. They don't do much except take a horse or two and as many cattle. Don't worry yourself sick. I'm so unconcerned that I plan to go back to my farm tomorrow. If I was really upset, I'd take you and Hilda back to my farm. I just wanted you to know that if they come, you stay out of their way and don't do anything foolish."

Rebecca thought about the Indians that night as she prepared for bed. She would be simply too terrified to do a thing. George didn't have to worry about her doing something foolish, she'd probably collapse, she'd be so frightened.

The household was up early and George enjoyed the huge breakfast he requested. He was enjoying his third cup of coffee when horse hooves crushed on the drive. He hurried to join the group on horseback waiting for him at the front of the house. He told the women not to worry, assuring them that he would be back in about four weeks, "If you need anything, send Sam." He planted a healthy kiss on Rebecca's cheek, told her to be good and rushed out to join the small group of travelers. Later that morning, Sam, and then Clem, brought their pallets to the classroom and the farm settled back into a tense routine.

At the end of two days, Rebecca started to relax. George had said, over and over, that the savages probably wouldn't even come this far east. She went to bed that night content that her fear was for naught.

Early the next morning, a blood-curdling yell startled Rebecca from sleep. She grabbed for her robe and raced to the first floor, positive that her worst fears would be enacted before her eyes. As she ran for the kitchen she was conscious of the noise of several horses and riders in the back. The tableau before her eyes looked like a museum painting. Sam and Clem were kneeling beside the kitchen door, rifles against their shoulders. Seven saddleless horses were moving toward the barn. The figures on the horses were bronzed by the sun and seemed bent on destroying silence forever with their howls and yells. They wore leggings and their black hair stuck up from the center of their heads like the comb of a cock. One of the riders had several feathers sticking out from his top knot.

Suddenly the picture took on the appearance of a nightmare. The crack of the rifles exploded above the din and Rebecca screamed and fell to her knees. The savage with the feathers threw up his arms and fell forward on his horse, then slowly slid down the glistening flank to the ground. Rebecca gathered herself into a standing position and then dashed for Sam and Clem. "Don't shoot, let them have the horses, don't shoot." Both boys watched as the remaining Indians raced for the woods to the west, followed by the riderless horse. With no thought to her own safety, Rebecca raced to the injured savage who lay several yards from the barn. She didn't hear Sam yelling at her until she sank to her knees near the fallen man.

"No! Miss Rebecca, no! Don't go near him. Don't do it, no!"

Rebecca knelt beside the Indian and looked down into his unconscious face. He couldn't be very old, perhaps seventeen or eighteen at the most. His shoulder was covered with blood and a dark red stain spread across his naked chest and ran down into the earth. Rebecca pulled the knife he held in a death grip from his hand and tossed it behind her. She saw the two boys standing just behind her, their rifles trained on the fallen savage. "Put those guns down, both of you," she snapped. "You weren't supposed to shoot any of them. There were to be no guns at all. Put them down," she shouted.

"What you gonna do?" Clem asked hesitantly.

Sam, older and feeling at the moment proud of himself, for he was sure his bullet had felled the savage, raised his gun, "Kill 'im, of course."

"No!" Rebecca shouted at him as she reached for the gun. "This boy is hurt and you're not going to kill an unconscious human being, Indian or not."

Both boys stood as still as death, and Clem voiced his concern in a frightened whisper, "What ya gonna do?"

"You leave me little choice. I'll have to patch him up," she barked, furious now that they had disobeyed George's specific order.

"Let 'im die," came Sam's low growl.

"And have the rest of the tribe here for our blood? No! I'll see to his wounds until he's strong enough to join his tribe. This is your fault, Sam," she scolded. "Perhaps if I can get him on his feet fast enough, we won't be burned out by his vengeful family." She calmly picked herself up and turned to the boys who were only now realizing there might be a great deal of truth in what she just said. "Let's get him into the house and the sitting room. Clear everything out of the room so we don't have to worry about him trying to injure himself or us, until he recovers and we can send him home."

Sam was not convinced. "I'm not touchin' no Injun."

"Oh, yes you are, and you're going to help me in the sitting room as well," she said with a confidence she didn't feel. She was remembering the tales of horror she heard on the way to Philadelphia the year before.

They got the Indian to the sitting room, then cleared everything out of the room except a table and a chair. Rebecca had Sam bring a pallet from the barn while she got her herbs and gathered the utensils she needed to get the bullet out of the Indian's shoulder. Hilda came to the door of the room, once, her mouth in a tight line and her face white. "Do you know what you do?" she spit the words out at Rebecca from between her clenched teeth.

Rebecca replied, "I've not time to argue with you now. Tell Sam I want one of those boys in the room with me at all times." She looked up from her preparations and smiled weakly at Hilda. "I'll be careful. Now, get one of the boys, please."

Both boys arrived quickly, and Rebecca announced that she was ready. "I have to get the ball out of his shoulder. You'll both have to hold him."

She worked for a long time, but the Indian never

regained consciousness. After she found and removed the ball, she cleaned the wound and sighed, "That takes care of that." She placed the prepared poultice over the hole in the boy's chest, bound it in place and stood up, "He's lost a lot of blood, but with sufficient care, I think he'll recover."

Rebecca sat with the Indian and late in the afternoon, as he tossed and turned in his pain-filled dreams, she confessed to Sam her greatest fear, "If his family or those friends of his return, they'll burn us out before they let anyone explain. Do you know if any of these Indians speak English?" Sam only glared back at her. He thinks I am a troublesome foreigner, she thought.

Rebecca stayed with the youth through the night and into the next day. The fever she knew would come, brought incoherent mumbles in a language Rebecca had never heard. She bathed him and forced liquids through his parched lips. Sam or Clem stood uneasily just inside the room at all times, relieving each other frequently. The door was locked, a precaution that Hilda had insisted upon. As Rebecca watched the boy toss and turn in his delirium she smiled to herself. He wouldn't have the strength to even reach the door, let alone try to open it. Sometimes, she decided, Hilda made too much of a fuss.

For four days the brave writhed and his fever raged. Rebecca slept little but spent most of her time bathing him down with water, changing the herbs on his shoulder and spooning clear broth between his lips. Hourly, one of the boys reported back to her that there were no signs of any other visitors, welcome or not. The one thing she feared was that other members of the boy's tribe would return for him before he was well enough to tell them that she had done him no harm.

When Rebecca rested, Hilda joined Sam and Clem in the sitting room. Together, they decided that no one, not even John, should know what Rebecca had done. No one must know about the Indian Miss Rebecca was caring for in the house. Hilda said many silent prayers that George would not return to check on them when he heard that the Indians were in their area, until the Indian died or left. She made no bones about the fact that she personally didn't care what happened to the injured brave.

On the afternoon of the fifth day, the fever broke and Rebecca awakened from a nap in her chair to find herself staring into a pair of wide, dark eyes. For perhaps a second, Rebecca thought she saw fear, then his expression became unreadable, and as she went about checking his wound and preparing something for him to drink, she talked to him. Quietly, she told him that she was taking care of him until he could travel, then he would be set free to return to his people. As Rebecca started talking, Clem who stood against the door grew tense, but Rebecca said, "He's come around. Don't try anything."

In the next three days, Rebecca cared for the Indian, feeding him, changing his bandage, and helping him move around the room. As she worked she talked to him, but he gave no sign of recognition and she decided that he either didn't understand her, or didn't want to hear her. By the end of the eighth day, Rebecca said quietly, "Tomorrow, you can leave. If you're careful, you should be able to get home."

The next morning, Sam and Clem escorted the Indian from the house where Sam had one of Quint's old nags waiting. They helped him up onto the back of the horse and Rebecca smiled as calmly as she could and said goodbye politely. The Indian moved the horse forward several steps and then turned around so that he faced Rebecca. He spoke slowly, but in nearly perfect English, "You gave Crying Wolf his life. He owes you your life."

Rebecca stood stunned. He could speak and understand English. She tried to remember all the things she said to him. As he turned to ride away, Rebecca sighed. Perhaps it was just as well that he could understand English. He must have known that she would turn him out of the house to travel home, when he was well enough. But his words, "He owes you your life," made no sense to her.

She shrugged her shoulders and moved back to the house. He was gone and Sam, Clem, and finally Hilda said good riddance. None of the neighbors found out and they succeeded in keeping Rebecca's doctoring from the others on the farm. Slowly the farm returned to normal. No more Indians were reported and there were no other signs of Indians around the farm. The classes started again, and Rebecca tried to forget her brush with a savage.

July faded slowly into August and once again George came to check. "No news is good news," he told her when she asked if they had heard from Quint. To her questions about Susannah, George smiled, "She is blooming. She can hardly wait for Quint to return and for the two of you to come visit."

Sam, Clem, and Hilda all agreed that the Indians came, took a horse, and left. George seemed satisfied with their version and asked only a minimum of questions. The only real difference in the household was Hilda. She had been sullen since the morning of the attack. Daily, she cornered Rebecca, "When Mr. McQuade come, I tell. No one else I tell. But him, from Hilda he find out about the savage and what you do."

Rebecca followed her established routine. In the morning she worked with the children in the classroom and in the afternoons, she worked on the dwindling pile of Quint's shirts or planned the lessons for the next day. As she worked, the return of Quint and her relationship with him occupied most of her waking moments. She lectured herself, denied her feelings, gritted her teeth and started again. She would not, could not, be his mistress. Oh, there was no question. She would love him forever, but she would never tell him that, and she would never find herself in his arms again. Even if they did live in the same house, and she was bonded to him by that piece of paper, somehow, she would stay away from him.

Word of the classes spread to the other farms and early in August, the two oldest children from one of the nearby farms crowded into the classroom. She worked hard trying to cover as much with all of the children as she could before classes were called to a halt for the harvest.

However, by the middle of August, the children were needed at home and Rebecca admitted that Hilda needed her help as well. Classes were cancelled and Rebecca went to work with a solemn Hilda. They were so busy that Hilda stopped reminding Rebecca that she intended to tell Quint about the Indian. Rebecca forgot about the episode.

After several days in the kitchen with Hilda, John came to fetch her. His youngest boy had been picking pears and fallen out of the tree. John was sure his arm was broken and Rebecca, John said quietly, was the only one he would trust to care for the child. She added the responsibility of the boy to her busy schedule, spending an hour or two with him each day. While Bette went about the near frantic work of preserving their food, Rebecca and the boy read.

As she worked, Rebecca thought continually about Quint and his arrival in two or three weeks. He said the middle of September and August was ending quickly. She missed him terribly and admitted that she would be overjoyed when he returned. Of course, she would have to stay out of his way, and very definitely, out of his arms. But, at least she would know that he was safe. She intended to serve out her full indenture time and she made some painful decisions about her own future. With her experience, she decided that she would open a classroom in Philadelphia like the one she had here on the farm. Her future would be spent in educating children. Constantly, she fought a tiny voice that kept whispering to her, "You love him. Let him love you in return, let him take you in his arms and make you feel like a woman again. It's what you want."

For a short time, she even considered returning to England. But she knew that, no matter what, she couldn't go back to Arthur. He would only sell her again. She was no longer a virgin and she was sure her worth was not great. Any husband that her brother could find would be worse than the life she had planned for herself. With her decisions made, she waited breathlessly for Quint, dreading the day he returned.

She took to traveling on foot to John's cottage, simply because Sam wasn't available often to hitch up the wagon. She made better time through the fields, anyway, she told herself. Late one afternoon, as she plodded home, she reviewed her careful plans. There were two more days in August and then, two or three weeks in September, before Quint would return to try her resolve. She brushed away a tear, he probably wasn't even interested in her anymore.

She glanced at the sun. Her charge had taken to reading to her and he'd done so well this day, she forgot the time. She was very late and Hilda would be angry with her again. She frowned. Hilda was always angry with her over one thing or another lately. Well, perhaps when Quint returned, Hilda's disposition would improve as well. She strolled on in the warm August sun.

Chapter Twenty-one

As Rebecca neared the barn yard, she saw Sam leading three horses toward the entrance of the stable. One carried a saddle and was covered with foam, as if he had been ridden long and hard. Another horse carried several packs on his back and he was foaming at the mouth. A third horse, a beautiful young mare, with a chestnut coat was wet with sweat although she carried nothing. Sam wore an expression that chilled her to the core. Before she had a chance to wonder about the horses, he raised his hand to push her out of his way, "Quint's back and Hilda told 'em. We are in big trouble. You an' your damn healin' ways."

Rebecca stood paralyzed, Quint was back, but it wasn't even September yet. She wanted to dash into the house and throw herself into his arms, but the scowl on Sam's face urged caution. As she started toward the back door, she stopped, unable to think for a second. She took a deep breath and scolded herself. For the better part of two months she had been telling herself that at all costs she must avoid him and the instant she learned he had returned, she pitched all her advice through the holes in her head. Then again, she thought, as she tiptoed forward, if he was as angry as Sam seemed to think he was, she might find it easy to stay out of his way. In fact, maybe she should not see him at all for awhile. Tears welled up in her eyes as she dragged herself around the kitchen and the back door of the house.

She was just past the kitchen door, when Hilda stuck her head out the open door and glared. "In his study, he waits. Angry with you he is!"

Rebecca lowered her eyes and wondered where she could hide. Hilda looked furious enough to drag her into the house. She panicked. She couldn't see him now.

With a glance back over her shoulder to see if Hilda would force her forward, Rebecca made it through the dining room and to the open doorway of the study. She stood before the space for several seconds. Quint's back was to the door and he leaned against the fireplace mantle, his body supported by the oak beam. He seemed deep in thought and she was loath to disturb him. Just the sight of his broad back caused her heart to flutter in her chest and her resolve was threatened once more.

She tried to decide how best to enter the room. Should she knock and wait for him to tell her to enter, just walk in, or knock and then walk into the study? She decided on the latter and tapped on the door. Before she took a step, Quint swung around and gazed at her. Carefully she watched, trying to understand the emotions that she saw on his face. She thought she saw pleasure, pride, desire and anger, but the anger remained as he took a step toward her.

"Woman, do you know what you did?" his angry words brushed over her. The tears that were forming before she reached the house, slid down her pale cheeks. She lifted her arms in a gesture of pleading and opened her mouth to answer his charge, but the words would not come. Quint covered the distance in three steps and pulled her into his arms, holding her tightly. He muttered against her hair, "How I've missed you!" Tilting her head up and gazing into her teary eyes, he ordered in a husky voice, "Don't you ever befriend a savage again." He hugged her tightly, and whispered against her ear, "If you do, you and I will have a session that neither one of us will ever forget." He pushed her away from him so that he could look into her yes. "Do you understand me?" She nodded her head as she clung to him but her confusion was obvious.

He tilted her head back and slowly lowered his lips to hers. As she returned his kiss with all the spirit she wanted desperately to deny, her world careened around her. He was back and she was nestled in his strong arms, safe and secure once more. Even though he was angry with her, a great warmth filled her and she forgot every lecture she gave herself. Instead of moving away, as she promised herself she would, she struggled to get closer to him and to fit her slender body into his larger muscular one. Suddenly, she felt him tense and then push her away. She opened her eyes and looked up at him in surprise.

As if he could read the unasked question in her eyes, he muttered softly, his husky voice trembling ever so slightly, "If you keep kissing me like that, I won't be able to control myself."

He took her hand and led her to the couch, then waited for her to sit. He sat down next to her and taking both of her hands in his larger ones, he sat there staring at her. She could read the naked desire in his large blue eyes and she lowered her head, knowing that the warmth she felt was a vivid blush. Quint let loose of her hands and placed one arm around her shoulders. With the other hand he held her chin up so that she was forced to look into his eyes. He gazed at her solemnly as he said, "I did miss you terribly, you know. Did you miss me?"

She closed her eyes, afraid he could read more than she wanted to tell him and trying to turn her head away, she wondered how she could admit to him that every day dragged by without him. She couldn't tell him that and not admit that she loved him. There was only one course of action for her. She said nothing.

Quint was hurt. Her kiss told him what he wanted to know, but she obviously was not going to tell him. He mused to himself that with everything that happened to her and the way he had just greeted her, she was probably having second thoughts about his affection. He had at least another six weeks before he left again. Now was not the time to push her.

"Tell me about the Indian," he pulled away from her and rearranged himself more comfortably on the couch. That should distract them both.

She explained what happened, how the Indian was shot and what she did to care for the boy. He questioned her about the number of Indians in the raiding party and what George said. He quizzed her about any signs of a return by the savages and if any people other than the household knew of her care of the brave. She tried to answer his questions, but the concern over what the others knew brought her own anger to the fore. "Why is everyone in this house so concerned about what the neighbors think? He was hurt, and all I did was take care of his wound."

Quint patiently tried to explain about the period between the death of William Penn and the War. He told her all about the fifties and the sixties when there were abuses on both sides. Then he told her about the massacre at Wyoming in '78 and some of the problems with marauding bands of Indians venturing into the more populated areas for slaves. "People right now are not too happy with Indians. Everyone around here has a relative or friend that was captured or killed by one tribe or another. We're trying to make peace with most of the tribes, but nothing has come of it. You helped one of the enemy, so to speak." He sighed and then asked about the classes and how the children were doing with their skills. He seemed very pleased when she told him about the two children from the neighboring farm who were coming to classes. She started to ask about his trip when Hilda, still looking grim, came to the door to announce dinner.

The meal was very quiet. Rebecca and Quint were silent as they both tried to sort through their thoughts. Quint wondered about her failure to answer his question. Fearing that he misread their last night together, he swallowed over a tight lump in his throat. Only her kiss gave him any hope, for it was full of want and he was sure she could not have feigned that. While Quint was trying to analyze Rebecca's reaction to his homecoming, she was busy trying to remember all the words of her daily lectures with herself. She was ashamed of the way she threw herself in his arms the minute he walked up to her and she fought a constant battle with herself over her prospect for a future with him. She kept reminding herself that a life with him meant heartache. She would be truly lost when he set her aside.

After dinner, Quint asked her to join him in the study for coffee and tea, but she told him it had been a very hard day and she needed her sleep. She escaped to her room quickly, but then she spent hours pacing back and forth. Nothing would have pleased her more than to run to his arms, but she had no assurance that he felt anything but desire for her. If she gave in, she alone would be hurt.

Below her Quint paced his study, trying to decide if she truly felt something for him. She didn't want to spend time with him after supper, and that worried him. She hadn't responded to his question about missing him, and that bothered him, too. He didn't buy her excuse that it was a hard day. She almost made it sound like his return had made the day a hard one. He decided that he could not formally propose to her until he was certain that she held him in her affections. Angry now, he stomped off to bed.

Rebecca gave up trying to get some sleep shortly after dawn the next morning. She had tossed and turned all night, but her resolve was still tenuous at best. She struggled into her clothes and when she got to the dining room, part of her was relieved that Quint had already had his breakfast and was in the field with John. Rebecca's face showed the strain of her sleepless night. Dark circles underlined her black eyes, but she went about her work with a vengeance. Hilda kept her comments to herself, she had already argued with Quint over dinner.

Afternoon came and Quint and Rebecca sat across from each other at the table, but there was a strain in the conversation that had not been there the night before. When Quint asked her if she would join him in the study after dinner, she again refused, using the excuse that she didn't feel well and needed to rest. Quint was in turn worried, then disgusted, and finally angry. Each afternoon for three days, Quint asked to speak to her but she firmly gave him one excuse after another. He was livid.

Everyone in the household felt his sharp mood. Rebecca spent the last two days cloistered in her room, but others were not so fortunate. She heard him railing at each in turn. He yelled at Sam for not exercising the horses and then for exercising them too much. Angrily, John left the house one day after lunch. Rebecca heard them shouting but she couldn't understand what they were yelling about. Finally, Hilda plodded up to Rebecca's room.

Hilda didn't even give Rebecca a chance to answer her knock. She forced the door open and shuffled into the room. "That man! This whole house, he is upsetting. I think back to the boat he should go!" Angry words spewed from her lips.

Rebecca tried to be consoling. "What has he done to you?"

"My biscuits, he say they are *too* tender. Fall apart, they do when the butter he puts on. Of course, the butter he puts on like he is trying to beat them up. For sure, they come apart if attacks them, he does." Hilda looked at Rebecca, the sparks flying from her eyes. "Because you not talk, he angry. Tonight, you talk. When study, he say, you say yes!" She folded her large arms and glared at Rebecca.

"No!" Rebecca cried. "I can't talk to him. I have to stay away from him."

Hilda gazed at Rebecca in surprise, "Why you have to stay away from him? You he likes. Plans he wants to make with you."

"I don't want to be included in the kind of plans he has. He can just find himself another mistress!" Her eyes sparkled with tears and her voice was full of pain.

"Hilda her mouth she promised to keep shut, but not now!" she mumbled more to herself than to Rebecca. "How do you know his mistress he wants you to be? Did he say mistress?" she hissed.

Rebecca stood very still for a moment, then she whispered, "But, he said he wanted me to . . ." How had he worded his request? She had been so sure that he asked her to live with him without vows between them. She couldn't have misinterpreted his remarks!

Hilda gave her no more time for reflection, but grabbed her arms and started dragging her from the room, "Maybe, talk to him, you do now, before the meal."

Rebecca pulled away. "I can't talk to him, not about that. I can't see him like this," she pointed to her calico dress. "I must freshen up," she whispered.

Hilda's face wrinkled into a determined frown. "Five minutes. Five minutes I give you. If the stairs you don't come down, back up I be." She stomped off down the stairs mumbling as she went.

Rebecca tore out of the calico dress and pulled on a green silk before she brushed her ebony hair then tied it back with a ribbon of matching silk. She splashed water on her face and dried with a cloth. After a quick perusal in her mirror, she sighed. There was nothing she could do with the dark circles under her eyes. Afraid that Hilda would march back to her bedroom, she stole down the steps to the sitting room to wait until dinner. She needed to collect her thoughts and she had to remember what Quint said to her about living at the farm. Hilda seemed to be so positive that he was asking her something else. But he never indicated a permanent relationship. What was she to think? Hilda was wrong, she had to be wrong.

She went into the dining room and sat down across from Quint. He glared at her for a moment and then said firmly, "We will talk after dinner this night, Mistress Ranserford, if I have to drag you into the study by your hair."

Rebecca glanced at the dark blue eyes that crackled with authority, and swallowed quickly. She looked down at her table setting. "Yes, Mr. McQuade," she answered softly. Quint glared at her but neither one of them said another word through the long painful meal.

The clang of the tableware against the pewter plates and the banging of the tankards on the wodden surface of the table resounded through the whole room. Before Hilda cleared the table and served dessert, Quint got up from his chair and walked to Rebecca's place. As he pulled out her chair, he turned to Hilda, "We'll have our coffee and tea in the study."

He grabbed Rebecca's arm none too gently and dragged her toward the door of the dining room. He shoved her to the study. She tried to move with some grace, but as he yanked her toward the door, she almost lost her balance. She did lose her temper.

"I said I would come and I agreed to talk, but I will go to my room if you drag me another step!" she snapped as he pulled her toward the door. She might as well have saved her breath. He paid her no attention at all and pulled her around to one of the leather chairs before the fireplace. Putting both his hands on her shoulders he tried to push her into the chair, but she sat down of her own accord and stared up at him. Some of her anger dissolved, and fear took its place. He looked furious!

Quint moved directly in front of the fireplace and stood staring at the empty hearth. After a minute or two, he spun around almost as if he expected to see her trying to leave the room. She was much too afraid to move. He was very angry and she really didn't know why.

After what felt like an hour, Quint turned around and clasped his arms behind his back. He squinted at the buckles on his shoes. "I want some answers to several questions, Mistress Ranserford, and I want them tonight, before you leave this room." Just then, Hilda entered the room with the coffee and tea. She placed the tray where he indicated and then she ran from the room. Rebecca watched her go and thought to herself that she had never seen Hilda move so fast. After the cook had flown from the room, Rebecca sneaked a glance at Quint. An enormous scowl cut into his face. No wonder Hilda left so quickly she thought.

She waited several more minutes, hoping that he would

at least pour the coffee or tea or suggest that she do it, but even that action did not provide the respite she sought. Quint just stared at her. Finally, he cleared his throat and said "I want the truth, no matter how you think it will affect either you or me. Is that understood?"

Rebecca only nodded her head. He looked so stern and foreboding that she wanted to follow Hilda's example and run from the room. Only the threat he issued her at dinner about dragging her into the study by her hair kept her in her seat.

Once more, Quint cleared his throat and turned back to the empty fireplace. "I want to know how you feel . . . about . . . about me." His head was lowered and Rebecca began to wonder if he stopped breathing. Still she hesitated, he wanted the truth, but she didn't think she could tell him the truth. It was very obvious that he was not going to allow her to say nothing. She couldn't admit that she had fallen madly in love with him until he gave her some hint as to his feelings. "Well," he spun around and glared at her again, as he waited for an answer.

She looked down at her hands and twisted her fingers together. "I . . . I care . . . I am. . . . I am . . . fond of you," she managed in a whisper. Her throat felt like it had closed up completely.

"Only fond?" he said.

"I . . . care for you a great deal," she murmured in an even softer tone, and tears began forming in her eyes.

Quint moved then and crouched in front of her chair before she could blink. "Then why in the hell have you been avoiding me? I told you we would talk when I came home and I certainly can't talk to you when you dash off every time I get near you!"

He sounded angry again, but his eyes seemed to be pleading with her. He put his hands on her arms and moved until his face was only an inch or two from hers. "Rebecca," he said tenderly, "I want you to be my wife. Do you care enough about me to marry me?"

Rebecca blinked several times. She was stunned. Marriage! She had not even considered marriage. He was joking, of course. She was a bondslave, and he couldn't marry a bondslave.

Quint waited and watched for several minutes, but she just sat there staring at him. He stood up to counteract the dive his heart took as he watched her. His eyes spoke eloquently of anger, confusion, hope and fear. Rebecca found her voice and whispered soulfully, "You can't marry a bondslave. What will your sisters say?"

He looked down at her anguish, "I don't give a damn what my sisters say. I'm not asking my sisters, I'm asking you. Will you marry me? Yes or no?"

"Yes!" Rebecca whispered. "Yes, I'll marry you," her voice now strong and happy. A sigh escaped Quint and he leaned back over the chair to kiss her gently. She slid her arms around his neck and he stood without withdrawing from the kiss. He pulled her into his arms and she melted against him. Quint broke away, and took a deep breath. He smiled down at her in relief, "My sisters will all love you, but even if they don't, it won't matter. I answer to no one."

Quint lowered his lips to hers and kissed her so tenderly that she thought her heart would explode. Then he guided her to the couch. "How am I ever going to stay away from you?" he said.

She tensed and Quint followed her thoughts. "Why did you stay away from me?" he asked softly. "You wouldn't talk to me. I think I went a little mad. We could have had this settled days ago."

Rebecca blushed and looked away to stare at the empty fireplace he found so fascinating before. Her voice was thin and quiet with embarrassment, "I thought you wanted something other than marriage from me."

Quint laughed, "You and Hilda. She told me months ago that you would never by my mistress. Is that what you thought I wanted?" Rebecca nodded her head and looked back at him. "Rebecca," his voice caressed her softly, "If I made you my mistress, you could tire of me and leave me for someone else. I want you always."

Rebecca sucked in her breath and stared up at him. He

had just said he loved her, even if he hadn't spoken the words. She smiled and leaned into him, happier than she had ever been before in her life. She turned her face up to his and he responded to taking her lips gently.

Quint set her away from him and stared down into her liquid brown eyes. "I think," he tried to calm his husky voice, "It's time for coffee."

Chapter Twenty-two

Rebecca poured coffee and tea, then cuddled up next to Quint on the couch. "First," Quint said taking a sip of coffee, "We must decide when we want to go south. I want to tell Susannah and George about the wedding and there's time to visit before the harvest."

Rebecca frowned and moved away from him, still a little hesitant. "When did you want to have this wedding?" she said softly.

Quint gave her a half smile. "I wasn't going to say anything yet, Rebecca, but I have one last trip to London to make. I have to leave in November. We can be married in February, right after I get home."

Rebecca looked at him, concern shadowing her eyes, "I thought that the sea was rather vicious in the winter."

"It is, but I'll not wait until spring. I have sound ships and skilled sailors. Storms shouldn't cause too much trouble."

Rebecca tried to smile, but a chill rushed through her that she couldn't explain. However, he was confident and he had been sailing for many years. He should know what the ocean could do in winter. She tried to relax. "You'll be back in February?"

"The earlier, the better," he grinned. "At the most, three and a half months. I'll take my ship over and return on a vessel that will be loaded and waiting to sail. I'll spend whatever time I need in London arranging things with my agent. Then, I'll sail right after Christmas. I have a feeling Susannah and George will want you to spend

Christmas there, and there are the classes and plans for the wedding. You won't even miss me."

"Yes, I will!" She glanced at him, her curiosity piqued. "I didn't know you had an agent in London."

"I've employed the fellow for several years now, but he never had much to do. I went over nearly every year. However, from now on the poor man will earn his money."

Rebecca looked up from her cup, puzzled. "Is business that good?"

"Yes, business is that good. I'm building two more ships. That makes seven all told. The man will have to do the work I've been doing. I won't be taking any more trips to England, at least not for business. I know that I'll miss you too much."

Rebecca blushed, then chuckled softly, "I'll bet you were a tyrant on this last trip."

"Not quite. At the time, I didn't know that you were not going to talk to me when I got home."

She turned a brighter shade of pink still, "But, I thought . . ."

"I know, love. I hold myself responsible for that misunderstanding. I should have made my proposal clear. And, that reminds me. I promised you something before I left." He strode over to his desk and took a packet of papers from the top half of the desk. "Here," he handed her the papers.

She recognized them immediately and her face paled. Carefully, she opened the packet and stared down at her signed contract. Quint had written across the face "Paid in full," and it was dated May 31, 1790, the day Quint left for the trip to the Caribbean. "I don't understand. The date . . ." she murmured.

Quint smiled at her. "I did that so that if something happened to me, you'd be free. I told George. He would have seen that you got them. So you see, my love, I'm not marrying a bondservant after all." Quint urged her to her feet, and kissed her gently. "You had best retire so you can get rid of those dark circles. Why, Susannah will accuse me of . . ." he stopped abruptly and under his bronzed skin Rebecca was sure she saw a blush. "I'll see you in the morning," he pushed her toward the door, his voice husky. Rebecca smiled up at him, he was trying hard to mask his desire. In that instant, she loved him all the more.

Raising herself up on her toes, she pulled his head down to hers. She kissed him softly on the lips, murmured, "Good night," and floated through the door.

Quint ambled over to the decanter in the corner of the room and poured himself a hefty glass of rum. He took several large swallows before his hands stopped shaking. He was in for a devil of a time trying to stay away from her. Just the thought of her possible rejection of his proposal had almost made him forgo their talk. He slouched down in a large leather chair. He never thought he would fall so completely in love. There had been little love visible between his mother and father, but then there was George and Susannah.

He thought about the trip to England. Winter was definitely not the best time to be in the Atlantic, but he was confident that what he told Rebecca was fact. His ships were sea-worthy and his crews some of the best men available. Those two facts were reason for the increase in business. But, with a wife like Rebecca at home, he had no desire for more travel. Business was excellent. After this last trip, he didn't really need to sail the seas. He could get married and enjoy his beautiful young wife. In time, they would start their family, a son or two and perhaps a black-haired daughter, like her mother.

He finished his rum and wandered through the main floor of the darkened house. The house was in good shape, but perhaps he should tell Rebecca to redecorate. He started up the stairs to his room. Hilda would have to be told and he wondered if the older woman was fond of children. Smiling slightly, he walked to his own chamber, trying very hard not to pause at Rebecca's door. He sighed as he opened his door. He could wait. Stretching out on the soft feather ticks, he wondered at his contentment, and drifted into a peaceful sleep.

Early the next morning, Quint strolled into the kitchen and Hilda took one look and knew that all was well in Quint McQuade's world. He ambled over to the hearth, poured out a cup of coffee and turned to face the friendly cook. "Do you like children, Hilda?" he said impishly.

She glanced up at him from her task and her surprise turned to anger for one second. Quint followed her line of thinking. "Now, wait a minute before you give me a tongue lashing. Rebecca and I are going to be married in February when I return from England. Nobody's having children now. I was curious, that's all.

Hilda smiled at him with what Quint thought was the broadest smile he had ever seen. "Married, you gonna be? Thank God! And children I love." She bristled slightly, "Married, I not be, but children I love."

Before Quint finished his coffee, Rebecca was at his side. Shyly, she glanced at Hilda, and the smile the cook bestowed on her was, if possible, even broader. "He told you, didn't he?"

Hilda nodded her head and left her work to embrace Rebecca and kiss her affectionately. "And," she chuckled, "Already, children he is mentioning." She laughed out loud. It was hard to determine who blushed a brighter red, Rebecca or Quint. Rebecca giggled a bit herself and followed Quint to the dining room for breakfast.

The next days flew by. Hilda was told about the trip to the Beal residence that would take place at the end of the week. Hilda refused to go, saying, "Leave my kitchen, I will not!"

Quint informed the families that classes were cancelled until further notice. After her angry objections, he explained to Rebecca, "I'm not about to share you with someone's children when I only have two and a half months. Harvest will take three weeks as it is." Rebecca quit arguing with him. The children were all needed at home for weeks after harvest.

For two days Rebecca packed for the trip to Susannah's. She folded the gowns that she had never worn into her trunk, smiling at Quint's excesses. He told her about his business successes and she smiled warmly. It was a good thing, she thought, as she smiled at his generosity. The day of the trip dawned bright and clear. The weather had been warm for mid-September, but this day was more than comfortable, Rebecca thought, as she checked her new dark brown traveling suit in the mirror above her washstand. She tucked the exquisite lace stole around her shoulders and under her jacket and adjusted the pearls she wore, another gift from Quint.

Trying to shake her embarrassment at meeting George and Susannah now that she and Quint were to be married, she thought about the trip. What would Quint's relatives say about their marriage? After all, she was his bondservant. He marked her papers paid in full to please her, but she was still bound to him no matter what he said. They were living together in the same house, too. That would surely cause gossip. True, Hilda was in attendance but that had not stopped them before. . . . She blushed at the train of her thoughts. A quick knock on the door drew her from her reverie and she grabbed her matching brown purse and opened the door.

"Downstairs, he be waiting to go. Are you together?" Hilda asked impatiently.

Rebecca smiled at Hilda's choice of words. "I'm together," she answered softly and made her way down the steps to an equally impatient Quint. As he guided her out the door to the waiting carriage, he gave final instructions to Hilda and they were quickly off. Sam drove the carriage and Quint sat beside Rebecca, pointing out places of interest as the carriage traveled the road to his sister's farm.

Quint and Rebecca arrived at the Beal farm by midafternoon and they were greeted by an enthusiastic group. Susannah scolded her brother for waiting two weeks before bringing Rebecca for her visit. She had a look of serenity about her that surprised Rebecca but the rounded stomach that even her gown did not cover left Rebecca speechless. George followed Rebecca's gaze, then affectionately patted the protrusion. Both women blushed.

When everyone was introduced to the young Beals, Susannah ushered her family and her guests into the kitchen. They sat around a large table and dinner was served. Rebecca was shocked that Susannah's kitchen was connected to the rest of the house, but as Susannah explained, with the cold winters in Pennsylvania, the warmth from the kitchen was more than worthwhile.

Rebecca sat next to Quint and after the meal, Quint covered her hand with his own, gave her a little squeeze and started to speak. "We have something to tell you," he began. Rebecca looked at him a little startled. He was going to tell them immediately! She missed the knowing smiles that passed between Susannah and George. "Rebecca and I will be married as soon as I get back from London," Quint said proudly.

Susannah laughed in delight and George left his place at the table and walked over to put his arms around his wife. He smiled down at Susannah and then turned a large grin in Quint's direction, "We're not surprised, you know."

Rebecca's stunned glance delighted George and he roared with laughter. "You knew?" she whispered.

Susannah answered for her husband, "We sensed the feelings you had for each other the first day we met. We felt this announcement was coming soon. We are delighted." The room burst into happy sounds with congratulations for everyone and George dragged out the barrel of rum Quint sent the Christmas before.

The week went by much too quickly. Rebecca was happier than she had ever been and she blushed frequently at both George's and Quint's teasing. The three Beal children and Rebecca began a love affair the minute they met and they hung onto every word she said. The baby, Anna, followed her around everywhere she went.

They tiny tot insisted that Rebecca tuck her into her bed each night. Rebecca had limited experience with children and Anna's obvious devotion thrilled her more than even she would admit.

Their last evening with the Beals, Susannah insisted that they talk about the arrival of the new Beal heir. The babe would probably arrive about the week after Quint left for London and Susannah admitted shyly that she would dearly love to have company right before the baby and after the birth. By the end of the meal, everyone agreed that Rebecca would return to the farm with Quint, then he would travel on to Philadelphia to sail and Rebecca would stay with Susannah and George until the child arrived. Then, she would go back to the farm and start winter classes.

The next morning Rebecca and Quint said fond goodbyes to everyone. All the way home, Rebecca was bubbly, describing her admiration of Susannah and her delight with the children and the way they accepted her. Quint sat back in the carriage listening and responding to Rebecca's happy chatter, satisfied as he never had been before and contented to the fullest. They would have a wonderful life with frequent visits between the two families. There would be children in great number, he promised Rebecca, adding, "I'm very fond of children."

They were back at the farm for less than twenty-four hours when the harvest began in earnest. Quint spent most of his time out in the fields, overseeing the workers. In excited tones, he bragged to Rebecca that the farm would see a large profit this year. "Another success story," she teased him. While Quint was in the fields, Rebecca, Hilda, Bette, and the new wife of one of the workers Quint had hired in the spring worked from sun-up to sundown to feed the army of men.

The days disappeared almost too Quickly to count and Rebecca tried to push the separation she knew was coming out of her mind. The days were so full and the work so demanding that at the close of each day, both she and

Quint crawled upstairs to their separate bedrooms, grateful that they could sleep for a few hours before the crush began again.

Then, one day the harvest was in, the extra men gone on to the next farm and Rebecca realized that in only two short weeks they would leave once more for the Beal farm and Quint would journey on, not to return for more than three months. That evening, after a late dinner, Quint sensed Rebecca's depression and asked softly, "Walk with me?"

They strolled past the maple trees at the back of the house, now decorated in the orange and red glory of a late fall, to a small stream that meandered near the woods to the west of the property. For some reason, Rebecca thought about the Indian, who had passed through these woods on his way back to his people. She hoped that he had managed to get home without further harm. Quint's conversation drew her back to the present. They talked about the trip Quint was going to make and the agent he would see in London.

They turned and started back toward the house, and Quint smiled down at her, "While I'm in London, do you want me to deliver any messages? I suppose you'll want to inform your family about the wedding."

Rebecca's eyes snapped black. "I have no messages and there's no one to inform."

Quint glanced away and back. "What kind of a ceremony do you want? I've not had much time for church services in several years, but I'll see the church official if you want. And, who do you want to invite?"

"Only your close friends, and all of the Beals, of course," Rebecca told him quietly. "I never cared much for big fancy weddings. They're too much work, and the ceremony gets lost in all of that pomp and display." Quint hugged her close. She was marvelously practical.

Just before they reached the house, Quint pulled her into his arms and kissed her resoundingly. She clung to him for countless breath-stealing kisses knowing that his control and her own were stretched almost to the breaking point. He held her tightly and reached down to caress the full flesh of her buttocks. He sighed, then whispered, "This will have to last a long time," he sighed again and added, "But, it will be worth the wait." He let her slip from his arms and they both laughed a little in their nervousness. "You sorely test my metal, woman," Quint whispered as he tugged at her black hair which hung in a fat braid down the middle of her back.

Rebecca prayed that the days would move more slowly, but there was so much to be done that they slipped by too quickly. There were just five days left before they had to leave for the Beal farm and Rebecca spent every spare minute she had packing her things for the extended visit with Susannah. The sounds of an approaching carriage disturbed the late morning calm. Quint was in the barn with John making preparations to leave. Rebecca continued with her packing. Hilda would see to the door.

Hilda opened the door to a tall handsome woman of about two score dressed in fashionable velvet. She asked to speak to quint and only to him. Her tone of voice brooked no argument and Hilda shuffled off to get the master of the house. Rebecca heard him come in from the back of the house and she quickly finished her task. She wanted to share what little time that remained with him. She forgot all about the carriage and their visitor. Rushing down the stairs she started for the study but stopped when she heard angry voices. She suddenly remembered the visitor and wondered who Quint was yelling at and why.

She started to turn to go back to her room, but she heard her name mentioned by a high-pitched female voice and she froze. The door wasn't closed completely and she stayed to hear the exchange, not even considering that she shouldn't be listening.

"Margaret, I really don't want to hear your accusations," Quint said angrily. Rebecca tried to remember if Quint had ever mentioned someone named Margaret. She couldn't.

The feminine voice laughed in a loud coarse way, "You know that you have disgraced us completely. It was bad enough that she is a bondslave, but to live out here with her in the same house. Have you no shame, man?" She didn't even pause to give him time to answer. "Why are you marrying her? Mary Jane was spouting some gibberish about mutual feelings of fondness." There was such a stress on the word fondness that Rebecca cringed. "I can't believe that. You're doing this just to spite us aren't you? What did you do, rape her and now her family is insisting that you marry her?"

"Margaret, take your filthy mouth and get out of here," his voice shook with rage.

"I'm not leaving until I've had my say. I have already talked to some of the sailors who sailed with her and their remarks were highly unflattering. You have a little slut, brother dear, and I'm not going to let you marry a whore. I'll see you dead before I let you further disgrace us like this. You got the estate that was rightfully mine, and now . . ."

Rebecca couldn't move. This was his sister?

"Get out of here!" Quint yelled, "Get out of here before I do something I may regret."

The tall woman marched from the study and glanced at Rebecca standing frozen by the door. "Harlot!" Margaret screeched. "And, a sneaky one at that." The woman hurled the words at Rebecca with such viciousness that Rebecca felt like she had been stabbed.

Quint followed his sister to the door of the study and saw Rebecca glued to the spot, her face ashen, her eyes blank, staring at nothing. For the first time in weeks they were black. Quint lurched forward two steps and reached her just as she slumped toward the floor. She was no longer aware of the hall, Quint, Margaret, or even the bright October sunlight that streamed into the house.

Margaret stood at the front entrance and watched her younger brother cradle the tiny black-haired girl in his arms and take the stairs two at a time to the second floor. As a distant door closed, her thin lips curled into a sneer. "I won't kill you brother dear, as much as I might want to, but you will never marry that piece of trash." She laughed as she made her way out the door to her waiting carriage.

Chapter Twenty-three

Margaret McQuade slumped into the carriage seat, furious with herself, but devastated by the news Quint gave her. Her own brother was marrying a strumpet and worse, a bondslave. If Mary Jane, the youngest of the three older sisters, had her facts correct, he was even madly in love with the jade. Her back straightened slightly and her face broke into a sneer. She probably handled that confrontation all wrong, but she'd lost her temper. He took the inheritance away from her and now he was going to marry and live happily ever after. She could not let that happen. There would probably be a dozen children from that kind of a union and no whore's offspring were going to get her farm. If some people got hurt as a result, then that was a shame, but he wasn't going to get the farm.

Margaret sat up and glanced out the carriage window. She was a tall attractive woman with reddish-brown hair touched with streaks of gray. She had the characteristic long straight nose of the McQuades but her chin was more pointed and her lips were thin. Her smile looked much more like a smirk than a grin. She smiled as she rested from her tiring useless journey. Now, at least she had all the facts and she needed only to put them together. Removing her hat pin, she lifted her hat from her head and let her agile mind turn the facts around and around. Slowly a plan began to form.

For months after the reading of that ridiculous will, her husband had tried every legal maneuver there was to break her mother's last testament, but it was impossible and she accepted the defeat only several weeks ago. Mary Jane returned from her latest visit to Susannah's farm. Shy mousey Mary Jane came to tea. She was the family visitor, traveling the rounds of her sisters and keeping them all informed about what was going on. The day she arrived, she was full of news. Susannah was going to have another baby, Quint was building two more ships, and he had acquired a female bondslave. He was farming between his sailing endeavors and Susannah hinted that the bondslave would become Mrs. Quinton McQuade come spring.

Margaret straightened up in the carriage. Never, came her silent scream. She felt ill just thinking about it. That woman would never be mistress in the home that should have been hers. Her original plan had been to find out all about the girl and discredit her before Quint. But she had lost her temper and Quint wasn't interested in anything she had to say. All that time and money! It had taken her the better part of two weeks to find out what she had. Mary Jane offered only one tiny bit of information, but it was at the beginning of the girl's sordid story and that was where Margaret started.

Luck was with her for the *Venture* had been in port for several weeks, with a sailing date only two days away. She met the first mate, a Mr. Landis, but the man was reluctant to discuss anything that happened on the voyage that brought Quint and Rebecca to Philadelphia. If he wouldn't talk about the voyage, then Margaret knew something unusual must have happened. She found a seaman from another vessel, a very distant relative of her husband's who remembered the voyage in question. He was only too willing to tell her about the rumored rape attempt on the girl and how the sailor had been taken ashore, half-dead, the day the *Venture* tied up. Margaret was sure there was more to the story and she retained the man with promises of gold coins if he would ply Mr. Landis with enough liquor to loosen the man's tongue.

It cost her dearly, but she got even more than she anticipated. She spent an hour with the still-grieving Rachel Hill, an old maid, with a vengeance to match Margaret's. She convinced the old woman that her husband and Mr. Hill were business acquaintances and Margaret explained smoothly that they had been out of the country and only learned of Stephen Hill's demise that very day. Both she and her husband were so sorry. Was there anything they could do? And the young widow? Rachel Hill reacted violently. Margaret verified the sailor's report and as she listened to Miss Hill rant and rave, Margaret tried not to smile. Miss Hill had much to say about the woman her brother bought. She announced that she didn't care if the chit bonded herself. It wasn't anymore than the little tart deserved. She, Rachel Hill, was not going to pay a pence to send her back to her brother.

After her visit to Rachel Hill, Margaret decided to take Elizabeth Ann into her confidence. Elizabeth Ann was the oldest and she was as upset over the will as Margaret. Elizabeth Ann was not as daring as Margaret, though. However, given the method . . . She went to see Elizabeth Ann.

It was Elizabeth Ann who found out all about Bud Worthman and Arthur Ranserford. There was much to find out. When they met for lunch, days later, Elizabeth Ann had the whole tale of Bud Worthman, at least some of his companions' version and she had the name and address of Arthur Ranserford. "In case," she told Margaret.

Margaret pursed her lips, "I don't suppose we can talk to this Bud Worthman, can we?"

Elizabeth Ann paled, "The man is in prison!"

Margaret laid out her plans to Elizabeth Ann. "The first thing is verify Mary Jane's story about the romance. I'll travel out to the farm and see for myself. If Quint has that trollop in the house, I'll find out if a wedding is planned and then I'll tell him just what kind of creature he is planning on marrying. That should end the whole thing right there."

Margaret watched the scenery pass before her eyes. She had left her home before dawn to get to the farm and then back to Philadelphia before the end of the day. Elizabeth Ann was not going to be pleased that she lost her temper. Well, she smiled to herself, Elizabeth Ann could help with her plan. She chuckled, her new idea would work beautifully. In fact, it probably would separate the young lovers permanently.

Quint took one look at Rebecca's face, her glazed eyes, and scooped her into his arms, wondering just how much of his sister's tirade she overheard. After he placed her on the bed, her eyes fluttered open and she looked up at him, confused at first, then tears filmed her eyes and she looked away.

Speaking softly, he pulled her face toward him so that he could see her eyes. "I've already told you, I don't give a fig what my sisters think. That one," he jerked his head toward the road, "is so angry with me because my mother left me this farm that she'll say anything. She's an unhappy creature and she delights in making everyone else as miserable as she is. She can't do a thing to us, unless we let her destroy what we feel for each other."

"She threatened to kill you. Your own sister wants to see you dead. Doesn't that bother you?" she whispered in disbelief.

Quint grinned. "She always was a bit dramatic." He laughed, a deep musical sound. "Don't you see, she is venting her anger at both of us. She wanted to upset you, upset you enough that you would run from me. She won't do anything, she's just making noises. Don't worry. I've had nothing to do with my older sisters for a long time now and after we marry I see no reason to change my attitude toward them. Love, don't worry, she can't hurt us." He pulled her into his arms and held her close, waiting for her tension to ease. As she relaxed, she let her head rest on his shoulder, and he tilted her head back. He wiped her tears from her face, then he kissed her gently.

After giving her instructions to finish the packing, he left to continue his own preparations for the sea voyage that he would begin in a week. Rebecca tried to continue with her packing, but Margaret's words kept pounding through her head. Finally, desperate to forget the incident, she consoled herself with the fact that Quint didn't seem to be anything but annoyed with his sister. Rebecca shook her head, this Margaret, his own sister, was very different than the sisters she'd heard about.

The day ended and Rebecca crawled into her bed exhausted and not yet convinced that Margaret was not planning to do something diabolical to her love. Morning dawned and she couldn't seem to rid herself of the feelings of despair that pressed on her. Though she tried hard to forget the previous day, the hateful words that Margaret shouted as Quint kept repeating. Rebecca knew she would never forget the savage language. Again, through dinner, Quint tried to assure her that Margaret could do nothing, but Rebecca noticed that he seemed reflective and somehow subdued. Every time she glanced at the front door, a shudder went through her, and she couldn't hide her feelings from Quint. They had been so happy, but now the reality of what she had become and what people might think of her weighed heavily on her mind. The minute Hilda cleared the service from the table, Rebecca excused herself and fled to her bed. She really hadn't accomplished much and she needed to finish her tasks. When she thought of the trip to the Beals, she smiled grimly. Susannah was going to have a lot of questions to answer.

For the first time in weeks, Rebecca felt alone and she was truly frightened. She had endured so much since her arrival in this strange country and she had convinced herself that her reward was Quint's love. Now, even though he was discounting it completely, the very life of her love was being threatened. It was more than she could bear. She was no longer a bondslave, not technically. Quint had freed her. Perhaps it would be best if she left the farm and secured a position as a tutor, as she originally planned. But all the plans she and Quint made in the moonlight nagged at her. Now she'd never be able to forget just how his touch produced the most marvelous tingling feelings and the maddening rush of her blood when his lips touched hers. How could she leave him, how could she forget their dreams?

Sitting on the floor before her trunk with small stacks of scarfs and chemises surrounding her, Rebecca laid her head down on the edge of the trunk and let the anguish she felt flow through her. The tears ran silently down her cheeks and she gave into the utter desperation she felt. She would have to leave. She could not let Margaret carry out her revenge. Quint might think it meant nothing, but Rebecca loved him too much to ignore Margaret's warning.

Quint closeted himself in the study immediately after dinner, intent on finishing the ledger that was an essential part of every voyage. All of the words and the figures seemed a jumble on the pages before him. Concern over Rebecca was wreaking havoc with the task he needed to complete before he retired. He watched her throughout dinner and instinct alone told him that she didn't believe him about Margaret and her insults. He couldn't help but notice the tiny shudders that shook her shoulders every time she looked at the front door.

He tried to force himself back to his paperwork, knowing that in time, Rebecca would see that Margaret could do nothing. But her eyes, filled with hurt and anguish, swam before him on the sheets of the ledger. He stood up in disgust. There was no way he could finish his work this night, not when the love of his life was suffering as he knew she was. He paced the room for a few minutes, amazed that the small slip of a girl completely filled his thoughts. If she ever left him he would probably never function again. He smiled to himself, even with her in the same house with him, he wasn't doing the greatest job of handling his affairs at the moment.

He left the study frowning. He would never let Margaret know what chaos she created. Damn the woman anyway! How successful she had been. He made his way up the stairs but before he walked to his room, he stopped at Rebecca's door to tell her goodnight. An unfamiliar sound disturbed him. If Margaret had made her cry . . . He clenched his fists, trying to think of a justifiable punishment. Carefully, he listened, and what he heard made him curse quietly.

Quint didn't bother to knock but pushed his way into her room. He wasn't surprised to find her sitting before her trunk, her head on her outstretched hands, sobbing as if her world had broken into fragments. Scooping her up into his arms, he sat down on her bed, and cradling her close, whispered soft words to her. He pulled his handkerchief out of his pocket and wiped at her tears. When her crying slowed, he lifted her chin and gazed into her black eyes. The pain he saw there tore at his heart. "Love, what's wrong? Why are you crying so? Surely, not because of Margaret?" he asked even though he knew that Margaret had to figure heavily into her tears.

She reached up and pulled his hand away from her chin, then looked down at her lap, twisting his handkerchief back and forth. "I can't marry you . . ." her sobs started anew. He waited for the flood that followed her words to stop once more. When she had control again, she continued, "I must find a job. I'll not be responsible for what your sister will try to do to you just because of me. I must leave . . ." her voice broke and she was crying again.

Quint sat stunned, unable to do more than hold her. Because of Margaret and her vicious tongue, Rebecca wanted to leave him. She would call off the wedding, deny her own happiness to protect him. If Margaret had been close at the moment, Quint wondered if he could have controlled himself enough to keep from hurting his own sister.

When Rebecca made an attempt to pull away from him, Quint came to his senses, "Now, you wait one minute." He tightened his hold, angry now. "Do you want to marry me? Do you still love me?"

Rebecca nodded and he relaxed a bit. "Then, there is no reason for you to leave and we *will* be married." As an idea began to take form in his mind, he started to smile and his grin grew broader and broader. He squeezed her gently, "In fact, we'll be married tomorrow afternoon," he said firmly.

Rebecca gasped, then held her breath. Tomorrow? He wasn't thinking logically at all. They couldn't be married tomorrow. "Susannah and George are expecting us in two days. We can't get married tomorrow. I told you, I won't do anything that would hurt you. I must leave," her voice trembled and Quint was afraid for a second that she would start the tears again.

"Love, listen to me! Obviously Margaret has upset you a great deal. Perhaps, she'll try to force you to leave. As frightened as you are, she might even succeed. I must go to London and there is no way I can take you with me. My men would mutiny with a beautiful woman on board." He glanced down at her confused expression, "Rebecca, do you want to marry me or not?"

She gave him a half-hearted smile, "Of course, I want to marry you, more than anything. But I don't want to be responsible for something terrible happening to you, all because of me."

Quint laughed, "Margaret wouldn't dare!" Then, he added almost to himself. "But, she might try something here. If we're already married, there's not a thing she can do." He lifted her from his lap and sat her on the mattress. "We'll leave for Susannah and George's first thing tomorrow morning. We'll be married there." He stood up. "I'll send a message to George this evening. He knows my older sisters well, and he'll understand when I get a chance to explain it all to him. Now, come on,

Sweetheart, smile! Tomorrow is your wedding day."

Quint pulled her to her feet and kissed her soundly, "Now, get packed quickly, I have messages to send and much work to do. Shall I tell Hilda? Would you like some help with your packing? You meant what you said about a big wedding, didn't you?" He fired questions at her in an excited tone and so rapidly that she didn't get a chance to respond. He was out the door before she decided which question she'd answer first.

She went to her wardrobe, pulling out several of the fancier gowns she'd planned to leave behind. Trying to decide which one she'd wear for her wedding, she took out a soft cream ball gown. She looked at it carefully. It was a beautiful gown, but it would require too much pressing to serve her purpose. She brought out a soft silk of the most brilliant emerald green she had ever seen and eyed it cautiously.

"That a wedding dress will make." She turned quickly to see Hilda standing in the doorway dabbing at her eyes with a handkerchief. "Mr. McQuade just told me and to help you pack, I have come. He says I go, we hurry we must, then I pack me." She paused and raising her round chin a bit, "But, home I come the very next day. I, my kitchen will not leave for two or three weeks." Rebecca ran to hug her friend. Hilda held her tightly for a minute and patted her cheek, then murmured in a soft whisper, "Come, pack you up, we must. Late for your own wedding you don't want to be."

A short while later, Rebecca stopped her chore and listened to the prancing of a horse against the crushed stones of the driveway at the front of the house. Quint's voice floated up the stairs and then she heard the horse move on quickly. Hilda left the room and came back with several more candles, "A long night of work, we have before us." Even in the shadows Rebecca saw the grin on the cook's round face.

Dawn came much too soon for Rebecca. She had toiled long hours with Hilda to see the trunks packed, and with the sun lighting the sky, she and Hilda prepared to close the house for several days. It was longer still before all the trunks were loaded into the two carriages Quint decided to take. Through most of the preparations, Quint was alternately shouting and then cursing that they must be on their way. By mid-morning everything was ready and with Sam driving one carriage and John driving the other, they left for the Beals.

Quint tried hard to get the drivers to move faster but both refused. Finally Quint gave up, admitting sheepishly that they really couldn't move at a faster pace with any safety. He calmed down and sat with Rebecca watching the scenery pass by. Rebecca smiled at her soon-to-be husband and teased, "Are you trying to get away from a hangman, Mr. McQuade? Or are you giving this idea of marriage some second thoughts?"

Quint stared at her for a moment, then sighed. "Rebecca," he tried to explain, "If George didn't get my message, we'll have to wait until tomorrow to get married, and I have to leave the next day. . . ."

Quint watched her for a second and then pulled her into his arms, hugging her tightly. "It's just that I don't think I can wait another day, Love," he whispered for her ears alone. He kissed her with such tenderness that her soft brown eyes glowed with happiness.

She whispered back, "He got your message. I just know he did."

There were several carriages in front of the Beal residence when Quint's entourage arrived after four that afternoon. George came out of the house immediately and after short preliminary greetings, he pulled Quint over to the side. "Why the rush, man? Susannah is worried sick that Rebecca might be with child."

Quint stared at his brother-in-law. He hadn't even considered that his sister and her husband might draw the wrong conclusions. "No! Margaret came, and caused a ruckus. Let's get all of these things inside and while Rebecca's dressing and I'll tell you all about it."

Trunks were unloaded, and Hilda was introduced to the children and made comfortable in a room next to the kitchen. Rebecca was taken up stairs to the room that she and Quint would share for the next two days and where she would change for the ceremony. Quint drew Susannah and George aside and told them about Margaret's visit. "I don't trust her," he said quietly. "She won't do anything to me nor do I believe that she would try to hurt Rebecca physically, but I wouldn't put it past her to try to force Rebecca to leave the farm. This is the only way I have of protecting her until I return."

George volunteered, "I think, since Margaret has already made Rebecca so uncomfortable, perhaps, wedding or not, she should spend the whole three months with us. At least, that way, she'll be safe from Margaret's vicious tongue."

Quint frowned, "I thought about that, but I want the classes she's started to continue. It gives her a purpose and it's great for the farm. I know her well enough to know that she won't stay here unless she feels she is truly needed. I'll be back by the end of January, if everything goes well, and if she stays for several weeks after the baby arrives, or even through the holidays, she'll only be alone at the farm for about four weeks. Margaret can't cause too much trouble in that amount of time, can she?"

Quint glanced over at his very large sister. "Susannah, I forgot completely about your babe until we arrived. I'm sorry, I hope you didn't do too much."

Susannah tried to smile. Her suspicions were not relieved by their conversation, "No one would let me do a thing. Quint? George and I talked about this. Rebecca isn't . . . you're not marrying her because . . ." her blush spread over her face as she tried to question her brother.

"Susannah," Quint spoke slowly and quietly, "I'm marrying Rebecca because I love her. I'm marrying her today because of what I'm afraid she might face with Margaret while I'm gone."

Susannah still looked a little dubious, "You didn't answer my question." She put her open hand over her brother's grim mouth, "And, it's none of my business, is it?"

Quint finally grinned at her, "Right!" He turned to George, "I need two more things."

George groaned, "Only two more?"

Quint, grinning broadly now, continued, "I want you to give Rebecca away. She asked me to ask you." He looked at his sister, "You offered me some of mother's jewelry once. Did you, by any chance, keep the small gold band with the ruby in it?" When she nodded, Quint smiled, "I would like to give it to Rebecca, at least until I can replace it with something more appropriate."

"I kept most of her things. I thought someday I might want to give some of them to our children. The rings were all much too small for me and I'll never wear any of them. Perhaps there is something that you'd like better?" The conversation was interrupted by the arrival of the pastor who had been summoned once the carriages were sighted.

Hilda informed Quint that Rebecca was almost ready and Quint dashed up to his nephews' room to change himself. The few guests, friends of George and Susannah, assembled in the large parlor. George went up the steps to lead the bride to the groom who was now waiting with the smiling clergyman. One of the servants picked some late golden mums for Rebecca to carry, and George presented his arm to her.

He brought Rebecca into the living room with great solemnity and gave her to Quint. The room grew hushed and the pastor asked the questions first of Quint and then Rebecca. When Quint placed the small gold band on her finger, he leaned toward her and whispered, "On our first anniversary, I'll get you another ring, if you want." She smiled up at him and shook her head, no. He kissed her tenderly and then it was over. Mr. and Mrs. Quinton McQuade turned around to receive congratulations from friends and relatives. A late dinner was served and before long the guests started leaving so that they could get to their own homes before it got too dark to travel.

Quint thanked Susannah and George and then made his excuses. Before he started up the stairs after his wife, he glanced over at his sister, "Susannah, if you love me, you will not have that babe tonight, please." He could hear George's laughter as he hurried up the stairs.

Chapter Twenty-four

Margaret raced back to Philadelphia muttering to herself. There had to be a way to stop that wedding, but how? Quint said they would marry in February so she had only three months to stop the affair. She pondered her alternatives. The girl was pretty, dainty in a fragile sort of way, and many men liked the type. She never thought her tall muscular brother would be enamored with that kind of girl. Evidently Stephen Hill also preferred her kind as well. Imagine, selling a sister! But, if this brother from England sold her once, he might be interested in selling her again. It certainly bore some thinking about. Yes, the brother might just be the key. She rested her aching head against the back of the carriage seat. Tomorrow Elizabeth Ann was coming for tea. They could discuss the whole matter then.

When her sister arrived at her house the next day, Margaret urgently explained in detail what took place the day before. "When I suggested that perhaps he ought to find out more about her and wait a decent time to plan a marriage, he threw me out of his . . . my . . . our house."

"How soon before this wedding?" asked Elizabeth Ann. "How much time do we have?" She lowered her voice and her tone was conspiratorial.

"He says they'll be wed when Quint comes back from England. Sometime in February I believe," Margaret frowned trying to remember everything Mary Jane brought back from Susannah's. "I believe Susannah mentioned that our 'gallant' brother is planning one more trip to England before he settles down."

Elizabeth Ann gasped. "February? We don't have much time. I hope your next plan is better than your last."

"I think we should contact the brother you mentioned and explain that Rebecca is in trouble."

"But she's not in trouble."

"Elizabeth Ann, use your head. He sold her before, and I'll bet he has no idea that the marriage didn't 'take'. If he sold her once . . ."

"He'll sell her again! But are you sure he doesn't know about her indenture?"

"He's done nothing about it. I can't imagine someone as crass as he not taking advantage of the situation. We can only hope." Margaret smiled at her older sister. "We're going to let him know what has happened. If he's the kind of man I think he is, he'll be here in time to stop the wedding. If you make our letter sound bad enough, then . . ."

"Me?" Elizabeth Ann looked at her sister over the tea service.

"You write better than I do."

When it was finished, both women decided that Elizabeth Ann's letter was a work of art:

Dear Mr. Ranserford,
Your poor sister is presently being held by my roguish brother. I fear that she is being held against her will and that his intentions are not honorable. He will not release the girl to me, and he vows that he will not release her to you. Believe me, sir, I have tried. We are not in a position to help her, but as her dear brother, whom she cries for, you must come to her aid. If you could come for her, we would be most happy to share our humble home with you until you can make arrangements to return to England where, I'm certain, you can find a

suitable match for her to one of your fine country gentlemen.

Your humble servant,
Margaret McQuade Harrison.

Margaret turned to Elizabeth Ann, "I hope you haven't overdone it. I don't want him asking himself a lot of questions before he gets here."

Elizabeth Ann looked confident. "I can't believe the man is too bright. You may end up having to tell him how to find another candidate for the girl. I don't like the part about him staying here. If she doesn't want to come with him, Quint could cause trouble for you."

"But if he's here, I'll know what's going on. I can keep Quint out of the picture if that wedding doesn't occur. After all, until our little brother is her husband, he'll have no say," Margaret looked pleased with her logic. "Now, I'll have to find a fast ship to take this to England. It has to arrive before Quint gets there. Let's hope it does the trick and this Arthur has already left for Philadelphia before Quint arrives."

"Margaret?" Elizabeth Ann wore a frown, "I'm not so sure about Quint. If he comes looking for her, there could be trouble."

Margaret smiled smugly, "I hadn't planned to tell you this, but since you asked, Simon trades with Indians. There are some business deals that I know about and I'm not above telling my dear husband what he has to do," she laughed a hard brittle laugh. "Simon will do as I ask, and I intend to ask him to stage a Indian raid." When Elizabeth Ann gasped and turned white, Margaret continued, "Don't look so worried. I said stage. I'll have it look like the Indians took her, not that they will. I wouldn't wish that fate on my worst enemy. No, it will only look like Indians took her. Quint will assume that that's what happened and he'll travel into the wilderness to find her. While he's gone, she and her brother can sail back to England where they belong."

Elizabeth Ann left and Margaret hurried to the wharf.

In a matter of an hour, she found a fast mail packet that was leaving with the evening tide. Arthur Ranserford ought to have her letter by the first of December.

The next afternoon, Margaret was busy with menus for a dinner planned for the end of the week. A persistent knocking at the front door sent one of the girls running. Margaret smoothed her dress and then her hair, wondering who would come calling this late in the day. Elizabeth Ann's impatient voice brought Margaret from the pantry in a hurry. "What are you yelling about? What has happened?"

Elizabeth Ann's face was red, and her full lips were curved down in a decided mark of displeasure. "This came this afternoon. I am to share it with you," she handed Margaret a stiff piece of parchment.

Margaret felt the hairs on the back of her neck bristle and she glanced at the missive. She recognized the handwriting before Elizabeth Ann commented, "It's from Quinton."

Margaret read and then reread the announcement. "Married," she gasped. "But it was supposed to be February." She glanced at Elizabeth Ann, "He can't do this."

"Well, he has," her sister snapped. "My God, what will we do? The letter to her brother!"

Margaret set her teeth into her lower lip, fighting for control. It would not do to lash out at Elizabeth Ann. "Something will work out. It must!"

Rebecca stood at the window gazing at the moon which hung over the harvested fields. Her fingers twisted the gold band that encircled her finger, in nervous anticipation. As the moonlight highlighted the browns and greens of the Pennsylvania landscape, she remembered the fun she had riding with her father across the English countryside. She thought of the servants who depended on her medical skills, her clothes that had been hers without a thought, and the things of her mother's that Arthur had stolen from her. She felt again the hurt she experienced the night the ship left for Philadelphia and Arthur dumped her on Captain Hemphill. Tears gathered as she remembered the betrayal she felt when the captain explained her position that day on the *Venture*.

Quint moved quietly to her side, watching her facial expressions in the soft glow of the moonlight as it filtered through the window blinds. She looked so sad, and when Quint glimpsed a small wet crystal bead slip from her eye and slide down her cheek, he turned her around gently to face him. His voice was husky when he whispered, "What are you thinking that would cause you to shed a tear on your wedding day?"

She gazed into his deep blue eyes, wondering if she could share her thoughts with her new husband. No, she told herself. Her thoughts were just too private to share until she knew him better. She gave a quick shake of her head and turned back to the window. Would she find happiness now, she wondered, or would it too be stripped from her just as she tasted its sweetness.

Quint sensed some of her fear, and pulled her around and into his arms. He held her gently against his strong body and tenderly kissed her hair, her eyes, tasting the salt of her tears, and slowly his lips captured hers in a delicate taking that spoke of love, and hope, and faith in their future together. Her arms slid up around his neck and she returned his kiss with a fervor that surprised them both.

Quint instinctively deepened his kiss. Soon the throbbing demands of his lips as they caressed hers made all thought an impossibility. His tongue slipped into her sweetness and she groaned in pleasure. As his gentle hands skimmed over the fabric of her dress, she remembered the pleasure she experienced before with him. As he cupped her breasts, trailed his hands over her shoulders and kneaded her buttocks, she tried to imitate his motion. She discovered that she derived as much pleasure from touching him as she got when he touched her.

She fought the tiny tingling twitches as his lips moved from her lips, down her neck to her shoulder. He nibbled his way back again and she heard him whisper her name. It sounded like a breath of wind fondling each syllable. That wind whispered of a love for all eternity and she melted into him.

At some point, she didn't know when, her clothes fell away and his hot flesh touched hers. His hands spared no part of her trembling frame as he explored and stroked every part of her. Holding her in his arms, he picked her up and moved to the soft surface of the bed which became a cloud on which she was being transported from the earth and into the serenity of the heavens. A tension started in her center and spread to her veins, pulsing up and out until she felt like she was a flame that only he could extinguish.

His kisses never stopped and for an instant she wondered if he was trying to draw her out of herself and into him for a perfect union. He played with her, petted her, adored her until she felt sure she would faint from the pleasure that pulsed through her. He bent his head to touch her breasts and she purred in delight. She held his head to her breast, knowing that soon she would explode into a million shards of bliss and she would never again be whole. He left one breast to caress the other and she twisted under him, sighing out her wants.

He seemed to understand the language of her sighs and he spread her thighs and knelt before her. Pausing, as if to beg entrance, he gazed into her eyes. She threw up her arms to welcome him home as a bittersweet longing coursed through her body and she waited for the joining that would make them one. He surged forward and a pleasure spread through her so intense that she once more feared that she might faint. They came together then as tenderly as his first kiss had begun, but soon their passion, already a white heat, flared out of control. He thrust into her with a growing sense of urgency. The explosion came and she felt herself burst into a thousand tiny sparks as she cried out his name. He collapsed against her and she realized that she never knew when he too had tasted ecstasy.

They lay together for long minutes as Rebecca felt herself float back to earth. Suddenly, with a dexterity that she didn't know he possessed, he rolled them over to their sides so that they were still intimately joined. He stroked the ebony velvet from her face and replaced it with tender kisses. With his arms still holding her tightly, she drifted off to sleep.

Sometime during the night, in the soft darkness, she awoke to more clinging kisses and tenderly whispered words of love. She rolled closer to him and whispered, "You need your rest."

His haunting laugh denied her complaint, "How can I rest when you are in my arms?" He pulled her even closer and placed his lips on hers, and once again her senses awakened to the heat of his body and its hardness as he pressed against her. The flames of passion, just extinguished, burst forth into a roaring blaze that separated her from the world of reality. As she floated back she realized that his breathing was deep and regular. For a fraction of a second he tightened his grip on her and then she too drifted into the perfect peace of sated sleep.

The early morning sun of the crisp fall day shone through the slats of the blinds as she opened her eyes. She was curled in the arms of a warm body and she cautiously moved her head so that she could gaze into the still sleeping face of her new husband. Husband! The word played across her mind and she smiled. In spite of the tragic turn her life had taken after her father died, she could now draw a deep breath and taste her happiness. She gazed at the man responsible. His luscious dark brown hair ruffled and curled against his face. His mouth was open slightly and his full lips were spread into a half smile. The long classic nose just seemed to need her caress and without conscious thought she reached out and ran her finger down the length of his nose.

Suddenly the lips moved, "Is there something wrong with my nose?" His eyes were still closed and Rebecca had a strong suspicion that he had been awake for quite some time.

Rebecca giggled, "There's nothing wrong with it, in fact, I was just letting your nose know how much I like it."

Quint pulled her closer and without opening his eyes, he ran a finger across her breast. Without warning, he opened his dark blue eyes and grinned into her eyes, now a soft liquid brown. "Let me tell your breast how much I like it."

She laughed softly and reached for his ear, running her finger around the edge. "There! Now, your ear feels loved, too."

Quint kneaded her stomach, expressing his affection and so the game continued, as they each exchanged touch for touch, until once again their passions demanded a feeding. Again, for a short time they slept, still joined with arms and legs entwined.

The sun shone brilliantly through the window when they stirred again. He kissed her energetically and suggested loudly that he was starved. "Woman, you'll have to feed me. I must have food!"

Rolling out of his arms, she stretched. "Tell Hilda. She's the one responsible for that feeding."

Quint made a lunge for her and grinned as he managed to snag a thin ankle when she leaped off of the bed. "I think not," he said, chuckling.

Rebecca tried to turn but he still held her ankle and she laughed, "I can't feed you if you keep me captive."

Quint crawled across the bed still clutching her ankle until he reached the edge of the mattress. He stood and pulled her into his arms. No longer smiling, he gazed at her with eyes that were at once bright and serious. He bent his head to capture her lips once more in a tender kiss, and he breathed against her mouth, "I love you."

She returned his kiss and stood for a moment feeling drawn into his deep blue eyes. "I love you," she murmured just as softly. For a moment, she thought her joyful heart would explode from her body.

They dressed quickly, and Quint led the way down to the kitchen which seemed to be the favorite room in the house. George was sitting at the table drinking a cup of coffee and glanced up at the couple, smiling warmly, "So you finally decided to get up, did you? You missed all the excitement. John left an hour ago with Hilda."

Rebecca glanced around the warm cheerful room, and when she did not see Susannah, she asked quietly, "Is everything alright? Is Susannah alright. She's up, isn't she?"

George looked so serious for a second that Rebecca was genuinely alarmed, then he snorted, "She's still abed. We were kept awake all night," he said looking at them sternly, "by many strange noises. I do believe we have been invaded my mice."

As a blush spread rapidly over her face and a small pained sound escaped her, Rebecca sank into a chair. She looked up at Quint who was standing in front of his brother-in-law. She got no consolation from her new husband when she realized that his face was as red as a beet. Quickly, she glanced at George and then watched with fascination as he worked his teeth against his lips, struggling to keep the laughter that danced in his eyes from bursting from his lips. He didn't succeed and he jumped up from the table, slapped Quint on the back, and left the room choked with mirth.

Quint sat in the chair next to Rebecca. She leaned toward him and whispered, "We didn't make that much noise, did we?" Quint, still speechless, simply nodded his head. Rebecca's face turned as red as Quint's had been and she put her hands up to cover her flaming cheeks.

George returned just then, and apologizing profusely, he added that he and Susannah stayed up and talked half the night away. They hadn't heard a thing he added quickly. "Rebecca, I didn't mean to embarrass you, but I have waited so long to be able to say something that would stop your husband completely." Rebecca smiled up at him. Her husband! It almost made the awful teasing bearable.

George turned serious and seated himself opposite the newly married couple, "We really were up half the night talking about your marriage. You know, when Margaret finds out what you've done, there could be fire works. Susannah and I are certain that the reason for her visit was to send Rebecca from your farm, or rather the farm she thinks belongs to her. I'm not too sure you know just how devious Margaret is. Susannah and I want Rebecca to stay here with us until you return."

Quint gazed at his wife and watched as her chin raised an inch. Her soft brown eyes glittered and then turned black as coal. Somehow he knew what she was going to say before the words slipped past her lips. "I have a class to teach. After the baby is born I am going back to the farm." Her chin came up another inch.

George opened his mouth but a quick look at Quint's shake of his head, George turned his attention to his cup of coffee and Quint and Rebecca turned to their meal. After breaking their fast, Quint suggested a walk. For an hour, Rebecca and Quint strolled about the property to the west of the home. They discussed George's proposal and Rebecca continued to object. "If Margaret does try something, I'll drag out my wedding papers and shove them in her face," she said heatedly.

Quint laughed, thinking of his tiny wife standing on her toes shoving her marriage certificate in Margaret's face, "Somehow, sweetheart, I doubt that you could do that."

Finally, she agreed to stay with Susannah and George until after Christmas. "They're only trying to keep me from worrying. They know I want you to stay until I come home," he added as she looked like she might want to argue. "If the winds are good, I might be home by the end of January but by the middle of February, I promise." That meant that she would only be at the farm for five, at the most six weeks. Surely, with George checking on her, and Hilda, John and his boys at the farm, she would be safe. Margaret couldn't do anything in that amount of time. Quint tried hard not to think of George's assessment of his sister's character.

They hurried back to the house to tell the Beals that

Rebecca would stay through the holidays. Susannah was enthusiastic, and George tried to bargain for the full time that Quint would be gone. George kept insisting, and once more her eyes turned dark brown. Before long, she began to object to staying with the Beals at all. Quint gave George a disgusted look and took his new wife out to the stable to see the fine collection of riding stock George was breeding.

Rebecca loved the stables, and she coaxed a small bay mare to the fence beside the barn. She soon had the horse nuzzling her for attention. Quint watched her with interest, "Do you ride?"

Rebecca looked up at him and grinned, "I used to ride every day. In fact, I think you'll find me a most capable horsewoman." Quint left her side and went in search of George and a saddle for Rebecca. The two men returned to the barn and when George found his new sister-in-law stroking the lean neck of the small horse, he looked from Rebecca to Quint to the horse and back at Quint. "Bring the bay around, and get Diablo for my brother." In minutes one of the young boys from the stable arrived with a big black stallion and began to saddle the horse.

With his expression serious, George questioned Rebecca about her riding skills as one of the stable hands began to saddle the smaller horse. George pulled Quint aside and murmured, "This little mare seems gentle enough but she has not been here long. I've had no chance to work with her, and I don't know how long she's been broken. Are you sure Rebecca should try her before I do?"

Immediately, Quint responded, "No!" He and George continued their discussion about the bay horse and then about another mount for her. Rebecca stood silently watching them for several minutes and again her temper flared. Her eyes snapped black and she muttered, "This is ridiculous. I'm an excellent rider, and they aren't even going to give me a chance to prove it." She was tired of waiting and she pushed the young groom away from the horse. The boy was already paying more attention to the discussion going on between the two men that he was with getting the small horse ready for her. She was not as unskilled as her husband and his brother thought, she told herself as she saddled the horse herself and then mounted, ready to ride.

When Quint and George glanced over at the small horse, shock registered on their faces, but Rebecca grinned and with just a hint of sarcasm in her voice, she commented, "If we're going to ride, then let's go!" Without a word to George, Quint mounted the black charger and watching Rebecca carefully, he pointed out the path away from the stable.

George watched them go and shook his head. That small black-haired beauty did pretty much as she wanted. Perhaps it was just as well if she did return to Quint's farm at the end of December. It would be next to impossible to control her and it would be a shame if he and Quint had a falling out over something she did.

Quint passed Rebecca on the trail after ten minutes out. He turned around often to watch, but he noticed that she was indeed a capable horsewoman. She seemed to manage the little mare with no problems at all. He grinned to himself, she was full of surprises. He watched as she held the reins tightly enough so that the frisky mare knew control, but she gave the animal enough head so that the horse could surge forward and enjoy the run. Rebecca didn't even seem to have a problem bringing the mare back to a slow trot so that she'd not become winded.

They rode for awhile and Quint took Rebecca around the perimeters of the farm. When they reached the edge of the woods bordering the farm, Quint stopped and informed Rebecca that they would rest themselves and the horses for a short while. Rebecca dismounted, stretched and then threw the reins over a small branch of a scrubby bush and murmured, "It's been so long since I've ridden, and I enjoy it so. May I ride one of your horses back at the farm?"

Without waiting for his reply she pushed on into the woods leaving Quint to secure his own horse and follow her. She ambled toward a small stream that wandered through the woods on the Beal property. Kneeling down by the stream she scooped some of the cold water into her hands and then to her lips. Quint watched her then he knelt down to get a drink, as well. As she glanced about the undergrowth something caught her eyes and plunging through the trees, she jumped the brook and ran for a large oak tree. When she reached her goal, she knelt down on the large brown leaves. Quint followed her out of curiosity. Then he spied a touch of pink. Rebecca began pulling away the leaves and pushed aside a small pine tree that appeared to be protecting the fragile blooms. In the middle of the forest, long past the first frost, Rebecca found a wild pink rose bush still blooming.

Quint was a little startled as she carefully picked the still perfect blossoms of pale pink. She smiled up at him, "I love roses, especially pink roses. I don't know why, but they always seem like such a happy flower." She brought the buds to her face and breathed their fragrance deeply, "Aren't they beautiful. Imagine, roses this late in the year. They'll only die here. I'll take them back so that everyone can enjoy them for another day or two."

Quint pulled her to her feet and placed his arms around her slender waist. "Are you happy, my little pink rose?"

She let her eyes wander over his face, watching the seriousness of his expression and the questioning look in his eyes. Smiling up at him, she sighed, "Oh, yes. Very happy." She reached up and pulled his head down to hers, then gave him a tender kiss. Quint took a deep breath and the sweet smell of the roses, combined with her special fragrance gave him a heady feeling. For one instant he felt drunk with pleasure, if such a thing was possible.

Rebecca looked up at him, with a blush coloring her cheek, "Let's go back now." Arm in arm they walked back to the horses, then mounted and rode back to the house.

As they rode, Rebecca clutched the roses protectively and while Quint saw to the horses, Rebecca rushed inside to show her treasures to Susannah. At dinner, a small crystal vase full of dazzling roses stood in the center of the table.

After dinner, Quint and Rebecca hurried upstairs to their own chamber where a small fire had been laid against the chill of the late October evening. In less than twelve hours Quint would leave for three months and Rebecca was filled with a bittersweet sadness she could not explain. She didn't try as Quint sat down in a large chair before the fireplace and pulled her into his lap. He felt as sad as she looked, and as if he could read her thoughts, he muttered, "It will only be a short time, then I'll be back." She said nothing and rested in his arms, willing this last night never end.

Chapter Twenty-five

Rebecca tried to force away the desperation that nibbled at her mind. Quint was still there and the night was just beginning. As he raised her face to his, she willed her mind a blank. She would love him as he loved her, she would not think of the morrow.

Quint's thoughts were just as troubled. He bent to the task of loving his new wife with an intensity that spoke most eloquently of his own despair. He placed a hundred soft kisses on her eyelids, her forehead, her ears and her cheeks. Pulling one of her hands up to his face, he covered her palm with gentle kisses, then reached for her other hand and held both to his lips. After he kissed each hand he placed them up around his neck. He stood, and cradling her in his arms, he walked the four steps to the edge of the bed.

Carfully he laid her on the quilt and slowly, as if he thought the night would never end, he began to remove her clothing, kissing each section of flesh revealed to him. When she was completely undressed, he removed his own clothing, while her eyes caressed the areas of skin he exposed. When he was as she was, he joined her in bed.

He drew her close and with a touch born of patience, he explored every inch of her body. Rebecca tried to reciprocate as she attempted to run her inexperienced hands over his shoulders, down his arms, across his ribs and down the flat plane of his stomach, but he held her so tightly that she couldn't reach nearly as much of him as she wanted.

He kissed her gently and pressed her close, afraid that if he released her she would vanish. Against her lips, he whispered, "I will miss you so much." She clung to him, and for one instant she was terrified that they would never have another night together. Suddenly, he was holding her so tightly that she struggled to breathe and she wondered if he felt the same foreboding that she felt. Almost as if he put her thought into words, he spoke, "I'm not going, I won't leave you."

"But you must go," she whispered back. "Your ship is waiting. Don't worry. Susannah and George will take care of me," she tried to reassure herself as well as him as she ran her hands through his luxurious beaver-brown hair. "You know you have to go."

He sighed, "Leaving you is much harder than I thought it would be." He tried to laugh but the sound was almost a sob. "I should have thought of this much sooner. Margaret will never know what a favor she has done me."

"We have tonight. What if you had thought of this on the way to London?" she tried to tease him out of his melancholy mood that threatened them both.

"I fear my sailors will wish I had stayed behind this trip," he mumbled as he began to kiss every inch of skin he could reach. She returned his kisses, causing him to twist and turn as she herself was twisting. He played with her, caressed her, touched her, until she was sure that she would lose her senses before the dawn arrived. Finally, after she begged, pleaded, in a voice so husky, she could hardly recognize it as her own, he eased himself into the moist velvet cavern that waited. Their passions had been stirred to the point of violence and he took her in hard quick thrusts.

Rebecca knew that before the explosion of ecstasy came, she would die in his arms. Quint vaguely realized that he was holding back, waiting for her, and as she cried out his name, he plunged deeply and moaned his own gratification to her. She wanted to hold him forever, but the thought could not be born out for her eyes closed and she drifted to sleep before he had rolled from her side.

Slowly, she felt herself surface and it took her a minute to remember where she was. It was still dark and she reached over to his side of the bed. It was empty! She waited for her eyes to adjust to the darkness of the room and then she looked around the chamber. His trunk was not next to hers, his clothing was no longer laying in a heap in the middle of the floor. She sat upright in the bed. He wouldn't have left her without a good-bye! Surely, he would not have done that!

A shaky laugh passed her lips, as once more she denied the thought. She jumped from bed and hastily donned her clothes, running from the room and down the stairs. Heading for the kitchen, she felt almost sick. He couldn't have left yet, he wouldn't do that to her. He couldn't!

As she reached the doorway to the kitchen, she saw him seated at the end of the table, silhouetted against the bright fire in the fireplace. Quint was there alone, and the sound of his spoon clanging against the cup sounded empty and somehow so forlorn that Rebecca felt tears start at the corners of her eyes. She watched him for a few seconds, through cloudy eyes, then blinking back the moisture she walked into the room. He wore such an expression of anguish that she wanted to run to him and tell him that he need not make the journey for her sake. When he glanced up and saw her he masked his emotions immediately. She decided that he did not want her to know how much leaving her bothered him and she drew the memory of his pain into her heart. She would act, for his sake, like he was only going to be gone for a day or two and would be returning soon. Perhaps, if she pretended hard enough, she would be able to get through the next few hours herself.

"Good morning, love," she said the words a little louder than she wanted. "You are up very early," her words tumbled one after another, and she didn't seem to be able to stop them. Quint seemed to understand and smiled up at her, easing a tiny bit of her pain.

Quint got up and pulled out a chair for her. He motioned toward the door, where she could see the early morning sun doing battle with a gray day. "George is bringing around your wedding gift. Until yesterday, I wasn't sure what you might like." Rebecca jumped up from the table and moved to the door that Quint indicated. George was leading the small bay mare that Rebecca had ridden the day before toward the kitchen door.

"She's mine? You're giving her to me?" she whispered softly as her new husband came to stand next to her.

Quint put his arm around her shoulders and pulled her even closer. "I bought her last night. I talked to George before dinner and he agreed to sell me the horse and the saddle, just for you."

Rebecca turned and hugged him tightly, "Oh, thank you! She is beautiful, such a beautiful little thing, and I'll enjoy her so much."

"She should help keep you busy while I'm gone," Quint smiled a bittersweet smile.

Rebecca couldn't remember much of the next half hour. It seemed to her that Quint had only waited until he could give her the horse before he left for Philadelphia. What she did remember was the kiss he gave her that burned on her lips for hours after the dust settled from the horses and the carriage that saw him away. The words of good-bye echoed in her head for hours.

He had kissed her and held her tight against his tension-filled body as he whispered, "You're mine, you belong to me, me alone."

Spontaneously, she responded, "I'll be here waiting for you when you return." He kissed her once more, with a kiss so fierce that it would be emblazoned across her mind forever. The tears gathered again and she wondered why she had been gifted with the love of such a man.

When they had finished dinner that afternoon, Rebecca pulled Susannah away from George and the children,

"The room Quint and I shared, it's your room isn't it?"

Susannah smiled, "Yes, but George and I decided to give it up to you and Quint and move to the downstairs bedroom. Now that I've gotten so large, the stairs are difficult. Please, don't think anything about it. We've moved downstairs with each of the children. It's so much easier being close to the kitchen with a brand new baby. We probably won't move back upstairs until spring."

Rebecca looked over at her new sister, a little embarrassed, "Would you be offended if I gave you back that room and requested another?" Her voice trembled slightly. George had just joined them at her astonishing request, and he opened his mouth to object, but Susannah laid her hand on her husband's arm to quiet him, "Would you take the room next to Anna? I will be so busy with the new babe, she may feel left out. If you were close to her, it might ease her little mind."

George stared at his wife in surprise, but when Susannah asked if he would help move Rebecca's things, he nodded and led the way up the stairs. Soon, all of Rebecca's personal items were transferred to the room next to Anna and Rebecca spent the remainder of the evening arranging her clothing and books to her satisfaction. Rebecca let Anna help with some of it and the bond between them grew. Because of her lack of sleep the night before and the hard work she had just finished, she fell into a deep and dreamless sleep and she was surprised when she woke the next morning feeling as good as she did.

Even with the care of the children which Rebecca undertook, the next several days dragged by but she tried to fill them with the Beal offspring and the care of her new horse. George asked the day after Quint left what she planned to call the animal and Rebecca answered without hesitation, "Petite Cadeau." George laughed over the name, "Rebecca, that was not a little gift. A horse could never be called a little gift and Quint insisted that he pay what I paid for the mare."

Rebecca lifted her chin, still not used to George's teasing, "The gift was not little, but even you'll have to agree that compared to your other horses, this horse is small." It mattered very little, for soon the animal was simply called "Cad" by all. As she settled into the routine of the house, her days grew full with household chores, plans for meals, parceling out the work for the servants and the time she spent with the children. Susannah rested and proclaimed that she had never been so pampered in her life. Even with all the help Susannah had, she admitted that she wasn't sleeping well at night and Rebecca assumed more of the household chores.

By the time Rebecca had been at the Beals for two weeks, the babe Susannah carried began its struggle to break free of its nine month prison. In a few hours, the household quiet was shattered by the lusty screams of the new addition to the family and Rebecca who assisted with the birth presented a new son to an excited George.

Now the days literally flew by as most of her time was spent helping to care for the new child and provide the other children with some kind of normal routine while Susannah recovered. Before Rebecca had given it much thought, November was gone and Christmas was only days away. Much time was spent in decorating the house and preparing the small pine tree that George brought into the home. George explained that many of the families in the area were German and the other families adapted the tradition of the Christmas tree. "It was easier to add a tree than to try to explain to the boys why the two families next to us had them and we didn't. Besides, we think it's a nice idea." It was almost, Rebecca thought, as if everything that was traditionally Christmas anyplace was also traditionally Christmas in the Beal residence. The whole season was filled with best wishes and good cheer and she enjoyed herself, in spite of the fact that she was alone and by now Quint was in England.

All of November and the first week of December passed quickly for Quint. They sailed through only two storms and neither one of them was very serious. The only damage they sustained was a torn sail. The winds were brisk and they reached the Thames eight days before Quint expected to arrive. On the trip over, he decided that he should make an attempt to meet Rebecca's brother. After all, in years to come, Rebecca might want to visit her home, and if he met the man . . . Now there was time to find out where the man lived and talk to him, in addition to meeting with his own agent and unloading his ship. He saw to docking and then went in search of his other ship. The smaller vessel left Philadelphia six weeks before his own departure and this was the ship that would carry him back to Rebecca. The cargo for the ship was already secured and within two weeks, Quint expected to be on his way home.

It took him several hours before he located the ship and when he found the *Sea Breeze*, he stared at it in horror. The main mast was shattered, several of the spars were broken and one was missing completely. Chunks of wood were missing from the deck and the bow gave the appearance that a giant sea monster had taken a mouthful above the water line. As Quint looked at the vessel, he wondered how it ever made port.

He found the captain in one of the shipyards and learned that they had encountered a storm of much greater intensity than the two storms Quint's own ship had survived. Two of the sailors were injured, the captain told him, and one mate was lost during the storm. It would be impossible for the *Sea Breeze* to leave before the end of March, and if they couldn't find carpenters immediately, it might be April before the ship could be made ready to sail. He signed the orders for the necessary repairs and started looking for passage on another vessel bound for Philadelphia.

Quint decided that the trip to London was ill-fated before the end of the second day. He couldn't find Arthur

Ranserford any place. The man still maintained the home in London, but the old servant who acted as butler and, Quint suspected, as valet, said Arthur was never there. The servant even refused to tell Quint where he was. He left his card, but Arthur Ranserford never responded. He waited one full week. His curiosity was aroused and he decided that he would just have to find the man to determine why he was so elusive. He wondered if the man was ill or a fugitive and if something had happened to him, it wouldn't do for Rebecca to find out that Quint had never investigated.

With his wife in mind, he started a search and soon had part of his answer. Arthur needed to remain hidden for fear those who held notes against him might find him and arrange for his imprisonment. Quint decided after a talk with the local banker that Arthur owed something to everybody in England except the king. On second thought, Quint mumbled as he trudged back to his inn, he might just owe that man money, too.

One evening, Quint and several of his officers stopped at a local tavern. Quint promised to buy dinner and a round or two of ale and the tavern was known to have a few honest tables of chance. After dinner, Quint stood off to one side and watched one man carefully. He was totally engrossed in a card game and Quint could tell by the expression on his face that he was not winning. He wondered if the man was a victim of the gambling sickness where nothing but the wager mattered. Quint had seen it before in the taverns of home. He watched and shook his head.

Several of the men at the table were preparing to leave, and Quint was stunned when one of the men referred to the man he'd been watching as Mr. Ranserford. When another man called the gambler, Arthur, Quint moved over to the table. It wasn't possible, he thought as he stared at Arthur's overbright eyes. Quint sat down and asked quietly if the game was finished. Arthur shook his head, "These gentlemen are calling it a night, but if you want to play, I'll stay over a time."

Quint let Arthur win the next three hands and from Arthur's reaction Quint wondered how much he had lost. Arthur raked in his meager winnings with such hunger that Quint became uncomfortable. He played one more hand and won back almost all he had lost. Arthur glared at him, "Just a bit of dumb Yankee luck. I'll win it all back in a minute." With the word "Yankee," every head in the tavern looked at Quint.

"This is the time to leave," he told himself. He pretended fatigue and called the gaming to a halt. Quint looked around for his officers. Only two remained, obviously in case he needed any help, and he smiled to himself. His men were loyal to a fault. Before he left this tavern, though, he was going to find out if this was his brother-in-law.

Quint gazed at Arthur, his expression questioning, "Sir, do you have a sister by the name of Rebecca, who left England a year ago to go to Philadelphia?"

Arthur had the decency to look uncomfortable, "That is none of your concern."

"I think it is. If you have a sister named Rebecca, then I'm your . . ." before Quint could finish his statement, Arthur swung at him.

Quint was not prepared and he tensed at the last minute. The punch was a solid hit and Quint staggered, more from surprise than for any other reason. He clenched his fist to retaliate but one of his officers pushed Arthur against the bar and Quint had time only to duck the left hook that another patron sent in his direction. Suddenly, the entire room seemed to erupt. Everybody swung at everyone else in the room. "Mr. McQuade, Mr. McQuade, sir, let's get the hell out of here," the youngest of his men pushed him toward the door.

Quint was pushed and dragged from the place yelling obscenities at Arthur Ranserford, into the arms of a waiting crewman. "Come on, sir, leave the bloke alone," muttered a man that Quint didn't even recognize.

"They're all crazy," Quint mumbled as his men pulled him away.

In the tavern, ignoring the flying fists around him, Arthur stood very still, "McQuade . . . McQuade . . . Philadelphia." Suddenly, Arthur remembered the letter that had arrived the first of the month. He stared at the door that opened to the dark night. The letter said something trite about Rebecca and a man named McQuade. It had to be the same man. Arthur scratched his head, trying to remember what the letter said, something about Rebecca being held against her will. Maybe that woman didn't have her facts confused.

He frowned as he remembered a most unpleasant visit several months earlier. The sea captain that took Rebecca to the colonies appeared at his door one afternoon, demanding that Arthur return the fifty pounds Stephen Hill paid for Rebecca. It seemed that the good Mr. Hill died before he received his bride and the relatives were refusing to reimburse the captain or to send Rebecca home. Vividly, Arthur remembered telling the man that that was his problem since he had, in good faith, sent Rebecca in the captain's care. That his rather dull sister had bonded herself to pay the debt was a matter that he would study, he assured the big man, as he pushed him through the front door. The captain made a nuisance of himself for three weeks, and Arthur had even been forced to seek lodgings away from his home for several days to avoid the persistent man. Eventually, the sea captain gave up and went away and now, here was this man, asking about Rebecca. Was there money in it for him? If this McQuade held his sister, there had to be something for him.

Arthur left the tavern, still wondering. He hurried home, the first order of business that letter. The next morning, Arthur went to the desk in the corner of his room. Where had he put that damned letter? He couldn't remember what the woman wrote. He began to pick up and discard note after note, his search becoming frantic.

Arthur spent the rest of the morning trying to find the letter from Philadelphia. When he found it, he read it over. It didn't make much sense to him. Obviously, there was something that the sister didn't know or didn't want to tell him. It was clear to him that Margaret McQuade Harrison didn't want her brother to have anything to do with Rebecca. He stared off into space, there had to be money involved! Why had the sister indicated in the letter that she couldn't help his sister. Maybe she didn't want to help his sister.

Arthur rubbed his hand across his brow. It was confusing, so confusing that he had a dastardly headache. If there was one thing he was sure of, money or at least property was involved some place. Rebecca didn't have any money, so it must be that McQuade was a wealthy man. First, he decided, he had to find out about the man he met briefly the night before, and then he had to get to America. That was where Rebecca was and where this Margaret Harrison lived and he doubted he would get any answers until he got to America.

He spent the next two days trying to find out about McQuade. He really wasn't too surprised when he found that the man was in shipping. What did surprise him was the amount of shipping the man did. He smiled in anticipation, there was more money involved than he could imagine. The man was wealthy beyond anything Arthur could calculate.

For the first time in years Arthur stayed away from the gaming tables. After he considered his options, he made an appointment to meet the family solicitor. It was worth the lecture he would receive from the withered old man to get to America. He frowned as he thought about the man, a friend of his grandfather, someone that should have been dead years ago. He held the purse strings to the estate, and even Rebecca never realized how much control that old lawyer had. Even the aborted marriage had not freed up the money the way Arthur had intended. But he was going to have another chance.

He dressed carefully the next morning and took Margaret's letter with him. That old fool must realize that he, Arthur, had to get to Rebecca as fast as possible. Of course, he would have to color some of the events of the year before to suit his own purposes but what were a few more tales when the rewards appeared to be so great. Arthur smiled to himself, that old rascal was always fond of Rebecca, if he remembered correctly. The lawyer wouldn't want her abused or enslaved by a savage American.

Arthur arrived a full ten minutes early for his interview. He endured an hour's lecture and several times during the one-sided discourse, he wanted to reach out and strangle the old man. He sat quietly, though, waiting for his chance. The money was worth it.

Arthur sat and listened to a long list of capital investments that Arthur sold off because of gambling debts. Grim faced, his thin lips drawn in a straight white line, the family retainer called Arthur one name after another, including thief. Then he went on to lecture him on the evils of wagering, until Arthur wanted to wrap his fingers around the wrinkled throat and stop the perpetual noise. Finally, when Arthur had had all he could take, the old man seemed to run out of air and Arthur got his chance.

He told the old man about the fine marriage that he had arranged and the failure of the husband-to-be to provide return passage for his bride. Knowing Stephen Hill was dead Arthur painted a picture of deceit about the contract that he signed. He got a little carried away as he described the trickery of the miserable sea captain who took Rebecca to Philadelphia, and he ended by telling the old man how Rebecca had been forced to pay her passage by bonding herself into servitude. He went on to explain what he had done to rescue his sister from the clutches of bondage. Arthur felt almost sick as he pleaded for the money necessary to pay the indenture fee and bring his own little sweet sister back to her beloved England where she belonged.

As the old man sat across from him, Arthur wondered if he laid it on too thick, but when the old man wiped his eyes and admitted that he, too, had dealt with some of these new Americans, Arthur felt sure he would be granted the funds to sail after the answers he needed.

The old lawyer was in a quandary. Watching the young man, he wondered if Arthur's outlandish tale might be true. Arthur had never shown any tendency toward the creative and it would have taken a very creative mind to dream up the tale he was being asked to believe. No, there probably was some truth to what he said, but he was not going to hand the last of the dwindling estate over to the young buck for him to squander again. He would make all of the arrangements for both Arthur and Rebecca and give the boy a bit of spending money. If Arthur had invented the story for money, then he would object and refuse. If his tale was true, he would accept the plan.

The old man explained what he would do, but he must sell one of the smaller farms to get the funds necessary. Arthur would have to wait for a week or two. When the lawyer contacted him again he would have passage booked for Arthur and return passage for him and his sister. In fact, the ancient barrister said, both the trip to and from America would be paid in advance by the lawyer.

Arthur listened to the old man's plan and started to choke. He was not a babe in swaddling clothes to be treated in this fashion. Arthur told the old man just that and stormed from the office. The lawyer was left with the impression that Arthur had made the whole thing up just to get his hands on more money. "Damn that boy," the lawyer raged to blank cold walls.

Several days later, Arthur again sat before the lawyer, ready now to accept his plan. If he didn't get to the colonies, there would never be a penny for him. He had to accept the old man's treatment for the greater gain. Once he got Rebecca away from this McQuade, he knew he could find some wealthy country gentleman, who would pay a tidy sum for Rebecca's hand and he would be in control again. He sat quietly and listened as the lawyer told him once again how Arthur would get to America, "It could take several weeks before everything is ready. Pack a bag and be ready to go at a moment's notice. As soon as everything is prepared, I'll send a message."

Chapter Twenty-six

While Rebecca enjoyed her stay at the Beals, she started a personal routine that kept her love for her new husband a bright and tangible thing. Each night before she crawled into bed, no matter how tired she was, she curled up in her chair and gave herself up to the memory of Quint. She saw him in his fields, working with John, she watched him ride up to the stable and she relived their last night together. His image was clear in her mind and she saw him smiling at her with his deep blue eyes.

Mentally she would calculate where he might be, on the sea, in London or meeting with his agent, and she prayed that he was safe. She put her arms around her body and felt that special closeness they experienced for such a short time. Then she repeated once more those words she said to him before he left, "I will be waiting."

Almost before she could draw a steady breath, Christmas was upon them and she began to make her preparations to return to the farm. She walked almost in a dream as she started to count the days until Quint's return. George and Susannah tried over and over to get her to stay with them at their farm until he returned, but she would not hear of it. George pleaded with her, telling her that the household could not function without her. She thanked him for wanting her and for exaggerating her usefulness so that she felt wanted but, she added quietly, she knew the Beal family needed to get back to normal without the added company.

By the fourth of January, Rebecca stood dressed in a

riding suit, her luggage packed into the boot of the carriage. The night before Sam arrived with the carriage, but she explained that she planned to ride Cad home. When George protested and refused to let her mount, she finally agreed to ride in the carriage for half the trip. George gave up. Even the weather seemed to be in favor of Rebecca's traveling back to the farm for it was warmer than usual and very clear.

Rebecca promised to return with Quint just as soon as he returned and they were settled. Then she kissed all of the children, hugged George, clung to Susannah for several minutes and then she was off, back to her home to await the arrival of her new husband.

Rebecca arrived home late that afternoon and she was delighted to be there. After a refreshing night's sleep, she sent word that classes would begin in two days and they would all have another short break when Mr. McQuade returned home. She supervised the cleaning of the house, moved all of her belongings into Quint's large bedroom and started classes. Two weeks after they began, Hilda began a week of non-stop cooking in preparation for the master's return. The whole farm waited.

The last week of January passed slowly, but the second day of February a lone horseman approached the farm, and for serveral minutes Rebecca knew a joy that could not be contained. When she identified him as George, Rebecca's heart sank. He brought a message that had just arrived. It came on the mail packet that left London the day after Quint had arrived there. The *Sea Breeze* was not fit to sail, Quint wrote, so he would have to make other arrangements. Rebecca was not to get upset if he did not arrive until the end of February. She swallowed her tears and called the children back to class. George, assured that everything was fine, went back home and the household settled into the normal routine.

Quint stood at the rail of the ship, looking west, and he

286

could almost hear his young wife whispering the words, "I'll be waiting." He thought back over the last week and frowned. When he got to the ship his trunk had been transferred and his first mate was waiting. The man had been insistent. This ship was not in good shape, in fact, the mate wondered if it was even sea-worthy. Quint found himself frowning and agreeing to go with the mate and see if other passage could be secured.

Quint had forgotten about Christmas in his rush to get back to his wife. Christmas was only two days away and because of that, no other ships were sailing for at least two weeks. Quint would not wait. The first mate had been more than a little surly. Frowning now, Quint knew he should have paid more attention to the man.

The days passed uneventfully and the vessel made good time. Why then did he have this feeling that things were not well? It was a feeling of foreboding that Quint could not escape. As the days slipped into weeks, and two small storms attacked the sea, Quint relaxed a little. The crew didn't manage the ship badly and they came through the storms with no difficulty. He forced himself to ignore his fears and concentrate on what he wanted to do at the farm. He started planning an office for himself and drawing plans for additions to the house. For long hours, he found himself staring off into space, thinking about Rebecca and reliving their few short hours together. How just the thought of her left him breathless! He willed the ship forward at an even faster clip and as if to answer him the great gray shrouds billowed with air and the vessel surged forward.

He blamed his failure to observe what was happening on his excitement of going home. They were just two or three weeks away from Philadelphia when he overheard two of the sailors talking about the falling glass and for the first time, Quint noticed the black clouds swirling just above the horizon to the southwest.

He watched as the crew lashed the kegs and casks to the deck and he kept an eye on the boiling black puffs.

This storm was going to be bad, something told him, very bad, and he watched the haphazard way the sailors were going about their duties. The vision in a green silk dress danced before his eyes and for the first time in his life he was truly afraid. He tried to shake the premonition that he might not live through this storm.

The first hours of the storm seemed not much different than other spring storms he had encountered in the Atlantic and he laughed at his concern. For a short time that morning he talked himself into relaxing, but before the storm was a day old, Quint was seized with such a sense of foreboding that he began to study his surroundings and question his own reasoning. The sailors did not seem to take proper care of the sheets and the lines that he knew were necessary to everyone's safety. The back of Quint's neck began to crawl with apprehension. He watched the tiniest movement each member of the crew made and the more he watched, the more worried he became.

By the second day, Quint began to make his own preparations for what he feared was now inevitable. The ship was short handed, something he failed to notice until yesterday. The sailors were sloppy and the vessel was poorly cared for. Quint knew a moment of embarrassment over his attitude toward his own first mate. "If I live through this," he muttered, "I'll have to apologize to the man." It was a sobering thought. He realized then that he might not live through the wreck he knew would come. If they didn't sight land soon and take refuge in a safe harbor, the ship would break apart in the gigantic battering waves.

He tried to make some calculations of his own about where they were, but he realized that he had spent most of the trip daydreaming about a woman that he might never see again. Increasingly concerned, he questioned one of two of the older members of the crew and discovered that they knew little and cared even less. They didn't know the danger of a storm at sea and a poorly prepared vessel.

Quint approached the only man he met on the ship that he thought had a modicum of knowledge, the first mate. He was more than helpful, and allowed Quint to see the charts of the area. Quint sensed that the man knew how desperate their chances were becoming. As they studied the charts together, they listened to the straining ship, and watched the sky, dark and heavy. They could make it if they headed toward the islands and Quint started to pray.

Toward dawn of the third day, the creaking of the ship became a crackling sound. Quint left his cabin and made his way to the deck. During the afternoon hours of the day before Quint had noticed the placement of the kegs and rope and other supplies that might be needed if the ship started to flounder.

The sky lightened only a small amount to signal dawn but Quint was so concerned with what was happening around him that he failed to even notice that. Two of the spars were going, the main mast was also giving way under the strain and they were taking on water. From the sounds below deck some of the bottom timbers were beginning to pull free.

Quint knew his timing was critical. He must not enter the water until there was no other recourse, but he would have to be far enough away from the ship when it broke apart, so that he would not be struck by falling timbers or pulled under as the ship went down. Yanking two pieces of deck railing from the fore section he lashed himself to them. He might have a chance if the mate was right about their position. But there was no chance for this ship and the men on it.

A tearing noise signaled disaster and he knew instinctively that a part of the stern was going. It was over. The ship was gone. He felt sick, but he knew he had to make his move. It was time. He threw himself over the side of the ship. Despite the whining of the wind, he heard the splintering sound that could only mean the main mast had toppled. Calmly, he wondered if he had waited too long. As he resurfaced in the boiling sea, he felt a sharp pain in his head as something from the ship fell on him. Suddenly, Rebecca's smiling face appeared before him. A dark void was trying to press down on him as a flood of water poured over his head, but he could still see Rebecca's face swimming through the water and the mist.

She seemed to be beckoning him and he tried to follow her but his arms felt like lead and his head hurt badly. Her face was so close that he thought he might be able to reach out to her, and he struggled against the weight of water holding him below the waves. He forced himself up and out of the water until he was above the boiling waves instead of below them. Over and over, as the waves claimed him, Rebecca appeared next to him as if to bring him back to the surface. It was almost as if she was calling to him, and he clung to reality, realizing that it could not be so. Still, her brown eyes and perfect oval face danced before his mind.

The thought that he must be dying entered his mind, but he still clung to the fading vision of the small black-haired woman who had been his for two days, the only two days of his life that mattered to him. Strange, he thought, as he tried to cling to consciousness, he had really only lived for those two days.

The storm that passed over the island had been a very bad one and Madeleine Hemphill and the two house slaves were out on the beach, searching for cargo that might have been pushed toward the island during the storm. Lucy, the youngest of the three, spotted the timbers and the rope before the three realized that a man was lying in the sand under the debris. The heavy surf still lapped at his bare feet and as the trio approached, Madeleine noticed that his left arm was twisted into a peculiar position. There was blood seeping from a cut on his head and he was very white. Probably dead, she thought, as they neared the body lying on the sand.

A soft moan startled all three women and they rushed forward. In one voice they exclaimed, "He's alive!" Madeleine sent Lucy scurrying off for three of the strong male slaves and a pallet as she and Betsy worked diligently to remove the ropes and timbers. Madeleine wondered if it was worth the effort to move him. He might not be strong enough to live. Usually, the ship-wrecked victims were so weak, or had swallowed so much water that they died within hours of being found on the beaches. Madeleine and Betsy turned him over as carefully as they could and both women were astounded at his size, "He's bigger than Father," Madeleine whispered in awe. It would be such a tragedy if this one died.

They waited for almost an hour before Lucy returned with the pallet and the male slaves Madeleine had requested. The man was rolled onto the pallet and gently carried back to the house which was four miles from the beach. Being the most westward island of the chain, they sometimes saw shipwreck victims, but all too often the bodies could only be buried. This one managed to get to the beach with some life left and all of the island medical knowledge would be used to save him. The natives and most of the slaves were very superstitious and they would see the man's survival as a good omen for the coming year. Madeleine almost believed it herself. Surely, he would survive, for he made it to the beach.

The pathetic form was taken to the big house and Mama Chee-che was summoned to attend the victim of the first storm of the year. His arm was broken in two places and he had a serious head injury, but Mama told everyone in the big house that although it looked grim, it was not impossible, she had seen worse and they had lived. She went to work, darkening the room, setting the arm and preparing the herbs and potions she used for head wounds.

After the man had been cleaned up and a slave posted to report the smallest movement to Mama who moved into the house, Madeleine entered his room. There was something vaguely familiar about this man. She had seen him before. He was a handsome man and she remembered the face. A sailor, perhaps, she thought. Perhaps someone who sailed on one of her father's ships.

The days passed slowly and the household waited with one breath. Daily, a small crowd waited outside on the large green lawn for a report of the man. Everyone on the island now knew. If he lived it would be a good year for them all. They waited. They waited for ten days, then eleven, but Mama still stayed secluded in the house and word was passed by the servants of the house to the crowd that grew each day, "No change!" On the fourteenth day Mama came forth from the sick room and told Madeleine quietly, "He lives!" The word was passed quickly and all who knew smiled happily. The victim of the first storm was going to survive. This year would indeed be a good one.

Quint fought a mist of pain. He was surrounded by water, nothing but water, and Rebecca smiled out as if to reach him then her face dived under the water only to resurface in front of him again. He tried to tell her that he needed her help, that he was hurt, but she only seemed to want to get away from him. He reached for her time and again but large cool hands forced his arms down at his side and ordered him to lie still. Every time he tried to raise his head to see where he was, a smashing pain brought back the black void that seemed to delight in swallowing him up into nothingness. Time did not exist and somewhere in his subconscious he was aware of people and soft linens. Cool hands raked over his hot body, trailing wet cold fingers, long and thin, and he imagined the fingers of death running over his body. His few thoughts were not coherent and he could only wonder why, if he was dead, he hurt so bad. Then the cold hands moved over his flesh and he sank into unconsciousness yet another time.

February was drawing to a close and Rebecca was living one hour at a time. She cancelled the classes once again and Hilda spent her time in the kitchen preparing all of her delicacies for the arrival of the master of the house. Rebecca was nearly beside herself in anticipation. Through January, as she waited, she was only suspicious, but now she was sure. She was going to have a baby. Quint told her on a number of occasions how much he liked children and she couldn't wait for his return so that she could share her news with him.

Each night, despite the chill in her room, Rebecca would disrobe and stand before the long mirror and look at her profile. Her breasts felt a little fuller, even if she could see no difference. Her stomach was a little rounded she thought, but there was nothing discernible. Into February she could see very little change in her figure and all of her clothes still fit the same. She was certain that her complaints were a direct result of a pregnancy, but her clothes and even her figure kept the knowledge a complete secret. She wondered if the stories she heard about her own mother were true and if she was going to be like her. One tale her father told over and over was how the two of them had gone to a fancy dress ball three months before Rebecca had been born. In the high waisted fashion of the day, not one person at the ball had the slightest suspicion that her mother was carrying a child. Her father confided that by the end of her seventh month, Rebecca's mother had bloomed and she was huge. Rebecca was pleased that her secret was safe for a while, but she couldn't help but wonder what Quint would say when she became huge and awkward like her mother. She giggled and knew she could hardly wait.

She felt wonderful. There had been a day or two of queasiness early in January but Hilda, who had noticed, laid the expected arrival of Quint and a good case of nerves as the culprit and fixed Rebecca some mint tea for her stomach. Rebecca wanted to share her secret with Hilda or send word to Susannah, but she dared say nothing until she confided her news to her husband. He had to be the first to know.

The end of February came and went but Quint didn't appear. Three days into March, Rebecca was annoyed but not yet concerned. By the end of the week, Rebecca was frightened. Each day, Cad was saddled and she rode her little gift around the property enjoying the cool brisk mornings that marked an early spring. If she couldn't ride in the morning then she traveled around the farm after the afternoon meal. There was only one day of heavy rain, and it fell for hours and hours. She didn't ride that day.

As she waited she was in a turmoil. She ached with fear and in desperation she sent for Susannah and George. They arrived in two days time and tried with reason and logic to persuade Rebecca that there was nothing wrong. Delays often occurred and a late arrival really was nothing to be alarmed about. It was still very early and she shouldn't get too concerned until more time had passed. George proposed that he make the trip into Philadelphia and see if there was any information about ships that left London in late December and early January. Rebecca thought that was a wonderful idea and Susannah and the baby stayed to keep her company. For the first time in two weeks, Rebecca relaxed. As much as she wanted to tell Susannah the news about her own baby, she said nothing.

George was gone for three days. His grim face proclaimed that his lips were telling lies when he said, "Nothing, yet." Later that night, when he and Susannah had retired to their room, Susannah demanded to know what was going on. She hadn't been fooled by her husband, although she prayed that Rebecca had been. Somehow, Susannah had managed to convince Rebecca that they should all retire early.

When they reached their room, Susannah turned on George, "What did you find out, and don't try to tell me, 'nothing yet.' I know you much better than Rebecca."

George looked glum, "The *Sea Breeze* is already in port.

The repair didn't take as long as they thought. The English ship Quint took was due in by February tenth. And, that's not all. Information from the islands, places a severe storm in the Atlantic in late January. That's all anyone knows."

Both he and Susannah jumped when a small gasp and a thump indicated that George's news was overheard by Rebecca as well. Susannah glanced at the open door and was struck with guilt. Rebecca must have come to check on them and with the door open she had heard every word.

Rebecca found herself stretched out on her own bed and George and Susannah were both leaning over her. "Rebecca," George said quietly, "We simply don't know. Anything could have happened. They could have had trouble and put into one of the islands for repairs. If there has been a shipwreck, then we have to wait for information from the islands. That can take weeks. Then again, Quint's ship could dock tomorrow."

Rebecca was dazed for several hours but after a good night's sleep she said simply, "Quint is not dead, so we'll wait." She insisted that George and Susannah return to their own farm. Planting was just a few weeks away and without being told, she knew that George needed to be at his own farm making plans. They exchanged assurances and Rebecca kissed them both good-bye. She concentrated on the classes and every afternoon Cad was saddled. She trotted around the property visiting the farmers and surveying preparations she ordered for spring planting on the McQuade farm.

She spent time thinking of the small token of love that Quint had given her, but she no longer watched her figure in the mirror. One or two of the dresses were a little tight but she did not look like she was carrying a child, and she kept her news a secret.

Logic told her that there was a possibility that if there had been a storm, Quint might not have survived, but she ignored logic. Quint was still alive. Somehow she knew that and he was coming home. He was going to have a son, and for that reason and that reason alone, he would return. It didn't matter that he didn't know about the child yet. He would come home! Rebecca refused to alter her routine and each day she taught her classes and went for her ride.

George and Susannah had been gone for almost two weeks when John was out working in the fields close to the house. In the distance, he saw a huge war party gathering in the woods in the southwest corner of the property. Quickly all of the families gathered together, and everyone ran to the main house. The women and children were herded into the well and John and his sons and the other two farmers started loading rifles and muskets. The Indians didn't seem to be interested in the house but John was taking no chances. For over an hour they watched and waited, but then the Indians rode off and the all clear was given.

Hilda ran screaming to John, "Rebecca, where Rebecca is?" John lined everyone up and it was clear that the young lady of the home was not with the women. She wasn't with the men either and when Sam went to check, he returned with the information that Cad was gone as well. Then, Hilda remembered, "She, riding went. Out there, she is."

Hilda went into hysterics even before John gave the order to search. For twenty-four hours, everyone on the farm and the neighbors from two close farms joined in the search, but there was no trace of the horse or the young mistress. John sent for George and he arrived in only sixteen hours. He came alone. Again, they explored every inch of ground. They found the tracks of the war ponies John told George about, and he declared them to be Iroquois. George pondered aloud why they came east and south. He couldn't believe that they had taken Rebecca.

Word was sent south and west of the property and even north into town. And, while they waited they searched again. When word came, George was as shaken as the others at the farm. The war party was sighted moving west. They had several white prisoners with them and one of the farmers, thirty miles west of Philadelphia, swore he saw a small black-haired white girl in a dark red riding suit with the party. Strange, he told George, when George questioned him, the black-haired girl was riding a horse. The other captives were pulled along on a tether line, but the girl in the dark red riding suit was on a horse.

George left the farm and made his way to Philadelphia to see what the government would be willing to do. He returned sick at heart. The government would try for a swap, a trade of some kind, but . . .

Chapter Twenty-seven

When Rebecca first saw the Indians at the edge of the woods, she was only annoyed. They had no business being on the farm. Surely, after all of this time they weren't there to avenge the savage she helped the year before. As she watched them milling about in a clearing near the massive oak trees, her annoyance turned to fear. The woods were dark and she could only make out their shapes. She kept her mare as quiet as she could, praying that they would pass the farm by and continue on their way.

As she watched and waited she counted the shapes she could see. There were at least fifteen and probably eighteen of them and she remembered what George had said about large war parties. She was trembling from fright and she wondered if they had spotted her. Her heart wrenched in her chest when she spied several white people standing in the back with several horses. She could only guess at what they were doing with the Indians.

Suddenly, without any warning, she was pulled from her horse and pushed to the ground. The daze through which she had moved for days now vanished and she fought like a cornered cat. She wasn't as strong as the Indian that unseated her, and she realized quickly that while he held her tightly, he was not exerting himself at all. That made her even more angry, but her struggles did nothing to gain her release. Her hands were lashed together in front of her, a rope was tied about her neck and she was led forward to join the others whom she now realized were captives. She looked at the two other women and the three men and a child and really didn't see their faces. They were all strung together, one rope loop fastened to the end of the next rope. The Indians moved on, pulling their captives after them. They moved quickly and Rebecca found that she almost had to run part of the way to keep the loop of the rope that hung around her neck from choking her. They traveled on for over an hour through one woods, then another, until they came to what appeared to be a small forest.

From out of nowhere came an additional ten Indians. Immediately, Rebecca recognized the leader of this group, and to her amazement, he recognized her. He led his horse up to her and sat looking down at her, but other than his recognition, she could read nothing else in his expression. For the first time, Rebecca was really frightened. If they were after the kind of revenge she heard about, she was certain that a very painful death was only hours away.

The Indian left her trembling and maneuvered his horse up to the leader of the larger group. The two men, one young and the other much older, sat on their horses and talked quietly while her Indian pointed to her several times. The young brave that unseated her, now on Cad, joined the group and for several more minutes it appeared that they were arguing. As Rebecca watched, the Indian on Cad jumped off the horse and stalked away, his face registering anger. He turned once and shouted something at the two Indians still talking. Her Indian grabbed the reins of Cad and guided the prancing horse to where she stood. Still holding the reins of Cad, he jumped down from his own horse and without a word, released the rope from around her neck, grasped her waist and swung her up to the saddle the Indian hadn't bothered to remove. Giving her a long look and still retaining the reins, he led her forward so that she was just off to his right side. Then, the march began again.

They moved through the trees and stopped twice during the night for a short rest. On the first stop, her Indian reminded her that he was Crying Wolf. She said her name was Rebecca. He lifted his hand and fingered her hair. "No! From now on, I call you Little Raven." He brought her food and water when they stopped the second time, but he said nothing else to her.

She was terrified. She was much too afraid to ask him any questions, but she did notice that the other prisoners where receiving very little attention and they were not being offered any food or water. Crying Wolf had said, "From now on . . ." She was too frightened to speculate on what his words meant.

When Rebecca was so tired that she knew she could go no further, she glanced over at her captor. As if he could read her mind, Crying Wolf lifted her from the saddle and placed her on his own horse. She could not help herself. Resting her head on his chest, she closed her eyes and drifted off to sleep.

When she awoke, he helped her back up on Cad and they moved on. In the distance, Rebecca could see people scrambling to hide themselves from the Indians but the savages seemed uninterested in any or the farms they skirted. Most of the time they avoided civilization. Once, when they got very close to one farm, there were several shots fired, but the Indians moved on as quickly as their captives could run and Rebecca tried not to think of the men and women being dragged behind her.

Again they traveled most of the night, stopping twice to rest. The terrain was now mountainous and the horses moved more slowly. By the third day, Rebecca was so tired and hurt so much that she began to consider death as an alternative to this nightmare. She prayed continually that if she did live through all of this, her baby would survive. For some reason they stopped much earlier on the third day than they had before. Rebecca was in a state of near collapse and fell asleep on the blanket Crying Wolf spread out for her before he tied up the horses. She slept soundly all night long.

She could see the pale light of dawn when Crying Wolf shook her shoulder the next morning. For no reason that she could understand, the two groups of Indians split up and the other captives were taken away with the original group of Indians responsible for her capture. One of the women screamed something at her as they ran past. Rebecca didn't understand her words but by the tone of her voice, something told Rebecca she didn't want to know. One of the young men with Crying Wolf wheeled his horse around and rode directly at the woman. He reached down from his horse and hit the woman squarely in the mouth. She went sprawling to the ground. The leader of the larger group yelled in their direction and the youth with Crying Wolf turned his horse around and moved back toward their smaller group.

Rebecca felt her chin quiver and the tears started to form in her eyes, but she decided that these savages would not see her cry. She squared her shoulders and tried to make her mind a blank. Crying Wolf glanced at her and for a fraction of a second, Rebecca knew that he understood what she was going through. As he glanced away, the expression on his face changed to one of total indifference. He felt some compassion, Rebecca knew, but was it enough to save her? She stared down at her hands, still bound. She wondered if her fate had yet to be decided. They moved on, but now they traveled in the opposite direction of the first group of Indians.

The sun was setting when they stopped for the evening meal. Crying Wolf pulled her from her horse and set her close to a large tree. She leaned back against the tree while he secured the horses. When he came back, he stood in front of her for several seconds as if he was trying to decide something in his own mind. Suddenly, he removed his knife from his breeches and Rebecca froze, stark terror written on her face. "This is the end," she thought and clutched her slightly rounded belly. Her child would never know a sunrise of the feeling of the wind in his face, or his mother's arms. But Crying Wolf hunched down and reached over to cut the rawhide strips that confined her wrists. When he was finished he put the knife back at his side and took her wrists into his hands, gently rubbing life back into her fingers. She looked up at him, the terror now gone. She wanted to ask him why he was taking care of her but she was too confused and she couldn't force the words over the cotton in her mouth.

While Crying Wolf tended to her, the other Indians built a fire and several skinned rabbits were brought out to roast. Crying Wolf sat directly in front of her and the other men sat as close to the fire as he did and in a nearly complete circle. After he had eaten, he handed Rebecca some of the rabbit meat and a flat pancake of corn meal. He brought her a skin of water and talked to the other Indians while she ate. She was starved and quickly finished everything he gave her.

Once she had finished, he took her arm and pulled her to her feet. "We walk," was all that he said, and she followed him without a backward glance at the other young men still sitting in the circle before the fire.

When they were far from the flickering flames, Crying Wolf turned to her, "In two days time we will come to my camp, to my people. I will tell you what I tell them. I will tell you how to behave. You will do exactly what I say." He waited to see if she understood what he meant. She nodded her head gravely.

"Women, squaws are the leader of our tribe. They pick the man to be chief. I am such a one. I was chosen by the women to lead my people," he glanced at her and in the darkness she could not see his arrogance, but she could feel it. He continued softly, "In two days time, I will present you to my mother and I will present you as my first wife. I will also tell my mother that you are carrying my child, my son," Rebecca rushed to deny what he was saying, "I'm not your wife and I am not carrying a child."

He cuffed her on the chin and not too gently, "Listen, white woman! I know this is not true and you know this is not true, but you are carrying a child. Without my protection, you will be a slave and the child will not live. You probably will not live. I have a plan. You will walk behind me, we will share the same lodge, you will fix my meals. The other maidens will not like this, for many have wanted to be my mate. They will throw things at you and they will pull your hair. They will do these things when I am not around." Rebecca's eyes were glistening with tears, but still he continued, "Do not give in! You are a fighter. Fight as you have done. Yell at them, throw dirt back at them, ask my mother where I am so that you may complain. Before the moon is new, I will tell my mother that you are not welcome in my tribe. I will take you away from the tribe, so that you may have my son in peace. I will tell my mother that I will bring you and the child back when you have recovered. She will understand this. We will leave, and I will take you to your home."

Rebecca looked up at the youth, tears glistening in her eyes, "Why are you doing this for me?"

He replied matter-of-factly, "You gave me my life, now I give you yours."

"What will your mother say when you return to your tribe without me?" she asked quietly, not yet able to believe her good fortune.

"I will tell my mother that you were not strong, that the child came early and you both died. There will be much sorrow and the women who hurt you will feel bad. It is the only way," he said softly.

All the pain and the hurt Rebecca had suffered since she left England was suddenly almost tangible. Then, to be treated so gently by what the New World considered its savages left Rebecca very troubled and in tears. She was being protected, almost revered, by an Indian. With her cheeks wet she reached up and pulled Crying Wolf's head down so that she could kiss his cheek. He reacted as if she had slapped him. Was that not allowed? she wondered. "I have never been kissed by a white woman," came his terse explanation, as he placed his hand across the cheek she had touched.

As she moved away from him, he reacted, grabbing her left arm. "Wait! You wear a symbol of another man. My family knows of your customs. We must get rid of this," he took her left hand and twisted the small gold band with the single ruby from her finger.

"No!" Rebecca cried as she watched Crying Wolf fling her wedding ring into the woods. That simple action seemed to sever Rebecca's touch with her husband and she slumped forward in tears.

Crying Wolf reached down for her, sorrow in his voice, "It is the only way."

For two days, they rode from sun-up to sun-down and both nights Crying Wolf walked with her after the evening meal. On the second night, she caught the knowing grins of the young men who watched the couple leave the camp, but Rebecca didn't even care. She glared at them, straightened her shoulders and followed Crying Wolf in the woods. She didn't miss his knowing grin, either, and she was certain that he was pleased with her.

Both nights, as they walked, Crying Wolf told her about things that she should know. He explained what would be expected of her and most importantly, how she was to act. Rebecca quickly figured out that an Indian could show temper when it suited, and she was going to have to show a lot of hers, he told her. Much better than to have to hold everything in. Fear, he explained was the only emotion Indians didn't show. She must never show fear, no matter how frightened she was.

Crying Wolf described the social structure of the tribe and Rebecca found other traditions that made a good deal of sense to her. The women owned all of the livestock, and the houses. They elected the chief, and could remove him if he didn't behave as they saw fit. The tribe went to war only if the women's war council said they go to war. Rebecca was fascinated. She wondered how the women of her acquaintance would view a role in politics. Susannah, she admitted, was the only woman she knew that might be vaguely interested. As they talked, Rebecca asked a hundred questions and Crying Wolf patiently answered them all. On both nights, they returned to the circle of fire, long after the other braves had rolled up in their blankets.

The third day began just as the other days had started

but Rebecca was tense already. Crying Wolf said they would join his people on the third day. It was the middle of the afternoon when they rode into a group of four huts. The small buildings, called lodges, were nothing more than elongated boxes with curved roofs and a hole at each end so that the occupants could crawl in or out. There were about fifty men, women, and children in the group.

Crying Wolf led her up to an old woman dressed in a skirt and shirt made of animal skins. Rebecca had seen a few people dressed in a similar costume in Philadelphia and she wondered if she had been looking at Indians and didn't know it. The arms of the shirt and the sides of the skirt had fringe hanging from what might have been side seams. The old woman wore several necklaces of what Rebecca now knew was wappum, considered of great value to the Iroquois. Rebecca did not have to be told that this woman was an important woman in the tribe.

In his own language, Crying Wolf addressed his mother and then turned to Rebecca. He lifted her down from the bay mare and placed her before the older woman. Rebecca looked the woman in the eyes and then lowered her own as Crying Wolf had told her to do. The woman said nothing to her son or to Rebecca but turned and retired to her lodge. Rebecca stood waiting for the old woman to reappear. She glanced at Crying Wolf uneasily, he had not told her what to do if his mother rejected her and it appeared that she had done just that. He looked at her dispassionately and she squared her shoulders and looked around at the small area he called home. Somehow, she thought it would be much larger, and that there would be a great many more people than the small group of underfed humanity that watched from every corner of the camp.

Minutes passed and Crying Wolf and Rebecca stood waiting. Rebecca wanted desperately to ask what they were waiting for but Crying Wolf refused to even look in her direction. When she was positive that her trembling legs would hold her no longer a rustling noise came from the lodge and the old woman came out of her lodge. She stood in front of Crying Wolf and Rebecca. She's not happy, not the least bit happy, Rebecca thought. She handed the girl a shirt, skirt and moccasins just like the ones she wore. Rebecca turned hesitantly to Crying Wolf. He nodded gravely and Rebecca took the folded clothes from the old woman. She asked Crying Wolf how to say "Thank you," in his tongue. He told her and for the first time, he smiled, "My mother speaks your tongue as well as the Iroquois language. She taught me." With that, he jumped up on the horse and rode away from the camp, leading Cad after him.

Rebecca turned back to the old woman and murmured her thanks. Crying Wolf's mother led her into the lodge and pointed to a small area near the far end of the lodge, "You and my son may sleep there." As she bent to leave the lodge, she turned in Rebecca's direction. "Change!" she hissed and then she was gone.

Rebecca carefully removed her filthy riding suit and donned the skirt and shirt she had been given, then went outside to see what was going on and to find Crying Wolf. "I'll never be able to carry this off," she muttered. "Not if the old woman speaks English."

At first she didn't notice Crying Wolf. He was seated in a circle with several older men around a small fire that burned in the center of the camp. Somehow, Rebecca knew she should not bother him, but as she looked around at the dark eyes staring at her, she was afraid. She tried to keep her face a blank, they must not know of her fear, she told herself as she remembered Crying Wolf's words the first night they talked. But they had never talked about what she should do while he did whatever it was that he was doing. This first day, they never discussed in detail.

She wasn't sure what was expected of her, and she kept telling herself that she couldn't show them how very frightened she was. When a warm hand touched her arm, she jumped. She turned and looked up at the old woman who was standing at her side. Crying Wolf's mother seemed delighted at the shock that must have registered in her face, but Rebecca fought for control and grew much calmer. Now the old woman was looking at her with disgust, and Rebecca knew once again that Crying Wolf's mother was a most unhappy woman.

She led Rebecca around the lodge and pointed to a grinding stone and a pile of corn. Rebecca looked at her with surprise, but the Indian squatted down and showed the girl what was to be done. Rebecca knelt beside the old woman and took the grinding stone when she handed it to her. Rebecca began to tackle the task she had obviously been assigned to do. At least she now had something to do.

Not one of the other Indian girls in the camp made any attempt to get close to her for days. By the end of that first week, Rebecca was terrified, but not because she was being mistreated. None of what Crying Wolf said would happen had taken place. What if they never did anything to her? She would be forced to live here with Crying Wolf, as his wife. When the babe arrived, all of the Indians would know that she was not Crying Wolf's wife and then what would they do. She refused to think about Quint and the problems at the farm. Each day, she tried only to live through that day and think of nothing but her life with the Indians.

Crying Wolf slept beside her in the small area of the lodge that was theirs, but he did nothing more than put his arm around her before they slept. She was always too tired to object to this bit of familiarity at the end of her busy day. He took her to bathe in a nearby stream every other day, and he sat with his back to her watching for intruders, she suspected. She realized just what his protection meant but she couldn't put her feelings into words. He seemed to understand and Rebecca relaxed with him, but only with him.

The new week began and Crying Wolf told Rebecca that he and several other young braves were going hunting. "We'll be gone for several days," he spoke softly and looked at her intently. He was trying to tell her some-

307

thing, but she wasn't sure that she understood. Perhaps, now the other girls of the village would make their feelings known.

Rebecca guessed right and the very next morning, within an hour after the braves left to hunt, one of the younger girls dumped a gourd of water down Rebecca's back. She told her mother-in-law about the event in angry tones, but the woman ignored her. All day long, each girl in the camp tried to outdo the one before with taunts and tricks with which they bedeviled Rebecca. She yelled at them and called them names but attempted to ignore as much as she could. When one of the younger girls slapped her, she went in tears to her mother-in-law and demanded that she do something. According to Crying Wolf's plan, his mother would take her part for the major episodes and ignore the smaller things. But the old woman did nothing.

Rebecca was furious. Crying Wolf led her to believe that the trouble would begin as soon as they got to camp and it had not and now her dear mother-in-law was ignoring the serious things the other girls were trying. Rebecca wondered if Crying Wolf was playing a gigantic joke on her. For two more days, Rebecca tried to handle the insults and the minor attacks but her temper finally got the upper hand. When she went to get water, one of the older girls followed her and tried to push her into the stream. Rebecca grabbed at the girl and jerked her away. The girl fell into the stream. A smaller girl rushed at Rebecca and tried to pinch her. Rebecca grabbed her hands, looked at her with black eyes and deliberately pinched her back. All day long as each of the girls tried to do something to hurt her, Rebecca retaliated.

The next week was a living hell. Every woman and girl in the camp taunted or tried to trick her until she wanted to scream. She decided that being a captive could not be much worse than what she was forced to endure. The old woman was no help at all. "Just wait until he gets back here," Rebecca mumbled as she tried to finish her tasks.

When the hunters finally returned, Crying Wolf didn't

have a chance to ask her a thing. Even before he brought his horse to a halt, his mother was at his side, chattering at him in their Indian tongue and pointing to Rebecca. Crying Wolf held up his hand, jumped down from his horse and glanced at Rebecca. She had her hands folded over her breasts and the expression on her face was furious. "If he smiles at me, I'll scratch his eyes out," she thought as she watched the old woman drag her son into the lodge.

Rebecca waited outside the lodge for over an hour. When he followed his mother from the lodge he looked grave, and he took her hand, "We will walk." He led the way out of the village and Rebecca followed, a little frightened by what she felt the old woman told her son. Perhaps her position in the camp had changed and she was about to become a slave.

They walked for almost a mile before Crying Wolf turned to her and he grinned down at her. "My mother wants me to take you away. She says you don't understand the Indian way of life. Since the other women believe that you are my choice they will say nothing. What did you do to them that they are all afraid of you? I had to hunt. I did not leave you without protection. My mother . . ."

"Bah! Your mother, indeed. She ignored me completely and let me protect myself," Rebecca announced in an angry voice.

Crying Wolf grinned at her openly now, "You fight too well." Then he walked off and stood looking out over the small valley that lay at his feet. He came back to stand beside her, and he looked somber, "I am afraid of what might happen when I go on another hunt, and I must hunt. My mother does not think that we are married. She asked me why you did not share my robe and she would not accept my excuse when I told her I feared for the babe. My mother may decide to sell you to another tribe. I think I take you back to your home tonight," he mused almost to himself. Rebecca felt a tremendous weight lifted from her shoulders and her face lit into a radiant smile.

Before he led her back the way they had come, he

cautioned, "You must look very unhappy. If you can bring tears to your eyes all the better." Rebecca stared at him for a minute and then nodded her head. By the time they got back to camp, Rebecca was trying to keep from sobbing. On the walk back she let her mind wonder about what had become of her true husband for the first time since her capture.

Crying Wolf left her in the lodge, and spent another hour with his mother. He came back to the lodge and told Rebecca quietly to gather her things. He led her away to the horses, helped her mount Cad and again holding the reins, he mounted his horse and led them away from the village. Rebecca's saddle was gone and she rode her horse with only a blanket between her and the animal. The skirt the old woman gave her was split, but it took her many painful hours of hard work to stay on the horse comfortably.

The journey back seemed almost leisurely compared to the flight they had taken three weeks before. Rebecca and Crying Wolf traveled slowly through the forests, stopping every few hours so that Rebecca could rest. At night, Crying Wolf built a small fire and Rebecca cooked the fowl or whatever small animal he felled for their meal. If water was available, Rebecca took a bath. Often, after she rolled up in her blanket she found Crying Wolf watching her. At times she felt a tremor of terror race through her slender form. He had to be taking her back to the farm. But she only had his word for it, and she found herself arguing silently. Of course, he was taking her home. He was an honorable man, he said he would take her back. But would he? He was a savage. She didn't ask him any questions, in fact, neither of them said much at all. There didn't seem to be anything to say.

Rebecca let her mind drift as mile after mile slipped by. She was certain that Quint was back from England, now and she wondered what she would tell him. For a month, she lived with the Indians everyone was so afraid of and she was returning home, not much different from when she had been grabbed weeks before. There was always the chance that he would not want her back. She was tired and angry and she tried not to consider that a possibility, but she could not stem the tears that started to flow. If Crying Wolf saw or heard, he paid no attention. Finally drained, her eyes dry, she lifted her head and squared her shoulders. She could still tutor. She would be able to make her own way. No matter what happened, she had a part of Quint, a small tiny little one forming in her body as each step took them closer to the farm.

On the night of the seventh day of travel, while they sat waiting for the rabbit to finish cooking, Crying Wolf broke the usual silence and said, "Tomorrow we reach your farm. I take you close to the house, but you will walk from the woods."

Rebecca stared at him, "Tomorrow?"

He only nodded his head and then looking at her with dark intense eyes he added, "If you do not want to return I take you with me to the north. I go there to join my brothers. My village is moving north because there are too many white people ruining the land. You can have the child and then we can marry. You can be my first wife in truth."

Rebecca smiled at him sadly, "We live in different worlds. I thank you for the offer but I love the man whose child I carry. I will always love him. It would not be fair to you. I could never fit into your world . . ." her voice shook as she whispered, "even if my husband doesn't want me back." Crying Wolf looked away from her and they both sat for a long time staring into the small fire before them.

Once more Crying Wolf broke the silence, "I will take your horse."

Rebecca gasped, "You are going to keep Cad? Why?" her voice hinted at a sudden loss of control.

"When I return to my village, I will tell my mother the story I told you when we arrived. I must keep the horse, to make the story real."

Rebecca sighed and turned away from him. He had risked much for her. There was the chance that the women might want him to step down because of her. And he had asked to marry her. The horse was the only thing she could give him in thanks and it would salve his pride a bit. She turned back to him, "I want you to have the horse. It was a gift to me and now I give her to you. May she serve you as well as she served me." She could not say another word.

She sat quietly remembering the morning that Quint gave her the little horse. She was coming home, but what she was coming back to she did not know. A part of her was excited and happy and yet something in her was also very frightened and apprehensive. Since her arrival in America she heard tales about women who had been captives of the Indians. They were never accepted back into society. There was a very real possibility that Quint would not want her as his wife. Perhaps he would allow her to remain until the baby was born. She realized that she knew very little about the man she married. He had been so angry with her when she took care of Crying Wolf and that was in his home. Now she had lived with them.

Still, it was not her fault. They had taken her away against her will, and she had been forced to go with them. And she had not been mistreated, but could she convince her husband that she had not been touched. None of the Indians had touched her, she was the same as when he left. A thought stopped her heart. What would she do, if he didn't believe that the child she carried was his? Her fear quickly replaced any excitement she had and she curled up in her blanket and tried to sleep.

Try as hard as she could, sleep would not come and she spent a terrible night. The several times she dozed off, she awakened with a vision of Quint pushing her out the door of the farm house. Hilda was standing behind him in the background pointing a finger at her and she had a dark scowl on her face. Rebecca was up before dawn.

They finished the rabbit and were on their way. They traveled for almost four hours before Rebecca started to notice things that looked familiar to her. They finally moved through the woods and just before they reached the edge of the trees, Rebecca looked up and spotted the farm house. Part of her wanted to scream her relief and part of her shrank back, afraid to move forward. Crying Wolf seemed to notice her confusion but he only stopped his horse and dismounted. He quickly reached up and pulled her from Cad. As he moved away from her, holding Cad's reins in his hands, he looked back and smiled slightly, "You have your life back." He jumped up onto his horse and trotted away. She stood watching him ride toward the west away from the world she was now afraid to enter.

Chapter Twenty-eight

Arthur waited for over a month before he received word from the lawyer that a buyer for the small farm had been found and it took another three weeks before passage was secured on a ship bound for Philadelphia. Long before the lawyer informed him that a buyer had been found, he wrote to Margaret and told her that as soon as he could arrange his personal affairs and secure passage, he would be on his way to rescue his sister. By March tenth, Arthur was on his way to the provincial capital of America.

The voyage was long and tiring and Arthur did not adapt to the rigors of the sea. For the first two weeks of the trip, he was forced to spend his time in his bunk in the inexpensive cabin the lawyer had reserved. He was so sick he wanted to die. The only thought that kept him going was the amount of interest he generated among several old widowers who had expressed a desire to meet the young widowed sister he was traveling to see. He told them he had to return her to their beloved England, then when she was at home, they could meet her.

Arthur suffered no guilt pangs in referring to his sister as a widow. That description would explain to any future husband her lack of virginity and if this McQuade had not already used her, he would be able to arrange a much better settlement for her. He laughed out loud as he remembered one irate suitor. He thought Arthur should pay him something for marrying the girl. That was the way it was usually done, he told Arthur. Arthur explained, as carefully as he could, that Rebecca was not the usual young woman, and she did hold title to the one large farm they had left, northwest of London. The suitor had been unimpressed and told Arthur that he thought a bride price, farm or not, was tantamount to selling the girl. Arthur instructed the old valet to show the man from the house before he said another word.

Arthur decided very early on in the sea voyage that he would also charge a finder's fee from one of the two old gentlemen he finally settled on as the best possible candidate. Both men had properties, both needed a wife but most important as far as Arthur was concerned, both were more than willing to pay him the bride price he was asking for Rebecca. Arthur spent a good part of the voyage, after he was up and about, figuring out the best price for a finder's fee and attempting to justify the figures with expenses he would tell the old men he had to spend to bring Rebecca back from the colonies.

Quint slowly surfaced from his fragmented dreams. The minute he was awake he knew he was not in the water he had imagined. Instead, he was in a soft warm bed and a large black woman was leaning over him. She was wiping his wet skin with a soft rag and he was being pushed over so that the warm wet linens on which he lay could be removed. The enormous black woman leaned down, grinning at him, "You come back from the dead. You be fine now." He heard a beehive of activity behind him and he tried to raise his head to see what was going on, but the pain made him dizzy and sick to his stomach. The black face loomed above him again and the voice cautioned him to lie still and mend.

With his head throbbing like it held a large drum, Quint realized that he was very much alive and he hurt all over. He didn't know where he was and he wasn't certain that he knew who he was, but he was alive. Slowly, he sank into a deep dreamless sleep.

When he awoke again, he was aware that a warm sweet liquid was being placed in his mouth and he was told to swallow. The black face came into focus for a second, no more, and then he drifted back into more deep sleep. Once more, he awoke and when he opened his eyes, he blinked into a brilliant light which could only mean one thing. Sunlight. Slowly, he lifted his head, but this time a dull ache was all he felt. He laid his head back on the pillow and moved his legs. They moved but as he attempted to move his arms he sensed bandages and something heavy that made the moving of his left arm impossible. Jerking his head to see what was wrong, a sharp pain hit him between the eyes and he muttered a coarse, "Damn!" as he closed his eyes again.

Slowly, the pain receded and he opened his eyes again. Standing next to the bed and leaning over him so that he need not move his head, was a vision of loveliness dressed in white. The vision had startling gray-green eyes and thick curling hair the color of dark bronze. "So," the vision whispered in a sultry feminine voice, "You are well enough to swear." She laughed softly and moved from Quint's line of vision.

"Where am I?" he tried to force the words from his hoarse throat.

"Questions later, now you must get well," the vision was again leaning over him, running her cool fingers across his forehead and into his hair. Quint fought the urge for more rest, more sleep, but his need was great and he drifted into oblivion.

Slowly Quint found that he drifted into sleep less and less and when he moved, the pain in his head was replaced by a dull ache that seemed to stay with him forever. He began to recognize the people who worked around him each day. There was Mama Chee-che, self-proclaimed doctor who told him he suffered from a broken skull. There were two young female slaves and the vision with the bronze hair who called herself Madeleine. Each day, Madeleine took over more and more of his care, seeing that hot broths were fed to him, shaving him, helping him into a sitting position and trying to answer his question about where he was and how he got there.

He was nearly struck dumb when he found out that he had been delirious for a month and a week and Madeleine told him how she and the two slaves had found him on the beach. No one knew what ship he sailed on or if he was traveling to Europe or away from Europe. Quint could remember nothing. He didn't know his name, where he lived, or what he was doing in the middle of the Atlantic in January. But the more he and Madeleine talked, bits and pieces started to fall into place in the ever-expanding puzzle of his life. He remembered the strangest things, like a gaming room in London, yet somehow he knew he didn't gamble for his livelihood. When he told Madeleine, she was convinced for one whole day that he was an infamous gambler who had to flee England or lose his life.

Quint told Madeleine that he was certain that the sea figured prominently in his life. He decided that he had to be a ship's captain just as he was certain that the ship he was on was not the ship that had floundered near the island. One of his earliest memories was the ship breaking up. He didn't tell Madeleine about the black-haired angel that brought him through the sea. She was his special memory even if she never existed except in his mind.

At the end of two weeks, his head only occasionally bothered him and then only slightly. He was so weak and tired so easily that Mama insisted he stay in bed until she said he could rise. Continually, he argued with her but she refused to let him leave his bed. He had no idea his strength was so depleted until Mama declared that he could leave his bed while his linens were changed. Slowly, he sat up because Mama was at the side of the bed lecturing him at every move he took. He lowered his feet and stood up just as she ordered. Grinning down at her, he decided that she was much too cautious. Everything was fine. Then, suddenly, the large sunny room started to move in slow circles and he realized that he was very dizzy. He thought he moved back to sit down on the bed and was shocked to find himself lying on the floor. As always,

Madeleine was at his side and she and the two slaves got him back into the soft bed where he was quite content to stay for another two days.

Slowly, over the next week, he regained his strength and he started to move from his bed to the windows and Mama ordered solid food for him. Madeleine brought his meals and they ate together at the small table by the window. He had ample opportunity to watch the golden-haired girl. She was well-rounded and soft, with full beautiful breasts and she wore her dresses low so that the soft swelling was apparent above her gown. She was tall and her gray-green eyes crinkled in amusement most of the time. Her sultry voice sent small shivers of delight up and down Quint's spine each time she laughed. She seemed to delight in patting and fussing over him and Quint depended on her for almost everything. He enjoyed her company and looked forward to her frequent visits. She had a penchant for leaning over him so that he could get a good view of her large breasts. Quint wondered if that was part of the treatment Mama had prescribed to make him well.

His memory was still very vague and he could not remember who he was or why he had been in the middle of the Atlantic on a ship that he knew was not his. Mama kept reassuring him on her frequent visits that his memory would come flooding back when he least expected it. "Don't you worry none," she told him quietly.

By the first of April, Madeleine took him outside the large house to sit on the spacious veranda that completely surrounded the house. He also started having meals with her in the elegant dining room off of the veranda.

Shortly after he started eating in the dining room, Mama came to remove the restrictive splint from his arm. She gave him a hard look before she grinned her wide toothy smile, "You as well as you can be!"

He bowed low, "I cannot thank you enough. Without your help, I would have been fish food by now. But, are you sure that I'll remember who I am and where I came from? It seems that I'll never remember."

She only smiled harder, "You remember soon!"

After Mama left, Quint approached the chair where Madeleine perched while Mama unwrapped the splints and examined his arm. He pulled her into a standing position and placed his arms around her waist and drew her close. "I'm more grateful to you, I think, than I am to Mama. If you hadn't been out on the beach walking, if you hadn't ordered your people to take care of me . . ." He kissed her softly with a restrained passion that surprised even him. He really didn't want to kiss her and he wondered why.

She looked at him unhappily, "I don't want your gratitude." She put her arms around his neck, pulled his head down and kissed him with raw desire that could not be satisfied with just a kiss.

Something in Quint made him pull back. He didn't want this woman, and he didn't know why. She was throwing herself at him and every male instinct told him he was a normal man, but not with this woman. He wondered if the bump on his head had created problems of which no one had dreamed. Disgusted with himself a bit, he left her and walked in the garden for over an hour.

The next evening, Madeleine told him about her father, Joshua Hemphill, captain of his own ship. They were seated at the dining room table for the evening meal when Madeleine looked up at him. "My father will be arriving on the island in a few days. He is on his way to Philadelphia."

Quint glanced at her and repeated, "Philadelphia?" Something about the name of the city startled him and immediately he knew that it should mean something to him. Madeleine stared at him, her gray-green eyes filling with tears. "Don't you want me to remember who I am?" Quint asked quietly. The answer was plainly written in her eyes. She didn't want him to remember anything if it meant her losing him.

The remainder of the meal was strained for both of them. After dinner, Quint went out to the garden and Madeleine followed, for often after dinner they walked together in the garden. Tonight, though, they were both engrossed in their own thoughts. Suddenly, Madeleine grabbed Quint's hand and pulled him to a stop, "I want you to remember, I really do! It's just that if you should remember another woman, someone important to you . . ."

Quint pulled Madeleine into his arms and drew her chin up so that he could look into her eyes, "I think there is someone, Madeleine, someone very important."

Madeleine threw her arms up around his neck and pulled his face down to hers. "No!" she cried. She kissed him as hard and as deeply as she could and for one instant Quint responded. In that moment, a wisp of a memory floated across his mind. A raven-haired woman . . . A good-bye . . . Rebecca! Suddenly, he pushed the beautiful woman away from him and gazed down at her excitedly, "I remember everything! I know who I am!" He moved away from her and said softly, "I'm married, Madeleine, to a beautiful young woman who is at home, on my farm just north of Philadelphia."

Her stricken glance filled him with apprehension, "It doesn't matter, your being married, does it?" she asked in a whisper.

"Yes it does, and when your father arrives, he'll be able to tell you just how much it matters," he turned to walk away. She let loose with a tirade of bitter adjectives to describe his behavior, his attitude and even his own parentage. Smiling slightly at some of her colorful words, Quint made his way to his room. He stretched out and flexed the arm that had lost its cumbersome bandage only a day before. Soon, he would have that arm around Rebecca's soft warm body.

As he lay on the soft feather mattress, a vision of a small but delicately beautiful, black-haired vixen danced before his eyes. He loved her and she loved him. She had led him from a watery grave to the safety of the island and she would be waiting for him when he returned. He thought of the pain she must have endured when he had not returned when he said he would. He had to convince

Captain Hemphill that he must get to Philadelphia as soon as the man could ready his ship. Whatever it cost he would pay. If they left a day or two after he arrived, he could be in Philadelphia inside a week. He would make his way back to the woman who had tortured his subconscious dream. Despite his excitement, he drifted off to sleep easily and slept soundly for the first time in weeks.

Rebecca stood very still and watched Crying Wolf ride through the trees. She took a deep breath and turned back toward the farm. Forcing herself to move, she began to drag her feet forward through the edge of the woods and into the fields behind the house. She would not think about what waited for her, and she plodded on.

When she had covered almost a mile, Sam came charging toward her, his rifle at the ready. She looked up at him and said softly, "Sam! Put the rifle down."

He sat on his horse for what seemed like a full minute before he let out a yell that competed with anything she heard from the Indians. He turned his horse around and headed for the house at a full charge. Rebecca watched in disbelief. A thousand thoughts flew through her head, but before she wondered over much, the horse was reined to a stop so quickly that the poor animal reared up on its back legs. Again, the animal was charging for her. Sam stood beside her on the ground before the horse came to a stop.

"You shouldn't be walking, Miss Rebecca. Don't you have yer horse . . ." He shifted, embarrassed, but Rebecca felt that he was truly glad to see her. He helped her into the saddle and jumped up behind her. She tried to ask him where Quint was and what was going on at the house, but he kicked the horse and they were racing across the last mile so quickly that Rebecca had no opportunity to do anything but hang on and try to breathe.

They were still yards from the house when Sam started yelling for Hilda. When Sam slowed the horse and they finally stopped, Hilda was standing in the open door of the kitchen, a horrified expression on her face. Sam jumped down and carefully helped Rebecca from the horse. He placed her directly in front of Hilda and abruptly her large round eyes filled with tears and she was holding Rebecca tightly against her soft form, sobbing, "My baby, my poor baby . . ." Rebecca felt the tears slide down her own face as she looked into the weeping eyes of her friend.

Pulling herself free of Hilda's embrace, Rebecca looked around, and when she saw no sign of her husband, she tried to ask where he was, but Hilda was firing questions at her, one right after another. Hilda pulled her into the kitchen and sat her before the fire. "Tell me," Hilda whispered.

Rebecca smiled slightly, "Do you remember the Indian that Sam and Clem shot last summer?" Hilda nodded and Rebecca went on to explain everything that happened to her. When she finished the tale, she looked around. John was there, and Sam and even Bette stood in the doorway, tears running freely down her cheeks. She asked quietly, "Where is Quint?" No one seemed to hear her. Hilda started giving orders to everyone. Sam carried water to be heated for a bath, John was sent to the Beals, Bette and one of her girls went to the house, but all through the meleé, Rebecca asked about Quint. She was beginning to wonder if they weren't speaking the same language. Hilda pulled her upstairs into her room and directed the filling of the tub and left her to take a bath, "Clean up yourself, and food I will get."

Rebecca stepped out of her Indian costume relieved that Hilda had left her so that she could undress in private. She glanced down at her rounded stomach. Soon, everyone would know. Sinking down into the warm water, Rebecca let the warmth spread through her and she tried to relax. A minute had not yet passed when Rebecca sat up and looked around the room. Everything was just as she left it five weeks ago. There was nothing of her husband's in the room. She was home and she thought back over the excitement of the last half an hour. They weren't going to tell her where her husband was. Suddenly, it struck her that he could have gone searching for her, but no, if he did that, some of his things, at least his trunk would be in the room. It wasn't.

Even the warm water didn't help the chill that ran from her neck, down her spine. He was not there. She straightened her back and squared her shoulders. Grabbing the cloth Hilda left, she started washing her face. She really didn't want anyone to tell her that she had been abandoned by her husband, and she resolved not to ask another question. When they wanted her to know, someone would tell her. Until then, she would pretend that nothing had changed. She finished her bath and dressed in one of her own gowns and a robe. She sat quietly, waiting for the food Hilda mentioned and after she ate a little she laid down in the big bed and gave herself up to Morpheus.

When she woke, she glanced around the room, but it was so dark that it took several minutes before her eyes adjusted. The sun must have set hours before, for there was no light filtering in from outside. Rebecca wondered if it was after midnight. As she lay back listening to the night sounds, she wondered what had awakened her. She slipped from her bed and made her way to the door as quietly as she could. Slowly she opened the door and listened. Candles gleamed from the lower floor and she heard a masculine voice quietly floating up to her from the first floor.

Grabbing her robe, she raced for the stairs, one word on her lips. "Quint!" She was half way down the stairs when she realized that George Beal was approaching the stairs from the study. She looked at him, the disappointment registering in her face. "I thought Quint was home."

George looked away, distraught, as she descended the remaining steps. "Rebecca," he said, almost too softly, "Let's go into the study."

As she moved before him, she wondered if he had the unpleasant task of informing her that Quint didn't want a wife that lived with Indians. She was startled when Hilda stepped out of the study, "Tea and coffee?" The cook was dressed and she looked so grim that Rebecca knew George had bad news for her.

She glanced around the study ablaze with candles and she was startled when Susannah stepped out of the shadows. Dazed, she moved toward her sister-in-law, "Where is Quint?" she whispered. Susannah never uttered a word but held Rebecca as a stream of tears flooded from her eyes. Needing to say something, anything, Rebecca asked quietly, "Have you been here long?"

She forced her thoughts to how the Beals arrived so quickly. George couldn't have gotten to the farm before ten or eleven o'clock, the trip from his farm to Quint's took at least six hours on a good mount but Susannah would have come in the carriage and, besides, it was dark. She glanced over at George to ask about the time but he refused to look at her. Glancing over at the small clock Quint kept on his desk, she was shocked to see that it was almost five o'clock. She had slept through the evening and all through the night. Glancing back in George's direction, she muttered, "I slept eighteen hours?"

She didn't expect an answer and she didn't get one. George's hesitant step brought him to within a foot of where she stood. Gently, he pushed her toward a chair and just as carefully eased her down. Kneeling before her, he took her hands in his calloused palms. Several times, he cleared his throat and then with an emotional sigh, he murmured, "Rebecca, Quint . . . never came . . . home."

He waited for some reaction, but none came and so he continued in a whisper, "There was a bad storm, some of the wreckage of the ship he was on washed up on one of the islands. It is feared that all hands went down with the ship."

Rebecca stared at him, nothing he said made any sense. She turned on him, "You don't have to lie to me, George. I know he doesn't want me any longer because of the Indians."

George glanced at Susannah and then looked back at Rebecca in disbelief. Susannah's husky voice broke the silence, "Rebecca, Quint was not like that. He never even knew that you had been taken. He never came back."

Words started to swirl in her head. "Was not like that,

never knew, never came back, never came back, never came back . . ." Something inside her started to crack and she held herself rigid, afraid that if she moved a fraction of an inch, she would splinter into a million particles. This was one nightmare she was not prepared to face. She slumped forward in her chair and sank gratefully into a deep black void.

When she opened her eyes, Susannah and Hilda were both leaning over her. There was something cold and wet on her forehead and she realized that Hilda had applied a cool rag to her face. They helped her to a sitting position and she looked over at George then to Hilda and finally at Susannah. Their faces held looks of grief and pity. She sat on the edge of the couch and mumbled, "He didn't know . . . he didn't know."

She glanced back at the trio, they seemed to be waiting for something. Slowly, almost in a daze, she finished her sentence. "He didn't know that I carry his child. He was going to be a father." Somehow, she got through the next few minutes. Even George's eyes were wet as he asked the necessary questions. Somehow, she managed to tell them when the babe would arrive and then she moved toward the stairs, her eyes dry, her heart broken. She never knew how she got to her bed, but she did not faint again.

It was almost noon before Rebecca came down from her room. She held her sister-in-law in her arms and comforted her as Susannah wept. Rebecca had no tears left to shed. She moved through the next two days in a daze. George watched her carefully, and she would find Hilda gazing at her through wet red eyes, but she said nothing. On the third day, Susannah and George left for their farm and the haze Rebecca was in started to lift. Quint was not coming back!

Late at night, when she lay in the big bed, knowing that sleep would not come, she relived those two precious days that she and Quint had together and she smiled through her pain. She had his child and she and the little one would live on the farm. Eventually, she would tell her little one about the father that he would never know. It would be a boy, Rebecca never questioned that Quint had fathered a son. Quint's son was already letting her know that he would be a strong healthy child. In spite of all the sadness that filled her soul, she rejoiced in the brisk movements of her child.

She reminded herself every night, as she waited for sleep, that she would never be alone, that she would forever have the product of their love. Quint would live on in their child and she cradled her rounded stomach. Until the child arrived, she resolved that she would take excellent care of herself. Nothing must happen to her or to her son.

She made her plans. First there was the spring planting that had to be finished and after that was taken care of, she told Hilda that she planned to visit the Beals, that by the first of May, she would leave for a visit.

She threw herself into the task of making the farm productive. John secured several good men to help with the chores and she worked with the overseer just as Quint had done. The long hours and the hard work left her little time to think about the critical part of her that was missing. Everyone on the farm stood in awe as she gave the orders that changed the fallow ground into neat furrows. As she worked, she blossomed, and Hilda quietly told everyone that she would be fine. She didn't bother to dress for dinner and often ate her meals in the kitchen with Hilda. She let John do what shopping had to be done and Hilda helped her let the seams out of several of the good dresses hanging in her wardrobe. She would need those when she went to visit Susannah and George.

Each evening, after she retired to her room, she would stand before the mirror and in the soft candlelight gaze at her expanding figure. "When I go to the Beals, Susannah will be so surprised at how much the babe's grown," she smiled slightly as she cradled her stomach for the hundreth time.

As her child moved strongly, she remembered with bittersweet love how Quint had delighted in the movement of Susannah's child when they spent that first week at their farm. Resolutely, she shook away any moisture that threatened to fall and went about her tasks. She was more than grateful that the long hours and the hard work brought her deep sleep.

The month passed quickly enough and Rebecca surveyed the planted fields. It was time to visit Susannah and George. She started to pack her clothes and alerted John that they would leave at the end of the month.

Chapter Twenty-nine

Arthur watched from the railing as the ship docked early in the morning of the twenty-eighth of April, but it wasn't until early afternoon that he made his way down the gangplank and asked about the street Margaret Harrison named as her address. As he stood looking up at the imposing three story home, he wondered why Margaret was unable to help Rebecca, certainly not from a lack of wealth. He was admitted quickly to a room that resembled a study and Margaret greeted him with all the hospitality of visiting royalty.

Margaret ordered tea and folded her hand in her lap. She tried to smile, "I've some rather distressing news for you."

Arthur steeled himself and asked timidly, "Have they married already?"

Margaret stared at the man. He didn't know they had married, and he didn't know about the shipwreck. Margaret started to smile. If he claimed his sister, she could claim the farm. She said softly, "Rebecca was captured by Indians over two months ago. Don't look so upset, Mr. Ranserford, she has been returned and is apparently in good health. My brother, however, never returned from England. The ship he took passage on went down in January somewhere in the Atlantic. He did release your sister from her indenture before he left, so there is no hold on her here. However, the business with the Indians makes it imperative that you get her out of this country, just as fast as possible, and back to England so that she can be married. Our men here would never think of taking to wife a woman that had been captured by savages. I even imagine that if Quint had returned, he would have forgotten about marriage.... She's ... tainted."

Arthur was stunned. Margaret made it clear that she wanted the girl out of the country quickly and Arthur wondered if Rebecca's capture might in some way affect her value in England. He stared at the woman sitting on the couch before him. She had just told him that her brother had perished at sea and she didn't seem to be grieving at the loss at all. From the glint in her eyes, Arthur could tell that she already planned to take title to whatever possessions Quint might have had. "Greedy bitch," he thought to himself.

Margaret took a sip of tea and inquired, "How soon do you want to see your sister? She had been living at the farm since her return from her ... adventures."

After a lengthy discussion they decided that in three, or perhaps four days, Arthur could arrange return passage and then Margaret would accompany Arthur and a maid to the farm. The maid could help Rebecca pack her wardrobe, Margaret would wait in the carriage, "You need some time with your sister and I prefer not to be involved with your family affairs." And, I don't want to be on hand if the girl mentions her marriage, Margaret thought to herself.

Arthur spent two very busy days at the docks arranging transportation for Rebecca and himself back to England and the evenings were spent most enjoyably being wined and dined by Margaret. She was delighted that he seemed to have taken her suggestion and arranged a suitable marriage for the girl in her own dear England. On Friday, just after dawn, they left Philadelphia. Margaret assured Arthur that their trip would be all day, and with the maid shivering on the carriage seat with the driver, they traveled swiftly toward the McQuade home.

The day was bright and nippy and Rebecca dressed carefully, smiling slightly as she donned her dress. As hard as Hilda worked letting out the seams, it was plain that the dress could only be worn for three weeks more at the most.

She stood before the mirror and looked at her image. There could no question. She was going to have a babe. She remembered Hilda's arguments over the last two days. Hilda did not think she should be going to the Beals, "Let them come here. Travel you shouldn't, not in your condition."

"I'll be fine. Sam handles the carriage well and I don't intend to stay long."

Hilda frowned, "About this I don't feel right. Wrong, something will go."

Rebecca smiled, "Hilda, everything will be all right." Hilda had gone back to her kitchen muttering and Rebecca finished her packing. She looked around her room. It was much later than she wanted to get started, but they would make the Beals' home before dark. She stopped in the study and gave John her instructions while Sam loaded up the carriage. Hilda followed her out of the door shaking her head, "To go, you should not."

Sam helped her into the carriage, she waved good-bye to Hilda and settled back for her ride to the Beal farm. It would be good to relax a little, she thought as she brushed the ever present moisture from her eyes. The baby was due in six or seven weeks and it was time to slow down. She must get ready to have Quint's son.

Hilda went back to her kitchen and wondered at the sense of foreboding she felt. Rebecca had changed a great deal since she and Quint had married last fall. Now, the girl was stubborn and more than capable of making her own decisions. "All right, she'll be," Hilda mumbled to the soup she was stirring. She had promised Rebecca that she would take the soup over to the new man and his wife. The young girl had delivered a fine strapping boy only the week before and Rebecca had insisted that Hilda prepare the food for the new family until the woman was on her feet again. "It's the first of many sons for the farm," Rebecca had whispered.

Hilda left the kitchen shortly before noon and walked the mile and a half to deliver the soup. She smiled. Clem, who worked in the stable when Sam was gone, had come into the big room twice to make certain she left him a big bowl for his lunch. She glanced up at the sun, he was probably eating that soup right now.

Clem's meal was interrupted. A tall thin man with dark eyes and dark thinning hair wanted to know where Miss Rebecca was.

"Sam took her to the Beals this morning. They've been gone about an hour, hour and a half by now," Clem told the man. He frowned and thanked Clem, then left. Clem, anxious to get back to his soup, forgot about the man for the moment.

Arthur was trying hard not to lose control. Another set back! Arthur glanced around at the prosperous farm. Too bad Rebecca had not married the man, for if she had, Arthur would now be the brother of a wealthy widow. Damn, nothing ever seemed to work out right. Now he had to go chasing after the chit. Margaret had better know how to get from the McQuade farm to the Beal farm. He stormed into the carriage and told Margaret what the young boy in the kitchen told him. Margaret smiled through her heavily veiled hat, this might be even better. She told her driver to travel faster. If they could reach Rebecca before she got to the Beal farm, nothing could stop them.

Rebecca felt the carriage sway slightly and glanced out the window as Sam pulled up on the reins. "What's the matter Sam?"

"Miss Rebecca, I think the rear wheel is going. I better check it out. A carriage accident wouldn't help you along right now." Sam came around to the door and helped her down, then he turned to the wheel in question. Rebecca knew they had a problem from the language Sam yelled when he saw the wheel. He got out the mallet and the other tools he thought he might need and turned back to the wheel, "If this don't work, I'll have to go for help. I don't like leaving ya here."

"Don't worry Sam, if you have to go, I'll be fine." Rebecca moved away from the carriage and sat down against a large tree at the edge of the road. Sam went to work on the wheel.

Before long, Sam shouted over at her, "I think I can fix

it. Might take a bit."

Rebecca smiled, "We have all day."

The words were barely out of her mouth when Rebecca heard the splintering wood, and Sam yelled back at her, "I think we have a problem." Before he could offer any other comments they both looked up and back along the road they had traveled. In the distance, a team of horses were speeding down the road and Sam moved away from the road, toward Rebecca who got to her feet as quickly as she could. The driver saw them in plenty of time and sawed against the reins, bringing the carriage to a halt not ten feet from Rebecca. The door opened and Rebecca stared at the man who stared back at her.

Rebecca took a step forward, gasped out the name, "Arthur," and sank to the ground. Before Sam could get to her, the tall man had her in his arms and he was moving toward the open door of the carriage. "Don't worry young man, I'll take her ahead and you can join us when the wheel is fixed."

Sam relaxed for an instant and then realized the man had not said a word about where to join him. He dashed for the carriage, but it was moving already. In the interior Sam made out the shape of the man and sitting beside him looked like the heavily veiled form of a woman. Sam rushed for the harness. He had to get one of the horses unharnessed. Once he was sure Miss Rebecca was safe, he could get someone to come back for the carriage.

He almost had the last strap loosened when he glanced up. The carriage was turning around. They were coming back to tell him where to meet them. He stepped into the road. As he watched, the driver of the carriage whipped the horse into a reckless pace. The carriage was almost on top of him when he realized they were not going to stop. Something was wrong. Someone was kidnapping Miss Rebecca! He jumped out of the way of the swaying vehicle and swore.

In seconds, he had the harness off of the gray and was on the back of the horse heading for the Beal farm. George would know what to do. George had to know what to do. Someone had stolen Miss Rebecca.

332

Arthur stared down at his unconscious sister, a look of disgust spreading across his face. "My God, she's pregnant."

Margaret's face was hidden by the heavy veil but she was as horrified as Arthur. The girl was clearly expecting. She looked to be close to her fifth month. Margaret mentally counted back. It had to be the Indians. Mary Jane never told her when the girl was taken from the farm, only that she had been. Her lips curled into a smirk. Now it was imperative to get her back to England. No half-breed child would live to work her farm. Oh, if only her brother could see his precious bondslave now, a savage's brat in her belly. Margaret wanted to laugh.

Margaret said quietly, "This changes all of the plans. I want the driver to stop and I'll ride with him until we get to Germantown. I'll hire another carriage to take me to the house and I'll meet you there." The carriage pulled over and the maid and Margaret exchanged places. Arthur stared down at his pregnant sister. If she wasn't his sister, he would have gladly choked her at that moment.

Rebecca came out of her swoon slowly. The last thing she remembered was Arthur stepping down out of a carriage and the shocked look on his face. She felt the rocking of the carriage and she opened her eyes. She eased herself up into sitting position and looked across the carriage at her brother. He smirked at her, "Hello, dear sister. It would appear that you have a problem."

"Arthur, stop this carriage, immediately," she growled through clenched teeth. "You have nothing to say about my life now, I'm m . . ." Before she could finish her sentence, Arthur reached across and slapped her hard across the face. Her head snapped back into the frame of the door. Once more everything faded and Rebecca sank down into the carriage seat.

When Rebecca came to this time, her head was throbbing. She glared at her brother. "Whatever you think you are doing, you will not get away with it. Kidnapping is not something you can do, even here in America. I have friends and family now. You see, before Quint came to England, he . . ."

333

Arthur glared back, "Rebecca, say another word and I'll throw you out of this carriage. I don't want to hear about Quint or his friends, or any of the things that have happened to you. And, I am very serious. If you say another word, I'll open the damn door and throw you out." He was yelling at her and he looked so serious, that for a moment, Rebecca was certain he would do exactly what he said. For the sake of her child, she closed her mouth and looked out the window. When they stopped she would tell him that he had no control over her any longer.

Only once when they were close to a woods did the carriage halt so that Rebecca could relieve herself. She refused to get back in the carriage and demanded that Arthur listen to her, but, he tried to hit her again. She decided that she had better wait until they had reached a town before she said anything else to Arthur. Her head was still throbbing from the crack she had taken in the carriage. She settled herself into the carriage seat and despite her best intentions, she drifted into a troubled sleep.

It was dark when they finally stopped. Before Rebecca was completely awake, Arthur clamped his hand across her face and hoisted her into his arms. He struggled with her as he climbed out of the carriage and as he started up a steep flight of stone steps, he hissed into her frightened face, "Don't you make a sound or I'll drop you down the stairs." He carried her up the steps, through a large door, and into a brilliant hall. She had no chance to look around and his hand was over her mouth so tightly that she couldn't even bite his hand.

He carried her up two more flights of stairs and if she hadn't been so angry, she would have laughed. He was panting and huffing before they reached a door that suddenly flew open. He strode into the room, dumped her on the bed and walked out of the room. She heard the key turn in the lock and something snapped. Glancing around she saw a small room with angled ceilings and tiny upper windows. She was in some kind of attic room and her brother, her very own brother, had locked her in.

She yanked off her shoe and walked over to the door. At first, she yelled as she banged, until her throat was raw, then, she just used the shoe and banged on the door. Surely, there had to be other people in the house. In time someone would come to check on her. Arthur was not going to get away with whatever he planned.

On the first floor, Arthur stood at the window, listening to the muffled banging. "She's not the same sister. Something has changed. She never used to act like this. Oh, she used to get angry and occasionally she threw things, but never like this."

Margaret sat on the settee, sipping her tea. "Thank God, I had the foresight to give the servants the night off. I can just imagine what they would make of all this noise." She sat quietly for a few minutes, listening to the thumping from the room on the third floor. She cleared her throat and said softly, "It's evident we can't keep her here."

"And there's no way I'll be able to sail with her until I have some control. I'd like to know what your brother did to her? She was never like this. I had to knock her senseless in the carriage to get her to shut up."

Margaret bristled, "Well, she can't stay here."

"And, Madame, what do you suggest I do with her? I can't even talk to her. Her condition makes a husband a joke. Damn, I hadn't counted on anything like this." Arthur looked in the direction of the stairs. Rebecca had been banging away for over two hours and his nerves were raw. Nothing he planned ever worked out right.

Margaret glanced at her conspirator. Like most of the men she met, he was spineless and incapable of even the simplest decisions. She would have to take control. Damn Quint McQuade and damn her mother. She shouldn't have to be faced with this kind of a problem. The farm was hers by rights and she shouldn't have to fight like this to get it. If it weren't for the fact that Susannah told Mary Jane about the will that Quint left with George shortly before he left for England, she would have thrown Arthur Ranserford and his pregnant sister out on the street.

Sam raced for the Beal farm. George Beal was smart, he would know what to do. It was almost dark when Sam slid off of the tired horse and rushed to the door. George met him with a smile on his face. The smile faded quickly when he saw Sam's anxious eyes. "Where is Rebecca, Sam? What has happened?"

Sam took a deep breath and started at the beginning. He described the loose wheel and how he had stopped. When he got to the part about the man and the carriage, "Are you sure she said Arthur?"

Sam nodded his head. She had said that very clearly. "One more thing, I think there was a woman in the carriage, and, I've seen the driver someplace before, but I can't remember where. One more thing, there was a maid on the seat with the driver."

George frowned, "What did the woman in the carriage look like?"

Sam shook his head. George prompted, "Was it too dark?"

Sam shook his head again. "No," he said quietly, "She had a big hat on and the black stuff down over her face. I don't know who she was."

George looked up into the pained eyes of his wife, "Sweetheart, someone has kidnapped Rebecca." For a minute, George was afraid that Susannah was going to swoon but she pulled herself together.

Susannah walked into the room and glanced at Sam, "Rebecca has a brother named Arthur. You knew that, didn't you?"

George nodded his head and started for the stairs, "Sam, I'll have messages to send, but I want you to wait. I'll have to take you with me to Philadelphia."

"Philadelphia?" Sam and Susannah asked together. Susannah followed her husband up the stairs, "Why the city?"

George stopped on the stairs, "The man is undoubtedly her brother and he plans to take her back to England. Quint must have looked the man up and introduced himself. It must be obvious to you, her brother doesn't approve."

Susannah sighed, "You'll have to find her. Before Quint left he gave me the key to the townhouse. You had better go there. You can at least be comfortable while you're in the city."

"While I'm there, I'll get the men at the shipyard to begin a search of the docks. If this man has talked to anyone, we'll find out. I don't know how long I'll be gone."

Susannah was right behind him, "Just find her, George. We promised Quint we would take care of her and we haven't been doing a very good job."

Captain Hemphill and the *Venture* put into Barbados on the last day of April and Quint waited until Ephram, accompanied by his daughter, made their way up the hill and into the house that overlooked the harbor. The older man seemed aware that they had a guest in the house, but Madeleine refused to tell her father anything until she saw the two men greet each other. Quint said they were friends, but she needed to know just how friendly they really were before she told her father about her feelings for the man she helped bring back from the dead.

As Madeleine watched the two men greet each other, her heart sank. They were very good friends and Madeleine felt a bitter sense of disappointment. Her father would not take her part now, even if Quint seduced her. The tall man with the luxurious brown hair was lost to her forever.

Quint explained as best as he could the events that led up to his throwing himself into the sea and Madeleine took up the tale from there. Captain Hamphill offered Quint a brandy and the two men sat down to discuss the black-haired beauty that Quint told the Captain was now his wife. Madeleine was dismissed to see about dinner and Ephram and Quint spent the evening discussing the business of sailing ships.

Before the evening was over, Captain Hemphill agreed that as soon as he replenished necessary supplies and rounded up his crew, they could sail. They could be on the way to Philadelphia in two days, "It's the least I can do," Ephram offered quietly. Quint went up to bed that night content that in a little more than one week, he would have his wife back in his arms.

Two days later, Quint stood beside Madeleine on the

dock waiting for the Captain to tell him to come aboard. They were leaving for Philadelphia in less than an hour. He planted a brotherly kiss on her forehead and smiled down at her. His voice was husky as he said, "I can never thank you enough for what you did. You saved my life and I am forever grateful."

Madeleine, her courage starting to fail her, wiped the tears from her eyes, "If you ever come back . . ."

Quint shook his head, "My life is waiting for me in Philadelphia, in the form of a lovely woman. Madeleine, I'll never come back. I'm sorry, but you must understand. My life is there."

She brushed the tears away as she watched him jump aboard the ship. Silently, she stood for a long time and watched the ship until it was a dot on the horizon. Perhaps someday there would be a love like that for her.

Chapter Thirty

Rebecca slumped down on the bed. She had yelled until she was hoarse and banged against the door until her arm ached. Arthur was not going to pay any attention to her. Well, she thought, when he does come, he will listen to me. I am not having my baby in a dirty attic room. She frowned, not when she and Hilda had spent two weeks cleaning and fixing the room next to her bedroom at the farm. And Quint's son was going to grow up on that farm, if it was the last thing she accomplished.

She curled up on the bed and drifted off to sleep. Before she was fully awake, Rebecca knew someone was in the room with her. She forced her eyes open and stared at a frightened young serving girl. The girl mumbled, "I have your breakfast, Miss. And Mr. Ranserford, he told me about you. He'll be here as soon as you eat."

Rebecca thanked the girl and splashed some water into her face, then sat down to consume the meal the girl brought. She was hungry and ate quickly. Arthur would soon arrive and she would tell him what she thought of his tactics. After breakfast she paced the floor trying to plan her words, Arthur was going to listen to her today, or else. But the hour crept by and then another and Arthur never came. Rebecca picked up the shoe and started on the door once more.

In a matter of minutes, a tall grisly-looking man and a drab ugly woman were at the door. The man grabbed the shoe from her hands and Rebecca was so surprised she released her grip without thinking. The woman said softly,

"Oh now, Mam, you mustn't act like that. It ain't so bad. Come on, now." Rebecca stared at the woman. What was she talking about?

"Miss," the man addressed her, "This here note is from your brother. After you read it, we're to take ya to your new home."

Rebecca grabbed the folded paper from the man's hand and glanced at Arthur's scrawl. She sank down onto the bed, and read the note. That rotten man! How could he do such a thing? She read the note again, "Rebecca, these are the servants I have hired to take care of my sister. They had been informed that you are a raving lunatic as a result of your stay with the Indians. They came from the docks and they were not too happy with their positions, especially when I told them that the child you carry is the result of your stay with those same Indian friends. I would be very wary, if I were you, for the man's mother was killed by the Indians when he was a boy. He had to watch, so he doesn't think kindly of them. He knows firsthand what they can do to a woman's mind. They will accompany you to your new home. It's close enough to walk."

Rebecca glanced up at the grimy pair, "Did my brother say when he would visit?"

The man hesitated, then said quietly, "We're going to take ya to your new home now, Miss."

Rebecca gazed at them and decided that for the moment Arthur had won. If she ranted and raved as she would have loved to do, they would only think that she was as insane as Arthur implied. For the moment, she would have to play along with the ridiculous scheme. But when she saw Arthur . . . "Shall we go?" she said quietly.

The woman went out the door first, the man grabbed Rebecca's arm and they followed. They left the room and made their way down a narrow stairway. They led her down another back stairway, out through the empty kitchen, into a hall and out the back of the house. As they walked Rebecca tried to get her bearings, but it was useless. She had no idea where she was and they were traveling down narrow streets, past large and small houses. They passed three large stables and crossed two streets before the man led the way to the back door of a large old house. "Arthur certainly doesn't want anyone to know that I'm here," she mumbled as they led the way into the building and up another flight of stairs.

Once more, Rebecca was pushed into a bedroom, much larger than the attic room she occupied the night before, but this room was filthy. The door slammed and she heard the lock turn in the door. She turned around to examine her prison. Gritting her teeth, she promised herself, "I won't have my babe in his hole. I'll get out somehow and get back to the farm."

Rebecca walked over and looked out of the grimy windows and then she walked over to the bed. She was not going to sleep in that bed and she wasn't going to stay in a room that hadn't seen a bit of soap and water for years. She walked to the door, banging brought results the last time, and she lifted her shoe and started slamming it against the door.

She paused and listened every few minutes, but the shoe did not bring the results she wanted. She tried yelling but that brought no one to the room. "He can't get away with this," she raged as she sank into a chair. How long she sat she wasn't certain, but something broke through her thoughts. When she realized that the door was being unlocked, she bolted to her feet. The man stood in the doorway and behind him was the woman with a tray in her hand.

"Got yer lunch," he stepped aside for the woman.

Rebecca took a deep breath and pointed to the table. "After lunch, I would like to clean up this room and tell my brother that I will not sleep on those linens," she pointed to the bed. "I want hot water and soap and rags, and you can help me," she pointed to the woman.

The woman shrank back, "I ain't no maid."

Rebecca glared at the woman, "I will want a bath every night, and my brother will have to provide clothes. Tell him," she snapped. "Obviously, he doesn't have the courage to face me himself."

Hours later the man and woman reappeared and the woman had clean linens in her arms. She glared at

Rebecca, "I'm to do some of the cleaning tomorrow. But you ain't getting a bath every night. We ain't toting no water up two flights of stairs every night."

For the next three days, Rebecca supervised the surly woman as she scrubbed and cleaned. The man never came into the room and Rebecca tried a dozen times to talk to the woman, but she growled and huffed as she worked. Rebecca finally gave up any attempts at conversation. She would have to wait for Arthur.

Eight long days later, the *Venture* tied up to the wharf in Philadelphia and Quint made his way to Captain Hemphill. "Thank you for your help. If you ever need my help, please don't fail to ask."

Ephram liked the young man who stood before him, "What are your plans now, son."

Quint grinned at the man, "You see that ship over there and that fat man sitting forward on the deck sleeping?" He pointed out the *Sea Breeze*, "I'm going to tell those scoundrels to get back to work and then I'm going home to my wife."

Ephram glanced at the ship and then stared at it as if he was seeing a ghost, "You're *that* McQuade?"

Quint nodded happily. "And, Captain, the next time you're in port, look me up. I want you to see Rebecca and tell her what you told me. We'll have an evening to remember. I have the finest cook this side of Paris."

Once again he thanked his host and as the gangplank was lowered, he jumped down and made his way through the stacks of cargo lining the shore toward the ship he had just pointed out. "I'll do that, son," Ephram said quietly to no one in particular. He'd like to see the black-haired beauty again and he enjoyed McQuade immensely. And, who knew. Sometimes, someone as important as Quinton McQuade of McQuade Shipping was a good person to know.

Quint strode to his ship and yelled up at the old sailor sunning himself in the bow, "Ahoy on the *Sea Breeze*."

The sailor stirred and stood up to glare down at the man

342

responsible for disturbing his afternoon nap. At first he did not recognize the man on the docks below the ship, "Who ya be annoying, ya landlubber!" He squinted at the dark-haired man grinning up at him, "Well, I'll be damned." He started across the deck, "Capt'n! Where ya been? Heh, mates, the capt'n's back. Himself is here!"

Within minutes, Quint was surrounded by bedraggled sailors and workers from the yard. They were shaking his hands, slapping him on the back and yelling to others on the dock, "McQuade's back." Several of the older men in his company demanded that they celebrate in style, "A party, that's what we need."

Quint emphatically stated that he had been away from home and his wife far too long. The stunned expression that greeted his announcement had Quint chuckling as he hurried to the local livery. In spite of the poor roads and the unfamiliar horse, he was home an hour after midnight.

Clem stood staring at him when he rode into the barn and still had not found his voice when Quint made his way into the house. He chuckled. Everyone thought he was a ghost. He slipped quietly up the stairs and through the open door of Rebecca's old room. Nothing in the room looked used and his wife was not there. Quickly, he moved over to the wardrobe but there wasn't a single item of hers in that piece of furniture. Fighting down his panic, he stood in the room for several minutes before it occurred to him that, of course, she wouldn't be in this room. She would have moved all of her belongings to his room. He tiptoed down the hall to the master bedroom. His whole body was trembling with anticipation.

Cautiously he swung the door open and looked at the bed. It was empty! He glanced around the room. There was no sign that she occupied this room, either. He lighted several candles and investigated the wardrobe and her chest in the corner of the room. His clothes had been moved into several drawers, leaving three drawers nearly empty. There were a few of her things, but her gowns and her chemises were gone. He stumbled to the wardrobe and discovered his clothing pushed to one side. On the other side hung most of her dresses. Quint was too tired to make much sense of what was going on. He rushed down stairs and out to the kitchen. Standing in the soft glow of the banked embers, Hilda stood talking to Clem who was shaking from his toes to the top of his head. She was still in her gown and robe.

When she saw him, she ran and threw herself into his arms, screaming in his ear, "Mr. George, tell me you are dead, he does. Oh, Mr. Quint, thank God, oh, thank God!" The tears were running down her round face. She reached up and patted his cheeks with both of her hands.

Her greeting stunned him and he asked anxiously, "Hilda, where is Rebecca? Some of her things are gone, and so is the trunk. Is she at Susannah's?"

Hilda gave him a look of pure pity, "Her brother, he comes. Rebecca he takes away. Mr. George for her he looks."

"He took her away? Why?" Quint's voice was growing in volume.

Hilda shook her head, tears streaming down her cheeks, she couldn't answer him, she had no answers. Quint patted her arm, "I'm going to the Beals. I must get a little rest, and eat something. I'll want to leave in about four hours. Clem, have my horse ready," he turned and left the kitchen.

In exactly four hours Quint was ready to travel. Clem crawled out of bed only minutes before and he was fumbling with the saddle and the harness when Quint came into the barn. He looked over the animals in the stable while he waited. The little bay he purchased from George was not there. "Clem," he asked puzzled, "Where's Rebecca's horse?"

"Gone," Clem mumbled.

Quint glared at him. "Where is it, did she send it back to George? She didn't have trouble with the horse did she?"

Clem shook his head. He was not going to say a word about anything that happened. He didn't want the boss mad at him. Hurrying, he completed his job. All he wanted was to get Mr. McQuade out of the barn and on his way. Let George Beal tell him all about the Indians.

Quint left the barn yard scowling. Arthur didn't seem the least bit interested in Rebecca that night in the tavern.

Had he lost everything and come to Rebecca for help? It would be just like the man to decide that there was something in it for him. Quint's face was dark with anger, and he decided that that was just what Arthur had done. He had left his crumbling home in London and come to Philadelphia.

To make matters worse, he jerked on the reins. Rebecca didn't know that he was alive. Urging the big stallion into a run, he raced through the familiar scenery. George would help find her, he thought, as the dark shapes flew past him.

Quint saw the big man who was his brother-in-law from the road, stacking wood in back of the house as he rode through the front yard. He slipped from his horse and the two men stood for a fraction of a second before George let out a yell. Then they were both clasping each other on the shoulders and slapping each other on the back. Both sets of eyes looked suspiciously damp.

Susannah heard the noise and came out to investigate. By the time Susannah realized that George was hugging Quint, she was close enough for George to catch her as she sank to the ground. George scooped her up into his arms and Quint followed him into the house.

Susannah was unconscious for only a minute and when she saw Quint standing next to George, she threw herself from the couch and dashed for him, crying and laughing at the same time. The noise level increased as George and Quint both started asking questions at that instant. George finally got the floor and insisted that everyone be quiet so that Quint could ask the questions he had been shouting above Susannah's happy exclamations and her tears. The first question Quint asked was about his wife, "Where is she?"

George and Susannah exchanged uneasy glances and George asked softly, "How much did Hilda tell you." Quint repeated the conversation and George frowned deeply, "We know Arthur has her. She didn't mention the Indians?" It was more of a statement than a question.

"Indians?" Quint's forehead crinkled into deep furrow as he glanced from George to his sister's solemn face.

George poured a glass of brandy, pushed Quint into a

chair, and handed him the glass. "Remember that brave Rebecca patched up?" Quint nodded. George continued, "Well, about the middle of March, some of his relatives made a quick sweep of the area, looking for slaves. Rebecca was out riding and they grabbed her." Quint came up out of his chair, but George pushed him back. "She wasn't hurt. It seems the Indian she treated took her into his camp and told all of his relatives that she was his wife." George rushed ahead so that Quint could not interrupt. "He never touched her. Rebecca told Hilda that the brave was very considerate and he planned the whole thing so that he could bring her back to the farm without losing face. He did keep her horse."

Quint was so shaken and upset that for several long minutes he sat and just stared at George. When he finally found his voice he whispered, the words forming slowly, "Was . . . she . . . all right? They . . . didn't torture her?"

George glanced over at the ashen face of his brother-in-law, "Quint, she was only dirty and tired. After she had a day or two of rest and a couple of Hilda's meals she was fine."

Quint stood up and started pacing in front of the large fireplace. "She doesn't know I survived." He turned around and glared at George, "Tell me about Arthur!"

George explained as much as they knew about the attack on the road. "Sam and I went to Philadelphia and spent three days there. I got back yesterday. By the way, I stayed at the townhouse and I left Sam there. I planned on going back in another day or two. The only thing I found out was that a man by the name of Arthur Ranserford talked to a Captain Bertrand of the *Maryland Belle* about passage for his sister and himself, but he never came back with the fare. That ship sails in four days. I planned on being in Philadelphia a day before she sails. The Captain knows the situation and he promised to contact Sam if Arthur came with the money for passage. He promised I could search the vessel before they leave for England."

Quint looked puzzled, "I know James Bertrand, he's a good man. None of this makes any sense. Rebecca doesn't know I'm alive. I don't know what Arthur thinks. I'm sure

Rebecca told him that we are married and he's the kind of man that would stick to a wealthy widowed sister like glue. It just doesn't make sense. Why is he so insistent on getting her to England? And if he is, he may have traveled north or south to another port."

George shook his head. "I don't think they'll do any traveling, Quint. There's something more that you need to know. Rebecca is expecting."

Quint turned his confused face in George's direction, "Expecting? Expecting what?"

"Rebecca is going to have your child."

Quint turned a pale pink and headed for the decanter of brandy. "A child? From . . . from . . . When I was . . . Oh, dear God. She's," he counted on his fingers, "eight months along."

George nodded. "But she doesn't show much. She says her mother was the same way. The baby is due in June."

Quint sank into a chair. "She's eight months along." He was out of the chair in seconds, racing for the door, "I've got to find her."

George grabbed at him, "We'll go first thing tomorrow."

Quint brushed George's restraining hand from his arm. "The hell we will! I'm leaving now."

George glanced over at Susannah. "We'll be all right," she said softly. "Go with him!"

George followed Quint from the room, "Damn it, wait up! I'm coming with you."

Quint and George arrived in Philadelphia late that evening. Sam had gotten help from the shipyards and he knew already that Quint had survived the sinking of the English vessel. His greeting was enthusiastic. He left to take care of the horses, and Quint and George made their plans for the search Quint wanted to begin that night. George convinced him that they couldn't find out a thing until the morning. George even succeeded in getting Quint to bed for several hours. Before dawn, they had broken their fast and were on their way to the docks.

They spent three days on the docks. James Bertrand tried to be helpful and he got Quint a list of most of the ships that sailed out of Philadelphia in the last two months.

None of the English-bound ships sailed within the last two weeks. Rebecca could not have left Philadelphia yet.

They traveled to all of the local inns and then to the taverns, but no one had seen the raven-haired girl, or her brother. They had disappeared.

They worked their way through Philadelphia and into the surrounding area. There was still no sign of his wife, and as the days slipped by, Quint grew more and more frantic. "I don't trust him. He wouldn't give a damn about her condition. If she's as small as you say, and he didn't bother to ask when the child was due, he might have tried to get back to England before the babe arrived. I have to check on some of the other ports. I want Sam to go south to Baltimore and I'll go to New York. You stay here, in case someone arrives with information." Within the hour, Quint was on his way to New York and Sam was headed south.

George and Quint had been gone for five days and Susannah was surprised and excited to see Mary Jane's carriage coming down the road. It would be a welcome diversion to spend an hour or two with her chatterbox of a sister. She put on the tea pot.

Susannah met Mary Jane on the front steps, "Oh, Mary Jane, I'm so glad you're here. I have so much to tell you. Quint is alive, and Rebecca has been kidnapped by her brother, Arthur." As she led Mary Jane into the parlor, she continued, "Quint and George are now in Philadelphia looking for her and what is really terrible, she's going to have a babe."

Mary Jane looked very confused, "From the Indian?"

"No! Quint is the father." Susannah and Mary Jane spent the rest of the afternoon discussing the love affair between Rebecca and Quint and speculating about Arthur.

As Susannah led the way to Mary Jane's carriage to see her sister off, Mary Jane said, "I'm going right to Elizabeth Ann and Margaret. They'll be so glad to hear that Quint is alright."

Susannah wasn't at all sure that Elizabeth Ann and

Margaret would be as enthusiastic about their baby brother's survival as Mary Jane seemed to think, but Quint was back now and he could handle his other sisters.

As the coach pulled out of the yard, Mary Jane laid her head back against the cushion. It was so nice that Quint had come back from the dead. Margaret wasn't going to like it. She didn't want to worry Susannah, but she knew that Margaret was already planning to take over the farm. Elizabeth Ann had complained to her several times.

Mary Jane sat up straight, she better see Margaret right away. It wouldn't do for Quint to get mad at Margaret again. She'd see Margaret on Monday and tell her about Quint. Margaret could just forget trying to take over the farm and the sooner she was told, the better for everyone. Mary Jane relaxed once more. Oh, it was such great fun to travel from one to the other with news. And this news was even more interesting than the tale about the Indians. She giggled in anticipation.

Chapter Thirty-one

Mary Jane glanced at Margaret's impressive brick home just after lunch on Monday. She could hardly wait to share her news with Margaret. A few minutes later, over a cup of sweetened tea, Mary Jane related what Susannah told her only two days ago, all about Quint's return from the dead, Rebecca's kidnapping, and the babe she carried. Margaret didn't react as Mary Jane expected. She was sure that Margaret would be angry but Margaret acted as if she was frightened. In fact, if Mary Jane hadn't known better, she would have declared that Margaret was terrified.

After only half a cup of tea, Margaret was making excuses and showing her out. Mary Jane was more than disgusted. Margaret usually listened when Mary Jane shared her news, but this afternoon, she seemed preoccupied. Mary Jane headed for Elizabeth Ann's home. Her oldest sister had to be told as well. Elizabeth Ann wasn't as intimidating as Margaret. She would listen.

Margaret had the coach summoned before Mary Jane's carriage had left the street. If Quint ever found out that she had anything to do with Rebecca's kidnapping, her life would be worthless. She had seen him angry before, and Simon, for all of his bluff, paid more attention to her brother than to her. If Quint was angry enough, he could convince Simon to make her life hell. No, Quint must never find out that she had anything at all to do with Rebecca's abduction.

As she rode the five blocks to the house she had arranged for Arthur, she thought back over her plans. They had been such good plans, but nothing worked out right and how was she to know that Quint could survive a shipwreck. She shuddered. Thank goodness she had put Arthur up in an old house that belonged to a business associate of one of Simon's customers. She had given him gold for several months rent so there was very little chance that if Quint found Arthur he could connect her with the house. Arthur would have to forget about taking Rebecca to England. In fact, at the moment, she didn't care what Arthur did as long as he didn't involve her.

The man had little back bone and Margaret was certain she could intimidate him so that if Quint ever found them, she would not be implicated. After she arranged the black veil over her face, she stepped down from the carriage and strolled up to the door. If anyone noticed her, they would only think she had come calling.

The tall, dirty man Arthur hired from the docks let her into the parlor and Margaret waited for the man to summon Arthur. She looked around, the house was really filthy. No, Quint could never find out that she had a hand in any of this.

Arthur was barely through the door when Margaret lifted her veil, "You have trouble Mr. Ranserford, big trouble." She wanted to get this meeting over with quickly and away from this place. "My brother is not dead as we suspected. Somehow, he survived and has returned. At the moment, he is tearing Philadelphia apart, looking for his WIFE. I failed to mention that he married your sister in October." She waited to see what effect her words had.

She wanted to sneer at the coward before her; he was actually shaking. Most of the color was gone from his cheeks. She could frighten him into leaving her name out of any tale he told. When he said nothing, she continued, "You are on your own, now. If he finds you, I will deny any knowledge of this scheme. No one saw her at my house and there is no way this house can be traced to me. If any comment is made about your coming to my house when you first arrived, I'll say that you told me you wanted to visit your sister and make sure she was happy in her marriage. And, of course, since I thought that most brotherly, I told you where you could find the girl. You are not going to involve me in any of this."

Arthur regained some of his composure by the time she finished her ranting. He growled, "Don't worry, I can take care of my sister. However, if you want your name left out of this mess, you better see that we have more than enough money to buy passage to England and for whatever we need here, until I can secure passage."

Margaret had anticipated his request and dumped a handful of gold coins on the table, "I will give you no more. I don't intend to ever see you again."

As she turned to leave, Arthur grabbed her arm, "I want to know one thing. What did you intend to accomplish when you started this charade?"

She tried to twist her arm free. She wanted out of this house and away from any connection to this stupid man before her. In her effort to get away, she threw the words at him, "I wanted his farm. My mother told me years ago that it was mine. With Rebecca married off and back in England, I could have claimed it."

He released her arm, "But when you thought he was dead, why not just send Rebecca back to England?"

She stepped back. "You sent word that you were coming. I saw no need to spend my money to send her to you when you were coming for her. Besides, with Quint gone, Rebecca had the farm. She would never have returned to England voluntarily." Margaret pointed toward the stairs. "Now," she pulled the veil down over her hat, "I'm leaving. I don't care what you do. If I ever see you again, I'll deny that I know anything about you. If I were you, I'd stay hidden for several weeks, and then get out of here as quietly as I could." She fled the room and Arthur was still standing in the parlor when the carriage rumbled down the street.

Margaret's words about claiming the farm ran round and round in his head. If Quint were to die everything would belong to Rebecca. He shook his head, he had to think. Somehow, he had to get his hands on the productive farm, but how? Quint was, according to Margaret, very much alive and he held the man's wife locked in an upstairs bedroom. Well, the child she carried couldn't be his. So he wouldn't know about the babe. He could use that, but how? Arthur sank into the nearest chair. He had to figure something out. There had to be a way.

He glanced up as he heard the door upstairs open and close. He hadn't seen her since the night he took her to Margaret's. The woman he hired brought her requests and her demands to him everyday. Rebecca was not the girl she had been. If he refused her requests for fabric, baths, food, she pounded on the door until he thought he would go mad. At first, the scum he hired from the docks had taken her shoes from her, but she used whatever she could get her hands on. Somehow, she managed to break part of the chair bottom apart and Arthur thought she was going to break the door down before they got it away from her. Then, hourly, she yelled for him until he had spent half of the funds Margaret provided to get the things she demanded. And, according to her keepers, she was getting bigger every day. If he gave up without a fight, he would never get his hands on any of the farm that his sister would own if somehow Quint McQuade was gone. No, he wasn't going to let McQuade have his sister, not without something for himself and if he could dispose of McQuade, so much the better. He went back to his planning.

Rebecca sat at the table, and gazed out the clean windows into the warm May sun. She could just see one of the neighboring gardens from her window. It was pleasant enough, but she wanted to go home. She was tired of sewing, tried of reading, and was uncomfortable. The babe would arrive in less than four weeks now, and if Arthur didn't let her out of the house and take her back to the farm, she wouldn't be able to travel at all. She glanced down at the enormous ball in front of her. There was no question. She was as huge as her mother was reported to have been during the end of her time. She cradled her stomach. "Soon, little one," she purred, "Soon."

Quint returned to Philadelphia the last day of May and Sam returned from Baltimore the day before. Sam hadn't found a trace in Maryland and Quint found nothing in New York. George had no news at all. "But, Elizabeth Ann wants to talk to you. She's been here once already. Susannah sent a note saying that Mary Jane came for a visit and Susannah brought her up to date so I suppose Mary Jane told Elizabeth Ann."

"I have no time for my oldest sister, not now. Rebecca is very close to her time, and if I don't find her before the babe is born, that damn brother may spirit her away before I get to her." He ran his fingers nervously through his hair. "Keep Elizabeth Ann away from me."

"What do we do now?" Sam asked timidly.

"We start over," Quint snapped.

For the next two days, Quint toured all of the inns and taverns he had covered before, and George and Sam made a tour of the ships in port. There was still no information. At the end of the third day, Sam and George were trudging up the hill away from the dock when Sam froze. They were across the street from one of the warehouses that lined the hills behind the waterfront. George glanced over at Sam and then looked at him closely. Sam was studying the carriage across the street. "Sam, what is it?"

Sam's eyes never left the vehicle and he said, so quietly that George didn't think he heard him correctly at first, "That carriage, that driver! I know that man. I know that man." He looked up at George and whispered, "That's the man. He drove the carriage that kidnapped Miss Rebecca."

George looked back at the carriage and then at Sam, "Are you sure?"

"I'm sure!"

George scowled, "I know where she is, let's go!"

In the rush to get to Quint, George didn't pay any

attention to the carriage before the townhouse. He dashed through the door and up the steps, and he almost collided with Quint. Elizabeth Ann followed her brother down the steps. Elizabeth Ann's eyes were red and it was clear that she had been crying and was still very upset. George took a quick look at Quint. His face was red with rage.

George asked quietly, "She knew?"

Quint snapped, "She says she guessed. She helped bring Arthur here."

George's mouth formed a circle as he looked up at his oldest sister-in-law, "How did you find out?"

George explained as he followed Quint to the horses Sam was holding, "Sam recognized the driver. Simon had the carriage and his driver at the warehouse. Sam said the man on the box was the man and I put it together."

Quint turned to George, "You don't have to come."

"The hell I don't!" George yelled. "As angry as you are at the moment, you might do something you'll regret."

Quint smiled a cold bitter smile, "Simon will take care of his wife. I won't have to do a thing."

George muttered as he threw his leg over the saddle, "No, just refuse to ship any more of his goods for him. The man would be bankrupt inside a month." Quint ignored George as he sent his black stallion into a bone-jarring race across the cobblestone streets.

They arrived at the Harrison home just before dinner. Quint forced his way through the door, knocking the serving girl aside in his hurry to get to Margaret. He burst into the dining room as Margaret was issuing orders to serve the meal. "All right, Margaret, you've had your fun! Now, I want my wife," Quint said, his voice controlled.

Margaret blanched and looked away from her brother. "She's not here. I'm not sure where she is."

"Margaret," Quint said quietly, still in control, "I know what you've done and I know why. Now, I want my wife."

Margaret straightened up to her full five feet, nine inches, and looked at her brother. He certainly did not look as upset as she thought he would be. She might get away

355

with her tale after all. "Quint, I don't know where Rebecca is. Her brother came here and I told him about the farm and he went to see his sister. The next thing I heard was that the man kidnapped her."

Quint's eyes turned a dark hard blue, and the lines about his mouth tightened, "I said I know what you have done! I know that you were in the carriage when Arthur took Rebecca; I know you brought her here; I know you were responsible for Arthur coming in the first place. Do not attempt to lie your way out of this, *dear sister*. At the moment, I don't care whether I beat the information out of you or you give it to me voluntarily. Either way, I will have my wife back with me tonight."

Margaret smiled a grim tight smirk, "Oh, I think not. Arthur has her hidden. Even I don't know where. However, I might be able to tell you where to find Arthur. That is all I can do."

Quint looked at George standing at his side, "Search the house."

Margaret froze, "No! You are not going to search my house."

"George," Quint said quietly. While he waited for George, Quint glared at the tall woman who was his blood relative. He stood in the doorway, waiting until George returned shaking his head, then he continued, "Why don't you make this easy on yourself. Just tell me where Arthur is."

Margaret glared at her brother. No matter what happened, she was not going to tell him about Rebecca. A cruel smile played at the corners of her mouth. "I seem to have forgotten where Arthur is. In a day or two . . ."

Quint stood calmly. "I spent a very interesting morning with Elizabeth Ann." He almost laughed when Margaret tensed. "If I was of an inclination, I could call my lawyer," He straightened up to his full six feet plus. "And, right now, Mrs. Simon Harrison, I know enough about you . . ." his voice trailed off. Margaret felt a little faint, surely, Elizabeth hadn't told him everything.

"Margaret, I know about the fake Indian raids, and I know about the serving girl Simon talked to last year. Elizabeth Ann told me about the old man in the prison. Now, where is Arthur?"

Margaret held on to the chair, her legs threatening to give out from under her. What did he intend to do with his information? Just above a whisper, she blurted out the address.

Quint nodded and he started for the front door. "One other thing I think you should know." He glanced back in disgust. "I'll be talking to Simon. My recommendation to him will be to take you to the frontier. Perhaps the savages you'll have to fight there will teach you something."

Margaret stared after him. No! Never! She was not leaving her home. Surely, he couldn't make her leave her home. As she stood in the center of the room, her shoulders sagged. The only person in the whole world Simon was afraid of was her brother. Whatever hold Quinton McQuade had over Simon Harrison, if Quint said the frontier, then that was where Simon would force her to go. Suddenly, she was very tired. Perhaps, if she was pleasant to her husband for a change, he would ignore her brother's order. She crept up the stairs to her room, no, there was no way out, Quint was sending her to the frontier. She had lost everything.

While Margaret was pondering her fate at the hands of her husband and her brother, Quint was charging through the side streets, looking for the house Margaret mentioned. It was growing darker by the minute and twice he considered going back to the Harrison house and making Margaret show him where the house was. When he finally stumbled on the dilapidated structure, hidden behind another house, it was well past the dinner hour.

Rebecca was depressed. Arthur still refused to see her and the man and woman, although they were not abusive, would not talk to her or take her messages to Arthur. She wanted to go home, and she brushed the wetness away from her eyes. After a bite or two of a tasty stew, she shed her clothes and curled up into a ball in her bed. Soon, the sleep she prayed for, came.

A short time after she fell soundly asleep, a banging on the front door drove Arthur away from his table. Quint was on top of him before he had the door fully opened. "Where is she?" Quint growled as he reached for the front of Arthur's shirt.

Arthur smiled calmly, in truth, he had been expecting the man for several days now, "She is not here."

"Where is she?" Quint repeated his question.

Arthur knocked Quint's hand away from the fabric of his shirt. Until that moment, he had not had a plan, but now he knew exactly what he would do. Quint pushed his way inside and Arthur moved aside. Another man, almost as large as the sea captain followed him into the hall. Arthur, his confidence building, looked at his brother-in-law and smiled. "I said, she is not here. I have her safely tucked away outside of town."

"And," Quint glared at him.

Arthur brushed off the front of his shirt, almost as if he was setting Quint aside with his strokes. "I doubt that you know what condition your precious wife is in." Quint lunged for him again, but George stepped up and held him back. "She spent some time with the Indians, you know. She carries a bastard savage brat in her belly. I'll relieve her of the child and you can have her back, for a price."

George couldn't stop him. Quint was on Arthur in a flash. He planted one powerful blow, before George got a good enough hold on him to pull him away from Arthur.

Arthur was reeling from the punch. He was stunned as well. Not in his wildest imagining had he expected Quint to react in that manner. The man was insane, and he had every right to call him out. In fact, as crazy as he was, Arthur might have a chance. He almost smiled. If he could kill Quint in a duel all the better. Then, he could take Rebecca back to the farm and claim the estate for her and the child. He would be rich beyond his needs. He straightened, shook his head, and said calmly, "I accept your insult. I will meet you at the appropriate time and place. My seconds will call on you tomorrow and make the necessary arrangements. Good night, gentlemen." He turned on his heel and walked back to the dining room.

Quint let out an anguished moan as George dragged him from the hall, out the door, and back to his horse. They moved off quickly down the street and Arthur smiled as he watched from the dining room window. He would get to pick the weapons. Quint had struck first. He straightened a bit more. Quinton McQuade didn't have a chance. He would choose pistols of course. He was an excellent shot and as upset as McQuade was it would be no contest, none at all.

Chapter Thirty-two

George followed Quint back to the apartment and neither man said a word as they trudged along deep in thought. Once they were back at the apartment and were settled in the study, George turned to Quint and said in a husky voice, "That was idiotic. You could have refused to meet the man. Just what do you hope to accomplish? You still don't know where Rebecca is."

Quint said, his voice a sneer as he peered at George above the brandy glass he was holding, "Why, I thought that was obvious. I'm going to kill the miserable bastard, and then find Rebecca." Quint took a deep draw from the drink he had just poured and turned back to George. "It would appear that the only way I'll ever get my wife back is to eliminate her brother."

Quint finished his drink and went to arrange a bath for himself. Then he informed George that one thing he needed was a decent night's sleep and he went to bed. George was not as fortunate for he found himself roaming through the apartment into the late hours of the night. Although he tried to sleep several times, he was up every hour or so to pour himself another brandy, or to have a cigar. He spent a good portion of time considering what Rebecca's reaction might be if Quint wounded her brother, or even worse, Arthur died. And, if Quint didn't survive, could he tolerate this Arthur. From what Quint said the man would foist himself on the rest of the family.

Of course, Rebecca might not be the loving wife Quint wanted if he was responsible for her only relative's death.

She had never said much about her family and George had no idea how close they might have been. His greatest concern at the moment was Susannah's reaction to all of this. There was no way she was going to understand. George knew that she was going to blame him for the present set of circumstances. He remembered her comments on more than one occasion when they heard news of friends or acquaintances involved in duels, that there never was a valid reason for that kind of murder. As the eastern sky grew pink with the coming dawn, George finally fell asleep.

When Quint got up the next morning, he glanced at the ashtray brimming with the dust of a thousand thoughts, and the half-empty brandy decanter. He told the temporary cook from the shipyards to let George sleep until late morning and left the apartment for a short visit to his banker and a stop at his lawyer's office. There were several minor changes Quint wanted made in his will. He composed a letter for Simon Harrison to be delivered to his brother-in-law after the duel. By the time he returned to the apartment, George had eaten breakfast and was waiting for Arthur's seconds.

"I've arranged for your other man," George told him when they were in the study. "I sent a message to Jonathan Cummingham, and he should be here in an hour or two." They didn't have to wait long, for Cummingham arrived before lunch. While they ate, George tried to explain what had happened and why they asked him to join them. "One day soon they'll begin enforcing the laws against dueling and this kind of meeting won't be necessary," George mumbled into his coffee cup.

Before they finished their meal, Arthur's seconds presented themselves and the terms were discussed. Arthur had chosen pistols, the place was to be a woods between Philadelphia and Germantown and the time of the meeting was set at dawn the next day. After the men left, George and Jonathan told Quint what the terms were and George added, "We're to see to the surgeon. Do you have someone in mind?" Quint nodded and added the name of an old family friend to the list of spectators.

When the apartment was quiet again, George turned on

Quint and sat staring at him for several minutes. He asked quietly, "For God's sake, tell me why you let him make a challenge out of this? I know what you said last night but somehow it just doesn't ring true. I can't believe that you thought this thing through. If you do kill Arthur Ranserford, what about Rebecca? How is she going to feel? Have you given any thought to that?"

Quint gazed at the glass he held in his hand for some time before he spoke. "If Arthur and Margaret are together on this, then I'll never see my wife again. Elizabeth Ann told me a great many things yesterday and I must apologize to you. Margaret is a very vicious woman. You gave her more credit than I, but we both were off the mark George, I don't even know where Rebecca is and Arthur is not going to tell me. The only hope I have is to eliminate him and then threaten Margaret with something so horrible that she will tell me what I want to know. Either way, it is really very simple, if I can't have Rebecca, then I really don't want to live."

George hesitated. Quint's confession shook him to his soul. "Then, you're going to shoot to kill?"

Quint didn't even look up at George, but answered in a flat voice, "I'm going to shoot to kill."

George pressed him for more but Quint refused to respond. Quint stood up and moved to the door. "I'm going down to the shipyards for awhile. I'll be back by dinner this evening. Don't worry about me." He walked out of the door and as George watched him go, he wondered if Quint had ever faced such a heart wrenching task. Either way, the man stood to lose a great deal.

George went into the study and slouched down in a chair. What he needed was his wife. He knew that he was going to send for her, but it would not do for her to arrive before they went to the dueling field. Quint would have him there the next day if he found out that Susannah was coming. He calculated the time involved and scratched out a note. Sam was summoned and on his way before George changed his mind. If his calculations were correct, Susannah would arrive at the apartment by early afternoon.

George went back to his chair and spent the next hour thinking about his brother-in-law and the man's reaction to the last twenty-four hours. Quint McQuade was not a violent man, and he seldom was angered. This whole affair was not Quint's style, not his style at all. And to declare that he was going to shoot to kill, that wasn't the Quint McQuade he knew.

Every man could take so much. Obviously, Quint McQuade had taken as much as he could. The corners of George's mouth turned up into a grim smile. If he were in Quint's position, no telling what he would have done. He would probably be in the jail, awaiting hanging for killing the bastard at the first meeting. George shook his head sadly. Quint had more patience than most. He could only hope that Susannah understood what was tearing her brother apart at the moment and why he had to fight.

George turned his thoughts to the choice of weapons. Quint was good with a rifle, but a pistol? He just didn't know. There was Arthur to consider. Most English gentlemen did a lot of shooting. Was Arthur any good? They still didn't know where Rebecca was. If Quint won and couldn't find her . . . The thought was not worth continuing.

Smiling grimly, once more he turned his thoughts back to Susannah. Knowing that she would be at his side the next day gave him some relief. She would certainly have much to say about all of this, of that he was sure. She would get over her anger and they would be together to share whatever tragedy the day brought.

Quint arrived back at the apartment after dark. George waited dinner for him, but he needn't have bothered. Quint ate next to nothing and there was no brandy passed that night. Just before they retired, Quint gave George a sealed letter. "In case Arthur's a better shot than I think."

George tried one last time, "Quint, let me call this off. You don't have to meet the man. With the information you have, we can have the man arrested. No one can steal another's wife, not like this. You don't have to go through with this."

Quint left George standing and talking to the closed bedroom door, as the younger of the two men retired for the night.

Both men were up before dawn and Quint wasted no time dressing and consuming his breakfast. He was hungry after the poor dinner he had eaten the night before. George on the other hand, pushed his food around his plate, and Quint had to wait a full fifteen minutes for George to finish dressing. "You may not be a nervous wreck but I am," George growled when Quint asked if he could hurry.

"I want this over," was Quint's reply.

They traveled by carriage through the dark streets and the only sound that could be heard was the clop of the horses' hooves and the rumble of the carriage as it rolled across the cobblestones of the paved streets. They arrived at the dueling site minutes before Jonathan Cummingham arrived with the doctor in tow. Arthur and his seconds were not far behind. The two groups were introduced and the regulations were explained to the combatants. The seconds paced off the twelve steps each man would take and they examined and tested the pistols, then both weapons were reloaded.

George drew Quint aside, but even as he opened his mouth, Quint told George, "Let it be."

Arthur and Quint took their places and the count began. The morning was cool for early June and the sky was a sheet of solid gray. A good morning to die, Quint thought suddenly as George counted, Four! Five! Six! Turn and fire at twelve, turn and fire, Quint kept repeating as he took the necessary steps forward. A gasp from George was the only warning that Quint had that something was wrong. He spun around after the count of nine.

Arthur was already turned and the pistol was raised. It was aimed at Quint, and the count was not yet ended. Quint's one thought was to fall to the ground but a thud and then a sharp burning in his chest, below his right shoulder followed immediately the loud crack of an explosion. Quint continued to sink to the earth, and he realized that Arthur's shot had found its mark. From some place far distant, he heard another pistol shot and then loud voices. The voices faded and blackness came to swallow him up. He heard no other sound.

George stared in disbelief. The pistol in Quint's hand came up partially as Arthur's ball found his opponent. The muscles in Quint's arm must have contracted because as he sank to the ground his pistol discharged. His shot struck

Arthur, who had fallen to his knees, when he took his shot. The ball found a lethal spot, slamming into the throat of the Englishman.

The doctor gave the dying Englishman a quick examination and declared that there was nothing he could do. . . . The large vein in the neck was severed, and Arthur's life's blood was flowing from him too quickly. He rushed to Quint's side and knelt in the spreading pool of Quint's blood. "He's still alive. Let's get him some place where I can work on him. As soon as I slow this bleeding, we must move him." George knew immediately that Quint must be taken back to the apartment. Susannah would be there in several hours and although she would be furious, she would help.

Arthur's seconds wrapped the dead man in a cloak and left the field. As soon as the doctor had bandaged the wound, George and Jonathan carried Quint to the waiting carriage. The doctor followed in the carriage that brought him to the field of conflict less than an hour before. The old man shook his head, such a waste of life.

It took almost an hour to get the injured man back to the apartment in Philadelphia. Before they arrived, Quint regained consciousness and in a hoarse whisper, he pleaded with George, "Find Rebecca. Tell her . . . what happened. Bring her to . . . me." He lapsed back into the half world of unconsciousness.

As the carriages pulled up in front of the house, George saw a shadow against the upstairs bedroom window. Instinctively, he knew Susannah had arrived. The thought flashed through George's mind that she must have started from the farm in the middle of the night. Even before Quint was lifted out of the carriage she was at his side. Tears spiked her dark lashes as she peered up into George's concerned face. She whispered in a shaky voice, "I knew something terrible was going to happen, I just knew it."

George waited until they carried Quint up the stairs and into his bedroom before he attempted to explain. Then he left. He had the note for Rebecca and Susannah's instructions. Margaret had to tell him where Rebecca was.

Margaret met him at the door. She listened to his tale and then hissed, "I don't know where she is and even if I

365

did, I wouldn't tell you. I will be much better off if my dear brother does not survive." She slammed the door in his face and George staggered back to his horse. He felt like a beaten man. Margaret was not going to tell them anything.

When he got back to the apartment, Susannah met him at the door. He couldn't remember when his wife had looked so angry or so upset. He dismissed the possibility that Quint had died. Susannah wouldn't have looked that angry if he was gone. He moved through the door and Susannah glared at him, "Where is she? That stupid man in there won't let a soul touch him until he talks to Rebecca. He's using up all of his strength just to remain alert. He sent the doctor home! Can you understand? Where is she?"

George swore loudly, "Margaret's refusing to say a word. She won't tell me a thing."

Susannah turned white and collapsed in a nearby chair. "George, Quint is seriously injured. If Rebecca doesn't get here soon, we'll have to wait until he loses consciousness completely. By then, it may be too late."

"We have been looking for her for days. Tell me what to do and I'll do it. Right now, I have no idea where she is, or how long it will take to get to her." George sank into a chair across from his wife and let his head drop into his cupped hands.

She stood up, suddenly, "We have to try. She must come to him today! He's still losing blood. I don't know how much more he can lose."

George offered quietly, "Could we get someone to hold him down while we work on him?"

Susannah glanced at him angrily and without a word headed for the bedroom where Quint was laying. When she returned she looked down at her husband's ashen face. "All right," she said. "Get me a carriage. I'll go. I know Margaret knows a great deal more than she is saying. You stay here with him until the men from the shipyard arrive and I'll go to Margaret. Somehow, I'll get her to tell me where Rebecca is."

George gazed at his wife in concern. He didn't want her exposed to Margaret's viciousness. He doubted that Margaret would tell her anything either. Running down the stairs, he considered ordering her to wait until he could go with her. No, Susannah would never let him prevent her from trying. The carriage was waiting downstairs when he returned to the bedroom, "I really don't want you to go alone. Can't we wait until some of the men arrive? I'll go with you then."

"If we wait much longer, it will be too late. I'll return as soon as I can. Don't let anyone touch him until I get back here, unless he completely loses consciousness." She kissed her husband's cheek and dashed from the room.

The morning was no longer young when the carriage pulled up in front of the Harrison house. Susannah charged up the steps and without knocking, she opened the large front door and strode into the hall. Margaret was coming down the front stairs as Susannah barged into the hall. The older woman's face turned a deep scarlet color and she glared down at her younger sister. "What are you doing here?" she snapped.

Susannah walked up to the bottom of the stairs. "I want Rebecca, now. You are going to tell me where she is."

Margaret smiled innocently at Susannah. "I don't know where she is. You and Quint both think I'm privy to information that I don't have."

"Margaret," Susannah threatened, her voice hard, "You are going to tell me. Arthur and Quint fought a duel this morning, and neither man came out the winner."

Margaret interrupted, "You mean our baby brother was engaged in something so terrible as a duel? And you are looking for his wife?" Margaret laughed. "I'm surprised that you'll have anything to do with him. I thought you hated dueling. You've commented about your feelings enough times."

Susannah took a step toward her sister, "Margaret, Arthur was killed. Quint was injured. Someone has to see to Rebecca. I'm sure you don't want to tell the girl that she has lost her brother and will probably lose her husband."

"I'm not going to tell her anything. I don't know where she is!"

"I don't believe you," Susannah said softly.

A firm male voice from the hall said, "I don't believe you

either."

Margaret turned in the direction of the voice, "Simon!"

"Tell her what she wants to know," Simon said quietly, in a tired voice. "If you don't and Quint dies, I'm ruined." He stepped out into the hall waving a letter in his hand. "Quint's man just brought this letter around. It was to be delivered if anything happened to Quint. It must be serious because this letter was to be given to me only if there was a question about whether he would make it or not." He looked back at the letter and then at his wife, "Margaret, if you in any way obstruct the Beals from finding Rebecca, or prevent her from claiming what is hers, Quint's lawyer will foreclose."

"He can't do that!"

"Margaret, seven years ago your brother bailed me out of a disastrous relationship with a local merchant. He bought off all my loans. If it wasn't for that brother of yours, and the fact that he's been shipping all my merchandise for half of what the other companies charge, we would be destitute. You do anything to keep Rebecca from Quint or from claiming what is hers, I'll do exactly what Quint suggested, I'll send you to the frontier. Of course, I'll have to go with you, because Quint's man will call in all of my loans. Tell Susannah what she wants to know."

Margaret dashed up to her husband. "I don't believe you. You never said a word, you . . ."

Simon took a step toward her. She grabbed at the paper in his hand but Simon jerked it away from her. With his other hand, he slapped Margaret across the face. He muttered, "I should have done that long ago."

Margaret put her open palm against the bright red mark on her cheek, then her shoulders sagged and she glanced up at Susannah. "Mother told me I was going to get the farm. Quint had no right to it. It was mine."

Susannah was losing her patience. "Margaret, Mother told each of her girls that the farm was hers. Mary Jane and I have laughed about that a dozen times. Imagine Mary Jane on a farm."

"She told Mary Jane . . . ?"

"Margaret," Susannah said softly, "Tell me where Rebecca is."

Margaret still appeared stunned. "There are servants, a man and a wife. They won't let you in."

Simon grabbed Margaret's arm. "Then, you'll go, too." He turned to Susannah, "You have a carriage?" Susannah nodded. "Then you can have your driver follow us. I'll have our driver bring the carriage around to the front."

Holding Margaret's arm tightly, he marched off down the hall, toward the back of the house to the stable. Susannah left by the front door. She sat quietly, waiting for the Harrison carriage and she thought about her brother. She was shocked that Simon Harrison mentioned Quint's help in front of anyone. There was no more time for speculation then, for the Harrison carriage pulled up beside her and they began their trek through the neighborhood.

They drove down two streets and turned into a narrow side street then the lead carriage pulled to a stop and Simon jumped down. He walked back to Susannah's carriage. "Margaret and I will take care of the servants. I'll signal to you." He walked back to his carriage and Susannah watched as he dragged Margaret down the steps. It was evident that the couple had had words on the ride to the house. Susannah watched as Simon pulled his reluctant wife up the walk, around a large building and to the side entrance of a small house almost hidden from view.

Susannah frowned as she left her carriage. This wasn't out of town and from what George told her, this was where they had come the night Arthur challenged Quint. Rebecca couldn't be here! Margaret lied. Susannah stood on the walk, watching the door, and waited for Simon's signal.

She started to pace the dirt path in front of her. How long would it take to find Rebecca, and would Susannah be able to convince her that Quint was alive, but wounded? And what about Arthur, where had the seconds taken his body?

Susannah was deep in her thought when the driver of the carriage called her name, "Mrs. Beal, I think they want you."

Susannah looked up, and Simon was waving her toward the house. Susannah rushed up the same path Simon and Margaret had trod moments before.

Before she reached the door, Simon was talking, "She's here. And, the seconds brought Arthur's body here. The servants, it appears, ran off when the body arrived." Susannah was through the door, but Simon wasn't finished explaining. "She's locked upstairs in a back bedroom. She doesn't know about Arthur, or Quint, and she's very confused. I thought you should talk to her first."

Susannah hurried past the parlor where she caught a glimpse of Arthur's body stretched out on the settee. "Simon, perhaps before I bring her down, you could arrange to have the body taken some place else."

"I'll see to it," he said quietly.

As Susannah moved up the stairs, she noticed Margaret sitting in a corner of the dining room. Her sister's eyes were red from tears and she looked like she had lost her last friend. She probably had, Susannah decided as she hurried down the hall to the back room that Simon indicated held Quint's love. "Rebecca," she called as she headed for the door, "It's Susannah."

It took Susannah only a few minutes to tell Rebecca what happened in the last several weeks since Quint had returned. She asked a few quiet questions and only once in the telling did Susannah notice her sister-in-law blanch. When Susannah told her about the duel and that Quint had been hurt, Rebecca's eyes closed and her face lost most of its color. For a second, Susannah was afraid. "Rebecca, don't swoon. As big as you are, I'll never be able to get you to the carriage."

Rebecca came alive then, "You have a carriage? Is he here? Is Quint at the townhouse, here in Philadelphia? Then, we must go. We must go, now!"

She was on her feet and Susannah gasped. There was no question, Rebecca was going to have a child and Susannah guessed that it would be very soon. They started for the stairs, Susannah leading the way. Simon held the door for them. Susannah glanced back at the parlor, the door was closed and Simon nodded at her. "I'll take care of everything," he said somberly. Margaret was nowhere to be seen. As they rushed out the door, Simon added, "Tell Quint, I'm sorry and I will handle my wife from now on. He has nothing to worry about, ever again."

Susannah bustled Rebecca into the carriage. The driver stared at the beautiful black-haired girl who was very much in a family way. Susannah said softly, "Take us back to the townhouse, as quickly as you can. But be careful." The man shook his head. There was no way he was driving as quickly as the situation with the capt'n warranted. He knew nothing about delivering babies.

Chapter Thirty-three

Finally, the carriage arrived at the apartment. Susannah helped Rebecca down, then hurried her into the house and up the stairs. Silently, she prayed that Quint was still fighting for his life. In the carriage, on the way from the house where Arthur had kept Rebecca, Susannah had filled her in on some of the details of Quint's search for her and she tried to prepare Rebecca for the condition in which she would find her husband.

As they came through the door, George came out of the bedroom and when he saw Rebecca, he sighed in relief. He murmured quietly, "Thank God! I don't know how he is hanging on."

Rebecca waddled into the room to the bed where Quint lay, still fully clothed. She could see the dried blood and the fresh stains on his jacket and she asked quietly, "Wasn't the duel at dawn? Why hasn't he been seen to?"

George looked guilty. "He wouldn't let anyone touch him until you came."

Quint opened his glassy eyes at George's words, and looked in Rebecca's direction, "I'm . . . sor . . . ry," he mumbled.

Rebecca sat down on the bed beside him and kissed his forehead tenderly, "My darling, let us take care of you. I don't want you to die. You can't die! You're going to be a father soon, so you mustn't die." Rebecca fell down on her knees beside the bed and tears she hadn't shed for several months came tumbling from her eyes, "Oh, Quint. You must get well."

Quint opened his eyes for a brief moment and tried to smile, then his eyes drifted shut once more. Susannah smiled grimly and went into action. With Rebecca's help, they managed to get his jacket and shirt off while George removed his pants. The men who arrived from the shipyards while Susannah was at Margaret's were sent scurrying off to get the doctor, candles for the sick room, water that had been heated much earlier in the day and the bandages that Susannah had ready. Rebecca refused to leave the bed where she sat holding Quint's left hand while they waited for the doctor.

Susannah watched her rub her back and she grew concerned. They did not need for the babe to arrive this day. She insisted that Rebecca rest for a while, at least until after the doctor finished removing the ball. Rebecca agreed to rest for a short time and went into the next room to lay down. George sent a carriage with detailed instructions to Hilda at the farm. She was to come immediately and bring Rebecca some clothes.

The doctor, the same man who had been present at the duel, arrived and went to work. The ball of shot was lodged against the large bone of the shoulder and although he could find no serious damage, the old man told Susannah as he applied fresh dressings, "This fool may not die from damage to an organ, but infection is a very real possibility. I should have removed the ball hours ago. I don't want to frighten you but I'd say his chances are very small to nothing." He gave instructions for cool baths to bring down the fever that was already climbing, and left something for the pain. Shaking his head, he left mumbling that a recovery would be a miracle.

Sam came dragging in Rebecca's small trunk from the carriage Susannah brought to the townhouse. It had been delivered to the Beals after she had been abducted. Susannah smiled in relief, and sent Sam and another man to retrieve the things Arthur had provided for her. Rebecca slept through most of the comings and goings, but when her trunk was placed in the room, she was out of bed as quickly as her distended shape would allow. She was into Quint's room before Susannah could stop her.

What she saw stopped her awkward progress and she

screamed for Susannah. Quint was thrashing about in his bed, fighting the stabbing pain in his chest, trying to pull the blood-soaked bandages from his wound. His eyes were open, but they were unseeing in their red-eyed torture.

Susannah was beside her in seconds and Rebecca rushed to the edge of the bed. As she struggled to keep him from ripping off the bandages, she talked to him quietly. Her soft words seemed to calm him and she stroked his head as Susannah applied another bandage. "He's burning up," Rebecca whispered. Susannah sent George to get cold water and Rebecca asked Susannah to get the packet of herbs in her small trunk. Susannah raised her eyes in disbelief, but she went in search of Rebecca's small parcel of precious herbs tucked in the bottom of her trunk.

When Susannah returned, Rebecca began to make a poultice of one kind of herb and then she set two different kinds aside and gave orders for a teapot of hot water. She carefully measured the herbs for the poultice into a pan of hot water and added a small amount of rum that George brought at her request. She gave instructions to Susannah and the older woman began to bathe the delirious man with rags soaked with more rum. George held Quint down as Rebecca applied the first of the warm poultices she had prepared. Quint's scream shook them all, but Rebecca assured her two relatives that it was the bite of the rum in the poultice that caused such a reaction. As the poultice cooled Rebecca applied another, but this time there was no scream.

All through the night, Rebecca, Susannah and George labored, sponging his hot feverish body alternately with rum and cold water and Rebecca mixed the poultices and applied them. Quint would gain a slight amount of awareness and Rebecca was there to dribble a tiny amount of the herb tea between his parched lips. Towards dawn, Quint felt a little cooler and the last of the poultices was applied and the teapot drained. Rebecca stood over her patient and put her hand to the small of her back, rubbing the painful spot.

George turned tired but anxious eyes toward his wife and then his sister-in-law, "Exactly when is the babe due?"

Rebecca had never been so weary and she didn't want to

figure out the exact time, "Oh, I don't know, in another week, perhaps two, maybe three."

George couldn't help it, he laughed. "Any time now?"

Rebecca nodded her head, and Susannah looked at her in concern, "You must rest! Go on. I'll watch until Hilda arrives."

"Hilda is coming? Here?" Rebecca was delighted.

"George sent for her last night. She should be here later today," Susannah answered. She was very aware of the large belly that protruded from Rebecca as she made her way to the door. Rebecca stopped and would go no further until both George and Susannah promised that they would call her if there was any change.

Rebecca tried to curl up in the bed she had used before, but she dozed fitfully and in only four hours she was back at Quint's bedside, preparing more poultices and making another pot of herb tea to spoon between his lips. His fever started to rise again and Susannah began the bathing of his restless form. He called again and again for Rebecca and when she reached down and touched his cheek or his head he quieted down for a time.

The sun was setting amid a ribbon of brilliant reds and blues when another carriage arrived at the Philadelphia townhouse. Sam helped Hilda down from the carriage and she scolded him as she climbed the stairs. Susannah met her at the head of the stairs and led her to the kitchen. As quickly as she could, she explained what had happened. Rebecca ran into the cook's waiting arms. "I'm so glad you're here." She brushed aside her tears and hugged the older woman.

Hilda hugged her back. "Travel for you I will." With Hilda to help, Susannah got to rest and Rebecca and Hilda took over bathing Quint and forcing tea down his throat. After much pleading, George and Hilda convinced Rebecca that she needed rest as well, if not for her own sake at least for the sake of the babe.

The next two days followed the first, as poultices were applied and tea brewed. With Hilda to add her support, Susannah got Rebecca to rest more often than she argued she needed. By the evening of the fourth day, Rebecca fell asleep in the chair next to Quint's bed while the other three went into dinner. She awoke with a start and stared across the room into the lucid blue eyes of her husband. Awkwardly, she pulled herself up from the chair and approached his bed. He reached out very carefully and laid his left hand on her large belly, whispering softly, "I vaguely remember a sweet voice telling me that I was going to be a father." He dropped his hand to the bed.

"Yes," Rebecca whispered tenderly. Quint closed his eyes and drifted off into a natural sleep. Rebecca rose from the bed and wandered out to the dining room. Hilda and George were out of their seats before Susannah even knew that Rebecca had entered the room. Their faces were etched with worry.

She smiled hesitantly, "He has survived the crisis. He is sleeping naturally." She turned and moved toward her room. Dinner was forgotten while Hilda put Rebecca to bed. Some time during the night Quint's fever broke and Hilda and Susannah changed his linens. Once he was assured that Rebecca was sleeping, he smiled at the two women and drifted back to sleep himself.

Rebecca slept almost eighteen hours and was slowly brought back to reality by the fierce movements of the babe. With a start, she remembered everything that happened in the last five days. She struggled out of the bed as quickly as her burdened state allowed and waddled into Quint's bedroom. He was sleeping peacefully. She ambled out to the kitchen where she heard Hilda's humming.

Hilda heard her before she was through the door, and held out a cup of fresh tea for her. "A lot you sleep. George and Susannah, home they go. Return, they will in a day or two." Hilda looked at Rebecca's extended shape and frowned, "Soon, come the babe will." As if she could anticipate Rebecca's next question, she grinned, "Improved, he is. Breakfast he had and a bath, and then sleep. Fine he will be."

After a light meal, Rebecca left Hilda to her new kitchen and took some of the unfinished baby clothes Hilda had brought from the farm into Quint's room. She sat quietly, and sewed while her husband slept. Rebecca was not aware that he awoke and lay watching her until she folded the little garment and put it on the table. She glanced over at the bed and was startled to see brilliant dark blue eyes watching her. She stood up and crossed to the bed. Bending, she felt his forehead. Smiling now, she whispered, "Your fever is gone. Can I get you anything? Water? Hilda made soup earlier today. Would you like some of that?" For some reason, she was slightly embarrassed.

"What I want, woman, is for you to sit down. We need to talk," Quint patted the side of his bed. Rebecca let a small smile play across her face as she sat down next to him. Quint spoke so quietly she had to lean forward to catch his words, "After the shipwreck, all the time I was in the water, I could see your face. You kept moving away from me. I could never quite reach you, but you saved my life. Even when I lay with my head splitting, I would still see you. Rebecca, you led me from the sea and brought me to safety. Sweetheart, I love you. I love you more than you will ever know. I'm sorry for all the hurt I've caused you, for thinking you were something you were not, for leaving you unprotected on the farm." His voice cracked slightly, "I didn't . . . mean . . . to . . . to shoot your brother, but . . ."

Rebecca put her fingers over his mouth, "Shh. It is finished. Arthur and Margaret did some very wrong things, and Arthur paid the ultimate price for his greed. Margaret will pay dearly because she will have to live with what she tried to do. You're going to be all right. That's what is important." Quint put his good arm up and pulled her shoulder toward him until he got his arm around her neck. He drew her down to him so that his lips could drink from the wellspring of his life. He kissed her with all the tenderness he could muster and she returned the kiss in full. He released her slowly and she sat with him holding his hand. Words were no longer necessary.

Hilda brought their supper on a tray and Quint insisted that Rebecca feed him. They ate their meal together with much play. Rebecca would first take a bite and then feed a bite to Quint. He teased her about taking the bigger chunks of meat and vegetable for herself and then he patted her rounded girth. Frequently, the babe would respond with a thump, which delighted Quint. Several times during the meal Rebecca rubbed her back and when Quint looked at her quizzically, she smiled slightly, commenting, "When your son is not content to play with you, he sits on my backbone."

After dinner, Rebecca told Quint about her four weeks with the Indians and the way Crying Wolf saved her from slavery. She cried a little as she told him how the Indian insisted on keeping Cad. With her urging, Quint told her about accidentally meeting Arthur in the London tavern and more about the shipwreck. He told her about Madeleine and how he remembered who he was and he explained that he had invited Captain Hemphill home for dinner the next time he was in port.

Hilda tapped on the door, "Tea and coffee, I have. Busy has been my day. Bed I go at a decent hour this night. Rebecca, bed you should go as well," she glanced at the young woman sitting with her husband, holding his hand.

"Rebecca will go to bed soon," Quint said, a grin covering his whole face. "I'll see to it."

Hilda looked at him, her expression one of disbelief and Quint laughed out loud. "Soon, Hilda." She shrugged her shoulders and closed the door quietly.

When they had finished the coffee and tea, Rebecca took the empty cups and put them on the tray, "I probably ought to take Hilda's advice."

Quint threw back the covers on the bed, and said softly, "I've been waiting for this. For nine months, I thought about little else but getting you back in my bed."

Rebecca frowned slightly, "I might hurt you."

"You can sleep on my left side."

"The babe moves a great deal, he may keep you awake."

"I don't mind," Quint said. "Don't you want to sleep with me?"

His voice was so much like a piteous little boy's, that Rebecca laughed, "I was only worried about you. Let me get my gown and robe." She was back in the room in a few minutes, dressed for bed.

Quint looked at her in the flickering candlelight and pouted, grumbling slightly, "You've already changed."

She threw her robe over the chair and commented, "I'll wait until I have my figure back, before I change in front of you." As she slipped into bed on his left side, he placed his arm around her shoulders and pulled her close to his side. She protested that he would hurt himself, but he would not release her and she snuggled next to him. Within minutes they both drifted off to sleep.

Twice during the night, she awoke to a strange drawing across her belly, but she dismissed the feeling because it wasn't her time yet and immediately she fell back to sleep.

Hilda found them still snuggled close together in the morning when she went in to check on Quint. Her chuckles woke him and she told him that she was going out to the market and would be back in a while. He asked her to bring tea for Rebecca and coffee for him before she left. For a few more minutes, he dozed and then shook Rebecca gently before he kissed her tenderly. "Wife," he whispered against her ear, "I love you." She opened her eyes and smiled up at him. "I would love you even more if you would get my coffee," he whispered.

Rebecca reached up and pulled his head down to hers, so that she could give him a kiss. She stretched and carefully rolled out of bed. "Coffee, sir," she said and started for the table. Suddenly she felt a gush of water running down her legs and onto the floor. She stood there for half a minute trying to decide what to do. Quint, alarmed at her hesitation, raised himself up on his good arm and stared at the stained gown and the puddle of water on the floor under his wife. Rebecca glanced at him and smiled at his panic. "It looks like our babe will be here today."

He responded with more assurance than he felt, "Come back to bed, love. Hilda went out shopping but she'll be back soon."

She crawled back into bed and as she lay down next to him the first pain spread across her stomach. She looked more surprised than anything and as Quint held her hand she tried to smile up at him. "I've never been on this side of a birthing. It's not as easy to relax with the pains as I thought."

Quint grinned encouragingly and continued to hold her hand. As the pullings continued, getting a little longer and a lot closer together, he talked to her quietly. He was not even aware that he was as tense as he was until he heard the door open and knew Hilda had returned. When the big woman stuck her head into the room, he gave a distinct sigh of relief.

She took in the floor and Rebecca stretched out on the bed with Quint holding her hand. The expression on her face said clearly that she didn't want to believe what she was seeing. Quint was now very relieved with the woman back in the apartment and he grinned up at her, "We're having a baby."

Hilda panicked. She rushed to the side of the bed and peered down at Rebecca. Rebecca tried a smile, but just then another pain arrived. Hilda rushed from the room, not sure what to do, or what to say. Only a minute or two had slipped by before she was back, "What to do, I do not know."

Quint asked calmly, "Have you ever delivered a baby?"

Hilda looked stricken, "No!"

"We're going to deliver one today," Quint said reassuringly.

"For the midwife, I go," she managed.

"Hilda," Quint shook his head grimly, "There's no time for that. This babe is in one hell of a hurry to be born."

Hilda gasped as Quint sat up beside Rebecca and said softly, "Sweetheart, if you feel like pushing, push." Rebecca panted and the contours of her face hardened. She was pushing, and she gripped his hand so tightly that he thought he might lose one of his fingers. As Rebecca labored, he gave detailed instructions to Hilda, telling her as he grinned at his wife, "Hilda, Rebecca has all the work to do. She's delivered babes before. She told me our part is easy."

Rebecca took a deep breath and waited for another urge. She turned her head and looked up at Quint, "How do you know so much about this?"

He smiled down at her, "I helped Susannah's second boy arrive. She wouldn't wait for anyone either, and as a farmer I helped with . . ." Rebecca gasped and again grabbed for his hand. Hilda's excited cry told Quint that his first child was on his way into the world. Twice more, Rebecca groaned, as she struggled to push the child from her. Then a wrinkled bawling baby boy rested on the stomach of a tired but satisfied new mother.

After Hilda cleaned up first the baby and then the mother, Quint moved gingerly from the bed to the chair that Hilda pushed close to the bed. Hilda handed him the small bundle and set about changing the bed and getting Rebecca a fresh gown. When the new family was settled back in bed, Hilda went out to the kitchen to fix coffee for Quint "Coffee, I need, too," she mumbled as she went through the door.

After his coffee, he climbed back in bed and laying next to his wife, admired his son. When Rebecca drifted off to sleep, he tentatively moved to the edge of the bed, swung his legs over the mattress and stood up for the second time that day. He tried a few experimental steps and then made his way slowly out to the kitchen. He nearly startled Hilda to death. Giving her instruction, he handed her the necessary coins and asked her to get back as quickly as she could, if possible, before Rebecca awoke. He left her grinning after him from ear to ear, her round eyes twinkling. For several minutes he wandered through the parlor of the apartment, but he admitted quickly that he was in no condition to be up for any length of time. He moved back to his room where his wife and son were still both sleeping. As he drifted off to sleep himself, he heard Hilda leave the apartment.

Before sunset, Susannah and George made their way back up the stairs of the apartment. They brought food stuffs and things that they thought Rebecca might be able to use for the babe if it arrived before Quint was able to go back to the farm. The apartment was very quiet and even Hilda's door was closed indicating that she, too, was taking advantage of the solitude. Susannah tiptoed into Rebecca's room expecting to find her sleeping. George swung the door to Quint's room open and grabbed his wife, pulling her to the doorway. As he pulled, he indicated with his finger over his lips that she mustn't make a sound. There in the bed was Quint, resting against the pillow on his side of the bed and across his face was a grin that could have served as a lighthouse beacon. His hand was extended so that the tiny form feeding from Rebecca's breast could grab his finger with a tiny hand.

Susannah glanced at the two young people enjoying their first born and then looked at the room. Her eyes filled with tears. On the table next to the chair and on the wardrobe were the biggest bowls of soft pink roses that Susannah had ever seen. "Oh look, George." Susannah tugged on his arm. "Roses for Rebecca!"

George never took his eyes from the serene face of his young brother-in-law and murmured, "And, a child for Quint!"

EXHILARATING ROMANCE
From Zebra Books

GOLDEN PARADISE (2007, $3.95)
by Constance O'Banyon

Desperate for money, the beautiful and innocent Valentina Barrett finds work as a veiled dancer, "Jordanna," at San Francisco's notorious Crystal Palace. There she falls in love with handsome, wealthy Marquis Vincente — a man she knew she could never trust as Valentina — but who Jordanna can't resist making her lover and reveling in love's GOLDEN PARADISE.

SAVAGE SPLENDOR (1855, $3.95)
by Constance O'Banyon

By day Mara questioned her decision to remain in her husband's world. But by night, when Tajarez crushed her in his strong, muscular arms, taking her to the peaks of rapture, she knew she could never live without him.

TEXAS TRIUMPH (2009, $3.95)
by Victoria Thompson

Nothing is more important to the determined Rachel McKinsey than the Circle M — and if it meant marrying her foreman to scare off rustlers, she would do it. Yet the gorgeous rancher feels a secret thrill that the towering Cole Elliot is to be her man — and despite her plan that they be business partners, all she truly desires is a glorious consummation of their vows.

KIMBERLY'S KISS (2184, $3.95)
by Kathleen Drymon

As a girl, Kimberly Davonwoods had spent her days racing her horse, perfecting her fencing, and roaming London's byways disguised as a boy. Then at nineteen the raven-haired beauty was forced to marry a complete stranger. Though the hot-tempered adventuress vowed to escape her new husband, she never dreamed that he would use the sweet chains of ecstasy to keep her from ever wanting to leave his side!

FOREVER FANCY (2185, $3.95)
by Jean Haught

After she killed a man in self-defense, alluring Fancy Broussard had no choice but to flee Clarence, Missouri. She sneaked aboard a private railcar, plotting to distract its owner with her womanly charms. Then the dashing Rafe Taggart strode into his compartment . . . and the frightened girl was swept up in a whirlwind of passion that flared into an undeniable, unstoppable prelude to ecstasy!

Available wherever paperbacks are sold, or order direct from the Publisher. Send cover price plus 50¢ per copy for mailing and handling to Zebra Books, Dept. 2745, 475 Park Avenue South, New York, N.Y. 10016. Residents of New York, New Jersey and Pennsylvania must include sales tax. DO NOT SEND CASH.

ROMANCE REIGNS
WITH ZEBRA BOOKS!

SILVER ROSE (2275, $3.95)
by Penelope Neri
Fleeing her lecherous boss, Silver Dupres disguised herself as a boy and joined an expedition to chart the wild Colorado River. But with one glance at Jesse Wilder, the explorers' rugged, towering scout, Silver knew she'd have to abandon her protective masquerade or else be consumed by her raging unfulfilled desire!

STARLIT ECSTASY (2134, $3.95)
by Phoebe Conn
Cold-hearted heiress Alicia Caldwell swore that Rafael Ramirez, San Francisco's most successful attorney, would never win her money . . . or her love. But before she could refuse him, she was shamelessly clasped against Rafael's muscular chest and hungrily matching his relentless ardor!

LOVING LIES (2034, $3.95)
by Penelope Neri
When she agreed to wed Joel McCaleb, Seraphina wanted nothing more than to gain her best friend's inheritance. But then she saw the virile stranger . . . and the green-eyed beauty knew she'd never be able to escape the rapture of his kiss and the sweet agony of his caress.

EMERALD FIRE (1963, $3.95)
by Phoebe Conn
When his brother died for loving gorgeous Bianca Antonelli, Evan Sinclair swore to find the killer by seducing the tempress who lured him to his death. But once the blond witch willingly surrendered all he sought, Evan's lust for revenge gave way to the desire for unrestrained rapture.

SEA JEWEL (1888, $3.95)
by Penelope Neri
Hot-tempered Alaric had long planned the humiliation of Freya the daughter of the most hated foe. He'd make the wench from across the ocean his lowly bedchamber slave—but he never suspected she would become the mistress of his heart, his treasured SEA JEWEL.

Available wherever paperbacks are sold, or order direct from the Publisher. Send cover price plus 50¢ per copy for mailing and handling to Zebra Books, Dept. 2745, 475 Park Avenue South, New York, N.Y. 10016. Residents of New York, New Jersey and Pennsylvania must include sales tax. DO NOT SEND CASH.